SHADOWS
OF THE VOID

SHADOWS OF THE VOID

The Quari Group Saga Volume 1

KEVIN WATSON

This book is a work of fiction. Names, characters, organizations, places, and events are either the author's imagination or used fictitiously.

Copyright © 2024 Kevin Watson

To request permission, contact the publisher:
permissions@yetiverse.com

E-Book ISBN: 9798989150007
Paperback ISBN: 9798989150014
Hardcover ISBN: 9798989150021
Audio Book ISBN: 9798989150038

First edition 2024

yetiverse.com

For Blue.

Not the color.

Nor the dog.

My friend and muse.

Thank you.

Shadows of the Void is a fantasy adventure that spans events from the formation of Earth to the present day and beyond. It touches various points in history, and the reader will encounter depictions of abuse, anger, anxiety, blood, bullying, classism, cults, death, graphic violence, guilt, incest, manipulation, poverty, racism, self-harm, sexual situations, stalking, torture, and war. The shadows can be a disturbing place.

I am born of the Mother. I am bound to Her living energy; it flows through me. Caring for the life She creates is my highest honor. I must never forget these truths and bind myself to these precepts.

- The Mother's living energy is sacred and shall not be squandered.

- All life has consciousness, though life infused by a soul is rare. I will tend to these forms of life above all else.

- I will only draw energy from a living soul within the confines of consensual ritual, and only to forge the eternal bonds of unity.

- When drawing energy, I will strive to limit the demand placed upon the donor. Life without a soul relies on my protection. I will honor its gifts and sacrifices with offerings of nourishment and care.

Life above all.

ONE

WHO NEEDS EXCALIBUR?

The bell over the shop door rang, tugging at the tangled knot of thoughts occupying Narah. A young man dropped a copy of the Edinburgh Evening News on the front counter, and she greeted him with a smile; one that would have been friendly, if not for the lingering haze in her eyes. He gave a quick wave and retreated through the door into the afternoon sun, drowning her words of thanks in the tinkling clatter of the bell.

Dropping her polishing cloth on a neglected silver tray, she shook off the fog of thought, and made her way through the shop. The antique furniture filling the store created meandering passages, encouraging visitors to explore. Silver-backed mirrors hung on the walls. Glass figurines and crystal stemware filled curio cabinets. Every nook and cranny held one treasure or another.

Narah reached the front counter and tucked a stray auburn curl behind her ear. She opened the paper, tapped the end of a pen against her pursed lips, and skimmed the adverts for rental spaces in Edinburgh. Her brow furrowed, causing the light smattering of freckles across her forehead to dance as she contemplated her options.

The township of Dunblane had been home for six years. While the small-town environment made her life more complex, it had been an ideal place to raise her son, Sean; until the school's tragedy. It had been two months since a gunman had entered the school, killing several children. Sean stumbled into the gymnasium during the chaos, witnessing the gruesome scene. Seeing the bloodied, lifeless bodies of his friends had left a mark, cracking the veil to a world Narah was not ready for her son to encounter. He began seeing creatures in the shadows, suffering night terrors, and a petrifying fear of dark places had rooted itself in the depths of his psyche.

Narah's eyes swept over the shop. Everywhere her eyes lingered, memories they had built rose from the woodwork. Phantoms of a past they must leave behind. The thought of abandoning their history made her uneasy, but the hope of helping Sean recover steadied her resolve.

The yellow glow of the school bus filled the shop window.

The distance faded from her eyes and a warm smile spread over her features. She would take Sean to a place he wasn't continually reminded of that horror. She would do anything for her boy, and no matter how it may disrupt her life, it was time for a change.

The shop door burst open, the bell clanging as a ginger-headed rush of energy barreled into the shop.

"Mu-um," Sean called at top volume.

"Here," Narah said, ducking behind the counter.

Sean spun, arms flinging wide. "Where?"

"Find me!" She watched him through the glass display, feeling his energy lift her mood.

"Marco!" His call resounded through the shop like a klaxon, making things near him vibrate, and he laughed.

She cupped her hand to her mouth, muffling her sound. "Polo!"

His tiny brow furrowed, his lips pursed, and a hiss of air whistled through his nose. "No fair hiding in something."

Peeking around a table, he spotted a large wardrobe standing in the corner. A smile spread across his round face, puckering his freckled cheeks and bringing out his dimples. Light blossomed in his blue eyes, and he dropped to all fours.

Narah watched as he crept between the legs of an antique desk, edging closer and closer to his prey. She stifled a laugh when he taunted her.

"Ya can't hide from me!"

He reached the base of the wardrobe, eyes creeping up the doors that towered over him. Rising to his feet, he stretched, grunting, lifting himself onto tiptoes, and wrapping his tiny fingers around the handle. "Found ya!"

Yanking the door open, he lost his balance and fell back onto his rump. He stared into the shadowy depths of the cabinet, eyes growing in fright.

Narah abandoned the game, rushing through the maze to reach him. "Mum's right here, Sean."

Sean scrambled backward into a pool of late afternoon sun, finding safety in the small patch of bright light on the floor. His tiny hands trembled, and he screeched at the darkness. "Stay away from me!" Horrified, his knees drew up against his chest, his arms locked around them, and his gaze remained fixed on the dark recesses of the wardrobe.

Narah stepped over him, approaching the cabinet. She hissed at the twisted forms lurking in the shadows, skewering them with her furious gaze. "Keep away from my boy!" The door of the wardrobe slammed with such force, everything around it shook.

Sean stared at his mother in awe.

Her anger melted away, and she knelt before him.

He sprang, wrapping his arms around her neck.

Gathering him close, she held him in the safety of her arms. "There now, we've sent those nasty tadgers away."

He held her tight. "Why won't they leave me alone?"

Thoughts of the power hidden within their blood and of the veil fractured by the grisly events at the school haunted her thoughts. She kissed his cheek, beaming at him. "Because you are my little knight." She rose and carried him with her toward the back of the store. "After all, in the stories, the bravest knights are always facing something ferocious."

Sean huffed. "I'm not brave. I hide."

Once inside the office, she sat him on her desk and sank into the chair. "Well, that's because you don't have the right equipment!" She patted him on the knee and picked up a long, thin box.

Sean eyed the package held before him. "What's that?"

Narah's eyes beamed. "Something special for my knight!" She lifted the box, offering it to him. "Well, go on. Open it."

He tore the top off with vigor. Inside lay an old, wooden short sword, covered in nicks and scrapes. He took the sword in hand, conflicted. He loved the sword but couldn't see how it could help him. "How is this supposed to keep the monsters away?"

"I know it doesn't look like much, but this sword is special."

"Why?"

"I'm glad you asked." Placing the box aside, she took the sword from Sean and turned it over, showing him the royal seal burned into the surface of the cross-guard. "This was a training sword used by the guards at the castle of Edinburgh."

Sean's interest in this news was clear, but he still appeared skeptical.

"Beyond that, it is the wood itself, and the other use for this weapon that makes it perfect for you!" She had him hooked, and she knew it.

He started babbling questions. "What's it made of? What's it used for?"

Laughing, she hushed him. "Give me time to speak, and I'll tell you." She made him sit still before continuing. "It's made of Lignum Vitae. I know it's a mouthful for me too. But they say it's the same type of wood that Merlin made his staff from!"

His eyes lit up. "The wizard?"

"Aye," she said. "What's more, it's said that once upon a time, Edinburgh Castle was teeming with things that moved in the darkness. Until one night, a brave knight, knowing Merlin's tale, took up this sword and set about securing the castle from those dark creatures."

Sean's eyes grew, and he examined the sword again.

"Now, every night, one guard patrols the grounds with a sword like this, keeping the grounds safe for all the visitors." She lay the sword in her lap and picked Sean up from the desk, placing him on the floor. "Kneel lad, that I may knight thee!"

Sean laughed, dropping to his knees in excitement. "Like this?"

"Aye! That is perfect." Lifting the sword, she tapped Sean once on each shoulder. "Rise, Sir Sean."

Sean scrambled to his feet and stood tall, chest puffed out and proud.

Holding the sword before him, she asked. "Now, brave knight, will you take up this sword and its sacred duty?"

Sean's head bobbled and flopped. "Aye!"

She leaned in, pushed her arms forward, and offered him the wooden blade. When he took the sword from her hand, she could see the awe on his face. He turned it this way and that, examining every ding.

"Now go," she instructed, "defend this realm!"

"Aye, mum!" he squealed, taking off through the winding maze of things in the store.

"Careful you don't break anything," she called after him. Standing, she followed, finding him mustering his courage before the wardrobe. She stopped, wanting to see if the sword would be worth the small fortune she paid to have it smuggled from the castle.

Sean lifted the sword, using its quivering tip to tug on the handle. The door swung open, and Sean took a nervous step backward, bringing the wooden blade to bear. "That's right! You better run! Sir Sean is here to end your scary ways!" He dove into the chest, hacking and thrusting at the creatures in the shadows.

Narah watched with pride as he found his strength, knowing now the sword would have been a bargain at twice the price.

In unity, we enshrine our new creed. Failure to abide by its precepts will result in the banishment of the offender and their family. May it keep the darkness of our past from dimming the light of our future.

—Queen Solyarra

Two

Nice kitties . . .

The staccato clatter of the carriage wheels sounded hollow; the cobblestones producing a rhythmic cadence which was absorbed into the peaceful stillness of the early evening. An army of ancient oaks lined the road, the thick cover casting long shadows and bathing the way in premature twilight.

A pair of children laughed, chasing one another around the thick trunks, parrying and thrusting with fallen twigs. Sean smiled, the playful duel stirring memories of his mother and the wooden sword she had given him nearly twenty-two years before.

Overhead, the canopy rustled. The early autumn breeze sighed through the leaves, and the upper boughs moved in gentle arcs; allowing glimpses of what lay ahead to peek through the thick cover.

Passing from beneath the shelter of the broad oaken arms, the Quari Gardens opened around the carriage. The headquarters of the Quari Group stood before them. A metal and glass pyramid clad in five identical facades. The sloped glass panels caught the last rays of the day's light, engulfing the structure in fiery radiance. The crystalline pinnacle exploded the sun's light into an array of colors, and Sean found it enchanting and beautiful. Though he had passed his first anniversary with the company, the sight remained breathtaking.

The gleaming pyramid of the Quari Group was less than five years old. Once, the village of Cordath had thrived here, an old-world town destroyed by a devastating storm a decade before. The incident remained a meteorological mystery. A front forecast to bring spring showers, stalled, grew in intensity, and dropped multiple funnels that chewed through the town. Tornadic winds devoured everything above ground level. The Quari Group lost a branch office, and in response, spearheaded an unprecedented humanitarian effort. The corporation found new housing in the surrounding communities for the displaced families, helped business rebuild near their new homes, and purchased the scared lots with generous offers. Weaving the town's history around the corporation's future headquarters, they left the cobblestone streets in place. LED reproductions replaced the mangled gas streetlights, a massive garden brought new life, and a sparkling pyramid served as the centerpiece.

The transformation had become a mecca for artists and tourists alike, creating a boom in tourism. Congestion and pollution led to a ban on motorized traffic within the gardens, and a fleet of horse-drawn carriages replaced vehicles.

Sean rocked as the carriage came to a halt. Gathering his satchel, he disembarked, lifting a hand in thanks to the coachman.

The coachman touched a finger to the brim of his hat and flicked the reins. The horse responded, and the carriage pulled away.

Fishing his phone out of his pocket, Sean reviewed the message summoning him back to the office.

```
RE: Promotion to Special Projects Team
Lead

Mr. Byrne,

Papa is most eager to speak with you
regarding your new position. As the
projects are of some urgency, he wishes
to meet this evening at 8:00 pm. Please
confirm your availability.

Ms. Iliescu
```

Sean checked the time, and the hint of a smile played at the corner of his lips. "I'm a wee bit early."

A towering panther statue stood watch at the entrance, and Sean admired its powerful, sleek lines. Excitement swelled, knotting his stomach. Between the massive paws, the doors beckoned. With a spring in his step, he went to answer their call.

< ᛉᛆᚾ ᚠᚱᛘ ᚪ ᛒᛚᛘᛋᛋᛁᚾX >

Ms. Iliescu, the right hand of the Quari Group's owner, deposited Sean in the executive conference room and left him to wait. A sizeable table occupied the center of the room, its top cut from the remnants of a massive oak toppled during the strange storm. The gaps and cracks of the grain were filled with resin, and the underside lit with a soft blue light. Its edges had been hand-carved with all manner of symbols, some familiar to Sean, while the majority were foreign. Around the table sat twelve executive leather chairs, with far more padding than the spartan knockoff at Sean's desk some forty floors below. At either end of the room, mahogany panels rose, trimmed in rails of brushed steel. It wasn't these things that captured his attention; it was the scenery.

The view from the executive conference room was breathtaking. From the sixty-third floor of the building, the lush, deep green patchwork of gardens and flickering lamps blended into the drapery of stars. Formed by a single pane of glass, the outer wall contained no lines to break the view or distract the eye. The high sheen of the polished black floor reflected the night sky, giving one the impression they were walking among the stars. The mirrored surface of the interior wall enhanced the effect. It was as though he were standing in space, protected by some magical force he couldn't comprehend. The ginger curls atop his head reflected in the surface, a fiery mess standing out amid this starry night. Sean was mesmerized by the picturesque beauty of the place.

The soft click of heels on the hard floors drew his attention to the door as Ms. Iliescu stepped into the room. She was a slight woman, in her sixties, with coal-black hair containing a silver-white peppering, which she wore with pride. Sean couldn't recall seeing the woman in makeup, yet she was still handsome, even if her features were too sharp for his tastes. Her gray eyes locked on him, and a shiver ran the length of his spine. While she was small in stature, she knew the power she held within these walls. The stern expression etched upon her features made it clear she would wield her authority like a cudgel.

Sean tried to resist fidgeting under the unsettling scrutiny of her lingering gaze. Eventually, she lifted a folder and flipped through its contents. "You've been a researcher in our corporate archeology group for over a year now, Mr. Byrne?"

"Aye. I started here after finishing my master's," he said, lifting his chin. "But my first work with the Quari Group was in Cairo, where I interned with the experimental archeology team."

Her brow rose, eyes narrowed, and she continued her assessment of him beyond the information provided within the file.

Sean's skin crawled under her gaze, and he couldn't shake the feeling she could see through him, uncovering things he would rather no one know.

"How did you find that work, Mr. Byrne? Was your internship fulfilling for you? Is it something you are passionate about?"

Sean swallowed, and his nervousness burned away under the excitement building inside. "I found it quite captivating. To use your research of historical events and places to recreate how things worked in times long-buried…" His smile bloomed. "It was exhilarating. When I saw a similar position open on the Special Projects team, I knew I had to apply." Color touched his cheeks when he realized how animated he had become, and he glanced away to hide his embarrassment. "Though I never thought I would be selected, being so new to the company."

Her finger tapped the folder while she contemplated his response. "It has been a rather short time for one to attain a promotion of this magnitude. Are you truly so skilled, or only adept at office politics?"

"I've never been one for playing games. Just working hard until the job is complete."

She flipped a few more pages and made a non-committal sound. "Humph. Well, your paperwork appears in order. I will have to pray you are less a fool than your predecessor." Her head canted to the side, and her gaze grew distant, as if she were listening to someone, though there was no one else present. Blinking, she snapped the folder closed. "The meeting is now to take place in Papa's private office."

Of course, Papa meant Djain, the young man who owned the Quari Group, one of the world's largest privately held companies. Sean had never heard Djain's last name, and if anyone tried to call him Mr., Sir, or any other title, he laughed and told them he was Papa. Sean had heard the man's spiel on the topic many times. '*I am Papa Djain, Papa to my family, Papa to my friends, Papa to my workers, and the Quari Group helps me to be Papa to all.*'

"Of course, Ms. Iliescu." Sean motioned toward Djain's office. "I can see myself over if you'd like. I don't want to keep you here at this hour."

Her eyes narrowed. "I will see you to your destination, Mr. Byrne." With that, she spun on a heel and entered the hall.

The abrupt departure caught Sean off guard, and he scrambled around the table.

She called back to him, her words muted by the growing distance. "After all, you have no inkling of where it is you are going."

A colorful wooden bird peeked out from behind tiny, ornate wooden doors on the clock above Ms. Iliescu's desk. Its solitary note marked the time as 7:45 p.m., and Sean verified its accuracy against his watch as they entered Djain's office. He came to an uneasy halt and watched her round Djain's desk, stopping behind its organized surface. His skin prickled under her studious gaze. He had been mocking her in his mind, thinking this was where he would have gone. The look in her eyes made him afraid she already knew.

He fidgeted with a button on his coat.

She let out a decisive, "humph."

Reaching for the desk, she pressed a small button. Her eyes remained locked on him and his expression as the wall behind her opened, revealing a private elevator. The soft, pleasant baritone chime that signaled its arrival reminded him of the ones in the main lobby below.

The doors opened, and Ms. Iliescu stepped aside, motioning for him to enter. "Here is where I leave you. I trust you cannot get lost inside the lift. Papa will be along. Touch nothing unless directed to do so."

Sean stepped into the brushed metal box and lifted his hands in surrender. "I'll not touch a thing."

The doors hissed, closing as she spoke again. "See that you do not. Not everything is as it may appear." The dire edge of her tone made the fine hairs on the back of his neck prickle and stand.

Gooseflesh was already creeping over his body when the elevator dropped, sending his stomach into his chest. His eyes moved over the smooth, unbroken panels, finding no buttons or displays to control the plummeting metal box. Taking hold of the rail, he closed his eyes, focused on the quiet hum of the descent, and struggled to calm his nerves.

< ᚠᚩᚱᛏᚾᛁᛗ ᛋᛈᛁᚾᛗᛋ ᛟᛏ ᛃᚱᚾ >

The lift slowed, settled, the bell chimed, and the doors hissed open. With one hand over his stomach, Sean made a hasty exit, thankful to be back on solid ground. Behind him, the doors closed, and the rock walls of the cavern surrounding him reverberated with the mechanical clatter of the locks.

The room was bizarre, filled with a discordant collection of paraphernalia. Metaphysical implements, alchemical tools, and archaeological treasures filled the space; surrounded by beakers and burners, candles, and cauldrons. The sight stripped away what little resolve he had mustered.

He turned back to the sealed doors. His hands moved over the smooth, uninterrupted surface of the cold metal, and his stomach churned. Like the interior of the lift, there was no call button, no floor display, no way to interact with the machine. Any hope of retreat had vanished.

He pressed his back against the metal. The cool surface radiated through his clothes, making him shiver. He sucked in a deep breath and wrestled with his thoughts, settling into a weak, but somewhat reassuring phrase. *'I'm a guest and everything's all right.'* Ignoring the imagery of horror movies flashing through his mind and the terrifying inner voice narrating his coming demise, he stepped into the cavern.

Natural stone walls had been machined down in places, expanding the space. Shelves lined the walls, formed by gouges milled into the rock. The ceiling rose high overhead and vanished into inky darkness. On either side of the room, misshapen, black openings loomed. Staring at the absolute darkness filling the passages made Sean uneasy. Whispers of secrets and things forgotten tugged at his thoughts.

Artifacts filled the shelves. The glint of metals and the sparkle of gemstones twinkled amid the artifacts.

Oil lamps ringed the room, and flames danced atop their wicks, covering the room in a flickering, warm glow.

Mounted on the far wall hung a vibrant tapestry bearing the Quari Group logo, a muscled black panther with amber eyes poised to pounce. A matching pair of masterfully carved panther statues framed the tapestry, sitting tall and exuding regal arrogance. The figures rivaled Sean's height, each bearing shimmering amber eyes with an all too real gaze that followed his every step.

A shiver ran down his spine and he stopped, staring at the statues. "Stop acting like such a feartie," he said, chastising himself. He forced his focus from the panthers and moved deeper into the space. Tension melted from his shoulders with every step. Feeling more at ease, he shook his head. "And stop talking to your damned self."

At the center of the chamber sat a large stone work table. The top surface was buffed to a high polish, while the edges remained rough-cut stone. The same collections of symbols that ringed the conference room table somewhere far above were chiseled along its upper edge. An eclectic array of items adorned the top: a selection of modern beakers and tubes; a well-used mortar and pestle; candles; decorative cloth containing old Celtic symbols and runes; several small bowls with unidentifiable contents, along with water and what appeared to be salt.

Sean spotted a pattern stained into the floor and discovered a pentacle covering the entire space. The outer ring contained various religious symbols; Norse, Celtic, Chinese, and Egyptian were among the few he recognized.

Between the points of the pentacle, smaller tables ringed the room, covered in odd collections: old leather-bound volumes; yellowing maps; scrolls; and papers from sources throughout history. Everything on display being a specimen requiring special care and storage. Sean's ire stirred until movement in the corner of his eye distracted him.

His head snapped toward the back wall. Blinking, he froze. The panther statues that had framed the tapestry were missing. His brow furrowed. "I would have sworn—"

Startled, he twisted, scouring the room for the missing statues. Finding no sign of the carved cats, a tinge of color burst onto his cheek. He gave a nervous chuckle, dismissing the confusion as a trick of the mind, brought on by the strangeness of his surroundings.

He moved toward what appeared to be a bronze age dagger shelved on the opposite wall. The leather wrapping on the handle had been replaced, but even the repair was aged and cracked, splitting from the tang. Sean's irritation stirred again at the lack of proper storage and handling.

Stretching his hand toward the dagger, another movement in his periphery pulled his attention. His head snapped toward the motion, and the color drained from his face. Fear gripped him as it never had before. The panthers now framed the elevator doors, heads angled, their amber eyes fixed on him.

Memories of things moving in the dark flashed through his mind. Long-buried fears whispered in his thoughts, and his heart raced.

"Don't be minding them none. They are Papa's pets, and they'll only eat ya if he tells 'em to." The unseen, gravelly voice sounded from beyond one of the gaping black openings.

Sean shrieked and plastered himself against the wall, dislodging several artifacts. The echo of his squeal was mortifying as it faded amid the clatter of the old copper bowl rolling around on the floor.

Sean stumbled toward the center of the room, distancing himself from the unidentified voice while maintaining maximum distance from the mysterious panthers.

A gruff little man stepped from the shadows of the leftmost passage, glowering at Sean and giving the panthers a dismissive wave.

Sean gestured toward the fallen items with an apologetic shrug. His head swiveled between this strange man and the large cats. Knowing they were alive did nothing to ease his fears. "I'm sorry for . . ." Sean moved toward the shelf, bending to gather the fallen items. "Let me help with—"

"No!" The word, an authoritative command, echoed in the chamber and brought Sean to a halt mid-sentence. Now quite grumpy, the little man crossed the room in a quick, waddling huff, placing himself between Sean and the things scattered on the floor.

Two dark, beady eyes stared from beneath bushy brows that were knit in agitation. The strange little man moved to straighten the items himself, grumbling at Sean over his shoulder. "Never touch anything down here unless told ta. Never!"

Ms. Iliescu's warning echoed in Sean's mind, bringing a puzzled expression flitting across the lines of worry etched on his face. His attention was focused on the two large cats, his confusion apparent in the tone and jumble of words tumbling from his mouth. "But you—they—but you are handling the items." Sean's words rang in his ears and he winced, giving his full attention to the gruff little man. "I didn't mean that to—"

"Fine!" the little man's rough voice interjected. "You want ta get yourself cursed? Hexed? Trans-located to gods only know what dimension?"

Grabbing the knife Sean had been admiring from the shelf, the stocky fellow marched toward him, dagger held in his palm. "How about gettin' yerself haunted by a spirit that'll whisper in yer mind nigh' an day 'til ya break an become the next Ripper?"

Drawing closer, the little man lifted the dagger on his open palm.

Sean backed away from the advance, mumbling, "I—um . . ."

Continuing to push, the man herded Sean around the room, offering the dagger time and again in little pulsating gestures. The crotchety cadence of his words cut Sean's stammering off. "No? Ya sure? If ya do, by all means, play with all the pretty, shiny little things. Then I'll not have ta be watchin' after ya!"

Backpedaling through the room, Sean tried to avoid the advance. His head twisted back and forth, glancing over his shoulder to avoid colliding with any other items while skirting the mysterious panthers. Sean's sense of panic was snowballing, churning in the pit of his stomach. His Scottish roots slipped free under the torrent of nerves, thickening his accent. "What—? Have—? Is yer head full of mince?"

The little man's cheeks reddened, and he huffed. "Is me head full of mince? Is me head full of mince!" The dagger came up, no longer being offered in an open-palmed manner, but now held tight, and pointed at Sean. The tip bobbed up and down, emphasizing the man's tirade. "Now see here, lad. When ya stepped off tha lift, ya done stepped inta a world ya know shite about. Now if'n ya don wan ta be feedin flies ta spiders ta try an take in more lives, ya best listen ta what yer told!"

Both men stopped and turned toward the deep, warm, rolling laugh that swept through the chamber. The atmosphere of the room shifted, heavy with the authority of the man still hidden in shadows. Ducking to enter the room, Djain eclipsed the opening behind him when he rose to full height. Towering over everything in the place, he stood a full head and shoulders taller than Sean, who reached the six-foot mark himself. Djain's steel-blue eyes stood in bright contrast to the rich depth of his ebony skin. The only hair to be seen lay in the coal-black peak of his sharp brows and the short, thin mustache and goatee that framed his mouth, accenting his square chin. The crooked smile on his face did little to soften the chiseled edge of his jaw.

He wore an off-white dress shirt. It was tucked into his slacks and loose at the collar. He had rolled the sleeves and pushed them up past his elbow. His forearms were powerful, and the musculature rippled beneath the skin when he greeted the cats, who appeared out of the inky darkness behind him.

The strangeness of this place was gaining a deeper purchase, unsettling Sean at his core. The dichotomous appearance of Djain, a man with an open and friendly manner and an imposing frame that loomed over the room, only added to his unease.

"I'm glad you found your way, Sean." Djain's deep voice boomed, resembling the rumble of distant thunder. His speech was slow, deliberate, and marked with a thick Caribbean accent, making it soothing to the ear. Anticipation swelled as Djain studied his uneasy guest.

Djain inclined his head, his appreciation of the gruff man apparent. "Rhoin, thank you for being here and looking after him." The cats purred their approval of his continued caresses along their sturdy shoulders. "We will take care of him now. You may be on with the rest of your evening. Please, give your family my best."

Rhoin gave Sean a dismissive snort, and Djain an almost ceremonial bow. Without another word, he crossed the room and placed the dagger back on the shelf before vanishing down a darkened passage.

Sean watched the little man leave and leaned back against one of the outer tables, returning his focus to Djain and his predatory friends. Swallowing, he tugged at the tail of his jacket, summoning the nerve to address the powerful man before him. "Thank you for taking the time to meet with me, um, Papa."

Djain chuckled and walked toward Sean. The closer the massive man drew, the smaller Sean felt. His voice locked in his throat, watching both Djain and the cats close the distance.

"Breathe, man," Djain said. "You are turning colors, and we have not even begun to discuss the good stuff."

Sean felt his knees quiver. A panther sniffed his trousers and almost knocked him over with a slow, delicate nudge. His eyes drifted closed, and he fought to maintain some semblance of composure, but when the rough, broad tongue lapped out, wrapping under his chin, and licking up his cheek, all hope of that failed. His arms flailed, and he slid along the edge of the table away from the creature.

Djain's calming tones broke through his panic. "Jacia, leave him be. He needs his wits for what is to come."

Sean blinked, his blue eyes bulging as both cats misted into vapor and vanished. Gone. Dismissed with nothing more than the wave of Djain's hand. His jaw was moving, his lips working, but no sound was forming.

"Rhoin may be gruff, but he is not touched." Djain backed away, giving Sean space to find himself. "It is you that needs to have your eyes opened, or more accurately, reopened." Settling in behind the central altar, Djain adjusted the items covering the top until they were more to his liking.

Sean watched the shuffling bowls and vials. Despite his nerves, he wondered what each might contain. Questions of their potential use filled his head, drowning out the voices of the past, whispering about creatures in the dark.

Djain brought a candle blazing to life with a puff of air. Taking a handwoven bundle from amid the items, he touched the end to the flame. After a moment, he snuffed the fire from the wrapped herbs. The scent of lavender, cedar, and rosemary filled the room, carried on tendrils of smoke that rose from the smoldering bale.

Eyes filled with wonder and curiosity, Sean eased closer. "Where . . . where did the panthers go?"

A smile lit Djain's face, and he clapped once. "Good. You are asking the right questions." He slid a stone mortar to the center of the table, placing varying amounts of the unidentified substances into the bowl. "They are still here with us. Only now, they inhabit the darkness, the shadows."

Sean's gaze swept the room, anxiety creeping back into his frame. He contemplated his feet and the pool of shadows surrounding them. Drawing in a quick breath, he took a step to his right, clear of the shadows cast by the altar. His eyes shifted from one shaded pool to another, while memories of his childhood resurfaced with a vengeance.

Djain's warm laugh rose, and he pointed toward the stone floor behind Sean. "Do not forget the ones you cannot leave behind."

Sean spun, finding his shadow falling in several directions. His shoulders tightened. He drew in a breath, and his eyes moved over the distance to the elevator doors. The soft sound of the pestle grinding the dry ingredients swelled in the room. Memories of the horrors lurking in the darkness filled his mind, solidifying the army of imaginary creatures he had slain as a child. "What did you mean when you said my eyes needed to be reopened?" he asked.

"You have witnessed things beyond the mortal veil before," Djain responded. "Though you were only a wee one and grew to dismiss the truth as nothing more than the fanciful stories of a traumatized child."

Stunned at Djain's knowledge, Sean stared at him. "How the bloody hell can you know that?"

"We have had our eyes on you since your internship," Djain said. "Even then, I saw your potential. Your interview for this position and our check into your history began years ago." Leaning over the table, he smiled. "I have been anticipating this conversation for some time."

Sean folded his arms over his chest and lowered his head in thought. His mind wrestled with itself, struggling with the implications, the reality, that there were things in the shadows and he had faced them before.

Fragrances from the concoction in the mortar permeated the room.

Djain watched as Sean formulated his next question.

Apprehension was evident, etched across Sean's brow. His curiosity to unravel and understand not only the mysteries dangling before him, but all he had encountered in his youth kept him rooted to the spot. Lifting his head, he fixed his gaze on Djain. "How did they vanish?"

The corners of Djain's lips edged upward, his eyes lifting from the powder forming in the mortar. "What you know about the world is only a sliver of the truth. For all the knowledge of the scientists, historians, and archaeologists, the lot of you are still naught but babes."

Djain set the pestle aside and tested the powder between his fingers, rubbing them together, ensuring correct consistency. "Tell me, Sean, have you ever felt eyes on you when none are there? Ever seen a thing, only to turn and find it gone? Known there was something in the closet or under your bed, and that knowledge set your spine to tingle?"

The hairs on the back of Sean's neck prickled, a chill rolled over him, and his head bobbed once. Feelings he had not encountered since his youth bubbled up. His hand dropped to his side, searching for a wooden handle that had not hung from his hip for many years.

Djain's head rose and fell with him. "Yes! There are other planes, and we are not bound to stay in one. That is where Jacia and Panji are, in the realm of the Shadows, where things that stalk the darkness dwell."

Sean tried to form words, but his throat had gone dry. He forced himself to swallow before rasping out, "I think I've seen these other things . . ."

Djain's jovial persona melted away. He stepped around the table, and Sean came face to face with the man's stern intensity. "You have seen a few, but there are many. I will be happy to teach you about it all if you wish. But understand, I can tell you no more until you decide if this world is where you wish to be. It can be bloody and cruel at times, but wondrous too."

Djain turned enough to pull a small vial from the various tubes on the table. He showed it to Sean, shaking it in slow, gentle arcs, letting the viscous red liquid slosh inside. "A bit of your blood from the monthly drive," Djain said. "I have tested it. I know you have the strength of blood to see. Maybe even touch forces you thought only mythical. Be warned. Once you start along this path, there is no retreat. Those who try, break."

Taking Sean's wrist, Djain turned his hand over and placed the vial into his damp palm. "There are many forces at work in this world, Sean. Like the Quari Group, some strive to make the world better for everyone, while others only seek to empower themselves. Make no mistake, we are talking about a struggle that will impact the fate of all."

Darkness filled Djain's eyes, his voice becoming cold and hard. "There is an artifact we seek, a shattered cube that, when reassembled, would give the holder access to unfathomable power. Another group seeks this cube, The Order of the Sacred Flame. They would use it to subjugate humanity and return the world to the elder races. This must not be allowed. They have already slain many in their pursuit, and only we stand in a place to prevent their victory."

Djain stepped aside, clearing the path between Sean and the altar. "Will you lend your strength and skills to our fight? Will you help us serve the greater good? Sean, you must now decide. Dash the vial on the floor, and return to the world you know, free of any memory of what you have learned." He motioned toward the stone mortar. "Or pour your blood into the bowl, and help me save this world."

Sean's fingers closed about the sample of his blood. Thoughts of ancient peoples and their savage rituals raced through his mind. His eyes moved around the room, lingering on the artifacts lining the shelves, thinking of all there was to learn and discover. Contemplating the knowledge lost to history because archeology was missing crucial information on forces science could not quantify.

From the black depths of the archways, a pair of luminous eyes blinked.

Sean's hand tightened around the vial. A long black tail wrapped about his leg, and he sucked in a breath through clenched teeth.

The truth of Djain's words gripped his core. The weight of the mission he was asked to join was suffocating, but the promise of learning so much more was freeing. Djain's call to help others resonated in his heart.

Behind Sean, the elevator's baritone chime sounded, and the swish of opening doors called, offering escape. His stomach knotted. The courage of a young boy, standing before the darkness with a wooden sword, prepared to risk himself to protect others, blossomed within. Pressing himself against the altar, he reached across its broad top, flipped open the vial, and poured his blood into the waiting maw of the mortar.

The doors to the elevator closed, and Djain smiled.

Excerpt from the Elven Volumes of Living Knowledge
Celestial Cycle 217.193417
in the First Reign of House Kryntan

Today I christen the first Volume of Living Knowledge. Wisdom dictates we maintain a record of what has gone before, so within these pages, the members of the ruling Council will jot their thoughts, curating the history of our people.

Much time has passed since our birth. With the guidance of an elder race, the Bright Ones, we have matured as a people, defined the rules by which we will govern, and formed the First Council to lead us into the future.

The Bright Ones have tutored us, strengthened our bond with the Mother, and opened our eyes to the power that courses within. We are no longer limited to the terrestrial flames of Mother's womb. We freely traverse the Astral and open doorways into the Heavenly Realms, walking among the eternal beauty of those lands.

I am humbled at being selected as our first Queen. I shall strive to further our relations with the Bright Ones, expand our knowledge, embrace what is yet to come, and honor the faith placed in me.

—Queen Kryntan

THREE

Djain's hands crashed together in a sharp clap. "Good! Good!"

Sean watched his blood pool in the stone bowl, picking up bits of the unidentified powders, and speckling with whites, browns, and greens. He dropped the empty vial, and it rolled across the polished surface. A tremble developed in his hands, and he gripped the table's edge to cover. The sharp corners of the rough-hewn stone dug into his palms, and nervous excitement coursed through him. He closed his eyes and swallowed hard to keep the churning contents of his stomach from escaping. His cheeks puffed slightly as he exhaled in a measured, steady release through pursed lips. When his eyes opened, he found Djain watching, waiting patiently. Sean responded with a nervous smile. "You said something about other planes?"

Djain moved around the altar, picked up the pestle, and worked Sean's blood into the powder, turning it into a thick paste. "That would be a good place to start.

You are in another plane now, and you have been since you stepped from the lift. It was more than nerves churning your stomach when you arrived."

Sean studied the walls and stone again, a hint of doubt falling like a shadow over his face. "Where is it we are supposed to be, if not in our plane?"

A knowing smirk twisted Djain's face, and he glanced upward. "You would not find the pyramid above us. Here, there is nothing but forest. Thick, vibrant, and filled with plants and creatures of which you have never dreamed. This is the realm of the Fae."

"How can you know that?" Sean asked.

Djain moved to a smaller table and retrieved a piece of parchment.

Sean crossed to the wall and scratched at its surface, comparing its makeup to his knowledge of earthen layers and their composition. "Nothing here looks different from what I would expect to see in any cavern in this part of the world."

"You will learn to feel it, sense it. The unease inside you hints at the truth. Your body knows it is not where it belongs, and learning to know what it is telling you will come with time and practice." Returning to the altar, Djain displayed the parchment to Sean, showing its deckle edges and textured surface. "The paper is handmade here. I want no surprises when doing spell work, especially of this magnitude, and in this place."

Running a finger over its surface, Sean inspected the page. "Spell work? You are talking about magic now?" His brow pinched, eyes moving to the crimson paste in the bowl. His tone bordered on mocking when he asked, "Are you going to do a spell?"

Without pause, Djain gave Sean a secretive grin. "No, Sean." He placed the paper on the altar and dipped his finger into the bloody mixture. "You are."

Sean almost laughed, but the sudden appearance of a sizable black muzzle at his side wiped the doubt away. Leaning over the table, he protested. "I don't know how to do any spells!"

Djain drew symbol after symbol on the paper. Some linked, others standing apart, seeming to demand their own space. One Sean knew to be a rune, but not its name or meaning. Most were shapes he couldn't recall ever having seen before.

"Do not fret. Papa will make it ready. Then I will guide you through the rest." Completing the last symbol, Djain studied his macabre work with approval. Motioning with the blood-smeared finger, he invited Sean to join him. "Now, come around here."

Stepping aside, Djain allowed Sean to take his place at the center of the altar. "What is it we are doing?"

Djain pointed toward the page. "To become part of Special Projects requires the ability to see certain magical markers. Many of the places we travel to, the things we access, are behind doors and magical locks. Some are formed by blending magic and machine. These are fundamental parts of the work we do to protect the world. The symbols I have written in a paste of your blood ensure the magics we are about to invoke are bound to you."

"Magic and machine?" The thought triggered a mixture of awe and excitement. Sean's worldview shifted further, and he struggled to accept the possibilities. "Will it hurt?"

Djain shook his head and moved the candle he had lit earlier, placing it before Sean. "No. There will be no pain unless you fight it." Fixing Sean with a severe gaze, he stressed the point. "Do not fight it."

Sean took a deep breath, the tension of the encounter knotting his whole body. "Aye. No fighting it."

A quiet laugh softened Djain's expression. "It is easy. Relax. No need to worry. Now, all you must do is clear your mind and focus on your intent, lift the paper, touch it to the flame, and say 'lift the veil from my eyes.'"

Sean repeated the phrase several times before Djain stopped him with a chuckle. "Use your own words. You are asking the spirits to open your eyes, to allow you to see beyond the mortal veil."

"If I have seen these things before, why do we have to do this spell? Why can't I see them now?"

Djain's head tilted to the side. "The veil was only fractured when you were a child, not lifted. And your aggressive defense of the spaces you inhabited eventually kept the creatures away, allowing the cracks to heal, which is why you stopped seeing them." He motioned toward the paper. "So today, we remove that block and let you see things you never imagined."

Sean thought of the nightmare creatures of his childhood, things he now knew were real, and considered his limited knowledge of their taxonomy. He fought to keep his imagination from birthing armies of unseen horrors in his mind. A shiver crept down his spine. His hand trembled, but he resolved to look beyond the unknown and approach the situation in a scholarly fashion. "So, I don't have to speak in Latin or some other archaic language?"

Djain chuckled and shook his head. "This is not Hogwarts. Your words clarify your intent." Djain's amusement faded, and he turned a hip to lean against the table. A weighty sense of importance settled in the room. "You can speak whatever language calls to you, make all the strange noises you wish—grunt, growl, even bark, so long as your intent is clear. You never want the spirits to guess what you are asking. The herbs and bobbles assist, provide a structure to focus and refine the magic, but at its core, your intent is everything. It is the very heart of magic. Do everything you can to be concise and clear."

The flapping of the spelled paper exaggerated the tremor in Sean's hand. He stared at the flame and muttered to himself, turning the words over, reforming the sentence until he was satisfied with the composition. He lifted the corner of the paper to the flame and spoke his invocation. "Open my eyes so I can see what others cannot."

The flames wrapped around the page, and Djain pushed an empty copper bowl toward Sean. "Drop the paper in the bowl." He motioned about the room. "Watch what happens as it burns."

The flames leaped from the paper as it settled into the curve of the copper. Orange tongues lapped at the air and brought the rich hues of the metal to life. The unpleasant smell of burning blood seeped into the air, and with it, Sean saw swirling tendrils of ethereal vapors appear around the room.

A cascade of golden flakes rained from the top panels framing the elevator. Where he expected to find buttons, a swirling mist was forming. Over the stone beneath the artifacts lining the walls, shades ranging from green to red sparked and trickled. As Sean turned, he saw a roiling, gray vapor filling the passageways through which Djain and Rhoin had entered.

Rounding toward the elevator again, what had been a golden shower of wisps was now well defined. Amid the cascading energy, a display of the date and time had formed, hovering over the brushed metal surface. The time caught Sean's attention, showing it to be 12:44 a.m. The swirling mass became a mystical call button in the shape of the pyramid he had left somewhere far above, in another realm. Sean closed his mouth, the soft sound of Djain's laughter making him realize it was agape.

Moving toward a display shelf, Djain pointed to the now visible labels. "The color of the name will show how dangerous an item is. We are studying these items, and you can help with that, but please mind the colors. Green means it is safe for you to handle; anything else, you best have Rhoin move for you."

Sean rubbed at the back of his head, noting that there were few green labels, and most were well into the orange and reds. "Is there special training required to handle them myself?"

"No. If only it were that simple. The genetics of humanity and how it interacts with magical energies when new life forms remain a mystery. Many fantastical races have emerged, among them the Dwarves." Djain pointed to the dagger Sean and Rhoin had been discussing when he arrived. A deep, blood-orange label denoting its danger level glowed in ominous warning below the blade. "Our Dwarven brothers and sisters have a special gift. They can neither invoke magic nor be touched by it."

"Oh." Sean swallowed. "I think I understand." Checking his watch, he pointed at the clock above the elevator. "Your clock appears to be wrong. I've only been down here about thirty minutes." He pulled his sleeve back and twisted his arm to show Djain the correct time.

Djain's head bobbed up and down. "So you have. There is more to learn about the realms than the names. Time does not flow consistently from one realm to another. Time in the Fae realm moves much slower. For every minute we are here, ten pass up there. That is why I have a clock. It is far too easy to lose track of time when you are jumping between realms."

"I—" Sean turned and studied the date and time hovering above the brushed metal surface in a warm amber glow. "Ten to one. I'll keep that in mind." Frowning at his watch, he sighed and tugged his sleeve down to cover the useless timepiece.

Crossing back to the altar, Djain dunked his finger into the bloody mixture in the mortar and slathered it into his open palm. He took a pinch of the ash from the burned spell and mixed them with his finger. "Now, you see the veil covering the tunnels?"

"Aye, I do," Sean said, moving closer and examining the shifting vapor.

"These ways are blocked to you. Go ahead, try to go through." Djain wiped the finger he used to stir the mixture in his palm on a towel.

Sean moved up to the misty barrier and stepped through, only to step right back into the room, facing Djain.

Djain laughed as confusion swept over Sean. His laughter evolved into a boisterous roar when Sean attempted to step through again.

"Isn't that interesting?" Sean mused, studying the edge of the energy field where it met the stone.

Pulling a bone-handled knife from the altar, Djain crossed to the other tunnel. "You cannot go through that one yet, but you need access to pass through this one."

Djain lay the blade across his palm and closed his massive fingers around the polished metal.

Sean winced when Djain yanked the knife free, slicing through the meaty part of his palm.

Blood dripped from the blade, vanishing into puffs of purple smoke; not a single drop reached the ground.

Djain smeared the bloody mixture over the doorway, invoking a new spell in a language Sean didn't understand. Purple smoke consumed the smeared blood almost as quickly as it was spread across the rock. The blood-laden paste soaked into the stone, vanishing like vapor on a pane of glass.

The dark curtain of energy drew back into the deep shadows of the passage, revealing the wavering image of another room beyond.

Djain laid the spotless blade alongside the candle, picked up the towel, and wiped his hand. "See if you can get to the other side of this one now. See where it leads you."

After giving the knife a second, puzzled glance, Sean stepped into the shadows beneath the stone arch. With each step, the shadows deepened. He glanced over his shoulder, where Djain motioned him onward, now oddly hazy and distant. He hesitated, peering at the room ahead, still unable to make out its contents.

Sean stretched his arms out and groped the empty darkness, batting away the memory of twisted faces that leered at him in his childhood. He searched for a wall or any form of structure to lend stability to the disorienting space. Cold sweat beading on his brow. A set of luminous eyes appeared before him, followed by a rumbling purr at his side. He froze, fighting his instinct to retreat backward. "Good kitty."

A low chuff sent a rush of heated breath spreading across his lower back, prickling the hairs along his neck. A firm nudge on his hindquarters caused him to wobble forward. He waved his arms to find his balance again. Fear tinged his voice. "Hey now—" he searched for the cat, discovering nothing but the empty air. "Either show yourself or leave me be."

In response, a tongue materialized, lapped at his cheek, and vanished. A tail brushed along the outside of his right leg, and a muzzle lifted him by the seat of his pants, pushing him forward.

"Oy—hey—wait!"

Sean stumbled forward, phasing through the wavering image. He reclaimed his footing in a spacious, occupied room. This new room was adorned in a modern industrial style: broad walkways, dark metals, patterned woods, and lots of glass. From amid the frosted glass panels, a dozen pairs of eyes fixed their gaze on him. The unfamiliar faces regarded him with a mix of confusion and amusement.

Wiping his brow and rubbing his hands on his pants, Sean laughed, color rising to his cheeks. He gave a quick wave. "Um, hello!"

A few of the onlookers returned the wave. One gave a head nod. They all smiled, and one by one returned to their work, putting the distraction of Sean's arrival out of their minds.

The sound of a baritone chime pulled Sean's focus to his right. Lift doors occupied the center of the wall, with amber mist floating above, displaying the date and time, 2:37 a.m. On the right panel, swirling smoke formed buttons that hovered over the brushed metal frame. The doors slid open, and Djain stepped into the room. Around the room, calls of greeting sounded. Djain found each of them with his eyes and returned their greetings with warmth.

Sean checked his watch and confirmed that fewer than forty-five minutes had passed since Ms. Iliescu had deposited him in the lift. He looked behind himself. A pair of spiral-trimmed trees stood to either side of a shimmering curtain of energy, and the distorted image of the room he had departed moments before.

Feeling Djain's presence, Sean turned to find him standing between the portal and the lift across the room. "Two ways to the same location. Which is . . . where? What realm?"

Djain's lips hinted at curling upward. "You tell me. How are all those butterflies in your tummy?"

Sean's head tilted, and he placed a hand over his stomach. After brief consideration, he faced Djain with an unsure gaze. "Our realm? The normal one. For us anyway."

"Terra," Djain corrected. "We call it Terra. In answer to where we are, this is the thirty-third floor, the Operations Center for the Special Projects department." He led Sean across the room. "All fieldwork and recovery efforts are managed from here."

They approached a strange table at the center of the room. It felt out of place and appeared to hover. Sean circled it, studied it, tried to find its secrets. A slab of rough-cut wood served as a tabletop. Living vines grew from its underside and stretched toward the floor, never reaching the tile. Atop the floating table sat a pair of sculpted, marble hands holding up a worn stone bowl of water. Intricate knotwork covered the outside of the bowl with copper pieces inset around the rim. A segment of the copper inlays appeared to have fallen out and lay on the natural wood beside the stone hands.

Sean motioned toward the copper shape. "Perhaps I can start by repairing this fine piece." As he spoke, he bent sideways and ran a hand through the vines dangling underneath, finding no supports or poles. Righting himself, he gawked at the confounding table. He pushed down on its top and found no give. "How is this not collapsing?"

Djain chuckled. "You keep asking good questions, but this answer needs to wait until you have . . . more experience in the world, now that you know the truth."

Reaching for the small copper object, Djain rolled it over in his hands, contemplating his next actions. "As for the bowl, there is nothing to fix. It is a tool for scrying, but it is among the most powerful I have ever seen. We keep this piece out, breaking the bowls' enchantments unless we are using it."

With a knowing grin, Djain offered the piece to Sean. "Take this and place it where it belongs. Look into the bowl and ask to see the Quari Cube."

Sean plucked the warm copper symbol from Djain's thick fingers. "Quari Cube?" He puzzled over the name. "Is that the name of the shattered artifact you mentioned earlier?"

"Yes, the Quari Cube. Your primary task will be to locate and recover the missing pieces. Perhaps we will get lucky, and the bowl will quicken to your command, showing you where to locate one of the remaining segments."

Studying the water, Sean edged closer to the table, inserting the copper piece into the bowl. "Show me the Quari Cube." As the words formed, something unfamiliar jumped between him and the basin. The exchange was shocking. He tried to pull away, but was bound to the device. Unable to release his hold, he found his focus locked on the rippling surface of the water. Images formed at the bottom of the basin. Brief blurry glimpses, churning the water into violent swells that slammed into the sides of the container. Icy droplets of water splashed across his hands, and a brilliant white light exploded from the bowl, engulfing him.

I am hesitant to reveal my thoughts, yet know future generations will require clarity of past; therefore, I submit to these living pages. Allow my first thoughts to be of our beginning. We were spawned in the Mother's living flames, Her soul, Her passion, breathing life into us—Her children. We were one with the fire. We bathed in the flows of the Mother's heart blood. We soared upon the currents rising from Her skin. We are one, and as she changes, so shall we.

— Councilor Jerandyl

FOUR

The light faded, and the world around Sean snapped into view. The modern office was gone. A wintery gale ripped at his clothing, driving tiny frozen crystals into his exposed skin. He pressed against the weathered stone at his back, gripping the icy surface. His feet skated along a ledge jutting from the cragged face of a cliff. Beyond its edge, the tops of fir trees reached toward him through an ever-shifting cloud of snow. A gust of wind carried the fine crystals past, whiting out the world. Instinct drove him against the frozen stone. The chill seeped into his joints and sapped the feeling from his aching fingers.

Straining to see through the blizzard, he called out. *"Papa Djain?"*

The response wasn't the basso, slow-paced lilt of Djain, but a sharp, heated, nasal drone that spat the words of some foreign tongue in fiery bursts.

Sean's eyes narrowed, confusion sweeping through him. He rubbed his hands along his arms and strained to find the unseen speaker.

The wind roared, carrying the strange voice away in its fury.

Frustrated and terrified, Sean eased along the snow-packed ledge, searching for the mysterious speaker and perhaps some answers.

A dark crevice in the stone face took shape through the blowing snow, and other voices, distant and muddled, joined the first.

Sean approached, slipping around the jagged edge of the opening with caution. Stepping into the crevice, he found the uneven walls of a natural cave. Water meandered along the floor in a thin stream, making its way to the edge, where it cascaded from the sheer drop, freezing in the open air and creating a crystalline fall. The passage was empty, sloping gently up into the mountainside and vanishing around a bend. An uneven glow lit the path, a flickering remnant of an unseen fire in the deeper recesses of the fissure. Now that he was protected from the whipping wind, the voices were more robust, though he couldn't make out their number.

"Hello!" Sean called, his voice reverberating in the stone chamber, creating an eerie echo.

The other speakers ignored his hail.

Unable to understand their words, he pressed forward, peeking around the corner. The rough stone floor plateaued before descending into an enormous cavern. Around the edges, formations had grown into thick pillars, and near the middle, the ground split. Several dark chasms gaped open, leaving only one easily traversable path across the space, and two narrow ledges skirting the giant formations. The broad path was littered with corpses in various states of decay. They ranged from scattered skeletons to a pair of fresh bodies, which, by appearance, were members of the group huddled at the cavern's edge.

A stone pedestal stood on the far side of the cavern. An onyx cube covered in iridescent blue symbols rested at its center. Sean was confident the strange object must be the Quari Cube.

He studied the men before him. They were draped in furs and leather, each carrying weapons; medieval swords and polearms, well used wooden bucklers bound with leather straps, and all bore the same crest. Three of the men held smoldering censers and stood in a rough triangle around the remaining half dozen. The costrels and leather satchels they had been toting were lying along the sides of the path, discarded as the group focused on their goal.

A monotone liturgy droned from those carrying the censers, their chant meant to bolster the group's spirits. Despite the effort, their fear was palpable.

The man with the nasal voice spoke again, giving a firm command and pointing right at Sean.

Sean stepped back, pointing at himself. *"Me?"*

One man turned and ran back up the path, dashing directly at Sean.

Still struggling to understand the situation, Sean braced for the collision. The hair along his arms stood on end and his body shivered as the man phased through him unhindered.

Tracing a warding symbol over his chest, the man paused and looked back through Sean. The lines on his face conveyed his unease, and his steps became unsure. He was still searching the shadows when he rounded the corner and vanished into the darkness.

The reality that he was still standing in the Quari Group building registered, and Sean's head ached. Rubbing at his eyes, he returned his attention to the strange happenings below.

Another man separated from the group and picked his way around the right side of the cavern. He hugged the columns and edged his way along the narrow path, despite the gaping chasm at his feet.

Determined to get a better view, Sean prepared himself for the numbing chill and passed through the group into the main chamber. The hairs on his arms rose. His stomach knotted, and a sense of dread swelled, intensifying the further he moved into the space. He stopped midway between the cube and the group, just beyond the gaping holes in the floor.

In the surrounding darkness, something moved.

Thoughts of Panji and Jacia flashed through his mind, and he searched the shadows, never finding more than lingering impressions of another presence.

Behind the man on the ledge, a pale face emerged from the stone. Fiery determination underscored the scowl etched on the newcomer's face, underscoring a terrifying ferocity.

Like a spirit emerging from a wall in a horror film, the man slid from the rock. He appeared human, but for the enormous, ashen gray wings that spread along the wall. The new creature stared at Sean, placing a slender finger over his lips, and rocking his head from side to side.

Sean cried out, *"Look out!"*

The creature's eyes narrowed to angry slits at Sean's interference.

Sean's legs trembled under the creature's glare.

A sadistic smile spread over the winged man. With horrifying glee, he stretched out his arm, and toppled the adventurer into the open maw of the fissure.

The cavern amplified the man's screams, and they crashed back in on themselves as the floor closed around him. The gruesome sounds of death echoed through the cavern, silencing the liturgical chant of the dead man's peers. Sean watched the men fight their urge to turn away. To a man, they kept their silent vigil until their comrade's cries faded, leaving only the sounds of their ragged breathing and the grinding of stone.

Blood seeped up through the creases in the rough stone, forming a crimson pool.

The murdering figure cast a hate-filled glance at the group. His focus shifted, and he stalked toward Sean, crossing the spreading puddle of blood without disturbing the surface. The wings were all that kept this creature from appearing human. He was naked and wore no jewelry, carrying only a sword of blue flame. Slowing, the beast sniffed at Sean, scowled, and dismissed him. Positioning himself behind the cube, his focus locked on the group.

The small party refused to buckle under their fear. One man spilled his stomach. Others stared at the crimson stain, visible tremors developing in their hands. A heated discussion broke out, filled with adamant gestures toward the cube.

Not a single man glanced behind.

A censer bearer lifted his hand, bringing the discussion to a halt. Kneeling, he removed his glove and tore open his finger with the tip of another's blade. Blood ran from his finger, marking the stone with a mystical symbol.

Sean moved closer, recognizing it as a mark he had seen on the conference room table and Djain's altar. Still, he couldn't place its origin or meaning.

Behind the stone plinth supporting the Quari Cube, the winged creature paced in irritation, his muscles churning with tension.

Gathering all remaining lengths of rope from the group, the priest tied the pieces together to create a single, long loop. Laying the cords on the bloody symbol, he waved the censer over the makeshift rope and chanted a short phrase. "Defendatu eta babestu." He encouraged the others to join until all their voices were speaking the words in unison.

Fury etched itself upon the creature's features. The blue flames danced along the blade, licking the air with vivid tongues of fire.

The circle of rope was wrapped around the group. Held by the priestly figures, they continued their cadence and moved across the room as one.

An otherworldly wail broke from the winged creature. The force of its cry carried such distress that even the chanting faltered. Realizing their error, the lead clergyman encouraged the group to lift their voices again, and they rejoined him with renewed vigor.

Taking to the air, the creature hurtled across the cavern, a blur of blue flame and ashen feathers streaking toward the group. The sword arced toward the priest's head and crashed into an invisible barrier. A shower of multicolored sparks exploded from the point of impact.

The party stumbled back a step, searching for the unseen attacker. What they found was a renewed surety. With confidence, they moved ahead, making for the cube. When the men approached, Sean moved out of the way, joining in their chant, cheering them on.

The maddened creature reigned fire and fury upon the invisible barrier in a relentless assault. Each blow landed in a different location, searching for weakness and turning the room into a cascade of ethereal light.

Once the party reached the pedestal, one man pulled out a stone chisel inscribed with unusual writing. He placed the tip against the onyx cube, and another drove it with a heavy hammer. The chisel sank into the cube, and a pained, tortured cry ripped through the room, tearing at Sean's soul. The hammer came down again, and the onyx box shattered into twelve irregular pieces. Even broken, the glowing symbols on the cube remained bright; the shattered bits vibrating, moving, and trying to reform.

The men in the group worked with haste under the priest's protective chant. Gathering each piece, they wrapped them in different bits of leather and bound them with hemp cords. Each member of the group was charged with carrying parts of the artifact, and the pieces vanished inside their tunics for safekeeping.

Outside the protective border, the winged man settled into a seething glare, studying each of the men with purpose and intent.

With the cube secured, the group moved to their fallen comrades. The leader bent and removed the medallions from the fallen. He tucked them away inside his garments with reverence.

Sean watched the group depart the cave, leaving him and the mysterious creature to study one another. He found the silence unnerving.

The bitter hatred in the winged creature's eyes set Sean's nerves on edge.

Moving to follow the group, Sean found his way blocked by a blazing blue blade.

The creature moved around him, a predator assessing its next meal. When it spoke, its sure, frigid tone sent shivers down Sean's spine. *"You do not belong in this place nor this time, and I shall not abide a witness to my failure. Time will see we cross paths again. You will grovel before me."*

The blade flashed, slicing through Sean's chest. The flames engulfed him in a deadly cold that chilled his soul. Pain swept over him, and he cried out, falling back as the blade was wrenched free. Before his head hit the stone, the frigid agony escorted him into darkness.

Excerpt from the Elven Volumes of Living Knowledge
Celestial Cycle 157.576109
in the Third Reign of House Jerandyl

I fear what we brazenly forget and reimagine in our histories. Children no longer know the truth of our origins. The heat, suffering, and long years that transpired before the gardens we call home bloomed. We sing fables—fanciful tales of life born amid silken petals. I can no longer condone our willful ignorance. There is solace in knowing the Mother remembers, and these tomes bear silent witness. Darkness lingers just beyond the horizon, and I can not endure. On the morrow, I join the Mother, giving myself without reservation. I pray you heed my warning. I have done what I can. Farewell.

—Councilor Zalitor Varunia

FIVE

Everyone gawk at the new guy.

A smokey, alto voice floated through the inky darkness, wrapping Sean in warmth.

"There you are."

Sean fought the ache in his head, focusing on the voice, trying to follow it as it grew distant.

"Back up and give him space. He's coming round."

Feet shuffled, clothing rustled, and other far-off voices took shape as Sean eased his eyes open. The false daylight created by the bright LED bulbs was diffused by a curtain of raven hair that hung around his face. A pair of compassionate eyes studied him through thick black lashes. The dusky tones of her eyelids, combined with the thin, dark lines of her sculpted brows, made their emerald facets glow.

A soft, caring smile formed as she watched him studying her features. "Haven't even gotten you into the field yet, and already I have to mend you." She gave him a playful wink. "I can already tell you're going to be trouble."

Though his head was pounding, instinct still drove him to return her smile. "What—ow."

The pain of moving his jaw caused him to wince, and she placed a finger over his lips. A spark arced between them and followed the path of her finger. She traced the supple skin of his lip, sending healing energy into him.

It tickled and thrilled.

Sean was enthralled.

"Shhh." She lifted her finger from his lips, and the connection snapped, only to spring back to life when her slender fingers slid along his jaw. "Rest a moment longer."

Djain knelt at his side, and Sean tried to turn his head, but the lady's gentle touch held him fast.

"Glad to see you are still with us," teased Djain. "How is he?"

The lady lifted her chin to answer. Her delicate strands of hair shifted, exposing the pointed tip of an ear. "He will be fine. It won't be long before he can tell us what happened." Her focus returned to Sean. Finding him studying her with quiet intensity, her eyes sparkled.

He pursed his lips. Questions crashed through his mind, each fighting for priority amid his struggle to organize his thoughts. Her touch was exhilarating. The shape of her ears brought to mind the myths and legends of the Fae, and the longer he focused on her, the more difficult it became to keep his thoughts in order. The soft rounding of her face, her high cheekbones, and the slight sweep of her nose as it narrowed to a tiny round tip were enchanting.

She noticed his careful evaluation and watched his lips twitch, forming involuntary little smiles while he traced her features with his eyes. Giving him a coy smile, she blushed. She leaned closer and spoke in a hushed tone, as though the cascade of her raven locks afforded them some form of privacy. "I'm Axylia. It's a pleasure to meet you, Sir Byrne."

Her fingers drew away from his cheek, breaking the tantalizing tingle of her touch.

With a playful brightness in his eyes, he whispered his reply. "Sean, please. I don't think being knighted by my mum counts, and the pleasure is mine, Axylia. Thank you."

Beside them, Djain cleared his throat and chuckled, causing both of their cheeks to darken.

Axylia sat upright, and the delicate strands of her hair brushed over Sean's face.

It tickled, and Sean regretted the laugh. Every part of him was cold and ached. Without the shelter of her hair, the brightness of the room stung. He turned his head and shielded his eyes with a hand. He grimaced and blinked through the discomfort, noticing the cloud of faces assembled around them.

Djain rose, addressing the huddled mass. "Alright, all of you, get back to your charges. We have family in the field needing your guidance." While he spoke, he lowered his hand, offering it to Sean.

Gradually, people returned to their stations.

Sean took Djain's hand and pulled himself to his feet.

Axylia rose, standing at his side. "Can you tell us what happened? What you saw?"

Sean's eyes moved over the length of her. The top of her head reached his shoulders. Her slender frame was draped with a sleeveless dress and belted about the waist. Natural fibers with bright colors were layered, giving the appearance of falling leaves around the hem, which came to rest mid-thigh. Her pale, shapely legs covered the distance to the floor, terminating at her bare feet. The sparkling sapphire polish on her toes glinted under the lights, and she wiggled them for effect, coaxing a smile from him.

Axylia's giggle snapped Sean back into the moment, yanking his gaze up to meet hers. He couldn't hide the jab of pain caused by the quick movement, and he rubbed the back of his head. "I'm . . . not sure where to start." His eyes shifted from Djain to the stone bowl and the copper piece lying beside it. "What is that? What did I witness? How did that creature see me?" He squinted at the floor, rubbing the base of his neck. "And what bloody well happened to my head?"

Djain's amusement became tempered with intense interest after the rush of questions. "Of course, we will answer all of your questions, but first, please, tell me all that you saw in the bowl. Never have I seen such a reaction, and I am eager to discover the cause."

Moving with fluid grace, Axylia pulled a chair from a nearby station. "Sit. Tell us your tale, and together we will find the answers."

With an appreciative smile, Sean sank into the chair. He sighed when he felt her fingers slip into his hair, wrapping around the back of his head. The energy he experienced before charged along his spine, and he relaxed into her touch. "What are you doing?"

"All Elves are gifted with ties to the cycles of life and death. Something has marked your spirit, your essence. I believe you would call it your soul." Axylia leaned closer, the heat of her breath moving the hairs along the back of his head. "I am easing the wounds left by this. Please, tell us what happened, so we have a better understanding."

Her voice soothed him, stirred him, and he swallowed down his reaction. "Of course."

Djain pulled up another chair, calling to a bystander. "Jason, please get him something to drink."

A man wearing a faded concert t-shirt and jeans scampered off toward the water cooler.

Djain settled in across from Sean. "Tell us everything that happened from the moment you touched the bowl."

Sean recounted his experience, telling of the white light, talking about the snowy cliff-side ledge, and finding the cave. He spoke of how he had called out to the men, but they couldn't hear him. When he reached the part where the man had moved through him, Djain interrupted, a quizzical expression on his sculpted features. "You mean it was as though you were there but unseen?"

The scrutinizing gaze and shocked tone of Djain's voice caused Sean's brow to rise. "Exactly." Concerned that something had gone wrong, he swallowed and asked. "I take it that isn't normal?"

Djain shook his head. He considered the bowl, then Sean. "The scrying bowl is a magical mirror. Flat. Hard. You see what it wishes to show you, but you are not part of the vision, unable to control the view, much like a moving picture show. Interacting in the manner you describe is unusual indeed."

Sean closed his eyes, feeling the healing energies flowing from Axylia's fingers. The pain was gone, and he briefly considered letting her continue. The thought flooded his mind with guilt, so he rolled his head back, eyes bright with appreciation. "No more pain, thank you."

Her smile was enchanting. Her fingers slowed and slid down to his shoulders. "You are most welcome." Pulling her hands away, she moved around and sat on the floor beside him. "Continue, please."

He resumed his story, picking up with the man pushed into the pit, though he left the graphic end of that incident out of his retelling. When he spoke of the naked creature, everyone's interest piqued. Others drifted over to listen, and gradually, the circle of strange face reformed around him.

Sean told of the bloody symbol and how he recognized it from among those carved into Djain's table. He explained the makeshift rope, the blessing, and how the group had crossed the room with the winged creature unable to harm them. He relayed the destruction and divvying of the onyx cube and the men's retrieval of their compatriot's medallions.

By the time he spoke of his confrontation with the strange man, anticipation buzzed through the group. When he told them of the flaming slicing through him, Djain and Axylia locked eyes.

"There was a Bright One there!" Djain said, an edge of excitement in his voice Sean had never heard before.

"A Bright One! That explains the state of him," Axylia said.

Dain studied Sean, his thoughts churning. "Knocked him out of the vision, out of consciousness, and back into his body."

Axylia placed her hand on Sean's leg, studying him. "And scarred his spirit. Dangerous business tangling with a Bright One."

Countenance darkening, Djain hissed a name. "Vitan!"

Sean held up a hand, glancing at the loose circle of people growing around them. "Wait. Vitan? Is he the winged creature? What the bloody hell is a Bright One? And what do you mean, he knocked me back into my body?"

"Vitan may be a Bright One, but he is the worst sort," Djain said. "A trickster, loyal only to self. He is, in some part, why this place is warded against Bright Ones. His help never comes without cost, and often, is laced with pain." Locking eyes with Sean, he admonished, "If you ever encounter him again, be wary of every word from his mouth, and take nothing at face value."

Axylia's slender hand slid to Sean's knee, giving him a comforting pat. Her eyes widened as she shot Djain a look. "Enough of dire warnings. Perhaps a bit of history is required to help our new friend understand." Her focus returned to Sean, her eyes locking with his. "Before time as we know it, the gods existed. The Bright Ones were the first race they ever created. You would call them Angels and Demons, but in reality, there is no delineation between them."

Djain leaned in, taking over. "The gods were bored, and bang!" Djain clapped his meaty hands, and it echoed in the room. "We have the cosmos as we know it." Looking around the room, he motioned the stragglers in, and the sloppy circle around them solidified. Some settled on the floor, like Axylia, and others knelt behind.

Jason returned and leaned into the group, passing a cold cup of water to Sean. With the attention on him, he shrugged and jumped into the conversation. "So now, in the middle of all these awesome explosions and stuff, the gods focused on random bits of rock and gas, forming them into living planets. That is how the Mother was born. Brimming with the magic of the gods and teeming with potential."

Across the circle, opposite Axylia, sat another slender woman. She had pointed ears which peeked through the dark copper hair that framed her sandalwood face. Her violet eyes held Sean, and he had the oddest sensation that he knew her.

His eyes narrowed, sweeping over the lines of her face, and he tried to find her in his memories.

"I'm Talaunia, and that," she motioned toward the young man who had provided the water, "is Jason. He hasn't enough manners to introduce himself, so you'll have to forgive him."

Catching Sean's studious gaze, Talaunia flashed him a secretive smirk while the others teased Jason and laughed. "The Mother was bursting with life, and she sprouted the loveliest of grasses, flowers, and trees. Forests, thick and full, in ways you would find difficult to imagine. Then, from the core of her being, she birthed her children." She brushed back the coppery strands of her hair with fluid grace, displaying the delicate point of her ear. "The Elves." Her eyes ignited something deep inside Sean, who remained unable to reconcile the odd feeling of familiarity she stirred within.

Djain jumped in. "It was then the gods took notice of their new toy. Interested in the Elves, they sent the Bright Ones to keep watch."

Talaunia nudged Djain with her elbow, picking right back up with the story. "Our society grew, and after a time, some of our kind mated with the Bright Ones. The Elevari came from those couplings; our mixed-blood cousins. The Elevari embraced a darker form of the magic we possess, and over time, corruption seeped into the Mother. Those in our society who copulated with them were shunned. It drove a wedge through families, ended eon long friendships, and eventually developed into a civil war."

"It was during their civil war that the Elves discovered how to open portals to other realms." A new face, sitting next to Talaunia, was now speaking. She wore her dark hair in pigtails. Her lips were painted with shiny black lipstick, and a silver chain wrapped around her neck like a collar. She was dressed in a black skirt, with a white top patterned with grey skulls. "Oh, I'm Sarah." She gave a quick royal wave and glanced at Talaunia, who rewarded her with a wink. Her eyes lit up, and she plunged ahead. "With the help of the Bright Ones, the original line of Elves ended the war in a single moment, and the world fractured forever. By using blood magic and bindings, the Elves expelled the Elevari and all their closest allies into another plane."

Jason took up the lesson. "Ok, so using all this magic at once kind of put the Mother into a sort of hibernation. No matter what the pure scientists tell you, that caused the first ice age. The continuing cycles are the phases of the Mother's healing, and now, we aren't helping."

Adjusting herself to lean against Sean's leg, Axylia turned her attentive gaze his way. "We weathered the changes, wondering if we had utterly destroyed the Mother. Then she stirred, coming awake. The ice pulled back, and life returned in force. Forests flourished again, and with this rebirth came all manner of creatures, among them, the humans."

"The Bright Ones learned nothing from their mingling with the Elves," Talaunia said, retaking control of the conversation. "Soon, they were copulating with humans, another race born of the Mother, but one that couldn't tap into her magical power. The mixed-blood offspring of the powerless humans and the Bright Ones had a somewhat less disastrous outcome. New races came to be, vampires and shifters, giants and succubi, as well as altered humans with the ability to sense and use the Mother's magic."

"Seers and mystics. Travelers and guardians. Witches like Sarah and me," Jason piped up. "We also have shaman," he dipped his head toward Sean, "like you."

"Like me?" Sean inquired. "What makes you think that?" His head tilted to the side. "And what's the difference between them?"

"I told you we tested the blood," Djain said. "The genetic markers do not lie. Each taint of Bright One blood alters the DNA in specific ways. I think you will find the path of the shaman comes to you with the ease of breathing." Pointing toward the scrying bowl, he added. "And seeing how that reacted to your request, I am eager to see how it manifests."

Talaunia leaned in. "As for the differences between the magically inclined humans, it is at its core nothing more than labels. You are all witches with the same access to power and ability, but some excel in certain areas. Those labeled as seers have visions of what may come. The mystics find it easier and less disturbing to talk with spirits. Travelers are gifted at projecting their consciousness to other places. Guardians are quite adept at elemental warfare and protection, with strong bonds to the Mother. There are healers, necromancers, shadow casters . . . the list seems quite endless." She paused. Her eyes swept over him, and Sean found her smile stirring the feelings of familiarity again. "As for the shaman, you lot are spiritual warriors. Often showing heightened abilities across many skills, especially those of an intangible nature."

Sean pulled his gaze from Talaunia, and it fell to Axylia. "And what of these other races—species you mentioned? Where are they? Why do we not see them?" He studied Axylia's features again. The effect the two ladies were having on him played itself out in the curve of his lips and the light in his eyes, giving him a boyish charm.

"There are many reasons," Djain responded. "The most prominent being that many find it difficult to reproduce. Long ago, they were known. You have all the fae tales that have become nothing more than a myth. When the humans spread, the other races distanced themselves."

"Belief in gods and magic faded," Sarah said. "Science became God, like capital g god. Humans mocked those with any belief in the divine or magic, and you see the results today. Humans have lost touch with magic and the Mother."

"Others, like the fae races, moved to another plane. The shifters are living among you, but they keep their natures hidden," Djain added. "Now that your eyes are opening, you will see they have been all around you, and you were unaware."

Sean studied the group, his eyes lingering on those who had not introduced themselves, wondering how they fit into this new world. His gaze settled on Djain. "I'm seeing what you meant about all our knowledge being but a sliver."

Djain chuckled, approval in his eyes. "You will be a quick study, I think."

"Let's hope—" Sean glanced sideways at the scrying bowl. "What about that Bright One, Vitan? You have never seen him there before?"

"No." Djain's eyes darkened, his jaw tensed, and he pushed whatever troubled him aside as his gaze swept across the faces of those gathered. "Everyone here has seen what you saw, but none of us experienced it the way you did. Nor did we see Vitan."

Axylia shifted. She studied Sean, a worried puzzlement creasing her brow. Her head snapped around, her eyes locking on Djain. "What happened? How did he not only see but interact and get struck?"

All eyes focused on Djain, expectation charging the silence. His brow knotted in thought, lips pursed in concentration until he replied. "I am uncertain."

There were audible gasps interspersed through the group, and most wore stunned expressions.

Talaunia was the one to comment. "I've never heard those words from you. You're the one who teaches us all!"

Djain turned to her and chuckled. "There is much even I do not know. We all continue to learn and grow throughout our path." He lifted his gaze and focused on Sean. "I have a theory, but it may well be wrong."

"Let's have it then," Sean encouraged. "At least we'd have something to work from."

Djain brought his meaty hands together in a single clap and laughed. "I like how you think!" Settling himself forward, he rested his elbows on his knees.

"The scrying bowl reacted to the shaman within you and pulled your spirit to the event rather than showing it." His eyes scanned the group. "More like he projected, rather than seeing a vision through the glass."

Axylia tilted her head in thought. "That would explain what happened. Why the blade affected his essence and how he could see what none of us did." She squared her focus on Djain. "But it doesn't explain how an untrained man could project, not only to another place but into the past."

A murmur of consent and agreement swept through the small group, and Djain lifted a finger to silence it. "I have a theory on this as well. Lineage, or more specifically, the strength of lineage."

Puzzled glances were exchanged throughout the room as Jason voiced their thoughts. "What do you mean by that? You think the Bright One in Sean's ancestral line is more powerful than the one in others?"

Djain held up his hands to settle them. "Not at all. More a question of generations." All eyes focused back on Sean. "Have you ever traced your family history? Everyone here has, going back generations, trying to find when the magic entered their bloodline. The most recent being Sarah, seven generations ago."

Sean stared at Djain dumbfounded, thoughts of his childhood rushing through his mind. "Could mom have been telling the truth?" Feeling the weight of their eyes upon him, Sean lowered his head.

Axylia peeked up at him with a curious glint, her hand stroking his knee encouragingly.

When Sean continued, he spoke to the group, but kept his gaze on her. "Whenever I asked about my grandparents, my mother told me that her father worked as a cobbler, and her mother was an angel. I always thought she was speaking in metaphor, meaning she cared for others and had a kind soul."

Eyes blazing with anticipation, Axylia swapped meaningful glances with Djain before nudging Sean. "Was that all she said of her?"

Sean lost himself in the facets of Axylia's green eyes, thinking, shaking his head. "No . . . she said something else that I thought was a winsome way of rhyming her mother's name. She said she had been borne of Alorn." He forced his gaze away from Axylia. "Does that mean anything to any of you?"

The group exploded with excitement.

Axylia beamed up at him, and Djain laughed, his eyes narrowing on Sean as if he were sizing him up for the first time. "It means much. Alorn is a founding member of The Bright Council. A group dedicated to overseeing relations between the magical races, protecting the Mother, and keeping her magic alive. It means your grandmother may be a Bright One."

Chaotic discussions surrounded Sean.

Djain sat across from him, watching, pleased, letting the conjecture rage unchecked.

Sean caught snippets of conversations, and it all seemed to be about him. Speculation about the purity of his line. Questions of power and the dilution of blood. Might it mean they could turn things around in their hunt for the remaining pieces of the Quari Cube?

Could it help them recover the fragments before the Order?

At his side, Axylia nudged Sean's leg. "How are you holding up? It is always overwhelming when your world is upended. Even more so when it's thrown at you like this."

Sean smiled, but there were still so many things he wanted to ask and understand. So many questions had been raised by everything he had learned, and it was making his head spin. Chaos had descended about his life, and it was written in the lines on his face, but he nodded with feigned confidence. "I'm alright. I hope I can retain all of this."

Axylia gave him a reassuring smile. "I'll be happy to go over it again with you sometime when there isn't such a crowd."

"Thank you," he said. He shifted his gaze to Djain. "I heard someone mention recovery, and you said earlier that I would be responsible for hunting down the missing pieces of the cube. Who were those men in the vision? What's so special about the Quari Cube?"

"Yes. That will be your primary task." Djain inclined his head, mulling over Sean's other questions. "You will recall the group I mentioned that works against us, The Order of the Sacred Flame. They seek to harness and control magic for their own power. Those men were part of that faction. The Quari Cube was created in a joint effort between others like ourselves, the Bright Ones, and the Elves. It is a bridge, a conduit to the magical forces safeguarded in the Elven Sanctuary. Whoever controls the Quari Cube has the power to transform the planet. We would see it used as intended, a way to strengthen the bond between the Mother and all of her children. The Order would wield it as a weapon, releasing the monsters the Elves banished eons ago and transforming the Mother into a place of nightmare."

Rubbing the side of his face, Sean struggled with understanding. "Why did they break it apart if it offered them the power they seek?"

Djain's brows lifted, a knowing light in his eyes. "Because the cube was created with protections. They were successful in absconding with the cube once before, but could not get past its wards. A Bright One, we now suspect to be Vitan, was tasked with protecting the cube after its creation. The original thieves were slain, and the cube reclaimed. When they came again, they shattered it, weakening its safeguards, and masking it from the Bright Ones. They scattered the pieces to ensure no one else could harness its secrets."

The weight of this new world settled on Sean, and he chuckled. "And here I thought I was going to be working on old coins and pottery, recreating ancient tech."

Understanding laughter rose from the group, and Jason spoke. "Oh, you'll mess with reworking plenty of old systems. Just worry about your training. You'll learn so much over the coming weeks, and there is no need to have it all in hand tonight."

Sean laughed. "That's good—"

Talaunia interrupted. "Djain, Papa, while department heads have not traditionally taken part in recoveries, I would like to take Sean on as my student and join as part of his support structure when he's in the field."

Many other voices erupted around them, all clamoring to be part of the team.

Talaunia stared at Sean with an intensity that made him both uneasy and intrigued.

Djain's eyebrow rose, and Sean felt Axylia go rigid at his side. From his view, he could only see the set of her shoulders, but the tension that had exploded between the elves was palpable.

Djain rose and stepped into the center of those gathered, placing himself between the ladies. He extended a hand to Sean. "We can talk about training and teams tomorrow. For now, I think our new friend has more than enough on his mind, and it is getting rather late." Djain motioned toward the array of clocks displaying times from around the world, and Sean noticed the hours had slipped away. It was now well past three in the morning. An exhilarated exhaustion settled on him. Djain saw the effect and continued. "Thank you for coming this evening and joining us. One never knows who will make it past Jacia and Panji." His low, rumbling laugh sounded. "I am glad you are one of them. Now go, rest, and we will see you again this afternoon."

Sean rose and took Djain's hand in a firm handshake. "I'm not sure how much sleep there will be, but I thank you for this chance, for showing me all of . . . this."

As he spoke, Axylia rose and slipped her arm around Sean's. "I'll show him out and see the others don't maul him."

Djain thanked Axylia with his eyes. "It is appreciated. The two of you get out of here and try to find some rest. Things are only going to get more demanding from here."

Sean thanked Djain again, and Axylia tugged on his arm, leading him through the crowd with ease. Nearing the lift, they found Talaunia standing before the doors. The ladies exchanged terse glances as Talaunia stepped closer to Sean, running a finger down his shirt. "Now, now. I hope you were not planning to leave without saying a proper farewell."

"Of course not. It was a pleasure to meet you." Sean searched her features again. The sense of familiarity was stronger than before, and he sifted through memories, trying to find the root cause. Involuntarily, he smiled.

Axylia reached around Talaunia and pressed the call button, and the soft baritone chime sounded, the doors sliding open immediately. Giving Talaunia an icy glare, she tried to end the conversation. "Have a good night, Talaunia. It seems our lift has arrived."

Eyes narrowed to slits, Talaunia sneered at Axylia. "See that you keep my new partner safe for me."

Axylia maneuvered Sean around Talaunia, and they stepped into the lift. "He's not property, Talaunia. The old ways are dead. Perhaps he'll voice his thoughts about the matter. There are several trainers, and he might prefer another. We wouldn't want other trainees to suffer if you were distracted, would we, boss?"

Talaunia puffed up, ready to reply, but the doors slid closed, cutting her off.

Sean's brow arched as Talaunia vanished from sight, and he turned, finding the tension melting from Axylia.

Once they were alone, Axylia sighed. "Please, accept my apologies. You should know many people will try to sway you or lay claim because of your lineage and the potential power within you. Remember that Papa Djain will always consider your desires and would never force you to attempt anything."

Sean's free arm moved, his hand crossing his body, coming to rest over the thin fingers she had wrapped around his arm. "Thank you for taking care of me today, for watching out for me now." His eyes searched hers, and his lips edged upward into a curious grin. "Are you one of the other trainers?"

A light blush touched her cheeks. "It was a pleasure, and yes, I am."

Light sparked in Sean's eyes, and he leaned toward her. "Well, that is good to know."

Excerpt from the Elven Volumes of Living Knowledge
Celestial Cycle 43.961153
in the First Reign of House Varunia

Visions involving the Bright Ones are often obscured, difficult to understand. I come to believe the cause is woven into the very core of their nature. While offering aid, they bring chaos and strife, thriving on the discord they sew. I caution all; be wary of their gifts and weigh any offers before accepting. We are pets for their amusement and you will dance for the treats they offer.

—Councilor Traxidor

Six

Books lay scattered across the library table, forming a crescent around Sean. He sat hunched over a yellowed manuscript, studying every discoloration, searching for the faded portions of the ornate handwriting. After reviewing the same line dozens of times, his eyes widened and a breathy "ah" escaped from the back of his throat. Grabbing his journal, he scribbled translation notes across the pristine white surface of the modern paper. Tension filled his shoulders and the rapid movement of his pen stopped. The fine hairs along the back of his neck bristled in warning, and his pulse quickened.

Time had slipped away, and the bright light of day had been replaced by the buzzing glow of fluorescent bulbs. The surrounding tables sat empty, creating small islands amid the deep shadows cast by the rows of towering bookshelves. The absence of the library's hushed bustle added to the eerie quiet blanketing the cavernous room.

Something lurked in the shadows.

Watching.

Stalking.

An empty chair spun in lazy circles at the attendant's desk, and Sean's skin crawled.

Headlights of passing cars swept over the frosted glass panels of the main entrance in bright bursts.

Movement drew Sean's gaze to the dark recess on his left. He dropped the pen on the table and slid to his right, feeling the unseen eyes tracking his movement. A nondescript mass of shadow shifted with him, following through the stacks. He stepped around the table and moved cautiously toward the main doors. The distance between himself and the unseen threat was disappearing rapidly, and he could feel the shadow's anticipation. At his current pace, the stalker was going to cut off the safety promised by the parade of lights beyond the entryway.

Tossing the chair next to him aside, Sean broke for the main doors. The slick leather soles of his shoes found little purchase on the glossy tile, and his foot slipped, throwing him off balance. Reaching for one chair after another, he scrambled toward the exit, straining to keep himself upright. A horrified glance toward his pursuer tightened the grip of fear around his chest. The apparition phased through the thick columns of books and wood, closing the distance with frightening speed.

Emerging from the shadows, its inky form was as devoid of detail in the light as it had been while lost in the murky darkness.

A spike of fear drove Sean forward with renewed focus. He found his footing and dashed toward the broken lights of the city. Heart pounding against his chest, he felt the icy grip of the specter on his shoulder. Throwing his weight into the crossbar of the door, it burst open, rattling under the force of the impact. Stumbling out into the night, he called out. "Fire!"

His shout echoed in the darkness. The safety of the crowded street had vanished with the library.

Disoriented and puzzled, Sean felt old fears worm through his chest. Fighting the rising panic, he searched for his stalker.

A blue, flaming sword materialized, blocking his path at the edge of a gaping chasm.

Sean stumbled backward.

The light provided by the blade illuminated his surroundings. He was inside the cavern that once held the Quari Cube. Dust-covered, rust-brown stains remained where blood had once pooled. The flesh of the fallen was desiccated and drawn, transforming them into a mummified memorial.

Vitan materialized before him, the blue flames casting ominous shadows across his features and ashen wings.

Sean knew he was still too unfamiliar with this world to defend himself. His left foot inched backward. Deciding he had no choice but to stand his ground, he planted his feet. Locking eyes with Vitan, he struggled to keep the fear from his voice. "What do you want?"

Hearing the crack in Sean's voice, Vitan's scowl turned into a mocking grin.

Sean drew in a deep breath and steadied the quiver in his leg. He shifted his stance and pulled his arms up in a poor imitation of a boxer. His entire body coiled under tension, and he repeated the question with more surety. "What do you want?"

Vitan's wings pulled in and tucked themselves against his back. Amused, he stepped to Sean's right, evaluating him.

Sean tried other questions, each more demanding and agitated than the previous. "Why am I back here?" He pivoted with his challenger. His left arm dropped, and he pointed to the mummified corpse. "Why did you kill this man?"

Eyes ablaze, Vitan leaned in, scrutinizing him, their noses nearly brushing against one another.

Sean closed his eyes and sucked air through his teeth, shaking from his effort to hold his ground.

The man sniffed at Sean like a beast before drawing back and circling to the right.

Feeling his personal space had been vacated, Sean opened his eyes, blinking as the strange dance resumed. "Do you know my grandmother, Alorn?"

The recognition in Vitan's eyes was banished as quickly as it appeared.

Sean's hand trembled in frustration as the strange standoff continued. Breaking past his fear, he barked his next question with fiery agitation. "What the bloody hell am I doing here?"

Vitan tilted his head and narrowed his eyes, replying in a whisper. "Child, the time has come for you to wake."

< ᚨᛟᚾ ᚠᚱᛗ ᛒᛟᛏᛇ >

Thunder clapped, the world shook, and Sean jerked awake. Lightning outlined churning branches in silhouette against the rain rolling in sheets down his windows. Wiping sweat from his forehead, he glared at the red numbers glowing in the darkness, 5:58 AM.

Throwing off the covers, he wiggled into a sitting position and dug his toes into the thick nap of the carpet. He pushed himself off the mattress, and the wooden frame creaked under the light strain. Even in his exhaustion, he smirked. "You and me both."

He rubbed at his bare chest with one hand and his eyes with the other, stumbling towards his bedroom door. His loose-fitting shorts hung from his hips, ending above his knees. The band of his crimson briefs winked in and out of existence with each step of his half-awake shuffle, their rich color a stark contrast against his pale skin.

Reaching the doorway, the bed groaned again, and he gave a half-hearted wave in its direction. "Aye—enough already." When he vanished into the hall, the center of the bed collapsed, caving in on itself, and the footboard's wooden beam splintered in two.

Hearing the sharp crack of wood, Sean stopped, shuffled backward several steps, and squinted into the room. His eyes went to the window, expecting to see a downed limb lying on the lawn, torn from a tree by the storm. Lightning flashed, and in the moment of illumination, he saw the crumpled pile that had been his bed. He groaned, and his brow pinched in bewilderment. He took a step into the room, but the early morning call of nature reminded him of other urgent business. Dismissing the mystery of the bed. He resumed his half-lidded zombie shuffle along the hall.

He tended to the call of nature and ended up scrambling for the plunger. The more he strained, the more stubborn the plug became, until, from behind, he heard a sickening gurgle from the tub. He turned and closed the curtain, avoiding the acrid cloud of stench and waste that belched out of the sewer. A smattering of thick, blackish-brown dots and smears speckled the shower and ceiling, making it look like a newly discovered piece by Jackson Pollock. "Bloody hell!"

Throwing up his hands, he spun and made his way to the kitchen while muttering curses on landlords and plumbers. Not bothering to turn on the light, he washed his face and hands in the kitchen sink before filling his trusty electric tea kettle with fresh water. He dug through the cabinet, found some Earl Grey, and dropped two bags into an oversized ceramic mug.

Sean rubbed at his face, his nose wrinkling as he sniffed the air. The sickening stench of burning wires filled the room. Sparks shoot from beneath the kettle, blackening the countertop. He knocked the pot into the sink with a string of rabid curses and yanked the cord from the wall to stop the meltdown.

Placing both hands on the counter, he shook his head. "I don't need this shit today."

Vitan's voice growled behind Sean. "Good. Now settle yourself and provide the attention I require."

Sean nearly came out of his skin and spun to face the intruder. Before him, in nothing but his natural glory, stood Vitan. Sean pointed at the door, stammering, his instinct torn between asking how the man got in or trying to throw him out. Deciding that either path would be his crowning achievement in stupid decisions, he clamped his mouth shut and glowered at the man.

Giving a cocky grin, Vitan spoke again, and his voice was smooth, cold. "I am Vitan. I killed the man because protecting that cavern and its treasure are my charge." Vitan drew in a slow breath, a taunting playfulness sweeping over his features. "Yes, I know, Alorn. The one from which your line was birthed. She is furious the council sent me to tame you, but this is not a family matter. She may seek you out when my task is complete, should anything remain."

Vitan crossed his hands behind his back, and the sword vanished. It was easy to see why the masters sculpted men of robust features, lean and powerful. For all Sean knew, there may be a statue of this man standing in Rome now. The thought birthed an inappropriate laugh. The dark idea of some priest taking a hammer and chisel to that statue's manhood provided amusement. Shaking his head, he stepped around the intruder and moved toward the living area.

Following, Vitan continued. "You were not at the location of my charge a second time, only dreaming, and this you did because I willed it. I require your attention. Yes, I shattered your bed, I clogged your waste chute, and I fouled your machine. What you humans decry as fate, or attribute to Murphy, is often nothing more than me and my brethren amusing ourselves."

Vitan took a moment to catalog the small living space. A single recliner sat near the window. Beside it, a small table with several archaeological journals stacked neatly on its surface. A short, well-worn sofa faced a modest television that sported a thin film of dust. Various odds and ends were displayed around the room: a cricket bat, an unopened puzzle, and pictures of family and friends among them. Vitan's eyes moved back to the recliner, and in a few quick steps, he sank into the worn cushion, shifting himself from side to side. "I detest sitting, but for you, I shall make an exception."

Sean's mouth dropped open, and he reached for the cricket bat, brandishing it in both hands. When he found his voice, the fullness of his Scottish upbringing broke through. "Yer bloody mad! Ye cannae go'n drag yer bare arse an' tadger on another man's shite!"

The outburst only increased Vitan's enjoyment, and he wiggled some more. "I can live to cause havoc in your life, or you can choose to accept things as they are and be free of me before the sun breaks the horizon."

Fists tightening around the stick so that his knuckles paled, Sean ground his teeth and sat on the sofa, glaring at Vitan.

"Wise choice for one so young." Vitan studied him, all mirth falling from his face, replaced with a stern glower. "I know factions are vying to reclaim and restore what I lost. As its protector, I would see this done if accomplished by the correct persons."

Sean's anger remained, but a pale rose color returned to his knuckles. "Am I one of the correct persons?"

Vitan's head inclined. "I recognized Djain's spell work upon you in the cavern. I would approach Djain, but it is near impossible for us to locate the man. He wards himself and his property with protective sigils we cannot see past, nor cross."

Sean's head shifted to the side, recalling the symbol the priest had drawn on the cave floor in blood; the same markings he had seen several times within the Quari Group headquarters. "If you want to help us regain the pieces, why did you attack me, my essence?"

"You were not of that time, so I branded your spirit, causing you to shine like a beacon. Once you cleared the grounds of the Quari Group, I knew when and where you were. Now, so am I."

Sean sat the bat aside and leaned back. "What is it you need me to do?"

Vitan extended his hand, and when he opened it, an ancient medallion slipped free to dangle from a worn leather strap.

Having seen glimpses of it before, Sean now saw the icon in its entirety, a hammered circle of metal surrounding a Celtic style cross set on a tongue of flame.

"The mark of the monks that stole my prize and have kept it from me these long years. Study it. Hunt them. Slay them if you wish. I care only that you return to me what is mine to protect."

With a flick, he tossed the trinket toward the coffee table. Sean dove to catch it, striking his lip on the table's edge, busting it open. "You can't bloody well throw around artifacts! They're fragile!"

Vitan shrugged. "You will do as I have commanded, or you and I will be at odds in this venture."

Plucking several tissues from a box beneath the table, Sean wrapped the medallion. "We'll see how this plays out. Do you know where any of the missing pieces are? If so, provide a sign of good faith on your part. Tell me, so that we may retrieve it."

Eyes narrowing, Vitan's tone turned cold. "Do not test me, ape."

Sean glared at him, dabbing at the blood on his lip with a finger. "I won't do anything for you on faith alone."

Vitan rose and placed a hand on the wall, and dark splotches formed in the paint. Bubbling little puffs of smoke wafted up from the discolored spots. Across the scorched latex, a series of numbers and letters appeared. "There, you will find one piece. Be warned; it is protected. Do not forget to learn your enemy's tactics and history first, or you will fail."

"Bloody hell! Did you have to burn it into my wall?" Wiping more blood from his lip, Sean rubbed it on his palm.

The result garnered a look of wicked amusement from Vitan. "Requests can be as deadly as a wish to a djinn. Best to mind your phrasing."

The hatred Djain harbored for Vitan was taking deep root in Sean. "How do I contact you when I know more?"

"I will know. I will find you. I have seared your soul, marking you as my chattel. Do not forget whom you serve."

Sean sneered. "I'm my own man, ya bloody prick!" Holding up his palm, the sigil he had seen around the Quari Headquarters and drawn by the priest in the cave was smeared in bright red on his pale hand. Dropping to his knees, he slammed his palm onto the floor and shouted. "Defendatu eta babestu." Almost as an afterthought, he added, "this house!"

Vitan roared, "No!" He dove towards Sean, his sword appearing out of nowhere, the blade blazing to life in his hand.

Without hesitating, Sean called out again in a commanding voice. "Defendatu eta babestu this house!" A strange power built within his core, twisting and churning, warning that he was calling on things he did not understand.

Vitan's forward motion stopped, blade frozen in mid-arc.

Seeing the effect spurred Sean onward. He shouted the phrase a third time, and a primal power surged from within. The wall of energy slammed into Vitan and hurled him through the window. Glass shattered, wood splintered, and the sound of the storm intensified. Wind and rain rushed into the room, and on the outside of the house stood Vitan. He was blazing in rage, throwing himself against the protective shield.

Explosions sounded as nearby transformers burst from the raw power crackling in the air, plunging the entire neighborhood into darkness.

Sean rolled back, sat on the floor, and leaned against the sofa. His eyes moved over the room, studying the aftermath of his morning amid the flashes of lightning. Bloody sigil on the carpet, GPS coordinates seared into the wall, rain pouring in and soaking his recliner while the carpet sucked up the rest of the water. And standing there framed by it all, a creature of power and light beyond anything Sean could understand, cloaked in blazing fury.

His hands trembled, and he turned, searching for his phone. Unplugging it from the charger, he wiped the screen over his pants to remove the blood he had smudged across its surface. Swiping a finger across the phone, it lit up, and with a few quick motions, his call connected.

"Quari Group, how may I direct your call?" The voice rising from the speaker sounded as though it belonged to a young woman.

"Papa Djain, please. This is Sean Byrne, from the Arche—from the Special Projects team on—" He patted the side of his head with his palm. "What floor was it? Oh, yes! On thirty-three."

There was a slight pause, and the woman's tone wasn't as polite when she spoke again. "We do not connect anyone to Papa via the front desk, especially not outside of office hours. Those who need his contact information have it. One moment and I will connect you to Special Projects."

"Thank you," he responded to the hold music.

After a moment, a terse-sounding young man picked up. "Ops."

"Good morning. My name is Sean Byrne, and I joined the team last night. I've had an encounter at my home and need to speak with Papa Djain."

The phone crackled with the sound of a hand covering the microphone, and a muffled discussion took place. To Sean, it felt like ages before a soft female voice came on the line. "Well, it didn't take you long to get into trouble. What's happened, Sean? Anything I can help with?"

The voice was familiar, but it took Sean a moment to place its owner. "Talaunia? Are you still there?" He tried to mask the discomfort from his voice as the magic worked through him, making him wonder if his insides were being twisted into knots.

She teased. "Night is my time. You'll know that soon enough. The best things always happen at night, Sean." She lingered on the words a bit too long, and while it may have thrilled others, it wasn't a game he wanted to play right now.

Curling up, he wrapped an arm around his stomach. He had most definitely done something inadvisable, and the tremor in his hand was getting worse. He ignored Talaunia's efforts at lighthearted banter, a gnawing voice in his head telling him he did not have time to flirt. "The Bright One, Vitan, came to my home tonight. I put up a protective ward but don't know how long it, or I, will last. Vitan is battering the barrier, infuriated. If this fails, I don't want to think of what he'll do to me. Also, I think I did something wrong when I invoked—whatever this is, my stomach feels like it's being ripped apart."

On the other end of the phone, he heard her draw in a breath, the concern in her voice unmistakable. "Blessed Mother."

Sean tried to speak more forcefully. "Talaunia, I need Papa. Now. I think I may pass out."

"No! Do not pass out! Whatever you do, stay awake. If you lose consciousness, the barrier will fail." Her voice became more distant and muffled, and he could hear her barking orders into the room. When she came back to the phone, she asked. "How were you able to put up that barrier?"

A flush of embarrassment washed over him. "I took a chance and guessed, piecing together, things I'd seen and the stories you all shared."

"Holy fuck. What an idiot! Brilliant, I might add, but still an idiot!" Behind her, he heard the deep rumble of Djain's voice drawing closer.

In another heartbeat, Djain was on the phone. "Sean, hold on. I am aware of your situation. With Vitan at your perimeter, we cannot use normal means."

Sean nodded, rolling his eyes at his mistake. "Aye. I understand."

"We are sending you an image. I need you to draw the sigil you see in the picture on a wall in blood. Exactly as you see it. Can you do that?"

He groaned, holding his stomach. "Um . . . Aye. I can. I can do that."

"Stay strong, and we will have you back here in a few moments. Here comes the sigil."

Sean lifted his phone and took a picture of the coordinates Vitan had seared into his wall. He smeared blood all over the tissue he had wrapped the medallion in for protection. The phone buzzed, and an image popped up on the screen. Rolling to all fours, he pressed his head into the floor before crawling to the nearest wall. Breaking the cut on his lip open again, he dabbed at the blood. It took him less than a minute to draw the symbol onto the wall. When it was complete, he rolled to his back and called out. "Done!" Clutching the phone against his chest, he concentrated on not passing out.

The droplets of rain carried on the wind peppered his bare chest, shocking and cold. Pain seared through him, and he curled into a ball. The wall shimmered and melted away.

Djain stepped through the wavering image and surveyed the scene. He stooped and cradled Sean into his arms, paying no mind to the streaks of blood smeared across his crisp white shirt. Djain fixed Vitan with a scathing glare, then pointedly turned his back on the enraged Bright One, carrying Sean through the portal to safety.

The portal snapped closed as they appeared on the Operations Center floor. Cheers rose from the group, and people swarmed in. Djain lowered Sean into a chair, where the cushions cradling his body.

A pair of supple fingers touched Sean, and a tingle of living energy flowed through the connection. He tried to twist his head, searching for Axylia, but it was Talaunia's violet eyes he found.

Hand trembling, he unlocked his phone, showing the picture to Djain. "May have found part of the cube ..."

Djain accepted the phone, handing it off to the technicians in the room. "Get a copy of this and summon his team."

Talaunia's other hand ran along his bare chest, sending healing energies into him. There was a devilish slant to her lips, though her eyes brimmed with concern. "Knew you'd be mine."

Sean closed his eyes, finding the disappointment of Axylia's absence softened by the comfort and safety he found in Talaunia's gaze. A smile filled with confused emotion touched his lips, and he offered her a quiet. "Thank you."

A shadow fell over him, and he opened his eyes. Djain was appraising his condition. "You are safe now, and you have done well. Let go, relax, and you will feel better."

"How?"

"Magic is driven by intent. You intended to protect yourself, and you did. Now accept that you are safe under my wards and let go of what you invoked."

Sean's eyes opened, and he glanced around the room. He knew he was safe here. Closing his eyes again, he sucked in a breath, deep and slow. With gentle coaxing from Talaunia, he repeated the process, relaxing more with each exhale. He felt the tension in him subside, and his hands ceased to tremble, just before the blackness took him.

Oh, how I wonder at the resilience of the Mother! The heavens bombard Her with the debris of creation. Enormous chunks of cosmic detritus, which She takes into Herself, claiming it as Her own. Among this collection of refuse, a liquid, which tempers the Mother. Her fiery blood withdraws, and She forms a thick skin, gathering the water discarded by the heavens into vast bodies. These waters churn, moving with unstoppable current and rekindling the thrill of riding the Mother's molten flows in our earliest days.

—Councilor Varunia

SEVEN

Sean stood looking out the window of Djain's private office and sipped on a fresh cup of tea. To the east, the pinks and golds of early morning gilded the lingering low clouds. The sun struggled against the gray skies, warming the world, and pushing the now distant storms off to the northeast. Lightning illuminating the dark shrouds of the cloud banks. "How do you ever pull yourself away from such views?"

Djain's gaze moved past Sean to the world beyond. "I would be a liar if I said it was not a struggle at times." His focus returned to the moment, and he settled into a guest chair. "Feeling recovered enough to tell me about your morning?"

Sean stared out the window at the storm, his head bobbing languidly. "Now would be one of those times." He sighed and looked at Djain.

Djain stretched over and patted a neighboring chair in invitation.

With only the faintest hint of lingering discomfort, Sean eased himself down on the edge of the seat.

"It will pass soon." Djain relaxed back into his chair. "Now, tell me all that transpired."

Beginning with the dream, Sean recalled the morning's events. Pulling the tissue-wrapped medallion from his pocket, he placed it on the edge of Djain's desk.

Djain stared at the bloody, crumpled tissue pile as Sean continued through the remaining events. When Sean spoke of casting the ward, Djain chuckled. "I knew you would be quick, but this was unexpected."

Sean searched around himself. "I have a picture on my phone if I can find it . . ."

"The techs already have your phone. You gave it to me when we returned. They will clean the blood from it for you and return it. The picture is already with your team, and we will meet them shortly to see what they have discovered."

"Oh—I don't remember that," he said with an awkward laugh.

Djain laughed with him, reassuring and comforting. "I do not find that surprising. You were unconscious moments after handing it over."

There was a quick double knock at the door. Without waiting for acknowledgment, a barrel-chested man entered. He sported reddish-brown hair, pulled back in a man bun, with long sideburns and day-old stubble. He was shorter than Sean and appeared to be in his mid-thirties. A thick bag hung from one hand, and a clean, pressed white shirt was draped over the opposite shoulder, where a folded newspaper was tucked under his arm. "Found you two some fresh threads," the man said, dropping the bag by Sean and handing the shirt to Djain.

"We appreciate it, Ryan," Djain said.

Ryan dropped the paper on the desk, folded to display an article on an inner page, with the title circled in bold red marker. "Ms. Iliescu wanted to make sure you saw this before getting too engrossed in today's business." He glanced at Sean. "It looks like someone else has been snatched."

Leaning forward, Djain skimmed the article. "She would not point it out unless she sensed it was not a mundane issue. She must be unable to see the cause." He held the paper out to Ryan. "Ask Jason to check the histories of anyone taken from the area in the last six months. Please, gather the rest of the team and wait for us in the conference room."

Ryan retrieved the paper, tucking it back under his arm on the way out the door. "On it!"

"Thanks," Sean said, but Ryan was already gone. He reached for the bag. "Where did they find clothing at this hour?"

"I would not expect much. Those came from the fitness center on the third floor." Djain pondered the bag and made a face before laughing. "I learned long ago to keep extra clothing around here."

With one finger, Sean pulled open the bag and peeked inside. "I'll do the same in the future." He slipped his hand in and pulled out a pair of black yoga pants with a white T-shirt bearing the Quari Group logo. "Not my usual style, but better than being half-naked."

Djain chuckled and stripped off the blood-smeared button-down. Sean found the man's presence even more imposing as the shirt came off. Djain's chest and arms had the well-defined shape and cut of a bodybuilder, his muscles shifting under taut skin. Hundreds of small mounding scars formed patterns across his chest and upper arms. Djain turned to pick up the fresh shirt. His back was covered in long cross-hatched scars, making him appear even more intimidating for having endured whatever caused the jagged marks. Pulling on the shirt, Djain used his chin and motioned toward his private water closet. "You may change in there if you wish."

Sean dropped the clothing back into the bag and slipped into the room. The pants were on the snug side, leaving little to the imagination, which made him self-conscious until he slipped into the T-shirt. The shirt hung on him, falling almost to his knees as it was a full two sizes too large for his frame. Tossing his sleep shorts into the sack, he rejoined Djain in the office.

Djain was hanging up the phone as Sean entered, and he suppressed a smirk upon seeing Sean. "I have ordered breakfast to be delivered to the conference room for everyone. Let us introduce you to your team. There is much to discuss."

Setting out for the conference room, Sean rushed to keep pace with Djain's towering form and brisk pace. He was puzzled as they passed the empty executive conference room. "Where are we going?"

"Ah, yes." Djain glanced over his shoulder. "You have not been given the tour." As they reached the main lifts at the center of the tower, Djain pressed the down button. "We are heading to the conference room on the thirty-fourth floor, which is also where your new office will be."

They entered the lift, and Sean felt it drop as Djain continued. "The Special Projects team covers floors thirty through thirty-four. On thirty, you will find our primary library, containing our most common books, writings, teachings on magic, and the history of the various species. Thirty-one is our magical pantry, where we store tools and ingredients used to make spells, such as the one used to allow you to see the mystical."

The bell sounded, and they stepped from the lift into an open area. Along the walls were individual, glassed-in offices. Right in the middle, on a raised platform, was the conference room. Sean could see people watching their arrival, some faces familiar to him, others he had not met. Surrounding the conference room were broad paths, dotted with small tables where groups could gather. Short bookcases had been arranged in the corners to create small alcoves with comfortable chairs for private study.

Approaching the middle of the room, Djain continued listing the floors. "Thirty-two is our training rooms, prep area, and where we build most portals for missions. Thirty-three, you have already seen, as it is the Operations Center."

Djain opened the door to the conference room. "And this is thirty-four. Welcome to the new world."

Sean noticed this table differed from the others he had seen. The glossy metal frame supported a heavy glass top that spanned the smooth black surface. Around the room, people sounded out their welcomes, some being polite and hiding their amusement at Sean's attire, while others laughed. All of them expressed their pleasure that he had recovered.

Djain pointed Sean to a seat next to his, near the head of the table. "Thank you all for waking and arriving so early." Djain stood before his chair and let everyone settle.

To Djain's left sat Talaunia. She stared at Sean, eyes alight with interest.

Next to her sat Ryan, the rugged-looking fellow that had delivered the spare clothing. His chair was kicked back, his boots resting on the table.

To Ryan's side was a new face. A man who looked to be in his early twenties, despite his ashen skin, and the silver sheen of his long hair and neatly trimmed beard. His icy blue-gray eyes were fixed on Ryan's shoes in tired resolve.

Across the table from the unknown man was Jason, the floppy-haired fellow who had provided Sean water the previous evening. After glancing up, he planted his face back into his folded arms on the table.

Between himself and Jason sat Sarah, bright-eyed and energetic, though every item she wore was dark and paid homage to death.

"Before we get started, has everyone met Sean?"

Everyone but the silver-haired man showed they had with a nod. Everyone but Jason, who grunted at the table.

The silver-haired man rose and turned to Sean. He was soft-spoken, and though his accent was nearly invisible, it reminded Sean of a friend that had grown up in Mumbai. "I am Gadyen. I look forward to serving with you."

Sean rose and stretched a hand across the table. "And I, you."

Gadyen focused on the hand lingering in the air for an awkward moment before turning to Djain. His brow rose in question, and Djain inclined his head. Gadyen reached out and took the offered hand, shaking it.

Sean tried to jerk away from the cold and leathery touch.

Gadyen's iron grasp held him firm. Giving Sean's hand two quick pumps, he released. "I see I am the first of my kind you have met."

Rubbing his leg to pull the chill from his fingers, Sean tilted his head. "Vampire?"

Gadyen flashed a toothy grin.

Sean noted the lack of fangs and felt a twinge of jealousy at the immaculate perfection of Gadyen's teeth.

Djain coughed. "We do not have time to play your games today, Gadyen."

Gadyen sighed and settled back into the chair.

Djain motioned for Sean to do the same. "Yes, he is a vampire. Forget what you have heard in the human tales, for they are filled with farce and fallacy. I promise you plenty of time to study all the races."

Sean kept studying Gadyen even after he sat. "In the library you mentioned?"

Djain's dipped his chin in affirmation.

Gadyen smirked, shifted his focus to Ryan's boots, and sighed again, heavier. "This is neither your home nor your castle. Do show some respect, even if you lack manners."

"Bite me," was Ryan's reply, but he lowered his feet.

Djain regarded Ryan and Gadyen. "Good. Now that we all know one another, we can start acting like a team. Together, you will recover the remaining pieces of the Quari Cube."

As Djain spoke, Sean could feel eyes lingering on him. His gaze swept around the table before locking with the intense scrutiny of Talaunia. The gnawing sense he should know her bubbled up again, and he frowned at the mystery.

She winked and mouthed a single word, 'Mine.'

He looked away, feeling the heat bloom on his cheek, and he smiled.

Sinking into his chair, Djain flipped a switch under the table, and the entire top flickered. A virtual keyboard faded into view before Djain, formed of muted amber light beneath the glass. Above, a display of files and folders appeared on an embedded screen. Hidden screens lined each side of the table, displaying everything as it appeared before Djain.

"Assigned roles. Sean will lead recovery efforts in the field and will head all research efforts here. Ryan and Gadyen will serve as security and manage Sean's martial training needs. Talaunia will ensure Sean receives proper mystical training and serve as the team healer. She is a cunning fighter herself should the need arise." Djain paused, staring at each of them with a pointed intensity. "History will not repeat itself."

Sean looked at Djain puzzled, but before he could voice his question, Talaunia caught his eye.

She shook her head with emphatic subtlety.

He arched his brows at her.

She pressed her lips into a thin line and narrowed her eyes.

Sean's shoulders fell. Files flashed across the monitors too fast for him to identify. When the last file loaded, he recognized the image all too well. The scorched wall of his living room loomed on the screens. Recalling his ill-cast ward, his stomach churned.

"Jason and Sarah will run missions from here in ops and assist Sean with research," Djain said. "Do you all understand your role in this group?"

After everyone had responded, Djain continued. "Good! Let us begin." He tapped the table over the picture of marred wall. "Jason, Sarah, do we have any information yet on the location provided by Vitan?"

Jason flapped an elbow in Sarah's general direction. "Not awake enough yet to process data. You tell them, Sarah."

Sarah bobbed her head. The black tips of her pigtails bounced around and the miniature skeletons dangling from her ears danced. She swiped around on the table, and the photo zipped off to the side, replaced by a satellite image zooming in on Europe and centering on a forested countryside. "Those coordinates point to the Villers Abbey in Belgium."

The image zoomed in further when she zipped her finger over the glass surface, showing a sprawling structure. "The high points. Founded in 1146 CE, abandoned in 1796 CE, and purchased by the Belgian state in 1893 CE. It was declared a historical site in 1973 CE. People *can* tour it, so public eyes may be an issue if on site."

After draining his cup, Jason lifted a finger. "Already sent out requests for information to the various historical societies and the Belgian Tourist Office Brussels & Wallonia, the agency covering that area. Have a spider running through social media to pull images of the place so we can combine them with satellite and make a virtual model of the site."

A light crept over Djain's face. "Excellent start. Let us move to the next item."

Sarah swiped again, and Djain's face hardened. A rotating, three-dimensional image of the medallion appeared.

Djain's voice was quiet and deep, taking on the ominous tones of a long peal of thunder you hear in the distance, warning of things to come. "I have a history with this group, so let me relay what I know." Taking a deep breath, he gripped the edge of his chair and began. "The Order of the Sacred Flame. A group of people like us, meaning they also share a connection with the Mother."

The knuckles across the back of Djain's hands paled, and the chair rails groaned under the pressure of his grip. "Unlike us, they are known to bind Bright Ones." He scowled, deep lines forming on his face. "Force them to do their will. They rage against any magic they do not control, decrying any unaffiliated uses as abusive and unsafe. All the while, they abuse it themselves, twist it to ensnare, to enslave, and corrupt others." His voice thinned out, spitting out the words as if they were bitter. "They gather magical artifacts. Hoard and harness their power. Believing it their sacred duty to restore those banished by the Elves. They are fanatical and dangerous."

"Jason," Djain said, bringing his intensity to bear on the still groggy man. "Do we have any information on the missing persons?"

Jason twisted his lips into a frustrated scowl. "I've got some basic numbers on the missing. There are a little over three thousand of them in the past six months. Going to take me a bit of time to sort through the lineage of them all."

"Form a research team to focus on those histories," Djain said. "What of your research into the Order's recruiting methods, any progress?"

Jason looked as though he were ready to crawl under the table. "Um, well—there are so many places to hide nefarious stuff." Attempting to lighten the mood, he lifted his finger. "But fear not, dude. I've got bots searching night and day. We'll find something soon."

Djain's countenance darkened. "We had better. Our enemy grows stronger, and we need to infiltrate their ranks to learn more about them." He took several deep breaths, locking eyes with each of them. "I know them. I have faced them before. Father helped create the Quari Cube, and was one of its protectors. In our childhood, the Order assaulted us many times, searching for the cube, but Father thwarted every attempt. As we grew, we fought alongside him, and when he passed, his duty fell to us. For a brief time, we withstood their attacks. I cannot number the lives given to this struggle long before the Quari Group was ever founded. Despite our efforts to keep it secret and safe, well, you know how that turned out." His lips pressed together hard, forming a pencil-thin line, and his chin quivered with rage. When he spoke again, his voice trembled. "I am certain they caused my sister's death, though I lack any direct proof. They killed her for her magic and the magic she protected."

A hard edge sharpened Djain's voice, causing Sean's spine to tingle. "The cube acts as a gateway, a bridge, between the Mother, and the vast stores of magical energy the Elves have secreted away. If the Order acquires it, the world as we know it will be consumed in darkness. Know now, this is as much of a hunt for me as an effort to preserve our world and recover what I am tasked to protect. Let their blood pave the way for the gradual restoration of magic. They are the ones who set the price when they took Oai'Quari. Now, let them repay that debt until Azrael is sated."

The room was quiet. For several heartbeats, no one moved, and all eyes were on Djain. The realization of where the Quari Group's name had its origin was universal. Questions swelled in all of them, and each leaned forward, prepared to break the silence with their inquiries, but not a single word was voiced.

Djain extended a hand and squashed their momentum. "I ask each of you not to share what I have confided in you. It is personal information. I feel you need it to do your job, and beyond that, the rest is my burden. If Sean thinks it becomes relevant, he can ask, and I will tell. Until then, the chapter of my past is closed."

Djain locked eyes with each of them, holding their gaze until a pledge to abide by his request was voiced. When he reached Sean, Djain continued. "Now you can see more fully why we recruited you. Why you must find the pieces before more fall under the control of the Order. Some books in the library allude to them, both outright and indirectly. We have already recovered those with obvious references, and you are now left with a difficult and weighty task. I will gather my journals that record my previous interactions with the Order for you as well."

Sean stared at Djain, unable to shake the thought that the hands of Fate were squeezing his chest. Lives balanced on his ability to scour history, find the hidden shards, and bring them back into the light. He swallowed, inclining his head. "I will handle your things with care." He tilted his head, thinking. "I saw the cube shatter into twelve pieces in the vision. How many remain to be found?"

"I have possession of three," Djain said in a somber tone. "We do not know how many the Order possesses, but they have been hunting far longer. We must assume we are behind in this race."

"I enjoy being the underdog," said Ryan with a bit of excitement in his tone.

"Dude, we'll snag the one at the Abby. That'll give us a third of them," Jason said.

"You are assuming it has not already been discovered by the Order," said Talaunia, giving Jason a stern glare.

Gadyen nodded. "We would be foolish to think the Order does not control several pieces, and we cannot divine from which locations those may have been recovered." Sweeping the group with his stony stare, he continued. "We must identify the hidden resting places of every shard and check them ourselves."

The enormity of their task settled on the group, drawing them into a weighty silence.

The door to the conference room opened, and a small table was brought in, followed by a buffet of breakfast items, plates, and a little portable cooler holding milk, juices, and iced coffees.

Djain thanked the servers as they departed. "Their timing was wonderful. I think we could all use a break. Please take care of your needs. We will continue after refreshing ourselves."

Excerpt from the Elven Volumes of Living Knowledge
Celestial Cycle 217.396811
in the First Reign of House Kryntan

The Mother has taken the elements from the cosmos, nurtured them, and created new life! Oh, the wonder of seeing these fragile, simple forms emerge. Our kin, for they too are children of the Mother!

The Bright One, Ceralon, has become a trusted friend and guide. She offers visions of what may come if we protect these simple creatures. Life! In abundance and variety beyond imagination. She whispers of new races, born of our merging bloodlines. The thought stirs my loin and enchants my mind. I am intrigued, and find myself eager to explore the potential!

—Councilor Syrdan

EIGHT

Over breakfast, Sean learned more about the Special Projects department. There were over a dozen active recovery sites around the world, with another half dozen in the planning and research stages. Despite the growing size of the department, Djain emphasized the importance of this group over all others.

After some time, Ms. Iliescu opened the door and stepped inside. Without a word, she gave Djain a demanding stare and tapped her watch.

Djain tipped his head toward Ms. Iliescu. "Ah, yes. Thank you for the reminder."

Before the door closed behind Ms. Iliescu's, the meeting was wrapping up.

"Talaunia. Sean needs to know the rules of magic before he tries something else and kills himself," Djain said, slipping directly into assignments. "In two hours, we will meet again to go over your training plan. Remember that he has tasks of his own to complete. No more than half his day is to be scheduled for training. You and Ryan must work out the details."

Talaunia turned a hungry gaze on Sean. She twitched her nose once. "I'll take him for a test drive this afternoon."

Sean appeared a little concerned with what she may have planned for him but brightened as Djain interrupted. "He has other things to accomplish today. You can begin his training tomorrow."

Talaunia's lower lip slipped out in a playful pout. She sighed, then flashed a dazzling smile. "That's fine. It gives him more time to anticipate being … under my tutelage."

Ryan and Gadyen glanced at one another, and both rolled their eyes while Jason laughed.

Sarah gave Talaunia a knowing smile. "Some people just need to be broken to discover themselves."

Talaunia's eyes flashed with a wicked playfulness, and she gave Sarah a wink.

Djain chuckled and lifted a hand. "Enough. You all have your work assignments. Now go, be about your business."

Everyone rose, heading toward the exit. Seeing the confusion on Sean's face, Djain motioned for him to hold back. "Wait. Let me show you to your new office." He chuckled. "At least you will know where you can hide from Talaunia's relentless pursuit."

Sean laughed nervously, his eyes tracking Talaunia until she was out of the room.

Djain led him past the little reading nooks to a corner office. He held the door open and motioned him inside. "This one is yours."

Sean drew in a breath, stunned by the space. The outside walls were sloped, and the view over the southeastern edge of the gardens was exquisite. Short, empty bookcases lined the inner walls. There was no desk or computer, and Sean gestured toward the barren space and looked at Djain quizzically.

"We have acquired a variety of desks over the years," Djain said. "Some bore witness to great feats of power and still harbor remnants of those effects in their structure. A friend will be along to give you a tour, and you may choose from our collection. Once you have made your selection, Building Management will bring it up. IT is already working on setting up your new computer. Gone are your days of working in cubicles on tiny monitors."

"I feel the need to thank you again for this opportunity and for placing such faith in me," Sean said, adding, "Papa."

Djain laughed, weighty and ominous. "We will see if you still wish to thank me by week's end." His mood lightened. "Take a few minutes. Enjoy the view. We will speak again later."

Smiling, Sean took in the gardens below. The gloom of the morning's storms had been banished by the rising sun. Golden light flooded into the room and he soaked in the comforting warmth. Behind him, the door closed, and he noticed the atmosphere of the room shifting. Intrigued, he turned, just in time to watch Djain step into the lift. The doors slid closed, and Sean sensed the lift's rapid descent as Djain's presence dropped away. Briefly, the room felt hollow, until the comforting atmosphere of the building rushed into the void.

Puzzled by the effect, Sean returned his attention to the world beyond the glass. He watched the activity of those milling about the garden. After the excitement and stresses of the past several hours, it proved cathartic, and he lost track of time.

A set of lithe fingers covered his eyes, punctuated by a breathy whisper in his ear. "Guess who."

Sean was startled at the touch. He spun, and his agile visitor twirled with him, maintaining their position at his back.

She laughed, prompting him again with a playful, "Guess who."

The silky-smooth alto of her voice removed the mystery, and Sean stilled, smiling. "Oh, well, I've been wondering where you've been hiding." He twisted around, seeking her eyes. "I'm glad to see you. Good morning, Axylia."

She stepped back, her hands lingering on his shoulders before falling away. Arching a brow, she examined him from head to toe. "And I, you. I hear you caused a raucous this morning, and from the state of you, I see the stories haven't been exaggerated." Her hand lifted and tugged on the front of his shirt. "Perhaps Papa will allow us to make a day of it and take you shopping for some real clothing." She stopped, and her chin dropped. "Papa wanted to talk to you about this himself, but you will need a few new things." She winced. "And a warding brand."

He gave a puzzled laugh. "What's bloody wrong with my old things? And branding? Like I'm some bit of chattel?"

She made a sour, apologetic face. "Oh, no, it's not like that. We can discuss it while we walk." Stepping to his side, she slipped her arm around his. "There is so much for us to do today."

Sean tucked his arm in, holding hers to his side. "Alright, what's our first stop?"

They made their way back through the small meeting areas.

"Basement level four. It sounds dark and dusty, but that's where the desks are stored."

"You'll have to help me pick out the right one." They reached the lift, and he pressed the call button. "Now, what's this about my old stuff and branding?"

"Well, I am sure you recall, there was this incident this morning between you and Vitan?"

The lift opened, and they entered. "Aye, not something I'll forget soon." Sean's hand hovered over the buttons. Unable to locate B4, he dropped his hand and looked at her with a quizzical expression. "I don't see a basement level four option. Is there a trick to this one? I don't see any of the magical—"

She dug the elbow tucked behind his arm into his ribs. "We don't speak of such things in public areas." Then she winked. "There is a trick, though." She pointed at a bare metal panel below the emergency call box. "You'll have to learn these symbols before you can use them, but all you have to do is trace the right one there, and you get an express trip to your destination."

She lifted her hand and gestured at the panel. "Now point, like this."

Sean extended a finger at the panel, and Axylia wrapped her hand around the back of his. Guiding his finger, they drew an invisible, intricate symbol on the wall. He laughed. "I'll need a cheat sheet for this. There's no way I'll remember how to draw that again."

The elevator started its descent, and she turned a pair of bright eyes up to him. "Oh, you'll have no problems remembering them by the time your training is complete." She let out a small sigh. "Now, about your stuff. After Djain brought you back here this morning, you passed out. When you did, the ward you placed on your house fell."

Sean's stomach knotted as the potential ramifications unfolded in his mind. "Och . . ."

"I'm sorry. Djain sent Ryan over to get some of your things, but he found the place a mess and came back empty-handed."

"Was nothing salvageable?"

"Ryan says that some of your smaller items, trinkets, and pictures might be ok. He had the window boarded up and locked the place down. You'll have to go see what you can find there later." The elevator slowed to a stop, and she gave him an apologetic gaze. "I'll go with you to help if you'd like."

He gave her an appreciative tip of the head.

"You can't go anywhere outside of this building until you are marked." The doors slid open, and they stepped out into the basement.

"So that's the branding thing. I've pissed off a Bright One, and I shouldn't chance him finding me again?"

"Essentially, yes." She glanced out into the room. "We can talk about all that ugliness after we find your desk. Let's go shopping!"

Her effort to lighten the moment earned a quiet laugh. Sean's eyes lingered on her a few heartbeats longer than necessary. When he lifted his chin, his eyes widened in surprise.

Artifacts were not only stored down here; they were cared for, preserved. Small glass rooms peppered the entire level. Each with independent sensors and controls to monitor air quality, maintaining the ideal environment for the treasures stored within.

Sean bounded from one display to the next, taking in the archived items. Books, scrolls, music boxes, and goblets. There seemed to be a bit of everything represented. "There must be an index somewhere, a catalog. Look at all of this!"

She tugged on his arm. "The records are right over here." She led him to a small terminal mounted on the side of a massive structural column. As he scrolled the index in wonder, she continued. "Remember, this is only one floor. There are several. They are already betting on how long it will take before you vanish down here."

They both laughed, and he forced himself to pull away from the screen. "Someone knows me too well." Glancing around, he sighed. "But today is not the day to lose myself."

Leading him toward the basement's outer edge, they came to a rather large, sealed room. Inside, an array of several dozen desks sat in neat, evenly spaced rows. Axylia pointed toward another terminal inside as they entered. "If you have questions about any of the desks, we can check the inventory."

Sean's eyes moved over all the options. "Some of these aren't your traditional desk." Spotting one appearing to have been carved into the segment of a tree trunk, he lowered a finger and drew it over the rough top, feeling the rings in the tree. A chill swept over him, powerful enough that even Axylia trembled. He lifted his hand. "What was that?"

Slipping her arm from Sean's, Axylia searched for the desk's details in the catalog. "That desk was recovered from the scene of a witch's murder. It looks like her books were locked away because she was into some dark stuff. The strange energy of the desk is why it's here, afraid that left out in the world it might have adverse effects on users."

Holding up his hands, Sean took a step back. "Think I'll pass on that one!" He flashed her a playful smile. "Perhaps this is a good way to check them. I'll see how they feel."

Unamused by his lighthearted approach, she admonished him. "Sean, you shouldn't play with these things. You never know what effect they may have."

Moving to the next desk, he lowered his fingers onto the dark walnut top. "This one is faint, seems sour. I'll try another."

Crossing the aisle, he stopped in front of a Victorian-style writing desk. Sleek curves, intricate woodwork, and a polished surface. "Don't think this one is me, but the craftsmanship is impressive." He touched the smooth finish, and a deep moan burst out of him. His hand jerked back, but the sultry heat of the desk had already caused his cheeks to color. Other parts responded as well, and he had to shift his hips as a heady aura of lust washed over him. "Och—" he grinned. Embarrassed, he twisted to face away from her, tugging at his pants, trying to make room for the sudden swelling.

"Are you alright?" There was concern in her voice, and she was already searching for the item in the catalog.

He glanced over his shoulder and held up a hand to keep her back, still working to adjust himself and regain control. "Aye. I'm fine."

She giggled, a slight blush tinting her cheeks as she read the description and realized the truth of his reaction. "Turns out that one belonged to the Madame of a brothel operated for decades in London."

"That clarifies some things." Rocking his hips, he took a few more steps.

The following desk was a simple wooden structure, four square posts, supporting side members, and a well-worn, slatted top. "This is basic, but has some promise." He dropped his fingertips to the surface. His hand jerked away and his face contorted in horror. "Where the bloody hell is that one from?" He hugged himself tightly, shrinking inward, head and shoulders sagging. "Such oppressive despair."

Her lips pulled down into a frown, and she turned to the console. "I wish you would listen and come read about these, rather than tempting the Fates." She paused and read the description, a hand lifting to cover her mouth. When she looked at him again, her eyes were shining and brimming with tears. "You can learn from this. Sometimes, it isn't great acts of magic that mark an item, but the events they witness. That was taken from Auschwitz."

Sean glowered at the table and shook his head. "The dark side of history has to be preserved, or we'll repeat it, but there are some artifacts even I would torch." He crossed back to her, still struggling to shake off the lingering effects. "You're right. I shouldn't play with this stuff. Let's read over the entries and find something interesting."

"There is a brain in that head after all," she said. Relief swept through her with his decision, and a playful light returned to her eyes. Tugging on his sleeve, she pulled him closer. "No need to read from way back there."

Her eyes were bright and warm, and he couldn't help but respond. He leaned on the table alongside her, their little fingers edging out until they touched while they studied the listings together.

They read each desk's story, making quips, laughing when the tales were light, and sharing in sorrow when the histories told of darker origins. There were only a handful of options left when Sean stopped her—pointing toward a desk near the end of the list. "That one. Let's see what it has to say about that one."

Axylia followed his finger and let out a happy, surprised sound. "Oh! Papa Djain's first desk." She clicked on the listing, and the inventory location popped up along with the history. "Last row, far back corner."

Sean drew his finger along hers, stepped aside, and headed down the aisle. "What's it say?"

"A mix of stone and wood, no metal. It says the desk has an odd balance of powers stored within. He inherited it from his father, a practitioner of darker magics. Still, he used it while first establishing the Quari Group, building alliances to help restore artifacts and links to the Mother, making it one of the few desks we have that hold such dichotomy." She turned, searching across the tops of the desks to find him standing still and smiling. "Did you find it?"

He was bouncing with excitement. "Aye! And it's wonderful." The legs were formed of gnarled wood with stone feet. The wood twisted around the stone to hold it in place, as if living roots had clasped themselves about the rock, claiming ownership. As it rose, the knotted and bent boughs turned and split along the underside of the tabletop, reaching out and entwining with one another to create the frame. Like so many other desks Sean had seen, the top itself was wood. The smooth surface was marred with symbols, some drawn and almost invisible from age, others etched into the grain. There were a few discolorations and stains, and Sean knew that each held a story, a bit of history that he wanted to learn. The right side and part of the top were scorched and discolored, but it did not diminish the desk's structural integrity. "This one!" he called out. "We'll tell them I want this one!"

As he jogged back up the row, she copied the inventory identification number from the record and sent the request. "Your new desk has been ordered!" She moved to his side, slipped her arm into his, and gave it a protective squeeze. "Now we have to deal with that warding business."

"Going to be that bad, is it?" he asked with an awkward laugh. "Then perhaps the condemned deserves a request."

A smile bloomed across her face, and she met his gaze. "What do you have in mind?"

"I would love to know more about you and the Elves." He pressed the ethereal call button as they reached the lift. "How different are we, the humans, our societies? Do you find it odd to be around us?"

"In many ways, your lot are barbarians, but in others, we are similar." The lift doors opened, and they stepped inside. "I think we have time for a quick tour." Axylia reached out and pressed thirty-five. "Let me show you our home away from home," she offered as the lift shot upward.

When the doors opened again, all Sean could see was a lush garden. A steppingstone path came right up to the lift, welcoming them. Sean exited the elevator, and his stomach twisted, the left side of his lips drawing upward. The building was gone, and he stood in a thriving place with thick foliage, crisp, clean air, clear blue skies overhead, and vibrant energy pulsing through him in waves.

Axylia tugged at his arm. "This way," she urged, guiding him along the path.

Ornate statuary and fountains appeared at regular intervals, the living archways allowing brief glimpses beyond the tall hedgerows as they passed. Flowers bloomed everywhere along the path, interwoven among the hedges, and sprouting from flowerbeds in dazzling displays filled with colors and blooms he had never seen before.

A towering canopy rose from what Sean assumed to be the center of this garden, and he could see the tops of other trees well off in the distance. Axylia giggled when Sean rubbed at the butterflies in his stomach.

"We entered another realm?" he asked.

She leaned toward him, running her hand down his arm and lacing their fingers together. "More of a pocket dimension, but yes, we are no longer on Terra. This is the realm of the Fae, a place between Terra and the Elven Sanctuary."

Other elves wandered the paths, and another group of beings, small humanoids the size of hummingbirds, zipped around the plants.

"Papa Djain helped us create this space, a place we can keep as close to our realm as possible. Many of the plants here and in our home cannot survive on Terra. The magic has grown too weak. So here, between the two, we maintain a small oasis. Perhaps someday we'll correct that imbalance and re-introduce them to the Mother."

Enchanted by the beauty of the garden and watching the surrounding activity, Sean was delighted. When he looked at Axylia, her pearlescent skin radiated an inner light, here, amid so much life. "I hope we do. I'm glad you shared this with me, though from what I have heard, I would love to visit the Elven Sanctuary." His eyes danced over her features before settling back on the bright emerald facets of her eyes.

She did not shy from his gaze, taking her time to study the textures of his face. The freckles sprinkled over his cheeks and nose, the dark blue of his eyes. Her brows edged upward with the corners of her lips.

A tiny creature flew between them, darting behind Sean's head. It was followed by a stream of others, and the sounds of laughter and play mingled with the buzz of their wings. Their voices were higher pitched than most humans, but not uncomfortable to hear. The small group raced around Axylia's head, swept down around her legs, and off toward the bushes nearby.

Once the group had vanished, the one hiding behind Sean's head zipped back around to hover between them. The little man bobbed up and down in the air as he spoke. "Axylia! You must stop being such a stranger. We all miss you, especially Lilly!" He fluttered over and poked Sean in the nose. "Is this the one causing all the buzz? Do you like picking fights with the pretty monsters?"

At such a close range, Sean could see the man much clearer. He had sandy blond hair, pulled back into a tail, and while his features were familiar, they were odd as well. His face was elongated, coming to a much steeper point at the chin. His brows were prominent and well defined for his small face, and his tiny ears reminded him of Axylia's, coming to a point atop the back of the lobes. The man was barefoot and wore snug-fitting pants that stopped mid-calf, along with a V-neck shirt made of some fabric that Sean couldn't identify. It was green in tone, but every time it moved, it shifted shade, hinting at reds, blues, and yellows as well, reminding Sean of a hummingbird.

Sean chuckled.

Axylia giggled. "He's the one!"

The little man drew back, his angled eyes sizing him up. The sound of the other pixies increased, announcing their return, and his wings sped up. "Don't get yourself squashed along with him. Oh, and neither of you saw me!"

The group burst out of the bushes behind Axylia and caught sight of their prey.

He let out a surprised exclamation and took off in the other direction, leaving a trail of glittering dust in the air. A cheer of renewed chase sounded, and the entire flock buzzed around Sean and Axylia, zipping off after their quarry.

Laughing, Sean lifted a brow. "Friend of yours, I take it. Fairy?"

"Pixie! Pixie!" She grabbed Sean's arm and laughed. "Never let Frost hear you get the two confused. He will torment you for a month!" She led him through an arched passage and into a small, private courtyard. A bench sat near a small pond with a water feature. The statue of a tree, womanly in form, holding an earthen vessel and pouring the water into a basin. "While you might see a fairy from time to time that appears to be about the same height as a pixie, they most often resemble you or me, but they can appear in a range of sizes."

She motioned toward the seat and settled in.

Sean sat beside her. "I'll keep that in mind. Do the fairies have any distinguishing features? I mean, Frost had notably angular features. Are fairies that way as well?" He shook his head. "What I mean is, if a fairy appears as the same size as a pixie, how do I tell them apart and not get myself a month of mayhem?" He laughed awkwardly, and she joined him.

"The fairies are much softer in appearance, like elves or humans with wings. You will not find a fairy with such sharp features nor a pixie with subtle ones, so if you can see their features, you can identify the two."

"Perhaps I'll just keep my mouth shut until I can spot the difference." He watched the water pour from the jar, his thoughts drifting.

She placed her hand over his. "What's bothering you?"

He shook his head in silence, continuing to watch the fountain until she placed her fingers on his chin and guided his eyes to hers.

"There is no need to shoulder the weight alone. That doesn't show strength," she admonished in tender tones.

He gave her a guilty smile and sighed. "I'm just struggling to wrap my head around everything I've learned. My entire life has changed over the past two days, and I've had no time to figure it out. I just know the world seems a lot heavier now than it did a few hours ago."

"I'm always here. To talk, listen, or just be an understanding presence." Her face fell, and she made a frustrated noise. "I don't want to pile on, but we cannot put off this discussion any longer."

He knew as well that they had lingered here too long. "No point in chewing on it. Let's hear it. Can't be all that bad, can it?"

She grimaced again. "We'll see. You should know you have two choices on how to have this ward applied. It is a tattoo, and you can either have it on the skin or the bone."

A dark, nervous laugh escaped. His brow knotted together, and his voice cracked, undermining his attempt to sound confident. "That sounds pleasant."

She winced, lifting her brows. "If you opt for what you would call a more traditional tattoo, you can have it placed wherever you like. But keep this in mind . . . if it ever gets messed up, chopped off, sliced through, if anything ever breaks the continuity of the symbol, the ward will be broken. You'll be vulnerable until you have another applied."

"Aye. So it's easy to apply, but it has the risk of leaving me out in the open if the unexpected happens. And what's the deal with the bone tattoo?"

She took a turn watching the falling water before speaking. "It is far more secure. You would be dead before it could be broken, as your bones, all of them, would have to be crushed to break the ward."

When he spoke, Axylia turned to find his eyes. "So it's a far more durable ward." His eyes narrowed with skeptical caution. "What's the downside? How do they tattoo the bone?"

A soft, concerned smile touched her lips. "My understanding is the process is harrowing. It is not used often because of the risks. The lucky ones pass out during the ritual and do not have to face the full brunt of the pain." She wrung her hands, pressing them into her lap. "More than one participant has been mentally broken."

"This new world is intriguing and wonderful, though frightening, and I feel so lost, like a child." Sean's gaze fell to her hands. "Like now. I cannot help but think I don't know enough of this new world to make an informed decision." He reached for her hands, and she draped her fingers over his. "You know this world far better. What do you think I should do?"

"I am afraid my thoughts may not be of much use, as they are conflicted." She offered an apologetic shrug. "Perhaps you should consult with Papa or one of the others before deciding."

Sean gave her hand a gentle squeeze. "I understand."

She rose with a sigh, tugging on his hand. "Perhaps we should go to him now. We've lingered here longer than I intended, and he is expecting us."

Excerpt from the Elven Volumes of Living Knowledge
Celestial Cycle 217.424379
in the First Reign of House Kryntan

The schemes of Ceralon and Syrdan have not gone unnoticed. The Bright Ones, Lucifer and Michael, have approached me, sharing concerns about the mingling of bloodlines. Their brother, Gabriel, rebuffs their concerns, heralding these unions as the way forward.

I am uneasy with the blind gusto with which Syrdan and Kryntan strive to embrace this effort. The prophetic visions regarding success are both inspiring and terrible. The council should reach an accord on this issue before fate and the actions of the rash determine our path.

—Councilor Arianelis

NINE

Full body tattoos for a thousand, Alex.

Arm in arm, Axylia and Sean returned to Djain's office. Ms. Iliescu chastised them for their tardiness and sent them to the Operations Center. When they reached ops, Sarah redirected them to the training rooms. The pair returned to the lift, laughing about their quest to find Papa.

When they entered the training room, Sean let out a low whistle. A half dozen portal arches stood against the far wall, well-spaced but lacking the energy ripple he was beginning to expect in such things. He could make out the lingering mists of energy around each, but was confident the arches were not in use. The left portion of the room was walled off with thick, padded panels. To the right was an armory. Weapons lined the walls and filled the myriad racks arranged in neat rows. There were sticks, swords, axes, knives, maces, bows, staves, and many implements he couldn't identify, all in various styles and sizes.

Hardwood floors covered the space, inlaid with a geometrically complex parquet pattern. Large pads, reminding Sean of the mats used for Olympic tumbling, covered the central portion of the room. Atop the pads, Gadyen and Ryan circled one another. Light bathed the area and drove all shadows beyond the mat.

Axylia led Sean toward the men, stopping well short of the light's edge. "I don't see Papa, so let's take a moment. You should see these two spar."

Ryan wore loose-fitting athletic shorts. His feet and chest were bare. The lights glinted off the sheen of sweat coating him, and his upper body bore a smattering of fresh cuts and scrapes. His arms and chest were covered in tattoos, and his hair now hung loose and fell to his shoulders. He danced around Gadyen, the dark strands of his hair swaying in rhythm with his steps as he searched for an opening.

Gadyen remained in a fixed position, his only movement a steady arc that kept him facing Ryan. He was barefoot, but clothed in a silver-white, asymmetrical angarkha with black trim and matching pants. His silver hair and pale skin blended into the clothing so well that if not for its colored edge, it would have been difficult to see the transition. Gadyen tilted his head toward Axylia and Sean, his eyes never moving from Ryan. "Welcome! Perhaps with cheering spectators, courage will find purchase and spur my opponent into action. Bring an end to his endless prancing about."

Ryan gave a mocking laugh, reversed directions, quickened his pace, and Gadyen responded, giving no opening.

"Fuck it," Ryan said. His shoulder dropped, and he charged at Gadyen.

The move was much quicker than Sean would have expected, but Gadyen was still faster. Sidestepping and only allowing Ryan to get a handful of cloth.

Twisting, Gadyen pulled the cloth free and taunted. "Oh! To have your goal in your grasp and yet let it slip through your fingers!"

Ryan planted his feet. His knees bent, and his forward momentum came to an abrupt stop. The muscles along his legs flexed, straining under their stored power, and he shot back toward Gadyen, a blur of skin and hair. This time, Gadyen was too slow. Ryan's shoulder collided with his chest, driving him across the mat and forcing Gadyen's foot out of the light.

Sean blinked, and Gadyen was gone. The lack of resistance caused Ryan to stumble into the shadows. Gaining his footing, Ryan backed toward the center of the mat, spinning, eyes moving all about the room.

Two different images of Gadyen appeared outside the light on opposite sides of the mat, but Ryan ignored them both, focusing instead on the empty places in the shadows.

From the left side, the image of Gadyen moved, but as it hit the light, the ghoulish form beneath the illusion broke through, and the twisted thing edged its way toward Ryan. "Dirty fighting old man," Ryan called as two more of the ghastly creatures broke from the shadows and made their way toward him.

Gadyen's teasing laugh rolled from the darkness, distant, ominous, directionless.

Ryan backed away from the creatures, avoiding the edge of the mat. His sharp eyes evaluated the situation, and he lowered himself, preparing for the coming scrap.

Gadyen appeared out of the shadows, a streak heading toward Ryan's back.

The two men collided and tumbled into the middle of the mat, and the three shadowy ghouls threw themselves into the fray.

Sean was amazed that Ryan seemed to hold the four of them at bay, even though he fought from his back.

Gadyen landed a blow, and the tide shifted.

Ryan was going down in a cloud of silver and smoke.

An animalistic roar sounded from beneath the pile, followed by the sound of rending cloth. Gadyen and his shady army were tossed away. Where Ryan had been, an enormous reddish-brown, shaggy maned bear rose, lifting onto its hind legs and growling its battle cry. Teeth glistened as Ryan fell back to all fours, snarling at his attackers.

Gadyen charged back in first, and the shadow creatures followed. Ryan made quick work of the others, paws shredding two of them, sending them up in vapors. The third he caught in his powerful jaw, tearing it apart with his teeth. It exploded into tendrils of mist, the smokey residue tickling his nose. He pawed at his nose, and it twitched and crinkled until he sneezed.

While Ryan dealt with his sensitive nose, Gadyen climbed atop his back. Wrapping one hand in the long fur, Gadyen wriggled and patted his flank. "Good boy!"

Ryan turned his head, teeth snapping at Gadyen and finding only air. He attempted to swat at him, but Gadyen was well out of range. Ryan reared up and bucked, struggling to dislodge his assailant, and Gadyen roared with laughter. "I shall never tire of riding you!"

Ryan threw himself over and rolled atop Gadyen.

Gadyen's grip loosened, and he groaned.

Ryan sprang back up and turned, placing his snarling teeth around Gadyen's throat.

Gadyen's slender, pale hand lifted and caressed the fur along Ryan's muzzle, and he whispered with a smile. "I yield."

Ryan released and drew back. In a heartbeat, he was lying next to Gadyen on the mat, nude. "Now, I'm fucking starving." Lifting his head, he turned a cocky grin on Gadyen. "Next time, drag something into the fight with some meat on its bones."

Gadyen patted his cheek. "I'll not allow you to waste away. Business first, then we can satiate your appetites later."

Ryan laughed and pushed himself up, his manhood on full display. Turning to face Sean and Axylia, he shrugged. "When you wake up naked every time you put on the fur suit, eventually you stop giving a shit about who sees." He tossed his arms out and spun. "Behold! And be in awe of my cock!"

Axylia shook her head and gave an exasperated sigh, and Sean laughed.

Gadyen rose beside him and sighed. "I fear the pursuit of manners in this one may well be what ends my long years. Go find something to cover yourself, then meet us in the war room."

"War room?" Axylia and Sean asked together before teasing and nudging each other.

Gadyen tilted his head toward the long, padded wall. "Our private name for the Training Coordination Office. More a comment on appearance than utility."

"Large map, a table in the middle, pieces to slide around. It looks like a scene from about any old war movie, ever," Ryan said, passing them on his way toward the lift.

With a graceful motion, Gadyen invited Axylia and Sean to lead the way. "The reality is much more mundane. We plot training scenarios and recovery missions inside," he said as they neared the door. "Papa Djain has been waiting to discuss yours."

Entering the room, Sean found it matched the picture he had formed based on Ryan's remarks, except to him, it seemed far more institutional than military. Rather than filing cabinets and war posters, this room had piles of books and various illustrations hung on the walls. Some cartographic, others resembled da Vinci's Vitruvian Man, but for other species. Djain was positioned at the head of the table, and around the corner to his left stood Talaunia.

Talaunia's eyes ran over Sean and Axylia, one shapely brow lifting. "I'll see to his needs now," she cooed at Axylia. "Be on about your business."

Djain's jaw set, his eyes hardening as they cut toward Talaunia.

Axylia's eyes narrowed, and she pursed her lips.

Gadyen chuckled, moving to the side of the table and reviewing the papers strewn across its top.

Sean let out a soft sigh and gave Axylia's arm a gentle squeeze. He cast an awkward glance at the two ladies before turning a bright smile on Axylia. "Thank you for all of your help and your company this morning. It's been a pleasure."

Axylia withdrew her arm from his and turned, lifting her chin, a sparkle in her eyes. "We must do it again soon."

Talaunia cut in. "Time is wasting."

Sean ignored her and continued to talk with Axylia. "Oh, we will. Don't forget, we have a date at my place, once the ward is in place, and I can safely roam beyond these walls."

Axylia's chin lifted. "How could I possibly forget?" Her gaze shifted to Talaunia. "Don't break him. We have plans later."

Djain cleared his throat. "We have things of importance to focus on."

"Of course." Axylia gave a respectful curtsy to Djain, then drew her finger along Sean's arm. "If you need me for anything, send for me. I will come." She gave a parting wave to everyone except Talaunia. The two ladies locked eyes, a silent battle of wills raging between them, until Axylia turned her back on Talaunia and breezed out of the room.

With a victorious smile, Talaunia spoke to Sean in a breathy whisper. "You'll have no desire to socialize when you are done pleasing me. Best cancel with the little harlot now before her attitude gets her fired."

Djain shook his head. "You are the one who has made it personal. Deal with your issues on your time." Dropping the matter, he shifted his attention to Sean. "Did you find a desk that suits your needs?"

Sean moved to stand beside him at the table. "Aye, Papa."

"Which did you choose?" asked Gadyen.

"Your first desk." Sean focused on Djain, watching his reaction. "Seems fitting to use it while trying to restore what they've taken from you."

Djain appeared pleased. "I look forward to seeing how it serves you. Now, have you decided on how you would like the ward applied?"

Sean's eyes swept the group, landing on Gadyen. Thinking of the sparring match he had just witnessed, his internal arguments resolved themselves. "I have. Tattoo the bone."

Gadyen's brows lifted, impressed by the resolve in Sean's voice.

Talaunia's violet eyes sparkled. "Oh, this will be a revealing day."

"You are certain?" Djain inquired.

Lifting his chin in resolve, Sean replied. "What I've already experienced, the stories I've heard of the encounters with the Order. Having seen the scrapes and cuts that covered Ryan after he and Gadyen finished their training bout on the mat, I don't see where there is any other choice. I'm only secure if the protection isn't easily compromised."

Djain's eyes narrowed in approval, one corner of his lip edging upward. "Very well. It is not a simple process. We should get started if we are to have it completed today." Giving direction to Gadyen, he continued. "It requires three casters. Can you find Jason and Sarah? Send them to the primary casting room."

With a formal bow, Gadyen slipped from the room.

"I should stay and assist. It can be trying, and Sean may need some tending when it's over," Talaunia offered.

Djain's eyes bored into her. "You best keep in mind what we are doing here."

Giving Djain a nod of understanding, she moved to Sean's side. "Come, I will help you prepare." She slipped her arm around his, mimicking Axylia. "You can be my escort to the ceremony."

Sean glanced at her fingers as they curled around his arm, an awkward expression settling on his face.

"It is the gentlemanly thing to do," she reminded him.

Sean's eyes lifted to hers, and the nagging sense of familiarity whispered in his mind again. "Of course." His smile became more natural, and he moved with her through the door.

"I must gather a few things from my private stores. I will return when I can. Get him cleansed," Djain said.

Talaunia nodded, echoing Sean's words. "Of course." Her eyes sparkled with mischief. "One can still have fun as they work, yes?"

Sean eyed her with suspicion.

Talaunia laughed, a bright laugh that was infectious. Tugging on Sean, she skipped a step. "I'm going to enjoy this." She hummed, pulling him into the light and across the mat. Reaching the other side, they stepped through a door previously obscured by the display of weapons.

Sean's stomach rolled as they crossed the threshold. "Did we change realms?"

She shook her head. "The casting rooms have wards to keep unwanted things out, and should something go amiss, in."

Looking around, Sean noted a small wooden table at the back with many of the same things he had seen in Djain's private casting area. Beakers, test tubes, stone pestle and mortar, copper bowls, a silver dagger, candles of various colors. Crossing to the table, they passed over the center of a rudimentary compass face, inlaid among the floor tiles.

"This is where you will stay, in this circle, when it's time for the incantation," Talaunia said. "First, we must prepare you, cleanse you."

"How do we cleanse me?"

Her eyes were bright and mischievous, alluring. "I'm about to show you." She moved behind him, and her hands came to rest on his hips. Her thumbs slipped under the elastic band of the pants, and she started pushing them down.

"Och!" He took a confused step away. "What the bloody hell are you doing?"

She bit her bottom lip, eyes sweeping over him. "Removing your clothes. Step one, get naked."

He gawked at her, a fierce skepticism flaring in his eyes.

She lifted one hand, placing the other over her heart. "I swear on everything I hold dear, no tricks. It is required."

He turned his back to her and peeled the shirt off, tossing the red mess of hair atop his head. She whistled, stepping closer and drawing a finger down his spine. "That's fine too. I can take it off for you or enjoy the show."

His shoulders tensed, a charge of excitement coursing through him at her touch. Taking another step away, he threw the shirt to the side of the room. "I can manage." He turned, unable to repress the nervous blush that spread over his face. "You just stay over there," he chuckled.

"As you wish," she said, leaning back against the table and ogling him. "I'm waiting."

He glanced over his shoulder at her a few times before hooking the yoga pants with his thumbs and bending to push them to his ankles. Standing, he used one foot to hold the pants to the floor. He removed one leg and reversed the process for the other, kicking the pants into a pile with the discarded shirt.

"Turn around," she commanded.

He crossed his hands before him, covering his manhood before complying. "Have you ever heard of harassment?" he asked, finding her eyes locked on his.

She winked. "We all see one another around here. This won't even raise an eyebrow." Her eyes fell to his hands, and an excited grin curled over her features. "In a few minutes, you'll be on display before the entire team, and half of them will use your body as an art canvas." She took a step closer and nibbled on her bottom lip. "Come on. You can give me a sneak peek."

"I think I'll wait for the others, thank you," he tried, but she was already a step ahead.

Twisting, she lit a candle on the table, picked up a dried bundle, and caught the end of it aflame. Turning back to Sean, she blew on the end seductively, extinguishing the fire. The scents of mugwort, rosemary, and thyme permeated the room. "We have to cleanse you, and Papa expects that to be completed when he returns." Smoke wafted up from the bundle of dried herbs. Giving him an earnest look, she dropped the teasing tones and gestures. "Now, arms out, feet shoulder-width apart. We have to bathe you in the smoke for this to work."

Embarrassment colored his cheeks. He set his jaw, closed his eyes, and after a moment of nervous teetering, complied, lifting his arms out to the sides of his body.

Talaunia let out a soft "Mmmm" sound, and her eyes remained fixed on his member. "Oh, yes, I can work with this."

She stepped closer and wafted the smoke over him, guiding it with a large feather around his head, face, and neck, and along his arms and chest before stepping behind and fanning it around the back of his head, arms, and shoulders. She worked down his back, over his ass, and kneeled to smudge around the backs of his legs.

"Turn," she said, and he complied. She cleansed his left leg, then his right. Reaching up, she fanned the smoke across his abdomen, moving down his hips into the pubic area. "Don't move," she whispered, leaning in.

She wafted the warm smoke so that it washed over and around his member. She studied his body with interest, kneeling before him, something more profound than a predatory hunger in her eyes. The tip of the feather grazed his inner thigh, tickling and sending a charge through his core.

It was involuntary, but he felt a twinge deep inside, and his cock twitched. Talaunia wafted more smoke over him, and his teeth ached from the struggle to keep his body from responding, but despite his efforts, he stiffened. Her eyes swept up his form, flirtatious and bright above her devilish grin. "It is nice to know at least one of your brains knows what's good for it."

The door opened, and their banter announced the sound of Jason and Sarah's arrival before the pair stepped into the room. Sean sensed their eyes crawling over his back, and his head dropped to his chest as the room fell quiet.

Talaunia leaned to the side, peeking around Sean's hip. She drew the back of her hand over her lips.

Sarah gasped. "Oops!"

Jason laughed. "Dude!"

Sean turned, his now rigid state on full display. "Nothing happened."

"Claim that shit, man! Damn," Jason said.

Talaunia stood and feigned embarrassment. "Please, don't tell anyone."

"There's nothing to bloody well tell," Sean said, face coloring in embarrassment.

"Sorry if we interrupted," Sarah said.

Sean could feel her eyeing him, and when he focused on her, he thought he saw discomfort in her eyes, and she couldn't meet his gaze.

With the shock of the new arrivals, Sean's manhood reverted to its flaccid state, and he lowered his hands to cover himself. "Sarah, there was nothing to interrupt. She was only performing the cleansing thing."

"Dude, stop trying to put the cat back in the bag. You were busted," Jason laughed.

Talaunia winked at Sean, and he took a step away, pointing at her with a nervous chuckle. "Is there anything else I have to do to get ready for this?"

Sarah's eyes flashed from him to Talaunia. "The cleansing is done?"

"Yes, he's cleansed," Talaunia responded. "He's just—frustrated." Then she purred.

Jason moved to the table, and the ladies followed. Talking over one another, they set about preparing some sort of pungent, inky potion.

Djain entered the room, his gaze sweeping over Sean from top to bottom. "Good, you are ready!" He carried a leather brush holder in his hand, rolled up and bound with thin straps. He crossed to the table with the others and laid it down, taking the concoction from each and examining it. "This is almost ready; now add mugwort."

Jason and Sarah both turned with puzzled expressions. "But mugwort is used for divination and cleansing," Talaunia interjected. "It has no place in this brew."

"Under normal circumstances, you would be right, but we will add a few extra things. Trying to extend the ward to cover him when he is projecting." Djain waited for each of them to understand and see the ramifications.

"Dude, this better work, or he's boned," Jason said, turning a concerned glance in Sean's direction.

"Lovely way to put it, Jason," Sarah chided.

"Am I to understand that this may not keep me hidden if I get sucked into another of those vision things?" Sean asked.

"I am confident that the changes we are making will keep you protected, even when you are traveling. I discussed the changes with Ms. Iliescu and Pretaris, both of whom are seers, and with Theran."

Talaunia's head snapped toward Djain, but he ignored her.

Djain met Sean's gaze, projecting reassurance. "Theran and Pretaris are the ambassadors of the Elves to Terra. They are among the oldest living Elves. They wield significant power and know more of magic than most could ever dream. I have confidence this will work and make what you are to endure worth the price."

Talaunia poked at Djain's shoulder. "You spoke with them?"

"They are not willing to discuss it. You must be patient." Djain turned a compassionate but stern gaze upon her. "And that ends the discussion. For now. We have pressing matters to which we must attend."

"It's been millennia; I think I've been patient enough," she huffed, hands going to her hips in defiance. She glanced out of the corner of her eye and found the focus of the others on her. Her gaze lingered on Sean. "Fine. You're right, more pressing things. Have to protect what I still have." Her head snapped back to Djain, and a finger shot out in his direction. "But don't think for a moment we're done!"

Djain chuckled. "I would never make that mistake. Now," he pulled a small vial from his pocket and set it on the table. "Once you have added the mugwort and mixed it in well, one drop from this."

"What's in it?" Jason asked, picking up the small vial to inspect.

"I do not know. Theran and Pretaris gave it to me. They mentioned something about the tears of the Mother being used to protect her child."

The sound of metal clanking drew their attention to the door, where Ryan and Gadyen were carrying in several heavy metal poles and a black duffel sagging under the weight of its contents. They moved to the center of the circle and dropped the heavy load.

"What's that?" Sean asked.

Gadyen's brow rose, his focus shifting from Sean to Djain. "Appears he still lacks a few details."

"It is a suspension device, a rack. We cannot have you pass out, fall, and destroy the spell work." Djain shrugged. "To ensure that does not happen, we are going to suspend you between the posts. Then no matter what kind of flopping around you do, the magic will still work."

Sean's mouth fell open, and around him, all conversation turned to the ritual. Gadyen and Ryan assembled the rack, which reminded Sean of an iron spider, while the others focused on perfecting the repugnant concoction. When the frame was finished, Talaunia used the smoldering bundle to cleanse it and each of the ropes tied to the anchoring points.

"We need him secured," Djain said once the rack was cleansed.

Flashing Sean a seductive smile, Talaunia beckoned him with the slow curl of her finger. "I'll tie him up."

The air in the room shook, bringing all activity to a halt. Sean watched the playfulness melt from Talaunia's face, and in confusion, turned to find Djain's fierce gaze leveled on her.

Sweeping the room with his eyes, Djain spoke. "If we are to accomplish our goals. If we are to help restore even a slim portion of what they have taken from the Mother, we must understand when it is time to put away our desires and approach our duties with the appropriate mindset." His head swiveled, making lingering eye contact with each of them. "If you are unable to afford this ritual the required focus, this is not where you belong."

No one moved.

No one breathed.

Lifting a single finger into the air, Djain twirled it in a small circle. In an instant, everyone was back at work.

Talaunia looked at Sean, nothing but business in her eyes or tone. "Please, join me."

Sean stepped into the circle.

"Spirits be with you," Gadyen offered as he and Ryan slipped from the room.

Limb by limb, Talaunia bound Sean to the frame, stretching him to his limits. His feet were bound just past shoulder-width apart, and his arms pulled up and out. He tried to pull against the ropes, seeking comfort for his already aching muscles, but Talaunia had done her job well. There was no give and no relief to be found.

Djain stepped into the circle and inspected the frame and bindings, ending by placing his hand on Sean's chest. "Now, we will begin. If the darkness comes, let it take you. There is no need to fight it. There is nothing to be gained by suffering more than you must."

Placing a hand on Talaunia's back, Djain herded her from the circle and called Sarah and Jason to join him.

The way they carried themselves now, faces tense with concentration, amplified Sean's nerves, and the weight of the situation settled into his stomach.

Djain stepped into the ritual area and placed his bowl and brush on the floor before Sean. He took small bowls and candles from the table and moved around the circle. The first bowl was stationed on the floor at the eastern point of the compass. A white candle stood in the middle of the bowl, surrounded by topaz and clear quartz. The next bowl was set on the southern point and contained a crimson candle surrounded by a mix of amber and clear quartz stones. Another bowl followed and was positioned on the western marker. From its center rose a blue candle surrounded by aquamarine stones and clear quartz. One last bowl was placed on the northern arrow, a green candle rising from a mix of onyx and clear quartz pebbles.

Standing in front of Sean, Djain held his gaze. "Once the circle is set, we will mark you for the ritual. Relax as best you can while we work."

"Trying to . . ." Sean said, pushing a nervous smile into place.

Djain scanned the room, taking stock of everyone's positions, and was satisfied with what he found. "Let us begin." He moved, standing before the eastern bowl, his eyes closed, and Sean watched him draw in a deep breath, releasing it over several long seconds. After exhaling a third time, his eyes opened. His hand drifted over the white candle, and it sprang to life. "Spirits of Air, we ask you here. Lend us your blessing and watch over us in this sacred space."

Sean saw a shimmer in the air over the candle. A calm wind blew across his chest and lifted the hair at Sarah's shoulders. He blinked a few times as a trio of faces appeared, hanging in the air along the arc of the compass, followed by muscular torsos that vanished into swirling mists below the abdomen. Their skin reminded Sean of smokey quartz, their eyes black pools with pearlescent irises, and their long, midnight blue hair was pulled back with golden bands. Power swelled in the room as the beings appeared, watching with guarded reverence.

Djain acknowledged their arrival with a deep bow before moving in sequence to each of the other three markers. Djain's invitation to each was personalized, and Sean was in awe as more spirits responded with each request.

The Spirits of Fire arrived, burning mirrors of their Air touched cousins, and the power in the room swelled. Their skin was the color of cooled magma, white-hot embers gave their eyes a searing heat, and their flame-toned hair was held back in obsidian bands.

When the Water Spirits arrived, Sean could feel the power in the room crawling over his skin and threatening to steal his breath. The aquamarine hue of their skin made their amethyst eyes stand out, while their deep sapphire hair was pulled back and bound in tangled driftwood.

The power swell that accompanied the Spirits of Earth made Sean afraid his chest would collapse. Their skin was the color of rich topsoil, their azure eyes peered from beneath mossy brows, and their forest green hair was bound with a living vine.

Sean couldn't stifle the groan that slipped from him, and he clenched his jaw.

Standing before Sean, Djain held his hand out flat, palm down, between them. He moved it in a slow, clockwise circle three times. "Now, we call to the Mother and ask her to watch over the spirits of her children."

The pressures in the room snapped into balance, and Sean could breathe. The air crackled with energy and power, unified in purpose and goal, no longer competing. Sean scanned the circle in awe. A protective barrier now hummed around them, its edge matching the outer rim of the compass. His gaze settled back on Djain's smiling face. "The circle is cast, and we thank the Guardians for honoring us with their presence."

Attempting to reassure him, Sarah drew Sean's attention. "The first circle is the hardest. You learn how to handle the power changes the more you do them." She cast a sideways glance at Djain. "Besides, I've never seen anyone pull as much power into a circle as Papa. No one else even comes close. So, you just medaled in the Olympics of circle casting."

"We can speak of all that after completing our work. Now, set your mind to the task." With that, Djain, Sarah, and Jason embarked on the painstaking process of painting various symbols, runes, and scripts along Sean's skin, covering the places above his bones. The process was slow and methodical, each of them asking others to check their work. Sean's muscles cramped and burned. His arms and legs felt as though they were being pulled from their sockets. Pain radiated from his shoulders and hips as the minutes dragged into hours. Gadyen and Ryan returned to check on progress before vanishing again. It took nearly three hours to complete the intricate work of marking the inscriptions on his skin.

Once finished, Djain looked him in the eye. "I know you are feeling pain, but what you are experiencing now is nothing compared to what comes. I will give you one last chance to change your mind. Once we take the next step, there is no stopping until the ritual is complete." Sean shook his head, and Djain pressed once more. "No one would think less of you."

Sean swallowed, glancing at the powerful planar beings that had responded to Djain's invitation. His head swung again, and through clenched teeth, urged them on. "Do it."

Dipping his chin toward the others, they moved into position, forming a triangle around Sean. After making one last check, Djain began. "The Mother rises now to build, around Her child, a shell. A ward that travels where he goes, all prying eyes to fell. Upon his bone, Her words remain, etched within his core. Wrapped in blood, sealed with his pain, hidden evermore!" His resonant basso voice sounded the words with authority. Everywhere the ink had been painted, his skin crawled, and he tried to squirm, to twist, but the ropes were unyielding. Djain chanted the passage three times, and with each iteration, the discomfort intensified, causing Sean to pull against the ropes with more fervor.

After Sarah joined Djain and their voices mingled in a unified chant, Sean felt the first real pangs of pain, and fear wormed its way into his chest. His temples throbbed, his heart galloped, and he screamed. The torment fed his fear, and his fear gave way to panic. Snapping his mouth closed, his teeth ground, every muscle in his body rippling and taut as regret painted itself amid the pain on his face. He struggled against his bonds, and the ropes dug into his skin. He felt the spreading warmth of blood as it ran down his forearm. His body ached with the effort to free itself from the binding. Again, Sarah joined with Djain, and the moment of regret Sean had was pushed from his mind, the agony driving all rational thought from him. All that remained was the base need to free himself, to escape this torture, but Talaunia had left him helpless to fight free of this web.

When they began the third round of the chant, Sean cried out in anguish. The markings on his skin bubbled and erupted, sending puffs of fetid smoke into the room. When Jason joined the droning chant, Sean's cries locked in his throat. Agony contorted his face, and the whole of the frame shook from the quavering strain of his efforts to escape. In searing waves, the intricate symbols atop his skin penetrated layer after layer of flesh, driven down through skin, cartilage, and muscle toward the bone at a slow, hellish pace.

Jason's third round ended, and for a fleeting moment, Sean dared hope that he had endured the worst of it; then, the three started in again, louder with more authority. His body screamed as though it were on fire, each part of him trying to jerk back from the flames, but there was no escape from the inferno raging under his skin. Sean's head tipped back, his eyes rolled up into his head, and the pain vanished into the peaceful emptiness of unconsciousness.

Excerpt from the Elven Volumes of Living Knowledge
Celestial Cycle 218.595901
in the First Reign of House Kryntan

I see potential the other councilors refuse to acknowledge, the chance to evolve beyond our current states. Mingling the gifts of our blood with that of the Bright Ones would allow us to bring a new race into being, melding the Mother's talents with those of the Heavenly Host. Ah! What could we accomplish for the Mother if we were to have such allies? Regardless of their narrow views, I have encouraged the Bright One, Iblis, to court the eldest of my daughters. May the Mother and Goddess smile upon their union.

—Councilor Syrdan

TEN

Evening had descended, and within the dusky twilight, the clear night sky promised a view of the stars seldom seen on Terra. Specks of light twinkled overhead, washing the Elven gardens in starlight and giving everything a delicate luster.

Sean lay in a patch of clover, his head across Talaunia's lap. The cool groundcover soothed his bare skin. Her right arm lay draped along his shoulder, fingers brushing over his chest, tracing the faint discolorations that remained. The healing energy of the Fae gardens seeped into him, aided by a tingling flow of familiar energy where her fingertips traveled.

Talaunia sped his recovery, guiding his restoration with her touch. Sensing him stir, she spoke in a hushed voice. "How are you feeling?"

Sean shifted, lifting a leg so that it bent at the knee. He grunted. "Better, but everything still aches."

Her left hand brushed the hair from his eyes, fingers trailing over his forehead. "By morning, you will be replenished."

One eye opened, and he rolled his head, squinting up at her. The other eye fluttered open, blinking away his confusion, and he searched the shadows that shaded her sandalwood skin. Catching himself studying the delicate curves of her lips, he forced his eyes to the stars overhead. "Morning?" The question puckered his face in displeasure. "There are things I needed to take care of."

"They will still be there tomorrow. Tonight, you are mine. Papa left you in my care, and I'll not release you until we are done." Her lips curled into a wicked smile. "Besides, I sent Sarah hours ago to inform Axylia that your plans had changed, and you were now spending the night with me."

Sean groaned, the sound spurred by an equal mix of discomfort and concern over the wording of her message. He closed his eyes and shifted, rolling away from her. "Bloody hell."

Her fingers moved over his side and along his back. "I thought you had better manners."

"Thank you for helping me," he said with sincerity. He twisted his head, staring up at her with a pinched brow. "What message did you send her?" He shifted his head to her lap once again, making it easier to hold her gaze.

"Have you ever desired something, Sean? Something you saw someone else trying to claim? Something that you were willing to fight and struggle for?" The depth of the shadows almost hid her tender expression. "Do not fault me for trying to attain what I desire."

Sean stared up into the shadows that masked her face until he found the deep violet of her eyes. He spoke, words filled with disbelief. "You know that makes you sound touched. You don't even know me. We've never even had a proper conversation."

She lay a finger over his lips, and a familiar warmth settled about him, his eyes following the delicate turn of her lips. "I know you far better than you realize, and deep down, I think you sense it. I can see it in your eyes at times, how you struggle to remember me." She kept her finger on his lips, tracing their contours as she continued. "We do far more than test the blood before introducing someone into this world. For months, my primary task has been to learn about you."

Sean tried to open his mouth, and she gave a soft "Shhh. Now is the time to listen. I spoke with your mother, trying to research your bloodline. She refused to answer, and now we know why. Being the direct descendant of a Bright One, she has many reasons to keep that information hidden." She pulled her finger across the coarse stubble covering his jawline. "Still, she was more than willing to speak of you. I have heard tales of your youth and your heart. Always adventuring, often foolhardy, but always gallant."

She ran a hand through her hair, pulling it all to one side of her head, and it allowed more of the soft light to touch her dark skin, showing the depth of her eyes. "You don't know it, but you've met me many times. You know, the awkward girl, Tammy, who sat several cubicles down from your old desk. She was such a strange one, but you always treated her with kindness and respect. Befriending her when no one else would. Defending her when others tried to bully or disparage her."

Sean's brows pinched in confusion, and she pressed her finger against his lips again. "Back in July, you met that redhead, Jenny. She was crying at the pub, mourning the loss of a family member. You spent an entire night comforting her, a stranger. She invited you to her hotel, but your eyes fell on her wedding ring, and you refused."

Talaunia's finger fell from his lips and traced along the side of his cheek, caressing the stubble, and his expression darkened. "The brunette, Kate, that you met in the non-fiction section of the bookstore. The two of you lost an afternoon debating the influence of the Celts at a coffeehouse. Days later, you lost another afternoon, discussing the influence of Egyptian architecture with her. The third time you met the day melted away amid lively historical discussions. You asked her on a proper date, though she stood you up, and you never saw her again." A heat simmered in her eyes, a wicked playfulness evident even in the sincerity of her expression, "I knew better than to see you again as Kate. You will find it hard enough to forgive these deceptions; never would you have forgiven me had I allowed us to become physical while I was under a glamor."

"What the bloody hell is a glamor?" Sean asked.

Her hand went to his chest. "It is magic that allows one thing to appear as another."

Sean's voice was thick and grew more heated the longer he spoke. "You're telling me you were each of those women, playing a roll to see how I would react? Testing me?"

She sighed. "In a manner of speaking. How better to evaluate someone?"

"By bloody well talking to them! That's how!"

"See, I knew you would be upset. I do know you. If you looked past the glamor, you would see you know me too, or at least parts of me." She smiled, recalling each of the guises. "The best characters have a bit of your soul in them, giving them life. With Kate, well, intelligent, strong, opinionated . . . surely, you see parts of her in me."

He let out a slow breath. The constant, nagging feeling that he knew her swelled into the forefront of his mind. His eyes flashed over her features, and he shifted, rolling away from her again, lost in his thoughts.

She ran her fingers through his hair and traced the edge of his ear. "I think the shadow of a beard fits you well."

Sean scratched at this cheek.

"I know you think him dead, but I met your father as well." She felt him stiffen. "I can tell you about him if you like. Your mother told me about him. That is how I know and how I found him."

His words were distant, questioning. "My father is dead. He died when I was a babe."

"No. Your mother told you that story to protect both you and your father." She placed her hand on his shoulder and coaxed him to roll to his back once more so she could meet his gaze while she spoke. "You know now that your mother is not normal. She is a succubus. For the safety of your father, she left and told you the lie. She did things she knew would cause pain to protect you both."

He shook his head, unsure. "She wouldn't hide that from me . . ."

"She did as I would, what was best for you. Based on her story, I found your father. Would you like to hear about him? I warn you; it isn't the most pleasant of tales." Her fingers drifted across his chest, gliding along his arm to his hand. She intertwined their fingers and waited for him to respond.

His eyes bore into hers, wrestling with accepting what she was saying. He shifted his focus to the night sky, but the sight of the stars troubled him further, and his eyes flickered back to hers. "Tell me."

She squeezed his hand, assuring him he wasn't alone. "Already knew that's what you would decide."

He let out a soft hiss of breath, which she ignored.

"Your mother knew where he was and gave me his name. I researched his history and found a wounded, mortal man. He spends his life in a small pub near the place they shared. More often than not, he spends his time lost in a bottle of spirits." Her fingers moved through his hair. "Should you decide you want to meet him, I will take you."

"What happened between them?" he asked.

She sighed. "I'm afraid that is their story to tell."

His eyes met hers, and he studied her, time stretching out unrushed by either of them. The diffuse starlight caused her copper hair to glow, and he found it captured his attention. "I think I need to speak with Mom," he said. "I'll wait for her to return. This isn't a conversation I want to have over the phone. She's on a business trip, appraising antiques for a family in Boston. She'll be back in a few days, and that will give me time to organize my thoughts and questions."

The subtle curve of her lips conveyed her understanding. "We will speak to her together, and for once, you'll be thankful to be in my company."

He rolled his eyes and settled in against her once more. He pulled their intertwined hands to his chest, asking questions about the research into his past, and she answered every one. The conversation was quiet and slow, hours passed, and Sean drifted off to sleep, quite unintentionally.

< ᚻᛗᚪᚾᛁᚻᚷ ᛗᚻᛗᚱᚷᚼ ᛋᚾᚱᚱᛟᚾᛏᛞᛋ ᚼᛟᚾ >

The sun peeked over the tops of the hedgerows as Sean woke. He stretched, finding a dull ache throughout his body, but nothing more than the stiffness one endures after a strenuous workout. Looking around, he found himself alone. Beside him, a pile of clothing waited, neatly folded, with a note peeking from between the garments.

Checking the pile, he discovered a fresh pair of tight yoga pants and another oversized shirt. Shaking his head, he dressed, speaking to no one in particular. "I bloody well have to go shopping."

Snatching the note up, he made his way out of the hedge maze, reading as the lift carried him toward his office.

Darling,

What a lovely evening! I trust you have found yourself in good repair. Here are some fresh clothes—we so need to take you shopping.

I would have preferred to greet you properly when you awoke, but I have been called to the war room to discuss your training. Papa wishes for you to start your day at your desk and has left instructions there for you.

Already, I look forward to the next night you spend naked in my arms. Before then, however, you must train. Our first session will be later today, when you will be all mine once again. How slowly the hours will pass until then . . .

~Talaunia

The doors hissed open, and Sean stepped from the lift, reaching his office without distraction. Once there, he dropped the note onto the recently installed desk and took stock of the other deliveries. Behind the desk sat a mesh chair with a high, broad back and wide base. Fresh plants covered the top of the bookcases, and beside them sat three desk sets, each themed differently. One was a more reserved design, with black backings, leather corners, and gold bindings. One was Disney-themed, with Mickey and Minnie holding pens and cards. The one he chose had a steampunk style, with copper and brass accents. Smiling, he carried it to the desk.

In the middle of the desk sat a pyramid made of various crystals. Sean picked it up, examining each face of the smooth surface. He thought he recognized the clear quartz that topped off the structure. The base was thick and black, and near the middle were layers of blue and red. Appreciating the weighty object, he sat it back on the desk.

A small stack of papers and a worn leather journal sat on the right side of his desk, with a brief note from Djain explaining that the journal was his. The documents below were translated excerpts from Djain's private book collection, highlighting anything they contained referencing the Order of the Sacred Flame.

Sean sat in the chair and tested it out, taking time to dial in the arm heights, seat height, lumbar support, and resistance. Then he opened the desk set and placed the holders for pens and pencils, business cards, paperclips, and tape in the left corner. Freeing the stapler from its wrapping, Sean positioned it beside the other pieces. He shifted the pile of papers and the journal to the middle of his desk, moving the notes from Djain and Talaunia off to the side.

Talaunia. Their conversation lingered in his mind. He couldn't refute anything she had said. With each encounter they had shared while she was under a glamour, she had read him flawlessly. It made him wonder how much weight that added to her comments about his father. Resolving that he could only answer that by confronting his mother, he picked up his phone. He stared out the window, sighed, and dialed her office line, knowing she wouldn't answer.

The answering machine picked up, and Narah's voice sounded over the phone. "Thank you for calling Yore Things. Our sales floor is temporarily closed and will reopen at eight o'clock on the twentieth. We look forward to helping you find all of your things when we return."

Sean shook his head at the cheesy message, but it brought a smile to his troubled face as the beep sounded. Taking a breath, he closed his eyes, "Och, mum. I forgot you were off on business. When you get back, let's have dinner. I've learned so many new things, and I look forward to discussing them with you. Be safe out there. Loads of Love."

Sean disconnected the call, his shoulders sagging. He knew his tone was off in the message, and his mother would pick up on it too. Hoping that she wouldn't decide to call him about it before returning, he sought a bit of comfort in the beauty of the gardens below.

Unable to find solace from the view, he returned to the desk and picked up Djain's journal. He admired the leather cover, running his hand over it, appreciating the craftsmanship. Upon seeing the pages of parchment inside, he gingerly placed the book back onto the desk. It lay open before him, and he leaned over it, splaying his hands atop the desk and examining the faded letters and quality of the skins. The journal was old, far older than Djain, like this desk. Sean's brow pinched, and he sank into the chair, considering what he knew about Djain. The discrepancies and contradictions floated in his mind, a puzzle demanding resolution. Thinking of Djain's youth, he focused on the crystal pyramid. The tip of his index finger traced the grooved line of a symbol carved into the surface of the desk. An odd tug pulled at Sean's thoughts, and he followed where it led. The world around him faded into the distance, and he was swallowed in a blanket of white.

Excerpt from the Elven Volumes of Living Knowledge
Celestial Cycle 218.836637
in the First Reign of House Kryntan

Reading what my fellow councilors have already committed to the living record, I feel compelled to respond. We are not blind to the vision shared by Syrdan and Queen Kryntan to merge the bloodlines of our people and the Bright Ones. We only council a slow and calculated approach to such an endeavor. The Mother is still in upheaval, as are we as a people, evolving, changing. We sense the new life She has cultivated in the depths of the waters collected upon Her skin, a simple being we must care for and protect. Is it foolish of us to undertake an experiment in creating life when we understand so little of its magic and mystery?

—Councilor Traxidor

ELEVEN

SOME THINGS YOU DON'T WANT TO KNOW ABOUT YOUR BOSS.

Sean felt himself carried on the wind, its icy grip holding him aloft as he soared over the snow-draped forest below. The purity of the snow reflected the pale moonlight, bathing the world in a surreal glow. A lone structure appeared, nestled in a small clearing amid the hardy, cold-loving trees. A trail of smoke billowed from the chimney, making promises of warmth to any who could make it inside. He descended through the snow-laden boughs and the wind lifted its voice, howling in frustration. The stubborn structure held against its relentless assault. Each gust broke against the thick, stacked stone walls, sweeping the powdery flakes into deepening drifts, threatening to bury what it could not overcome.

A solitary window sat hidden beneath a heavy shutter, locked away from the world until spring returned. To its side, a thick wooden door marked the entrance, standing guard against the frigid onslaught. Sean passed through the barrier unchallenged and left the cry of the wind outside.

Inside, a small fire burned, crackling in its stone hearth, driving the cold from the rustic home. The room was wrapped in quaint darkness. Shadows quivered in the flickering light, casting an old-world warmth over the trappings of a life lived around the central room.

Interspersed among the many Norse items in the home were a host of anomalies that piqued Sean's curiosity. Pottery and art, jadeite statues, bone necklaces, and wooden totems, all things belonging in a much warmer climate, not this frozen landscape. Sean thought of the warm Caribbean sound of Djain's voice and resolved to ask Papa about the apparent cultural conflict.

Looking deeper, Sean could see more questionable items scattered about, bones and strange jars with contents he did not wish to identify. In the corner sat his new desk, Djain's desk, much younger, far less scarred, and not yet singed with fire.

Two doorways sat opposite the main entry, one blocked by a wooden door with an inset latch, the other divided from the home's main body by a heavy cloth.

A sonorous snore broke the stillness, resonating from behind the closed door.

In response, a quiet giggle sounded beyond the fabric drape.

Sean's brow lifted in curiosity, and he followed the sound of laughter.

The house was small, but the fire's warmth did little to keep the chill from creeping into the smaller room.

The cloth over the opening was heavy and plunged the space into darkness. On opposite walls of the room, thick feather and hay mattresses lay on the floor, covered with heavy, fur-lined blankets.

To the right lay a dark figure, almost invisible in the deep shadows of the room. Eyes closed, head extended from beneath the heavy covers; Sean was confident it was a much younger Djain. In his mid-teens, the strong jaw of the man Sean knew was already developing, as were the powerful, broad shoulders.

Sean watched as a mound of fur to his left shifted, unfurling, so the outline of limbs and a torso became apparent beneath the pile. Long, thin fingers crept from under the edge of the fur, peeling it away. A mess of dark braids appeared, followed by the deep, dusky brown tones of a smooth forehead. A pair of sharp brows emerged, resting over a matching set of bright, inquisitive gray eyes.

The figure froze, and Sean could see her listening to the darkness, noting the subtle point of her ears. He could see her cataloging the sounds, the creek of the trees, the crackle of the fire, the howling of the wind. The blanket resumed its slow descent upon hearing the rumbling snore from the other chamber, revealing her long nose and high cheekbones. Beneath the point of her nose, a pair of plump, pouty lips became visible, two shades darker than the youthful skin they adorned. The face was of one still walking the transitional line between that of child and woman.

The girl shifted again, finding the new position cold and causing a chill to run through her. Her feather gray eyes peered through the darkness, searching the opposite wall. She swallowed, and her full lips pressed into a thin line before she whispered. "Big Brother."

To Sean, the language sounded Norse, which he didn't speak, yet somehow the words untangled themselves, and he understood their meaning.

"Are you sleeping? Tell me what he taught you today." Though her voice carried the same rhythmic lilt as Djain's, it was much softer, adding to Sean's puzzlement.

In the darkness, Djain's eyes fluttered open, his lips curling into the smile of one who had known she was there, of one who had been waiting for his cue. His eyes cut to the heavy drape, but he was listening beyond, gauging the cadence of the snores. Once satisfied she had not disturbed the unseen guardian; his pale blue eyes moved back through the darkness to find her silhouette. Even in the dark, he could see her tremble from the cold.

"You know I am awake." His voice was still shifting into adulthood. It was pitchy and making uncomfortable jumps, from the upper baritone of his early teens to the sonorous resonance that promised to bloom in him as a man. He struggled to speak at a low volume, finding it challenging, his body betraying his efforts.

Eyes darting to the drape again, he leaned towards her and whispered. "If you are cold, come and let me warm you." He was already peeling back his blanket, shifting his massive frame to create space for her at his side. "Then I will tell you about the day."

As the scene played out, Sean was certain it was a familiar routine for the pair.

A slender, crooked grin spread over her pouty lips. Her chin inclined, and her head pivoted against the pillow so she could eye the cloth drape. The fire's dancing light cast the subtlest of glows, outlining the thick fabric, and she traced its path with her eyes. Finding nothing out of place, she shifted, and a long, limber leg slipped from beneath the blanket. She wore thin, cream-colored pants tied at the mouth and hanging low on her hips. Her bare feet hit the floor, cushioned by the fur rug. A matching cream top covered most of her torso as she sat upright in bed, leaving a small track of skin to peek out from between the garments. Her budding breasts created subtle curves in the cloth. In the chill air, her nipples pressed against the cloth, and Djain's eyes lingered.

Grabbing the edge of the mattress, she rose to her full height, approximately five and a half feet, even at her young age. A long curtain of dark, braided hair followed her, falling halfway down her back. She crossed the narrow room with a single, graceful motion and slipped down into the space Djain had prepared for her.

Situating herself on her side, she faced him, and he pulled the blanket up over her shoulders. He was happy to have her at his side, and she made a quiet, delighted sound. Stretching, she placed a gentle peck on his forehead.

"Are you warmer now?" As if part of a ritual, Djain pressed his lips to her forehead, tender, lingering. He shifted beneath the blanket, his hips moving with the press of the girl against him.

Sean knew and even felt the struggle he could see in Djain, even if neither youth yet understood. He could feel the fire at his core simmering as the girl pressed closer to Djain. Sean could also hear the strain in Djain's voice, his attempt to keep the raging hormones bursting within him from being discovered.

Swallowing, Djain whispered. "What do you want to know this night?"

"Do you remember when Father brought back those rabbits? A couple of days ago. I heard him say to you something about—what did he call it?" Her voice was soft, and their noses touched from time to time as they spoke.

Sean could tell Djain had draped an arm over her, and she pulled in closer, holding him. Their legs moved, and the blanket came free, showing their legs intertwined.

"Reanimation. What does that mean?" she asked, having found the word for which she had been searching. "Has Father taught you that yet? What were the rabbits for?"

She gasped, eyes widening as some sort of realization struck her. Tightening her grip around Djain, she pressed herself into him. "Are you going to do this thing to the rabbits? How does it work?"

She squeaked in anticipation of his answer.

The sound pierced the quiet of the home, and Djain tensed.

Her head snapped up, and she sucked in a worried breath, her eyes fixed on the doorway, waiting, eager to see if she had roused the snorer.

Djain's eyes fell to the exposed, slender slope of her neck. "I hope Father didn't hear me," she muttered, wriggling and squirming around until she vanished beneath the blanket and lay eye level with Djain's chest.

Sean heard her gulp in a breath and felt his chest tingle, watching Djain's face contort in confusion.

The girl exhaled, her warm breath spilling over Djain's bare chest. "Hide me if he comes in," she whispered, a playfulness tickling her words.

Djain grabbed hold of that request, using it to focus himself in another direction. "You know I will hide you if I can."

A new fear was growing in Djain's eyes, and he stared at the cloth drape granting their privacy. The creek of wood sounded, and the pair clung to each other, relaxing as the sound of snoring returned in the next heartbeat.

She peered up at him from under the covers before burying her face in his chest to muffle her giggle, realizing it had been nothing more than a rafter settling.

After a long moment, Djain lifted the blanket, and a soft, agonizing groan escaped him. Their mingled scents had blossomed from the confined warmth and stirred something deep within. Wiggling and worming her way back up, she faced him nose to nose once more, and his hand rested on the small of her back.

"Rabbits," Djain squeaked. "You want to know of the rabbits? I can teach you about the rabbits."

Dropping the cover, he turned his head and took a deep breath. "Father is doing many things with them. And yes, he will use them to teach me reanimation, as well as to supply us with food and furs." He took another breath of the chilled air, trying to quench the heat in his chest. "Father first made me place the boys in one cage and the girls in another. While I did that, he told me that reanimation is a dark and difficult skill and that many things can go wrong. He also says the price is high, so high that most are not willing to suffer the cost."

Djain gained some measure of control over himself while relaying the events. Sean felt the fires within himself die down to embers, crackling and sparking each time Djain shifted at the hips to relieve tension. "Why keep them apart?" she asked.

Djain's brow pinched and lifted. "I asked Father the same thing, and he laughed! He made me lift the bar keeping the rabbits apart, and when I did, the boys were hopping all over the girls, like those wolves we saw last spring."

She gasped, her eyes widening.

"Father says, 'it not yet be time for nature to have its way with them.' Then Father made me pull them apart again. The boys were letting out an awful noise, and their cocks were all shiny and pink, sticking out past the fur. Father said, 'Nature. Remember, there be times for it.'" Djain shook his head and lifted his shoulder.

"And I still do not know what that was supposed to mean, but it had nothing to do with reanimation."

"Why'd he show you that? Why put the rabbits together if he wanted them apart again? That's silly." She huffed, annoyed, shifting in his arms to settle in against him again. "And why does he keep saying stuff like that about nature? I wish he would tell us instead of making us try to figure it out. Don't you think so?"

Djain whispered a soft "Yes," and his hand moved under the cover, sliding over her back. "Now, if you are trying to give life back to . . ." His voice trailed off, and he went rigid. He did not move. He did not breathe. Sean watched understanding click into place. Djain knew that what he had been struggling with since she entered his bed was 'Nature.'

Sean saw annoyance flare in her eyes, a reaction to his sudden stillness. The girl rocked herself back and slammed into him with a full-body nudge. "Hey," she hissed, her arms unwinding from his torso. Her hands landed on his chest, and she pushed away. Beneath her knitted brow, her gray eyes searched out the blue of his. "Why do you keep doing that?" Her harsh whisper sliced the cold air. "You know you do it because I asked Father once, and he knew you were doing it!"

She bolted into a sitting position. The heavy blanket fell away and cold air poured over their bodies. Swinging a long leg out and over, she pushed herself up and straddled Djain's hips. He moved with her lying on his back. She planted the heel of her palms into the firm ridges of his chest to pin him down. Hovering over him, she glared; the beads of her long hair grazed his skin, her pouty lips pressed into a thin line. Her tunic remained disheveled, the bottom of it rolled up to her lower ribs, the neck falling over one shoulder, exposing her skin.

"Father said this. Father said that. Father said you were doing this because we were growing up, and that's not fair." She leaned closer, nearly growling at him. "If you're going to act like this, then I don't want you to grow up. You are going to have to get over being mad at me too!" She pushed herself back, shoving against his chest, and her slight form loomed over him.

Sean felt the turmoil and emotion as Djain's eyes swept over his sister again. What little light illuminated the room accentuated every part of her. The curve of her hips seemed more pronounced when she sat atop him. The bare skin of her midriff tantalized him, and his fingers twitched at the thought of caressing her. Where the faint light caught her small breasts cast deep shadows, making them appear fuller. Her nipples pressed into the cloth, tugging at Djain's core, and Sean felt the depth of Djain's growing hunger for her. The curve of her bare shoulder swept up into her neck and made his lips tingle. Shadows kissed her face, strengthening her features and giving a glimpse of the stunning woman she was becoming. Djain cleared his throat and hissed back. "I am not mad at you!"

The girl rocked back, lowering herself to sit atop him, and ground herself across his erection. Djain's eyes grew into saucers. His hands gripped her sides, and she froze. She lifted herself and twisted, studying his lap, seeing the well-defined line of his firm form pressed against the binding fabric. Easing herself down again, she felt this strange, unknown part of him press against her, and her eyes sought his.

The embers of lust blazed to life inside Sean, an inferno of emotion boiling at his core, mirroring the tortured confusion within Djain. He could see further questions forming in her mind, and he knew Djain had no answers.

Another moan sounded deep in Djain's chest, and a creeping flush crawled across her cheeks, her skin darkening as heat rose to her face. Her hands lifted from his chest and hung in the air between them, and she struggled with her response. Her mouth dry, she tried to wet her lips, drawing the tip of her tongue across them before coaxing out her confused words. "You aren't mad?"

Her lips parted, and her breath came quick, catching, holding back the storm of questions spinning in her eyes. She gazed down at Djain, moving her hands to cover his, holding them to her. A wicked light flashed through her eyes. "Am I—?" She paused, lowering her chin so she could better study his reaction in the darkness. Her eyes narrowed, and she rocked her hips forward and back, feeling his hardness beneath her. "Making you like this?"

Her movements drew another moan from the depths of Djain's chest, and he responded with a nod, not trusting his voice to work through his sporadic breaths. Her eyes widened, his hands sliding up her side, his broad grasp covering her skin below her ribs. Biting on her bottom lip, her hands moved down his forearms, tentative, exploring. She caressed over the developing strength of his upper arms, and each saw the other in unfamiliar ways.

To reach his shoulders, she pulled her hips forward, grinding over him, leaning in. "How long have I done this to you?"

He drew in a breath, staring at her with something new in his eyes. "Since midsummer's moon," he croaked.

Her long braids cascaded to one side as she lowered herself and touched her lips to his forehead. "Does it hurt? You make these sounds when hurt, but they are different."

His head moved from side to side. Between ragged breaths, he responded, "No. It does not . . . hurt." The muscles along Djain's torso were taut with his struggle to remain still beneath her, while desires he did not understand raged inside. She shifted, sliding down his body. It was a slight movement, but it caused him to tremble.

Now locked eye to eye with him, she lowered her forehead to his. The tips of their noses bumped, and her inquisitive side flared to life once more. The question fell from her in a breathy burst. "Is this okay?"

Djain drew in a breath while she spoke and licked his lips. "Yes . . ."

Her left hand slipped from his shoulder, fingers moving along his collarbone. "Does Father know?"

Again, he responded in the affirmative with an almost inaudible, "Yes . . ."

Her fingers found the middle of his chest and traced the subtle crease forming between his developing musculature. "Will he get mad?"

A hint of fear, of uncertainty, flashed over Djain's features, and he gave a half-hearted shrug with the free shoulder. "I—am unsure."

Continuing to explore him, she lifted her head from his, her eyes moving down his chest. She rocked back atop him, pulling another deep sound from his core. Her fingers danced over his skin, over his abdomen. Her eyes flashed back to his, a new question burning in them. He drew in a sharp breath when she pulled herself down, so her weight rested atop his thighs.

His hands fell to the mattress, fingers taking hold of the cloth. The girl's fingers dipped past his belly button, and she toyed with the drawstrings holding his pants closed. Looking at his body, she asked her next question. "Can I see?"

Light flooded the room as the heavy drape drew back. In the doorway stood the silhouette of a man. The snoring had ceased, and neither of them had noticed.

Djain and the girl froze, squinting against the bright intrusion.

Father's head made a slow arc, examining the room, the situation. From the depth of shadows, he spoke first at Djain with a stern reminder. "Don't be forgettin' the rabbits." There it was again, that Caribbean flavor, but much heavier and thicker in this man's voice.

Father's foot reached out and kicked the mattress the girl had vacated, speaking again with a softer tone. "You spend more time in that bed than this one.

Tomorrow you be telling me why it is you need it or we be rid of it."

Reaching up, Father pulled the drape back over the door, plunging them into darkness again. His footfalls crossed the main room. The crackle of embers sounded with the addition of another log onto the fire. His door creaked, and his voice floated in through the curtain. "Be mindin the hour." His door closed and latched, and a quiet stillness settled in the room.

Djain looked up at his sister, seeing the deep blush that had colored her entire face, and felt a similar heat in his cheeks.

She met his gaze, giggled, blinked, and with a squeak, darted in sleek movement across the bear rug and burrowed deep under the covers of her bed.

Sean watched the scene unfold, breathless. So bound up in the emotional tide of Djain's experience, his heart raced, hammering away inside his chest.

Djain released the dread of his father's appearance, only to come face to face with the fear of everything new that swelled within. Laying in the darkness, Djain watched the outline of the blanket settle about her. He extended a hand, an invitation, letting it hang in the space between them, and Sean recognized the longing he could see in Djain's eyes.

A quiet giggle sounded from beneath the blankets, and one edge lifted. She peeked out, searching for him, her eyes coming to rest on his hand as she nibbled at her lower lip.

He shifted in the bed, turning to his side, and making room for her as he always had. He whispered to her. "Oai'Quari . . ."

Her hand snuck from beneath the furs, stretching across the space until her fingers curled into his. She slipped back out into the cold. Djain's eyes were watching her in a new way, and she was reveling in it. Crossing the small space in silence, she sank into the bed beside him once more.

Her arms coiled around his chest, and he draped his arm over her back. She kissed his forehead, and he kissed hers. In the dark, her eyes fluttered. Finding his gaze riveted on hers, her smile blossomed, and she whispered the familiar words. But now they seemed to mean so much more. "Big Brother."

Councilor Traxidor has stated my feelings about this well. If we wish to toy with the concepts of life, then let us do so with measured steps. In the Heavens, we have seen myriad forms of life and heard prophecies that tell of a future where the Mother one day supports an abundance of species—if we tend her with care. Let us focus on helping the tiniest, most vulnerable forms of life flourish before conducting trials in selective breeding.

—Councilor Daejor

TWELVE

The world snapped back into focus, and Sean closed his eyes, trying to recenter after the dizzying change of location. Pushing back from the desk, he lifted his head to find Djain standing across from him, watching with interest.

"Welcome back. What was it you saw?" Djain asked.

Sean swallowed, warmth flooding his cheeks. "I, um . . ." He cleared his throat and shuffled the papers atop the desk. "I saw the night you told your sister about the rabbits."

A warm light sparked in Djain's eyes, and he laughed. "I have not thought of that night for some time." He turned and sat on the edge of the desk, losing himself in the memory. "What a confusing night that was." He laughed again, the quiet sort of laugh that is filled with nostalgia. "There were so many things we still had to learn."

Sean squirmed, shifting in the chair while the heat remained in his cheeks. "Yes, but it was clear what she meant to you, what you meant to each other, even then."

Watching Sean's discomfort, Dain arched a brow. "Something else about the vision troubles you?"

Sean laughed, looking out the window. "The longer the vision played, the more I could feel your emotions and turmoil, everything you were experiencing. It was . . ."

Djain saw Sean searching for the words and finished the thought for him. "Intimate. Confusing. Frightening."

Sean turned back to face Djain. "On some levels, all of those, yes. Will it always be like that?"

Djain reached across the desk and tapped the journal. "There are no stories about that part of my life in here. How did you find your way there?"

Sean arched a brow, wondering why his question was ignored. "I was hoping you could tell me. I thought I had to have that scrying bowl to do that?"

"No. There are more ways to see what was, what is, and what might be than one might expect." Djain reached down and touched the pyramid. "This is a potent focus. A wonderful implement to aid a traveler. Where did you get it?"

Sean shrugged. "It was on the desk when I arrived this morning."

Djain rubbed his chin, eyes roving over the desk. "Tell me everything you did before the vision and what you were thinking."

Sean took him through the morning, taking the time to admonish Djain about the care of his journal.

"You should take better care of documents of such an age." He explained his thought process, describing how the disconnect between Djain's age and the document had led to questions about Djain's childhood. How he had spread his hands over the desk, focused on the crystal, and found himself flying over a snowy forest.

"There is the answer," Djain said, pointing at the pyramid. "This pyramid is made of crystals with special properties. The clear quartz amplifies the others, and black tourmaline can protect you from lower beings that will attempt to leach on and drain your energy. The blue iolite helps you better remember what you see. Each color in this pyramid has a purpose, and while you may not yet understand the mechanics of travel, this unlocked the path for you anyway. As you do not know how to protect yourself while traveling, it also allowed the emotional bonds to become abnormally strong."

Picking up the pyramid, Sean turned it over in his hand, studying it. "Then, I should be able to use this to travel to specific events that we need to see to find what we seek."

Djain laughed, bringing together his large hands in a single clap of excitement at Sean's sudden shift of focus. "Exactly! Though I hope you will do it with someone to watch over you until you are more knowledgeable. It would be advisable to practice constructing a few circles."

Sean's face contorted at the mention of the circle. "I'll have Axylia sit with me. I think I'm done with circles for a while."

"If you make a few yourself, you will be much happier inside one when working certain magics." Djain studied him, eyes lingering on the discolored skin where the magical symbols had been drawn. "These will fade soon enough. Did you see any sign of Vitan while you were traveling this morning?"

Thinking, Sean shook his head. "Actually, no, but I noticed something else."

Djain's eyes narrowed, a note of caution in his voice when he asked, "What did you notice?"

"Your Caribbean heritage colors your speech, and I noticed the same with your family."

Djain's eyes widened. Leaning forward, he asked, "Are you telling me I have an accent?"

The reaction caught Sean off-guard, "I—um—"

"Well, your Scottish roots are not well hidden either." Djain watched the shock spread over Sean's face, then filled the room with rich laughter.

Sean breathed, releasing the tension that had coiled in his gut, and shared the laugh with Djain.

"What about the vision made you curious about my speech?" Djain asked.

"Well," Sean paused, selecting his words. "In the vision, everyone spoke what I believe to be Norse, but even then, the Caribbean influence was clear."

Djain inclined his head. "We were speaking what is now called Old Norse. You wish to know how Father, a man from the Caribbean, wound up raising children in frozen forests far away from his tropical home."

"Aye," Sean said with intentional brightness.

Djain's eyes lit up at Sean's humor. "Father struck a deal with a Bright One and was translocated into Norway as part of that arrangement. Oai'Quari and I arrived afterward. As a group, we were feared and shunned; still, Father taught us Norse to aid our interactions with the villagers. All other training and instruction were given in Father's native tongue." He paused, thinking of the evening Sean had seen again, and his eyes glistened with a nostalgic light. "In the darkness, we often spoke in the regional tongue. I can not say why. Perhaps we longed for acceptance, and our nightly discussions gave us a false sense of accomplishment."

A hush fell over the two of them until Djain cleared his throat. "Have I sufficiently answered the riddle and removed the oddity of the mingled cultures?"

Sean smiled. "Yes. Thank you for sharing."

"It was a pleasure. I should reminisce on those days more often; there is much worth remembering." Djain knocked on the desk. "Best of all, you can now move about in the physical and the Astral without Vitan tracking you."

Sean straightened his back and lifted his chin. "Guess that means it's time for me to go shopping and check on my home."

Laughing, Djain inclined his head. "I suppose that would be the best use of your day. You should be allowed time to settle before digging further into this world." Djain rose from the table and headed for the door. "I will send Talaunia down to take you."

Sean hurried around the side of the desk. "Um, Papa? I had made plans to do those things with Axylia last night, and I've already had to cancel once."

Djain glanced back at him from the open doorway, a crooked smile on his face. "Alright. I will send Axylia." He paused, eyes dropping toward the floor, and he chuckled. When his eyes found Sean again, they were alight with a knowing brightness. "We cannot fight Nature now, can we." Giving a quick wink, he let the door close and strolled away, his warm laughter filling the space.

Sean's face flushed, and he was glad that Djain had turned away. He returned to his desk, a guilty grin spreading across his lips as he sank into the chair. He took a deep breath and struggled to separate the thoughts Djain's words brought to life in his mind and the memories of his morning adventure. Closing Djain's journal with care, he moved it to the side and picked up the top set of printed reports.

The cover held information and an image of the original work, the *Heimskringla*, commonly called the *Old Norse Kings' Sagas*, a collection of stories written by Snorri Sturluson in the 13th century. These pages were an excerpt from the saga of Halfdan the Black.

Through the document's texts, the parts of Halfdan the Black's marriage to Ragnhild, his second wife, appeared to contain the essential factors. The pair had a son, Harald Fairhair, who was loved by his mother but not by his father. Ragnhild was said to dream of things to be, and the document contained passages detailing one of her prophetic visions of a thorn growing deep and tall and branching to cover all of Norway.

The summary suggested Ragnhild worked with the Order of the Sacred Flame and that the Order strove to bring her visions to fruition. The partnership led to the Order supporting Harald and assisting his efforts to unite Norway for the first time and become King. In return, she fed the Order information via her special gift to help them gain power in other parts of Scandinavia.

Placing the pages on the *Heimskringla* aside, Sean picked up the next stack of paper. A much heavier report with an unmistakable cover, the *Malleus Maleficarum.* The manuscript which drove the great witch hunts in Europe. It was written by Henricus Institor, the Latinized name of Heinrich Kramer, a Catholic clergy member.

A special foreword had been added before the text, detailing how Kramer had been influential in the Order of the Sacred Flame. The organization had infiltrated the Catholic church, using its resources to further their power and to obtain relics of great magical importance. The *Malleus Maleficarum* was one such tool. Kramer often quieted away any precious artifacts held by the persecuted witches. It also proposed that Dominican Friar Jacob Sprenger, another name tied to the reviled document, was among the first to fight against Kramer and the Order. Later, the Order had Sprenger's name associated with the notorious work to undermine his efforts against them.

A soft knock on the office door drew Sean's attention. Placing the document back on the desk, he lifted his head, and the brooding lines covering his face melted away. Axylia stood on the other side of the glass door. She was wearing a flowing scarlet dress that ended at her knees and carrying a matching clutch, the sum of which complemented her pearlescent skin and raven hair in a tantalizing way.

He rose and moved around the desk.

She stepped inside, greeting him with a warm but reserved smile. Her eyes swept over him, lingering on the slight discolorations still marking his skin. Concern descended, drawing her brows together. "How are you?"

He continued to close the distance. "It was rough there for a while, but I'm alright now." His eyes moved over the length of her before locking on her gaze. "You are stunning." Holding his arms out to his sides, he glanced down at himself. "Somehow, I think I am underdressed. Are you sure you wish to be seen with me in public?"

She reached out and tugged on his oversized shirt. "I am getting accustomed to seeing you in this strange ensemble."

They both laughed. Sean twisted, searching the room, only to realize he had no other chairs in the office. He shuffled several plants from atop the short bookshelves. "I hated having to cancel on you last night."

Her eyes followed him, and she brushed a finger through her hair, tucking it behind her pointed ear. "I admit, I was disappointed . . ."

His head tilted, hearing something amiss in her tone. Reaching for her hand, he tried to draw her towards him and the makeshift seating. "How are you? Is everything alright?"

Axylia pulled away, giving her attention to the desk. "I see you are getting things organized."

Sean sighed and followed. "Aye. It was kind of Papa to provide these things."

Axylia eased into his chair, rubbing her hand over the desk's surface.

His eyes lingered on her until he forced himself to look away. He moved to the window, stared out over the park, and watched a flock of birds take to the air above the gardens.

Axylia flipped through the stack of papers. "Papa takes care of us. If you ever have a genuine need, he will see it remedied."

When Sean looked back over his shoulder, he found Axylia holding the note from Talaunia. Her expression was masked, but he thought he could see hurt lurking beneath the surface.

He moved back around the desk to face her. "It isn't how that note makes it sound."

"Sean, I have known her for an exceptionally long time. There has been bad blood between our families for millennia. I know how manipulative she can be . . ." She trailed off, her focus somewhere beyond Sean, toward the door. "And speaking of evil."

A puzzled expression settled on Sean's face, and he followed her gaze.

Talaunia stepped into the office dressed in a light blue sundress and wearing fiery red lipstick. She gave Sean an alluring smile. "Hello, Sweetie."

Axylia dropped the note on the desk and leaned back in the chair, arching a brow.

Talaunia's gaze flickered to Axylia before snapping back to Sean with a playful hunger. "Darling, it's time you send your little pet away. We can't allow any distractions while training."

Sean shook his head. "Axylia and I are going out for the day. We'll have to train tomorrow."

"It will not please Papa that you are ignoring your training." Talaunia stepped closer to Sean, taking hold of his shirt. "You should make better choices."

Smiling, Axylia spoke from the chair. "Papa is the one who sent me down. Sean and I are leaving for the day with his blessing." She flashed a black American Express card. "And his financial backing."

Glaring at Axylia, Talaunia tightened her hold on Sean's shirt. "Well. Then I will not delay your outing further." Her gaze shifted to Sean, a flicker of heat in her eyes. "You will be mine again tomorrow. Until then . . ." She lifted her chin and leaned in, pulling him to her and placing a quick kiss on the corner of his lips. "Think of me."

Surprised, Sean pulled back, wrenching his shirt free of her grasp. "What the bloody hell?" Acting on instinct alone, he wiped at his face.

Talaunia's smile became more wicked, and she looked at Axylia. "Have a good day."

Axylia's eyes were slits, her lips pursed into thin, tight lines as she watched Talaunia leave.

"I'm sorry," Sean said. "I did not see that coming."

"That was her intent." Axylia's eyes lingered on the corner of Sean's lips, and she sighed, pulling a tissue from the small purse she carried. Rising, she crossed to him. "She can be so vicious, mix truth and rumor with such efficiency. If she ever speaks about me, if you ever have questions, please ask me."

Sean tried to assuage her concerns, but she tugged on the front of his shirt, straightening it back out.

"Hold still. She left smudges of her smutty lips on you." Holding the tissue up, she paused. "Let me clean it?"

He lowered his chin, turning his face, so the offending smear was more comfortable for her to reach.

Lifting a tissue-wrapped finger, she rubbed away the offending lipstick. "Her words are a subtle toxin, seeping in unnoticed, until one day, you discover the undercurrents of her hate have dismantled all you held dear." When she was satisfied, the stain had been removed; she placed her hand on the middle of his chest, her eyes brightening. "Much better."

Taking a step back, Sean took her hand in his and lifted it, placing a tender kiss along the back of her knuckles. "Thank you. I'll not allow her to cause mischief. I still wish you were part of my team. It would have been nice to work together."

Her eyes sparkled, and her fingers tightened around his. "Papa wouldn't even entertain the idea. There was an avalanche of requests to join your team after the scrying bowl incident. People were playing politics, trying to gain your ear and influence. Papa drafted a memo to everyone involved with Special Projects, making it clear he had already assigned personnel to your team and forbidding anyone from approaching you about the subject." She sighed. "He has high expectations of what you will accomplish, so you are working with the head of each department." She dropped his hand to slip her arm through his. "At least I still get to help you in other ways. Why don't we start at your home, then we can move on to shopping."

Axylia led Sean down to the training rooms and over to an empty portal arch. "No one said I couldn't help you learn along the way." Taking a few moments, she showed him the basics of how to build a portal, gave a few dire warnings about never opening portals to places you have never been, and helped him open a passage into his living room.

< ᚪᚢᚾ ᚲᚱᛗᚪᛏᛗ ᚪᚢᚾᚱ ᚱᛗᚪᚾᛏᚪ >

Arriving at Sean's home, they surveyed the damage, and it was far worse than Sean had hoped. Every piece of glass in the place was shattered. Barefoot, Sean couldn't move from the entry portal until Axylia sifted through the mess and located a mismatched pair of shoes, and even they had holes torn into their sides. Once through the portal, Sean started the painful process of taking inventory of things now lost. The gouged and pockmarked surface of the walls was peppered with embedded bits of shrapnel, the shattered remains of his memories and keepsakes. What had once been his meager entertainment center was now a mishmash of tiny plastic bits and cracked circuit boards. The padding of his worn couch had been turned into confetti and mixed in with all the other debris. The only piece of furniture still intact was the recliner, still soggy from the rain. Positioned in the middle of the seat was a melting pile of what Sean hoped was dog shit.

Reaching the kitchen, Sean stopped in amazement. Every pot, pan, baking dish, cookie sheet, the racks from the oven, anything made of metal had been fused and formed into a metallic hand, middle finger extended to welcome him home.

Pictures, once hanging on his walls, had been ripped from their frames. They sat stacked in a neat pile atop the debris of his dining table, covered in rips, tears, bends, and creases. Flipping through the stack, Sean was awash with fury and loss. A sadness filled his eyes as he studied every defiled face, telling Axylia of who they were and what the picture had meant. Buck teeth, bunny ears, horns, and glasses appeared as frequent modifications, applied in black. When Sean was in the picture, a cock-shaped hat had been placed atop his head. "At least I have digital backups of some of them . . ." The photos trembled in his hand, the anger and hurt of the loss building upon itself. Holding his fist to his lips, he drew in a deep breath through his nose and dropped the ruined photos back into the clutter as he exhaled.

His cricket bat lay shattered amid the pieces of his weekend league trophy. "I was looking for an excuse to buy some new equipment," he said, trying to put on a convincing front. His words were flat and filled with an emptiness that was growing the longer he stayed amid the rubble of his life.

Peeking from under a pile of glass shards, a picture of him and his mother caught his eye, and he picked it up, dusting it off with care. "At least I still have this."

Axylia stayed by his side as they moved through the rest of the house, finding the destruction no less thorough in any other room.

In the end, the only item recovered was the lone picture.

Sean thanked Axylia for being there with him, and he was grateful for her presence. He wasn't sure how to process the loss, and seeing the destruction left him feeling violated. She held his hand as the depth of the damage settled into the pit of his stomach, reassuring, encouraging, and letting him take the time he needed to process the devastation and decide it was time to move on.

Using the portal, they returned to the training rooms and sealed the path to his old house. Axylia considered the situation, eyes brimming with concern and compassion. "Do you need some time? We can take a break if you wish."

Sean shook his head. "No. I don't think that would be such a good idea. Best to distract me for now, start rebuilding my life, so later, I have those things to reassure me as I process all of this."

"Then, on we go." Axylia gave his hand a gentle squeeze. "The Quari Group maintains flats in several major cities around the world. Today, we will visit the one in Covent Garden and use its proximity to the shops to help address your dire wardrobe needs." She gave a soft smile and tugged on his shirttail.

Directing him to a screen beside the empty portal, she pulled up a list showing each of the properties and selected the one for Covent Garden. The screen filled with information, the address, a landline number for the flat, names, and photos of the building manager and the doormen, and below it all was a series of symbols.

"The portal key for this location," she said. "Why don't you open it for us while I prepare." She slipped a ring onto her finger, and the glamor swept over her, changing her ears, their pointed tips vanishing into smooth, round curves.

His first attempt failed, his mind still on the tattered memories they had left behind, making his symbol work less than accurate.

She encouraged him to slow down, focus, and try again.

On the second attempt, the image of an unoccupied living space flickered before them and fell away in a shower of sparks.

After showing him the correction needed, he tried once more and found success. Arm in arm, they stepped into the London flat.

They spent the afternoon resupplying Sean's life. Axylia ordered a limousine, and in it, they moved through the city, visiting an endless array of shops. They sought clothing for fieldwork, casual dress, and a few suits for when the need arose. Axylia introduced him to several metaphysical stores and guided him through the basics, ensuring he had a well-rounded set of tools for use at home.

Mid-afternoon, they stopped for lunch. Sean insisted it was the best Italian food ever. Axylia assured him his hunger was swaying his opinion. After the meal, the shopping continued. He gathered personal care items along with a few other miscellaneous things Axylia insisted he must have, for no other reason than he liked them, and he needed to rebuild.

Axylia paid with the Quari Group's card at every stop, despite Sean's arguments that he was responsible for himself. It turns out a clerk will always reach for the black card when they see it, even if a red-headed Scott is trying to block the handoff.

The sun sank below the horizon, and Axylia directed the driver out of the city. Sean was taken aback as they eventually pulled onto a sprawling country estate. A stately home rose before them, imposing and regal. A touch of awe colored his voice. "This is where I'm staying?"

Axylia squeezed his hand, her smile filled with delight at his wonder. "Yes, and no." The car eased to a stop, and the driver exited. "There is a cottage on the property. It sets away from the main house, tucked into the woods along the banks of the Thames. They call it the Stony Brook Cottage."

Sean blinked, pulling his eyes from hers, in awe of the grandeur of the place. "I would have been happy in a Holiday Inn."

"Perhaps, but Papa takes care of his family, especially those who lose their homes in the line of duty."

The driver returned, and they made their way along the forested road. Sean's eyes fell to their entwined fingers. "Thank you," he whispered. "So much has happened the past few days. I cannot express what your friendship, your company, your presence has meant to me."

She squeezed his fingers, and in the dim light, he saw the corners of her lips lift as the car came to a stop. The driver exited and opened the door for them, Sean slipping out first, holding her hand as she followed.

The cottage was plucked from a fairytale. Steeply gabled roofs, intricate trim work with multiple chimneys lifting against the dark sky. A warm glow came from within, and the doorway stood open, welcoming them. Sean tried to grab the enormous pile of shopping bags, but Axylia pulled him toward the house, asking the driver to deposit them on the dining table.

A welcome basket sat on the table, along with the keys, a Quari Group branded box with a courier label attached, and a handwritten note welcoming Sean. The message informed him that the kitchen was stocked and ready for his use. It gave the number to ring should he find anything lacking and wished him a pleasant stay.

Axylia directed the driver to the main room with all of Sean's packages and tipped him. "Please give me a moment longer," she said to the man.

The driver gave a shallow bow before taking his leave.

Sean's brow pinched, and he gave her a slight pout. "Must you go?"

Her eyes lingered on his lips, and she took a deep breath, the traces of a smile brightening her gaze. "And what would we do were I to stay?" There was a question in her eyes, imparting more meaning than what her words alone conveyed.

Sean's smile lifted to one side. "Many things spring to mind. If you are looking for a professional reason, I could use some private tutoring in things I've already seen. If a personal reason will do, the same applies, though I may be far more interested in the tutor than the topic."

She pulled her lower lip between her teeth and nibbled at it, her eyes dancing over his features as she mulled his words. "Very well, perhaps a bit of tutoring on portals." Her grin became playful. "And to make sure you pay at least some attention to your lessons, there will be a test. Tomorrow, you will be expected to create a portal to work."

He laughed in response. "A challenge! I accept your terms."

She reached up, her fingers drifting across the soft cloth covering his chest. She patted twice and stepped away. "One moment, I must release the driver."

He watched her go before turning his attention to the items on the table. Opening the box, he found his new laptop and phone, with a note from the IT department outlining login procedures. He sifted through the bags and found the items purchased at the occult store, arranging them for study. He was examining a violet-colored crystal when she returned.

"Iolite," she said. "It's a sound choice to help you when you travel."

Placing the deep blue stone back onto the table, he rose and gave her his full attention. "There are stones that look like that in a pyramid I found on my desk this morning."

"They are the same type of crystal." She crossed to him, standing a little closer than necessary. "I had hoped you would like it."

He chuckled. "So you are the mysterious leaver of things on desks."

"Guilty," she beamed up at him. "I hope it will help when you are ready to project."

"Well, thank you for such a thoughtful gift, though I thought it was nothing more than a pretty paperweight when I first saw it."

She laughed, her shoulders lifting in subtle movements. "I hope you get much better use from it."

Sean's lips thinned into a knowing smile, and he gazed into her green eyes.

She fidgeted before her brows lifted in question. "What?"

"I already have. I used it to project this morning."

Her eyes opened in astonishment. "How? Where? What did you see?"

Taking her hand, he led her to the kitchen. "Let's find something to drink and relax. That is the best way to share a story, yes?"

She gave him a sly smile. "I think you are just looking for an excuse to keep me around longer."

"Perhaps."

They both laughed, splitting ways, Sean going to the stainless-steel refrigerator and Axylia moving around the center island. "We got bottled water and some juices in here," he said, rooting around in the frigid space. He pulled out a small tray of fresh-cut fruit. "And snacks!"

She laughed outright and ducked behind the island. When she stood, she hoisted a bottle of red wine in one hand. "There is a wine cooler over here; I may kick you out and stay here myself."

His brows lifted, and he reached up to pluck two wine glasses from where they hung upside down below the upper cabinets. "Kicked to the curb in favor of wine. I'll not forget that!"

She laughed again, and they both set to rummaging through drawers to find the corkscrew. Sean came across it first and cheered in victory, holding his other hand out toward her for the bottle. "Allow me."

He made quick work of the cork and poured them each a glass. Taking the bottle and the fruit tray with them, they entered the living area.

"Being in here makes me nervous. I'm afraid I might mess something up. It's all so elegant." Sean shrugged and laughed. "And I'm not."

He urged them toward the back deck, where they found a view overlooking the river. Sean placed the bottle and fruit on a small cedar table, and together they sat in a cozy, handcrafted wooden swing. It moved in a smooth arc, and they were soon gliding along its fixed path. After taking a sip from her wineglass, Axylia turned her gaze on him, a delighted light in her eyes, and she poked at his side. "I believe you owe me a story now."

Taking her hand, Sean related the events of his morning, touching on all the things culminating in his vision of the past.

He lowered his head, looking playful and apologetic. "I'm afraid I don't feel comfortable sharing the specifics of what I saw. It was a private moment from Papa's childhood. I can say that he either grew up in an impoverished area or centuries ago, which brings his age into question."

Axylia was staring at him, a touch of worry lining her face. "You must spend all the time you can training." She squeezed his hand. "It seems to be clear you are drawn into the mystical much easier than most, likely because of your bloodline." She shifted in the seat, facing him more fully. "There are so many dark things out there that you are not prepared for, Sean."

"I know I must train with Talaunia. However, I promised Papa I would ask you to watch over me when I try to project again." He adjusted the way he held her hand, his thumb caressing over the back of her knuckles in a small circle. "Would you be willing to help me practice? Perhaps of an evening?"

Her head lifted and fell almost imperceptibly. "I will."

Hours passed in easy conversation, filled with laughter, as they shared tales of their childhood antics. Axylia's presence had been a soothing balm to the wounds Sean had suffered that morning, and Sean felt a growing affection for her. She had drawn him into talking of all the things he thought lost and showed him the true value wasn't in the items from the past but within his memories.

She looked at the stars and sighed. "You have distracted me, and the hour grows late. Come, let me show you how to create the portal you will need in the morning."

Rising, she tugged on his hand. He feigned resistance before allowing her to pull him from the swing. They gathered the empty bottle and glasses, as well as the untouched fruit tray, and returned to the kitchen. Sean cleaned their dirty dishes and hung them as Axylia dealt with the other items. They both returned to the dining area, where Axylia drew a series of symbols on a pad. "This will open a portal to the training room from anywhere you are."

Sean studied it, creating the shapes in his mind. "Ok, I believe I have it."

She pulled him over to the closed bedroom doorway. "Our evening is coming to an end." She tapped on the door. "Make me a portal here, so we may part at the threshold, as I believe is customary."

Sean's lips curled upward. "Of course." He thought about the symbols and the procedures she had shown him earlier in the day. He traced the patterns around the frame, and the bedroom door shimmered, fading into a view of the training room they had left so many hours before.

Her gaze was inviting, her inner light shining as they locked eyes. "Excellent. Now do not forget it before morning."

He laughed, reaching for her hand again. "Today wouldn't have been nearly as bearable without your company. Thank you for everything."

She squeezed his hand, lingering to stretch the moment. "Thank you, Sean. It has been a long time since I have had such an enjoyable night."

His eyes moved over each curve of her face.

A blush rose on her cheeks at the intensity of his gaze.

"I'm not sure I'm ready for you to depart," he confessed, his voice a nervous whisper.

She responded with a slow nod, lifting a leg and stepping backward, passing through the portal. "Good night, Sean."

Swallowing, he dropped her hand and took a step forward. His arm slipped around her waist, and his hand splayed across her lower back. He pulled her to him, pressing their bodies together. His lips descended to meet hers in a lingering, heady kiss.

When their lips parted, their eyes fluttered open, and each drew in a breath. Smiles blossomed, and Sean leaned forward, carrying her through the portal, his body leaning into the training room before easing her feet to the floor. "Good night, Axylia."

He crossed back through the portal, his gaze lingering on the blurry vision of her. He saw her blow him a kiss before she collapsed the doorway, leaving him to stare at the eggshell texture of a door that led to an empty bedroom.

Fire and water are now tangible aspects of the Mother, and through our bond with Her, we can feel and manipulate their forces. The Mother's skin whispers. An unfamiliar voice, fresh energy, building between the roiling waters above and the rivers of her fiery blood rushing through her core. A change in all that we are tints the orange-hued skies. It's coming as inevitable as the cycles of the cosmos.

—Councilor Arianelis

THIRTEEN

What? No, CliffsNotes?

The portal inside the training room snapped open, and Sean stepped through the quivering image. He stopped short when he noticed Axylia, Djain, and Jason watching him with amused expressions. Sharing a brief, warm moment, Sean and Axylia said their hellos before he greeted the others. "Seems I'm running a bit late. I had some trouble getting the configuration right."

The rich laughter of Djain's deep voice filled the room. "We have been watching your attempts, seeing portal after portal collapse. We were discussing the need to dispatch a car for you."

Axylia held up the slip of paper with the symbols she had drawn and gave him a playful grin. "I don't allow any open book tests."

Sean laughed. "You wouldn't believe the state of the sitting room. I tossed every cushion in the place, trying to figure out what happened to that!"

"Dude, we believe you," Jason chortled, pointing past him to the wavering view of the Stony Brook Cottage.

The pile of pillows and cushions on one end of the couch was spilling over the side, a few threatening to vanish down the hall.

Sean turned and saw the mess he had left behind, distorted but discernable in the archway. He lifted a hand, waving it before the portal, and laughed. "Someone needs to show me how to close these things."

Axylia stepped up behind him, running her hand from his shoulder down his arm. "Like this," she said. She wrapped her fingers around his hand and taught him how to collapse portals.

As the portal shimmered and misted away, he turned his head, grinning at her over his shoulder. "Thank you."

Djain coughed.

Jason laughed.

Axylia and Sean blushed, and she stepped away from him.

"This morning, you will work in the library with Jason," Djain said. "He will help you acclimate and show you the results of his search in the archives. We have watched for any volumes that may relate to the Order or other groups of interest for some time."

"We got this man," Jason droned.

"Be certain to break for lunch before one. Talaunia is planning to begin your training at that time."

"Aye, Papa," he said. He nudged Axylia with his elbow. "Have lunch with me?"

Her lower lip protruded. "I can't. I won't be here."

Djain tapped Jason on the shoulder and motioned for him to follow. "Jason will wait for you at the lift." The two men walked away, leaving Axylia and Sean alone.

"Dinner? We can try to cook without making the kitchen as messy as I've made the rest of the house."

"I'm sorry," Axylia said. Her brow furrowed and a sad smile settled on her lips. She stepped closer, taking his hands. "Papa assigned me to a recovery effort in India this morning. The healer on their team was injured when a curse was triggered. They still have not recovered the artifact, so I must go assist. Papa allowed me to delay long enough to see you before I portal out."

With a soft sigh, his shoulders fell. "I'm glad he let you wait for me, but I don't want to delay you if someone's in need. When you return, dinner, and this time, the story will be yours." He cupped her cheek, his gaze sinking into the facets of her eyes.

"It's a date." She turned her head and kissed the palm of his hand. "You have two days to figure out what we are cooking." Stepping to the nearest inactive arch, she created the portal that would carry her away.

"Be safe out there," he said.

She winked. "If you try not to get into any more trouble while I'm away."

He lifted a hand. "I swear."

She was already through the portal and only saw the motion. She returned what she thought was a wave and blinked out of view.

He headed toward Jason and the waiting lift, but he was already dreaming of her return.

< ᛋᛟᚱ ᚦᛁᛚᛚ ᚠᛁᚻᛞ ᚭᛟᚾ >

The morning evaporated under a landslide of new tech and instructions, leaving Sean a little dazed. Jason had installed apps on his phone and computer, allowing digital access to the library's index and the text of every volume it held. Many of the documents were translated in multiple languages, and the software allowed Sean to study them side by side. After identifying dozens of potential tomes requiring examination, the men settled into a steady rhythm. They worked well together and lost track of time.

"How am I to begin your training if you never bother to turn up?" Talaunia teased, stepping out of the stacks. She leaned against Sean's side and peered over his shoulder. "I shall have to arrive at an appropriate punishment to ensure your future compliance."

"Oh, man, no wonder my stomach's been snarling like a possessed howler monkey," Jason said, checking his watch.

Sean shook his head, laughing. "Jason, can you have these volumes pulled and set aside for me? I know you gave me the app, but"—he waved his phone—"I have a thing about the texture and smell of books. I'll start researching them tonight."

"Sure, dude." Glancing at Talaunia, he leaned toward Sean with a smirk. "Best of luck. She looks especially spirited today."

Talaunia laughed. "Oh, he knows me too well!" Reaching out, she grabbed Sean by the arm and tugged. "You are now mine. Come along."

Shoving his laptop into a satchel, he hurried toward the lift. "I'm coming."

Somewhere behind him, Jason quipped. "Not till she says to you aren't."

He glanced back, but was pulled around a corner.

"I see you found a clothier."

Sean's eyes dropped, and he glanced at the new clothing. "Several. I can't tell you how nice it is to be in something I own."

She nudged him with her elbow. "I've seen you in your best suit. Everything else pales."

Her arm slipped into his, and she escorted him into the training area. The room had a new configuration since he passed through earlier this morning. The large center mat where Ryan and Gadyen had sparred was arranged with tables to either end. Various obstacles were erected throughout the center of the room. Beams and pipes were going in multiple directions, along with a set of cubicle walls that created a maze in the middle. Several potted trees dotted one corner, and opposite them, what had to be a magical storm rumbled, dumping torrents of rain that never made it to the floor.

"As you have proven yourself to be the sort that attracts trouble, Papa and I have decided that you need to learn defensive skills first." They stopped at the edge of the mat, and she turned to face him. "So today, you must stop me from landing my attacks." Lifting her hand, she drew a finger across the scruffy growth along his jaw. "Not to worry. If you fail, you know I can make it—" her cadence slowed, her words becoming breathy and seductive "—all better."

"Why do I get the feeling I'm going to wind up in yoga pants again before this day is out?"

Her smile became wicked, and her eyes flashed. "Perhaps you have a gift for the prophetic, too." She guided him around the maze looming on the mat. "Let's find out," she said, a sense of danger in her teasing tone.

They stopped by the long edge of a table, and across its surface lay various items, rings, necklaces, watches, and tiny vials that reminded him of mini test tubes. A pile of matches and lighters sat between a collection of candles and several stacks of loose papers covered with symbols that were becoming familiar.

"Here, we have a collection of charms, amulets, wards, and spells. You will learn about their particular uses and vulnerabilities."

Sean surveyed the table while she spoke, lifting a hammered bronze ring with a wooden inset.

She took the jewelry from his hand, placed it back on the table, and gave him a chastising glare. "These things are all situational, and a mistake can be disastrous, so stop fiddling and pay attention."

He arched a brow and gave a crooked grin. "Aye, no more fun for me."

"Today is about my fun, not yours." She pointed at the ring he had picked up. "The inlay has been charged with a glamor but not yet invoked. The spelled insets are chosen by the person preparing the charm, and they can be made of almost anything but are most often created with wood, paper, or cloth. Most of the jewelry pieces carry similar types of spells and are useful for disappearing into a crowd. They require a drop of blood to invoke, and once invoked, will remain effective until removed or dispelled."

He fixed her with a pointed stare. "Or for spying on people without them knowing you are there?"

"Yes," she sighed. "If you prefer to dwell on that, then yes, that is how I managed it."

"How do you dispel them? It seems that might be a key defensive tactic."

"Dispelling involves salt and some type of blessed water. So, unless you plan to run around with a super soaker hosing down random people, it's not an effective defensive technique."

Sean laughed at the imagery. "I see your point. How do you determine what you will look like when it is activated?"

"That is part of the creation process, but something from the person the spell has been modeled on is used, most often hair concealed within the charm." She moved her hand over the small pile of necklaces, copper, and silver designs, each having custom insets. "These contain spells for pain, healing, protection against things unseen. You learn to identify them based on their shape, and the symbols worked into the metals."

His brow knit. "I thought the jewelry was for disguises . . . glamours."

"The necklaces are an exception," she said. "If you want to know why there are books on the subject in the library, it's not important for what you must learn today." "The stacks of papers are spells"—she pointed at the thin, loose, vellum-like sheets—"written out and waiting for use. You invoke these with fire. Burn the sheet, and the magic is quickened. They can be powerful, but you must have fire to use them. Try relying on one of these during a rainstorm."

Sean's eyes moved to the rumbling torrent across the room, and he could feel her mischievous grin beneath her teasing words. "Yes, you'll be getting all wet later—if you survive phase one. But you can look forward to drying off afterward; it can be quite an experience." With that, she gathered a few books of matches and a pair of lighters, offering them to him. "Put these in your pocket. You'll need them."

Taking the items, he rolled them in his hand. "Do we need these? I have seen Papa spark fire with a wave of his hand."

"Papa has many skills that most lack. He has been well trained, and eventually, you might do the same, but calling the elements to life by will alone is something rarely seen."

His lips pursed into a resolved line. "It can be done. That's all I needed to know." The corners of his lips twitched upward, and he slipped the lighters into a pocket.

Pointing at the collection of candles, she pressed on. "These are not something you can use easily out in the world, but they make for wonderful additions to your home. Cleansing, purification, warding, using them to invoke magic that needs to be birthed over long periods."

Sean rubbed at his chin. "So I will need to set up something at home once I have that situation sorted out?"

She placed a hand on his right arm, and a bit of concern touched her face. "You don't have to, but I would suggest you do it, even now. Don't wait. Set up protections, even at the Cottage. You've entered this world now; you must always be ready."

Her playfulness returned, and she dropped her hand from his arm. She moved around the mat, hips swaying, drawing his eyes downward. "You stay. Better start figuring out what each of those does. Training has begun."

Rolling his eyes, he turned and searched the table, muttering. "Some kind of legend or key would have been helpful." He scratched his right arm and picked up a few of the necklaces, studying their shapes and symbols.

Turning them in his hand, he discovered runes inset in their backs. He now knew the characters to be part of an Angelic Script, though the meanings were still foreign. He scratched his arm again, thinking over the things she had told him. "Blood."

Patting the pockets of his jeans, he searched for his knife. The image of a great metal finger rising from a counter flashed in his mind, and he cursed. "Vitan!"

From across the room, he heard her voice lift in a taunting chant. "There are finger lances over here!"

His head dropped, and he chuckled. "Of course there are." He eyed the obstacles in the middle of the room. "I suppose I have to go through this . . . labyrinth to retrieve them?"

Her laughter was light and thrilling. "There are no minotaurs, don't be so dramatic. Come now, teacher's waiting."

He gathered a handful of the charms and draped them around his neck before turning and heading into the maze. Passing the first pipe, he heard a hiss, and the square filled with a fine mist. Dashing forward, he turned a wary eye toward the haze. He rubbed along the side of his pants, trying to remove the moist film and scratch all at once.

Turning back toward the maze, he continued through the cubicles, picking his way with careful thought. The head-high walls were packed in a dense grid, making it difficult to see a clear path and slowing his progress. Making a right turn, he came to a dead end. Looking behind himself, he considered turning back. Dismissing the idea, he placed his hands atop the wall, hopped up, and pulled himself over. Before his feet hit the floor, his whole body shook from the force of a jarring sneeze. His feet jerked out from beneath him, and he tumbled face-first into the mat.

Still struggling to get back on his feet, another sneeze wracked his body, and he heard Talaunia giggle. "You best hurry along before you hurt yourself."

One body-wrenching sneeze after another hit him as he continued to pick his way through the twists and turns. He scratched along his arm and over to his shoulder. Doubling over from another sneeze, he took several stumbling steps and used his left hand to steady himself. Turning the last corner, he was out of the maze, and he could see the lances on the table ahead.

He stepped off the mat, scratching at his right shoulder, the joints of his left hand aching under the action. Pulling his hand away, he stared at it, bewildered. He tried closing it into a fist, but his fingers refused to contract more than halfway, and he watched as they bent and locked in an arthritic pose. "Bloody hell."

Grabbing a finger lance, he dropped to a knee and began rubbing his right arm and shoulder against the side of the table. He pricked the index finger of his left hand. Lifting one necklace after another, he dabbed drops of blood on all of them, smearing it over metal and wood, but nothing happened.

Talaunia bent down, inspecting him. "Oh my, that rash is spreading quickly. I see you found a few other surprises on your way through as well. Too bad you didn't protect your spells better." She grabbed the necklaces around his neck and lifted them from his head. "These are worthless. That mist was a saltwater solution. Every step you took past that only carried you further from the things that will stop all of this."

He turned his face toward her, intending to glare, but at that moment, another sneeze shot through him, bouncing his forehead off the table's edge.

"Sweetie, you need to get yourself to the other table and try some of those amulets until you can figure out what ails you." She wrapped her fingers around his left arm and tugged him upward. "Don't forget your lances," she said, pushing him toward the maze. She caught him at the entrance, turning him aside. "On second thought, you best go around Darling. I'm afraid you might kill yourself if you try to go back through in your current state."

He rolled his eyes, which only made her enjoy the moment more. "Not taking any shortcuts. If I die, guess we all bloody well learn something." Sneezing, he turned from her and blundered headlong, back into the maze.

Behind him, he heard her laugh. He pulled his left arm up along his chest, the ache in the joints having descended to the wrist. His right arm was itching up past his shoulder, along his collarbone and upper back. The simple act of breathing hurt, his chest and ribs growing sore from the continual fits of sneezing.

He took his time and was careful not to touch anything else in the maze while he picked his way through its twisting passages. By the time he emerged, his back was hunched over, and he was hobbling like some twisted monster from a silent film. Talaunia was there, waiting, leaning against the table with an amused expression. "Stubbornness like this is why you attract all the trouble."

Reaching the table, he grabbed a handful of the charms and draped all of them around his neck. Fishing a lance out of his pocket, he pricked his left index finger several times before dragging the bloody tip across every amulet dangling from his neck.

The ache of his ribs and hand subsided. Another sneeze tickled his nose, but he choked it off and sighed in relief. The itching that had been creeping across his skin vanished, replaced by a strange numbness. Facing Talaunia, questions tried to form, but his mind was growing foggy.

Her eyes swept over the array of emblems, cataloging what he had used. Mirth spread across her face, and her eyes brightened. "Oh, my."

His focus fell to his legs, he stamped his foot, and it bent at an odd angle, sending painful jolts along the nerves in his leg. Confusion clouded his eyes. "What?" His head swam, disoriented and light. He lifted his chin, searching for Talaunia, and when he located her, she seemed so distant. The world wobbled and became a blurred streak of color, and he was looking at the ceiling.

Talaunia's foot was beside his head, and his gaze swept up her leg until it vanished into the slit of her skirt near her hip. "When'd you get so . . . tall?" he asked, struggling to focus on her face.

"It's going to be a long day," she laughed.

He blinked, trying to drive the deepening fog away, but his eyes refused to remain open any longer. Talaunia's hand rested on his chest, gathering the amulets as he drifted off to sleep.

< ᛏᚻᛗ ᛒᛟᚱᛁᛞ ᚻᛗᛗᛞᛋ ᛚᛟᛁ >

"Welcome back," Talaunia mused, playing with his hair.

Sean's eyes fluttered open, and he found himself once again laying with his head in Talaunia's lap. "What happened? How long was I out?"

She lifted a mess of charms, dangling them over his chest. "You took yourself out far quicker than any of my concoctions." She jingled the collection of swinging necklaces. "You needed one of these. You could have used three if done correctly—you used seven."

Embarrassment flooded his cheeks. "So you can have too much of a good thing?"

She sighed, a playful wrath glimmering in her narrowed eyes. "Watch it, or I'll put them all back on you." One by one she dangled the amulets over his chest, explaining their purpose before tossing them away. "This is the one you needed. It's a cleansing charm. It will banish most incidental curses, but has little effect on targeted spells or those of a more nefarious variety."

He snatched one of the discs from the air and studied the markings.

She picked up the next, continuing. "This one will act as a ward to block curses that are aimed at you, at least most of them. You should consider wearing one at all times, and perhaps a mojo bag." She lifted another and dangled it before him. "This one is for reducing pain. Some things magic cannot solve, but it can help." She tapped his forehead with a finger. "You used four. I imagine that is why you were stamping your foot like a bull. Things go numb, did they?"

"Perhaps." His eyes shifted from the amulets. "That's only six. You said I used seven?"

"Oh yes, we mustn't forget your crowning jewel." She lifted another necklace and dangled it over him. "This one isn't defensive. It has many other uses, but none that are valid for today. It is a sleeping charm. If you can't sleep, this can help. Have an injured patient that should sleep until things heal; again, this is a lifesaver. Never, ever use it on yourself in a defensive situation, or you know what will happen."

He sighed and chuckled. "Bloody hell, knocked myself out."

Her touch trailed over his forehead again. "Yes, Sweetie, you did." Her fingers drifted around his cheek and up to his lips, where they danced over the contours of the soft flesh. Her voice was breathy. "You really should learn to be more careful with my things."

Searching her eyes, he rebuffed her, though his words lack conviction. "I'm not yours."

"Not yet, but you will be." Her smile twisted, becoming dangerous and playful. "Now, I have pampered you enough. You still have many lessons to learn before the day is out."

Slipping from beneath him, she rose to her feet in a single graceful move, dropping his head to the floor with a thud.

He rubbed at the back of his head. "Gods have mercy on me now."

Talaunia laughed. "They aren't allowed here. If you are seeking mercy, you best grovel before the only goddess you'll see today."

The afternoon passed in a series of similar training sessions. Talaunia set him up to stumble and left him to find his way clear of the messes he created for himself. She made him carry sheet after sheet of spelled paper into the downpour until he generated enough fire to quicken the spell. Once he managed it successfully, he cheered. The magic dispersed the storm and left him a soggy mess. He had turned to her with a question he knew must have an answer. "Why don't we use this on hurricanes and other destructive storms?"

"All magic has a cost. If you mess with nature, you best understand the balance of things. You cannot force your will on the Mother in such a drastic way and not expect her to respond, to show you exactly where you fit in the scheme of things. All things must be kept in balance. Think before you cast. Otherwise, you'll wind up killing yourself or others."

Sean was puzzled. "We've been invoking magic all day. Where is the balance in that?"

She stepped to his side. "We have been invoking minor spells, and the balance was taken into account when they were created. The amulets have a limited sphere of impact; you paid the price for them in blood. Papa created this controlled storm, using his knowledge to craft the spell to banish it, knowing that your spell would restore the balance. Even here in training, the balance is maintained, even if you do not yet understand."

Before the day ended, Sean was spent, having suffered most of the curses hurled at him. The list was long and vile: boils, lesions, blindness, and an array of intestinally compromising curses.

"Remember, we take it easy on you here in training. Out there, the things that are after you are much darker and far more deadly." Talaunia had underscored the mildness of the training more than once, and it made him wary.

Returning to his office, Sean gathered the pile of books Jason had pulled from the library, grabbed his phone, and headed toward the lift.

Having no way to reopen the portal back to the Stony Brook Cottage, Sean made his way down through the lobby and into the gardens surrounding the building. Mundane travel would be his mode of transport tonight, and the Addison Lee driver was to meet him outside the southern entrance in half an hour. Strolling along the quiet paths, he turned and took in the starlight glimmering over the pyramid's surface. He reflected on how much his world had changed and about the new people who had entered his life. His thoughts lingered on Talaunia and Axylia, their warring personalities, and how each drew him in their own way. Letting out a slow breath, he smiled.

The Bright Ones have opened our eyes to the mystical powers flowing through our bond with the Mother. Using the Heavenly Gardens as our classroom, they have taught us to access the inherent abilities we all share, to commune with all living things, and manipulate living energy. They also taught us to access other gifts, which vary among us; I can see potential outcomes of specific events long before they transpire. Our future is thrilling or terrifying. I pray the Mother grants me the wisdom to use these visions to guide our people away from tragedy.

—Councilor Traxidor

Fourteen

Kitty cats, kitty cats, kitty cats, go!

The cottage was wrapped in peaceful silence. Sean was asleep on the divan, sprawled at an odd angle. An open book rested on his chest. His computer sat on the coffee table. A soft aura surrounded the screen, created by the bronze text of the library's interface. The cursor blinked with eternal patience, waiting for the parameters of its next search. Next to the computer, his phone sat atop a tower of books constructed during his research. The phone came to life, vibrating, buzzing, and screaming like a klaxon. A pulsing red light flashed behind the Quari Group logo and the row of glowing symbols beneath.

Sean jerked awake. The book on his chest toppled to the floor. The phone vibrated from its perch, crashing into the table. Blinking away the groggy confusion, he stared at the clock on the mantle, trying to make out the position of the hands.

2:37 AM.

Rubbing at his face, Sean rocked forward, pawing at the phone to silence the ear-splitting cry. He studied the symbols, a crease forming on his brow as he struggled to decipher the message. Through the fog of sleep still shrouding his brain, he decided the symbols must be a portal location. "Only one way to find out."

He stretched and groaned, stuffing the computer into his satchel. Hoping his instincts were correct, he traced the symbols around the bedroom doorframe and watched the wavering image of a busy room take shape.

When he stepped through, he found himself in the Operations Center. A makeshift refreshment table sat beside the lift. The scent of coffee and danish filled the air, and his stomach rumbled. The room itself was on edge. Tension lined every face as people dashed between stations. The main screen showed an infographic of India. Another was filled with climate information and the history of Baba Budan Giri. A live satellite image was projected on one wall, providing occasional glimpses of a lake through the clouds.

An unidentified voice barked into the bustling crowd. "Someone clean up this image. I need a better view."

Across the room, Jason responded to the command. "I'm not a damned weatherman, but I'm working on it, dude!"

Gadyen appeared at Sean's side, offering him a steaming cup of coffee. "Presuming you are like Ryan; this will aid your search for clarity." Gadyen was bare-chested, save for a pair of bone-studded leather straps crossing his chest. His hair was pulled back and bound with silk, and he wore a crimson fustanella around his waist that fell unevenly about his bare legs. A sword was strapped across his back, and an array of blades and charms dangled from his belt.

Giving him a once-over, Sean accepted the coffee. "Thanks. What's going on here?"

Ryan approached with a cup in his left hand, walking through the busy room without a stitch of clothing.

To Sean's surprise, everyone seemed unphased by the naked man shouldering his way through the crowd.

Giving an exhausted grunt of acknowledgment, Ryan shouldered up next to Gadyen. "I'm not awake enough for this shit."

Talaunia appeared from the other direction, stopping in front of the trio, her dark copper hair pulled back in a taut tail. She was dressed in a leather top and pants that hugged her curves. Along her arms and legs, an array of wards and charms were attached with leather strands. She, too, wore a belt overflowing with various items and a fan of daggers at each hip. "Morning, Sweetie," she said, her violet eyes bright. She leaned in and kissed his cheek. "Glad you got my summons."

"Your summons?" Sean's eyes flashed around to the various screens before returning to hers. "Why am I here?"

From behind, the weight of Djain's presence enveloped him, and Sean turned. Several heartbeats later.

Djain entered the room, flanked on each side by a large black cat. All vestiges of the businessman had vanished, replaced by a warrior wearing a loincloth. Every sharply defined muscle was on display. Over the scarred mound patterns covering his chest, ghostly white symbols were painted. The artwork covered his body, including skull-like imagery across his head and face. He held a gnarled wood staff in his right hand, the length of its ashen surface etched with runes stained a rusty crimson shade. From the bulbous top of the rod, feathers dangled, attached with strands of hair. In his left hand, Djain cupped the upper portion of a skull, the bleached bone inscribed with geometric shapes and magical symbols.

Sean swallowed. Djain was terrifying.

Djain's steel-blue eyes swept over the room, and when he spoke, a chill raced along Sean's spine. The usual warmth of his basso resonance was gone, replaced with icy authority. "We have family members on a recovery mission at lake Galikere in India. While there, they were set upon without warning. We will not leave them to face this alone."

"Is it the Order?" asked a technician.

"That we will determine when we arrive," Djain said. He turned to Sean. "Once we are inside the temple and can see the state of the artifact, you will help us evaluate what is needed for a safe recovery."

"Absolutely," Sean said. "Whatever I can do to help." Glancing around, he realized no one was meeting his gaze, and his stomach knotted. "Is the group under attack the one Axylia went to help?"

He touched Talaunia's arm and knew the answer before she spoke, though when she looked at him, he was surprised to see genuine concern mirrored in her eyes.

Talaunia hid her emotions behind action, draping dozens of charms over Sean's neck. "We'll get her back. Here, carry extra supplies for me." Reaching around him, she fastened a belt weighed down with other amulets, miniature scrolls, and vials. "Stay close and do what we tell you."

Sarah slipped up to him and tugged on his satchel. "I'll keep watch over your things."

He let the bag slip away. "Um, thanks. One less thing to worry about."

Djain watched the exchange, his head shaking. "Sean will not be with us until we have secured the area around the artifact. His training is far from complete, and I will not lead him into confrontation until he is prepared."

Eyes darkening, Sean protested. "I know how to take care of myself."

Talaunia chaffed at Djain's declaration as well. "What better way to see how we work together than to see us in action? I'll keep him with me." She stepped toward Djain, her words pointed. "You know I won't let anything happen to him."

Leaning forward, Djain fixed his fierce gaze on Talaunia. "We do not have time for pointless debates. Sean will remain here until we call for him."

Lip curling in displeasure, Talaunia ran her hand down Sean's arm. "Sorry, I tried. I wish you were coming." She angled her chin, ensuring Djain would hear the acidic bite in her tone. "It would help with your training."

Djain whistled, and the chaos of the room came to a standstill. "Here is what we learned before contact with the team in India was severed. They have secured the area surrounding the artifact but have not yet made the recovery. They are surrounded and have raised a defensive circle. It falls upon us to reach them and break the attack before their protection crumbles. This we *will* do!"

A cheer rose from the room, and Djain let it roll.

"Whoever attacked pinned them in, cast wards to cut off our communications, and prevent their escape. We will travel to the site through the same portal, positioned along the hillside well above the Galikere shore." Djain pointed at the glowing portal on the wall. "It remains open and must rest outside the perimeter of our attackers' wards. Once there, this team will make their way to our family and bring them home."

Another round of cheers went up before he continued. "Be watchful. Be mindful. And 4be ready to tend to one another. We will all be back, but some may require care. Prepare!"

Djain turned, evaluating his team. "Everyone ready?"

Ryan tipped up his cup and drained what was left of it. "Could use more coffee."

Sean glanced at the untouched cup in his hand. With a shrug, he offered it to Ryan, who accepted without pause.

After draining it, too, Ryan smirked. "Better. Let's go fuck 'em up!"

Gadyen inclined his head.

Talaunia checked her belt and weapons, her eyes lingering on Sean. "Got everything I have to take with me."

Without another word, the fearsome persona of Djain led them through the portal.

< ᚴᛰᚿ ᚺᚠᚾᛗ ᛏᚻᛗ ᚲᛰᚿᚱᚠᚷᛗ ᚴᛰᚿ ᛏᛗᛗᛤ >

The group stood atop a mountain. Deep green grass speckled the ground, and patches of short brush grew wild over the slope. Below them, an earthen path circled a small lake. The air was thin, and visibility was limited. The haze of the cloud bank surrounding them held back the early morning light, prolonging dawn's arrival.

Djain signaled for silence and dipped his head toward Gadyen.

Gadyen vanished into the mist.

The group listened for any sign of their opponents, but only the water's soft lapping against the moss-covered rocks below reached their ears.

When Gadyen returned, he materialized out of the mist itself. "One sentry in the cloud wall to the south." His whisper was so quiet, it forced them all to lean closer. "Three casters ring the lake. They face away from the water and perform the containment ritual. I cannot check further until we end their casting."

Djain scratched behind Jacia's ear, thinking through the situation. "Panji, stay with Talaunia. Distract the guard at her command." The cat mewled and nuzzled him before moving to stand behind Talaunia. "Talaunia, you will deal with the guard. Silence him, bind him, and we will collect him for questioning. Panji will let us know when we are free to act."

Talaunia pulled objects from her belt, her expression telling Djain she understood her assignment.

"Once the guard is down, Gadyen, Ryan, and I will dispatch the active casters." Djain peered out into the fog, considering their next action. "We only need the sentry—Gadyen, feast. Restore your strength and prepare for what is ahead. Regroup at the guard's position."

Gadyen gave a bow and backed up a step, vanishing into the fog.

Djain leaned in closer to Talaunia. "The Mother is with us." Spinning, he moved north, well above the water's edge, with Jacia at his side.

Flashing his bare ass at Talaunia, Ryan followed.

Talaunia cataloged her items in urgent silence. She pulled a butane torch from her pocket, and slipped a bit of parchment with a silencing spell from a small pack at her waist. She checked the zip cuffs hanging from her hip, the sleep potion in her hand, and touched the amulet around her neck.

Glancing over her shoulder toward the sentry's post, she tucked the vial containing the sleep potion into her left palm, and grasped the spell paper between her fingers.

She signaled Panji, who passed through the haze in silence.

Talaunia crouched and moved with sure footing across the dew-covered grass. Ahead, the dark outline of the guard formed in the mist, and she slowed, watching.

It was apparent when the watchman caught sight of Panji in the fog. His whole body tensed, and he pivoted to follow the cat's path. Seeing him focused on the giant cat, Talaunia smiled.

A click sounded sharp and clear in the still morning air. The ignitor shattered the peaceful serenity, and the flame roared to life with the intensity of a jet engine. The guard turned, trying to cry out his warning, but the paper had already been consumed.

Absolute silence fell.

Talaunia launched herself at the man, taking his knees out from under him. In seconds, the man was face down in the dirt. The spry elf perched atop his back, knee pressed into his spine, digging in with all her might.

The man's face twisted with anger. He struggled and yelled, but no sound escaped; even the lapping of the water had been swallowed up within the perfect silence.

She popped open the vial and dumped it over the back of the man's head.

Blinking in confusion, he relaxed, and fell into a deep sleep.

Talaunia climbed off and wrestled her target into a sitting position. She bound the man with zip cuffs and draped the sleep amulet around his neck. She pricked the tip of her finger with a dagger and activated the charm. Slicing the leather cord, she cinched it around his neck, securing it like a choker, ensuring it wouldn't fall off, even if the man rolled over.

With a pop, the sound rushed in, leaving an uncomfortable pressure on her ears. She stretched her jaw this way and that, contorting her face into a series of odd expressions to counter the effect.

Panji padded up, sniffed the bound man, and nudged Talaunia.

Talaunia gave the cat a firm pat on her flank. "Well done, girl. Let them know it's clear."

The panther purred softly and melted into the mist while the sound hung in the air.

Long minutes passed, and Talaunia paced nervously. She checked her blades and potions and stared into the ever shifting cloud bank. An enormous form took shape in the swirling mists, and she froze. Tensing, she prepared to douse the mysterious creature with a potion from her belt.

The approaching figure twisted and shifted until the outline of a man took form, and Ryan stepped into view. Blood glistened around his mouth and ran down his chest. "That circle has been fucked all the hell up!"

After another few moments, Djain reappeared, the cats licking their muzzles at his flanks. He studied the crimson stains dripping from Ryan. "Panji and Jacia enjoyed the hunt as well."

Gadyen stepped from the mist, as pristine and polished as he had been before his task, but there was something different about his presence. He bowed toward Djain. "It is done. I stand ready."

"Good. After me." Djain led them down the slope, over the brown dirt trail, and to the water's edge. A moss-covered mound of stones lay along the bank. At its head, a tall beige rock stood like a marker, a monument. The rock seemed out of place in the rich colors of the area. Its surface was stained with symbols akin to the runes used by the Norse.

A pair of torches stood alongside the shrine, bright strips of cloth flowing from beneath the bowls where the flame lapped at the air. "The child of a god struck the Mother with his mace here. The lake formed within the impact crater." Djain stepped up to the shoreline between the candles. "Beneath these waters stands a temple, built before the lake formed. Within those walls is where we will find our family. Let us go to them."

"How are we to enter?" Gadyen asked. "While I can stroll the depths with ease, you more fragile creatures require breath."

Djain planted the end of his staff into the water. "I will make a path. Let us be quick about our business."

Gripping the staff with both hands, Djain closed his eyes and lowered his head. He chanted under his breath, and the winds along the shore stirred, whipping about them in growing torrents, pushing the cloud bank up and away. Raising the staff above his head in one hand, his eyes snapped open, and he struck the surface of the lake. Water exploded in the air. The wind raced past Djain, swirling itself into a vortex, lifting the water up and over the spinning gale. A tunnel opened along the lake bed, forming a path to the temple resting beneath the murky depths.

A thin layer of water rushed over the tunnel base, slipping between the rocks in rapid little streams.

Ryan gave Gadyen a grin and darted into the watery tunnel. "Fuck yeah, let's go!"

Gadyen sighed and followed on Ryan's heels.

Talaunia chased after them, her eyes darting here and there, apprehensive about the watery walls.

Below, Gadyen and Ryan reached the structure and vanished underground.

Glancing over her shoulder, Talaunia saw the panthers' shadowy forms barreling down on her. Djain followed, the waters of the lake knitting themselves closed behind him, sealing them in. Eyes widening, she quickened her pace.

As the structure's outer wall neared, Talaunia spotted a staircase leading below the foundation. She dashed down the stairs, her boots hitting shallow puddles, and the splashing echoed off the rock walls. The stairs leveled out into a long tunnel, with another set of rising stairs at the far end.

Ryan and Gadyen were waiting at the ascending stairs, peering up into the unknown. From behind them, Djain's voice strained when his bare feet hit the tunnel, and he saw the others waiting. "Move! Now!"

The sound of rushing water resonated along the stone tunnel. Behind Djain, the waters were pouring in, filling the cramped space.

"Fuck me," Ryan called from ahead. Grabbing hold of Gadyen, the pair dashed up the stairs.

Talaunia rushed to catch up, hearing the sounds of alarm ringing from ahead.

The clash of metal echoed down the stairs.

Adrenaline surged, and she scrambled to reach her friends.

Atop the stairs, Gadyen stood sword in hand over the twitching body of a dying man. Another sword lay on the ground, discarded by the man desperately grasping the gurgling slit in his throat.

By the time Djain and the panthers had entered the small room, it was cramped. The water rushed up to fill the hole and cover the stairs, sloshing out onto the floor, but it held just below the floor's surface. Talaunia stared at it until Djain assured her it wouldn't come any further into the structure.

"I bet Sean would love to see the architecture of this place," Talaunia said, taking in the room.

Pointing at the water, Djain refocused their attention. "That threat is behind us; the real one lay ahead."

There was no direct light source, the stone radiated a luminescence that cast everyone in a pale blue-green hue.

The passages branched off from the small room to either side, and Gadyen's gaze shifted between them.

He pointed his sword at the fallen man. "He sounded the alarm before I could quiet his tongue."

Blood seeped from the deep slit across the man's throat, pooling around his still body.

Talaunia's sandalwood skin had taken on an ashen pallor.

Djain touched her arm. "What's troubling you?"

Her eyes found his, and what he saw reflected there twisted his stomach into a tight ball.

She pointed to the corners. "There is no life here, aside from what walks and speaks."

Djain's countenance darkened, and he checked the corner she had indicated, finding nothing but wilted, rotting plants. Turning to the other corners, he saw more of the same.

Calling the cats to him, Djain spoke to them in a foreign tongue, and they vanished. "They will scout our path."

Ryan's brows knotted, concern fueling his ire. "How long?"

"These have been dead for days; things further in were living until recently." Her eyes cut to Djain. "What life force I can feel of our people is faint, and there are others present." Her eyes darkened, fear and anger flashing in her eyes. "Elevari."

The tension in the entire group elevated.

"We will not give up, nor will we leave them behind. They are going home with us."

Gadyen gave a solemn nod as the cats reappeared.

Talaunia caressed the withered leaves and they crumbled in her hand.

Djain communicated with the panthers.

Ryan and Gadyen stood by the passages, watching for any signs of activity.

A somber silence hung in the air.

Indicating the opening to the right, Djain spoke. "This is our path. Let us see to our grim business. Move with urgency but caution. There may yet be surprises ahead."

< ᛕᛖᛗᚠᚲᛗ ᛋᛁᚱᚱᛟᚾᛏᛒᛋ ᛚᛟᚾ >

The floor of the Operations Center was organized chaos. People were yelling status updates in a give-and-take style. Others were barking orders to no one in particular, but somehow, the correct individuals always seemed to respond.

Sarah dashed over, gently guiding Sean up against the wall. "They will bring the medical supplies over here in a minute. When they do, stand at the head of the first gurney. If it's needed, you can be the one who pushes it through the portal."

Sean felt like a child, taken by the hand and guided through his first big event. It irritated him, but he understood.

"I will. Thank you, Sarah."

She flashed a smile and rejoined the circus on the floor.

Sean paced against the wall. Unable to understand the cryptic codes being tossed around, and wondering how his new friends were fairing. He was concerned for all of them, but he was focused on the ladies. Talaunia was all fire, more a fighter than a healer, and he had fewer concerns about her. Axylia, on the other hand, struck him as a pure healer. Yes, she had a spark all her own; he only wished he knew more about her combat skills.

Two gurneys rambled to a stop before him, and Sean stepped to the head of one. He latched ahold of the frame and squeezed, attempting to release the tension building inside. Staring at the inactive arches, he wished they would spring to life.

〈 ᚼᛩᚠᚱ ᛋᚳᚠᚳᛗ ᛁᛋ ᛁᛗᚳᛩᚱᛏᚨᚾᛏ 〉

Gadyen was first into the hallway, followed by Talaunia. The panthers wisped away into the shadows with a wave, and Djain fell in behind. Ryan was the last into the tunnel, acting as their rear guard.

The first passage was clear and traversed without incident, running about seventy-five yards before hitting a hard left turn. Gadyen held up a hand to halt their progression.

Talaunia watched as a second Gadyen ghosted into existence: one safely behind the corner, the other standing brazenly exposed. The effect only lasted seconds, and the two figures blended back into a single form.

241

Signaling for them to follow, Gadyen vanished around the corner, leading them deeper into the temple.

They traversed the new passage without incident, though it was shorter than the first, and ended at a set of stairs. The steps rose with a gentle curve toward the structure's middle. At the base of the stairs, a dagger protruded from the wall, its tip driven between a pair of stones. Gadyen studied the path ahead and pointed at the handle. "Do not disturb this blade."

Each took their turns, slipping past the handle and moving up the stairs. Hundreds of tiny holes dotted the surface of the wall. "Darts," Talaunia said. "Probably poisoned, and that dagger is likely keeping them from skewering us."

Bringing the group to a stop, Gadyen pointed to an opening above. "We will be exposed once across that threshold."

Each of them understood the implications and took stock of themselves, preparing for whatever conflict lay ahead.

Gadyen checked his belt and brought his sword to the ready.

Talaunia drew a pair of silver daggers from her belt with dark runes set along their blades.

Djain loomed, a dark god, soaking in the strange light.

Ryan stood askance in the hallway, gaze fixed on the path behind. His chest rose and fell in deep breaths, the low warning sound of the bear within rolling down the staircase.

As a group, they rushed into the room.

A domed ceiling soared overhead, and several other passages stood open around the room's perimeter. A stepped platform rose at the center of the space, with a stone plinth in the middle. The pedestal was carved from the same type of stone used to create the moss-covered shrine on the shoreline above, and atop it sat a wooden mask pulsing with mystical energy.

The room had been filled with living plants, but the stench of decay was heavy in the atmosphere. Rotting leaves covered the ground, and the tall grasses filling the box planters along the walls had wilted. Overhead, the hanging plants had succumbed. The bushy vines spilled over the sides of their containers like skeletal fingers.

Talaunia paled. "Oh. Mother, please. No—" She reached out, touching Djain on the arm, a horror-stricken look on her face. "These plants were killed intentionally. Fucking Elevari left her nothing to draw from." Seeing Axylia across the room, her eyes misted, and she shifted her gaze to the others.

On top of the platform, the original team from the Quari Group held their ground. Two were down and unmoving. Axylia had another propped against her chest, both of them muttering and pale. Axylia herself did not appear to be weathering the situation any better. Her pearlescent skin was dull and mottled with gray; her raven hair shot through with ash, crimson, and burnt orange streaks.

Feeling Djain's eyes on her, Talaunia lifted her chin and met his gaze. Her lips pressed into a thin line, her chin quivered, and she shook her head, tears of fury brimming in her eyes.

The original team was inside a circle. The candles marking the cardinal directions sputtered and struggled for life. Still, the magic held against the onslaught of power pummeling the protective barrier. The circle lacked the power and presence of Djain's, but it refused to yield.

Five strangers stood around the platform—their attempt to shatter the protective circle ending as they shifted to face the new threat.

Both sides squared off, and a tall, skinny fellow with a thin oval face, pointed ears, and a sharply angled goatee lifted a long tube to his lips. A soft pop sounded, and a slender dart left the pipe on a whiff of air.

Gadyen's sword flashed in front of an unflinching Djain, deflecting the dart which shattered against the stone wall.

Djain lifted a brow, a wintry smile forming, directed at the man across the room. "I have been informed of your underhanded and abhorrent destruction of the plant life within these walls. There are doors behind you, and I will give you one chance to see yourself out. That is the only mercy I am inclined to offer. If you remain, there will be no quarter."

One man eased toward the passage behind him, and the gaunt fellow snapped. "Hold!" He turned a hawkish gaze to Djain. "We will leave, only with the mask in hand. Tell them to release the circle. We'll take what should be ours and be on our way. They will not last much longer."

"That will not happen." Djain sighed, resigning himself to what lay ahead. "It saddens me you did not save yourself."

The thin man shrugged, his narrow features twisting in a self-confident smirk.

"Fucking Elevari," Talaunia hissed.

The gaunt man's eyes flashed to Talaunia. "Ah! Cousin." He gestured toward Axyila. "How nice of you to join your friend for a lesson."

The two men flanking the Elevari leaped forward. Where their feet should have hit the ground, two long tails unfurled, and the group faced a pair of towering pythons.

Without hesitation, Ryan pounced, transforming in mid-air. His bulky, ursine frame landed atop the first snake, driving his claws into the writhing mass below him. The serpent's tail lashed out, and the pair rolled off to one side, each trying to best the other.

Djain whistled and pointed.

Panji and Jacia pounced atop the other snake from the shadows, and the room devolved into the chaotic sounds of enraged beasts locked in deathly struggles.

In a blur of motion, Gadyen stepped into the shadows and vanished, only to reappear a moment later behind the man that had tried to flee. He grabbed the man about the chest with one arm and forced his head to the side with the other. He sank his teeth into the man's neck. There were no fangs, no romanticized beauty, no surgical punctures, only the rending of flesh with incisors and canines. The man screamed when his neck was torn open, blood gushing into the air in quick spurts as his heart pumped the life from him. Gadyen lapped at the hot crimson liquid, the color a stark contrast to his silver hair and pale skin.

Talaunia hurled her knife at another attacker, following its path on foot and throwing herself into the man. The force of their collision drew guttural sounds from each as their struggle began.

The room was a cacophony of action and noise. Tossing his blowgun aside, the gaunt man pulled a short, thin dirk from his belt along with a bag that he dangled from his left hand. Muttering an incantation, he used the dirk as a focus, shooting a bolt of energy at Djain.

Lifting his left hand, Djain caught the bolt, and it split, rolling down his arm and across his powerful chest.

Beginning a confident, steady march toward the Elevari man, Djain taunted. "For your sake, I hope you know something aside from air magic. I am born of the air, and it is but another part of me."

The thin man swallowed hard and took a step back before trying again, building a more significant charge of energy and unleashing the crackling bolt of lightning at Djain.

Again, Djain caught the bolt, dispersing the energy across his frame.

The musty scent of decay faded under the fragrant swell of ozone.

Djain continued closing the distance between himself and his attacker. The deep rumble of his voice colored with disappointment and resolve. "You do not fathom the depths of your mistakes, do you?"

Ryan moaned, the sound laced with pain.

Gadyen's head shot up, chin streaked with crimson, and he dropped the lifeless man in his arms.

The body collapsed on itself in unnatural angles, the ravaged throat gaping open, allowing what blood remained to dribble onto the floor.

Ryan sank his teeth into the soft flesh of the python's side.

The long, muscled body of the serpent wrapped around Ryan's bulky chest. Skin rippling with the effort, the python constricted, and the sickening sound of cracking ribs echoed through the chaos.

In the next instant, Gadyen was there, hacking at the snake with his sword.

Jacia and Panji continued to wrestle with their snake. One moment they were there, twisting and rolling across the floor; the next, they were gone, dragging the serpent with them into the Shadows.

Talaunia plucked a vial from her belt and cracked it open, pouring the contents over the man's head, and he laughed with twisted glee. Talaunia glanced at the vial and cursed. "Shit! Wrong fucking potion!"

The man's strength and agility heightened, and he pressed his advantage. Grimy fingers knotted themselves into the lacing of her leather top. Turning her clothing into a handle, he pulled her around like a rag doll. His other hand latched onto her hair, and he yanked her head back. He leered at her. "Give me a kiss, gorgeous!"

Talaunia tried to force her lips closed, but his brutal kiss was unrelenting and his tongue wormed its way through to slide across her clamped teeth. Rage boiled inside her, and she opened her mouth, pulling his lip between her own before clamping down and forcing him to pull back.

Blood welled on his lower lip, and he smiled. "Worth it, doll, so very worth it!"

Talaunia spit a chunk of his bloody lip back into his face, and slammed her fists into his beefy frame.

The man held fast, his dark eyes roving over her, filled with hunger. "Think I'll have myself another taste."

She struck at him with all the fury she could muster, her blows seeming to have no impact.

He twisted her, torquing her head to the side, opening her neck for his bloody lips to latch onto the soft flesh.

The muscles in her side spasmed, complaining about the forced position, but now she could reach her belt. Ignoring the discomfort, she pawed at the assortment of vials in desperation, groping for any potion that may help.

Djain closed in on his opponent.

The Elevari lunged, striking with the dirk and opening a gash on Djain's forearm.

Blood ran from the wound, streaming down Djain's arm to drip from his fingertips. Not a single drop hit the floor. Wisps of purple smoke shrouded the blood, devouring it, and leaving nothing behind.

The gaunt man's eyes widened, the pumpkin shade of his eyes now visible. He stammered and pointed, watching the gaping wound on Djain's arm seal itself, healing over in seconds. "But how?"

Djain fixed the man with an icy stare. "You did not listen, and now you will never know."

The main swung at Djain again, but this time Djain caught his arm in an iron grip.

Looking down at him, Djain reached out, calling the air in the man's chest.

The man choked and gasped. Pawing at his throat with his free hand, he uncovered a shining metal emblem that had been hiding beneath his cloak.

Djain stopped, and the man gulped in the air. "I can make it quick if you prefer." His eyes landed on the mark of the Order dangling from the man's neck. "I offer this kindness, though none who do the Order's bidding deserve mercy."

"Go to hell, you half-breed bastard," the man sneered at him.

Djain's eyes narrowed. "Such vitriol and bigotry from one with your heritage." He curled a finger in front of the man's face. "I told you I was a child of the air. You will no longer find it your ally."

The sound of breaking glass echoed in the chamber. Talaunia's palm was under her attacker's jaw, and his mouth had been driven closed around a glass vial. Blood ran from the corner of his lips, and the manic, happy glee he was experiencing vanished in a wave of terror. He dropped Talaunia and fell to the floor, rolling onto his back, gurgling and gagging on the foam erupting from his mouth.

Talaunia planted her boot in his ribs and stood over him, spitting in his face. "I'm no man's plaything!"

Gadyen seized the snake's head, one hand wrapping around the upper jaw and one around the lower. With a fierce yell, he pulled and split the snake's skull in half. The body fell limp around Ryan, and Gadyen peeled away the dead weight.

The man before Djain fell to his knees, eyes enlarging, bulging as he struggled for air. Red specks appeared in the man's eyes from the strain of suffocation. Djain wiggled his finger before the man again. "Go. Find peace."

Air rushed in, and the man's chest swelled. The rending of bone could be heard, and crimson spots soaked through the man's garment where the pressure building in the confines of the chest had forced shards of ribs through the skin. Two wet, muffled pops sounded, and the man's chest fell, the excess volume of air rushing down into his abdomen when the pressure equalized.

Shoving the man over, Djain bent and tore open his tunic. Pushing down on the surrounding flesh, he broke off a piece of the protruding rib. After rummaging through the man's robes, he located the pendant bearing the Order's seal, and yanked it from the corpse. He handed the bloody mess to Talaunia. "Keep these safe. We will use them later to learn more about the Order."

Talaunia stared at the slick, warm bone in her hand and the cold metal medallion.

Djain was already moving past her toward Gadyen and Ryan. "How is he?"

Ryan tried to wave them off. "I'm fucking fine. Leave me alone."

Gadyen shook his head. "Of things that might happen, that is not among them." Turning his gaze up to Djain. "Ribs and an arm. I heard them snap."

Talaunia moved to his side, invoking a pain amulet.

Djain shifted so he could see Talaunia and Gadyen. "Get the portal up and get him back home." He stared into the circle, continuing to issue directives. "Have Sean and Rhoin come. Send the stretchers. Be quick!" He looked at Talaunia. "Dispatch another team to gather up the guard you left on the hill. We will want to speak with him."

Talaunia paused, "Papa." Her brows rose over her troubled eyes, and she tipped her head toward Axylia.

Djain followed her gaze. "Yes, notify the Traxidors, but for the sake of all, use a messenger. We do not need your conflict injected into this moment."

Talaunia sounded almost meek. "Of course." Turning, she set about helping Gadyen with their assigned duties.

Panji and Jacia came bounding back into the room, heads high. Each held part of the snake dangling from its maw, blood and entrails hanging out the severed parts as they dropped them before Djain, who smiled and purred his approval.

< ᛏᛟᚾ ᚠᚱᛗ ᛒᛗᚠᚾ ᛏᛁᚠᚾᛁ >

Sean's foot was tapping in anxious rapidity when the portal flared to life. Like Sean's foot, the entire room came to a hushed standstill, and all eyes faced the shimmering air within the arch.

Gadyen was the first through, his clothing and hands stained and smeared with blood. He glanced at Sean and the two stretchers on his way past, moving toward the center of the room. "Someone summon Rhoin! He is needed in the field. And find more stretchers!"

Sean's heart skipped a beat at Gadyen's call for more beds, his worry spurring him to push forward with the gurney. Talaunia's return prevented him from making it to the portal. Hope flared in his heart when he saw her, until her expression registered, knocking him off-balance.

Talaunia moved to Sean, placing a hand over his. "They need you. You must hurry, but I have to warn you, it isn't good. When you get there, don't use any pain amulets. They are too far gone." Her eyes locked with his, and she could see the question swimming in his mind. He stared at her, and it raked at her heart to be the one to tell him. "Axylia is beyond hope. Go. Help the others and give her some comfort."

She shifted, placing her hand behind Sean, shoving until he snapped out of his shock, and pushed the bed toward the portal at a run.

ᚲ ᚼᛟᚾᚱ ᛒᛟᛥᚼ ᛁᛥ ᚲᛗᚱᚠᛗᚲᛏ ᚱ

Djain was beside Ryan when Sean appeared, and he took the bed as Sean spun, surveying the carnage in the room.

Spotting Axylia on the raised platform, he ran headlong into the protective bubble around them and fell back a step. "Axylia, it's me. You need to let the circle go. The threat's gone."

The girl in Axylia's lap stirred, speaking, but Sean couldn't make out the words. Djain appeared at his side, encouraging the ladies. "Yes, Becca. Keep going. Papa is with you now."

The candles marking the circle's perimeter were spent. Sean sensed the barrier collapse as one after another the flames guttered. Columns of white smoke rose from the blackened wicks.

Together, he and Djain rushed the platform.

Djain knelt beside a still form, checking on the man's condition. "Conner, we are here."

Sean crossed to Axylia, and the girl he assumed was Becca.

Djain was dour, moving from Conner and shaking his head.

Sean recalled Talaunia's admonition and pulled out a pair of cleansing charms. Finding a lance, he pricked his finger and activated them both.

Djain snapped his fingers and held out an arm toward Sean. "I require one of those for Jamie."

Sean handed one to Djain and tried to drop the other over Axylia.

She rolled her head away and whispered. "Becca first."

Displeased, Sean followed orders, slipping the charm around Becca's brunette hair and letting it dangle over her chest.

He couldn't tell if it was doing anything for her, but Axylia seemed to know. She tried to move Becca out of her lap, and Sean helped, easing the girl onto the floor.

Another team with a stretcher arrived, and Djain signaled them over to Jaime, helping to load the limp man onto the bed.

Sean sat behind Axylia, and she leaned back against his chest. "Tell me how to help you," he said in a pleading whisper.

"You can't," she responded, her voice weak. Relaxing back into him, she folded her arms over his. "Need living . . ." Her head lolled forward, her body going slack.

Djain was frowning, watching the exchange transpire, and he barked at the stretcher team as they headed for the portal. "Tell them to move with haste—and bring plants!" He turned his attention to Becca, crossing and preparing her for the move.

Sean placed his lips against Axylia's ear, talking low and urgent. "I'm living. Please, draw from me."

Djain stopped what he was doing, fixing his attention on Sean. He spoke a stern warning as gently as he dared deliver it. "You do not know what you are offering, what you are asking of her. She cannot."

Sean glowered at Djain. "I can heal as well as her. If it helps, she should lean on me, physically and for the energy she needs." He pursed his lips. "I can feel her slipping. I can't understand it, but I know it."

Djain lowered his head, a somber tone in his voice. "I see it too. It is Nature, and Nature is cruel."

Axylia jerked, her body tensed, and she shook her head.

Sean's arms stiffened, pulling her against his chest. "We have a date tomorrow. You better not miss it."

His eyes swept the room, thoughts colliding, feeding the torment growing within. Rage swelled at being forced to remain behind. He was angry at himself for the time wasted on shopping instead of training and furious that he wasn't prepared to help those lying around him. Feeling Axylia tremble in his arms, an icy resolve solidified the storm within. He would not be left behind again, wouldn't fail his team when they needed him.

With effort, she lifted her chin and sought his eyes

Sean's jaw tightened when he saw the bright green of her irises had faded to a dull, black moss shade.

Axylia forced a smile.

"Please," he begged her. "Use me." He lifted her hand and placed it on his cheek.

Djain glared daggers at him for pressing the situation. He drew in a breath to lash out, but the next stretcher arrived, loaded down with potted plants, saving Sean the brusque tongue lashing. Djain and the attendants moved with urgency, placing the ferns and grasses around Axylia. With a glance, Djain urged Sean to help her.

Pulling her hand from his cheek, Sean moved it to a plant and wrapped her fingers around it. "Here. Plants. Just for you."

The others moved Becca onto the stretcher and headed toward the portal as all the plants around Axylia browned, withered, and became blackened husks in seconds.

Their sacrifice gave her enough strength to seek Djain and make a request. "Take him. He need not see this."

Rhoin approached in somber silence. The room's atmosphere kept him from speaking as he stopped beside Djain.

Sean shook his head. "I'm not going anywhere without you. They will be back with the stretcher in a moment. We can take you to the gardens, where there are plenty of plants."

Djain shook his head. "The Mother cannot heal her now. She gave too much of herself away, and the Mother does not have the strength of magic to intervene."

She squeezed his arm. "He's right. If I try to heal now, I risk endangering the entire region. It would destroy so many lives."

"But the gardens—" he protested.

"Would be no less devastated," Djain said.

Sean blinked away the tears threatening to form. "There has to be something we can do."

Another stretcher arrived, and they gathered Connor's still form.

Djain stepped over to the pedestal, and Rhoin followed, staring at the stone tower and the mask which had brought them all there.

Djain studied Sean with an apologetic gaze. "Sean, we need your expertise." His eyes shifted between Sean and Axylia. "I know you do not wish to leave her side, but this is why you are here."

Sean refused to move, his concerned gaze never leaving Axylia. "I would think that could wait."

Shaking her head, Axylia responded. "The mask is ready for retrieval. Becca dissolved the binding to the guardian before casting the circle. Jaime studied the pedestal and tried to dismantle the traps." Her breathing slowed, and she swallowed hard, forcing herself to continue. "He triggered it, and a plume of poison sprayed the others."

Djain motioned for Sean to remain. "It seems we subjected you to this for no reason. You have my apologies." He spoke in compassionate tones to Axylia. "Thank you for letting us know."

"I'll place it in your private study," Rhoin said in a solemn tone. Lifting the mask from the stand, he turned and gave Axylia a low, lingering bow before clearing his throat and making his way back to the portal.

Once Rhoin departed, Djain pierced Sean with his gaze. "Say your farewells and come home. We need to close this portal."

Djain gave a deep, respectful bow to Axylia. "It was a privilege to know you."

"And you," she whispered.

Djain walked with somber resolve, stepping through the portal without glancing back.

That other world seemed far away to Sean, so foreign, so unknown as he gazed down on Axylia. "We are only getting to know one another, and now we must say goodbye?"

"All things have their limits, their times. I've had millennia." She gave him a soft, pained smile. "Saved the best for last. I'm glad they let you come."

He brushed a finger through her hair. "I have amulets if you—"

She placed a finger over his lips and mouthed, "No." She played with the stubble along his cheek. A faint light flickered in her eyes, fading far too quickly. Her fingers slid past his ear and sank into his hair. She cupped the back of his head, and using what little strength remained, drew him closer. Her lips brushed his. "Go now. Please."

Every fiber in him demanded he stay and keep her wrapped in the shelter of his arms, but he released her and summoned the strength to rise. Lingering at the edge of the platform, he gazed at her for the last time. Eyes misting and jaw taut, he struggled. A storm of emotion churned inside, birthed by all the changes thrust upon him, and loosed by her loss. Through force of will, he pulled his eyes away and moved down the stairs.

Two new figures stepped through the portal, entering the underwater temple. A male and female elf, each tall and regal in appearance. Sean felt them evaluating him as they met.

The male turned away, moving toward Axylia.

The female paused, her gaze matching the cold and demanding tone of her voice. "Leave us. She should be in the company of her kind."

Sean's teeth ground and he stared daggers at the pair before stepping back into the Operations Center. The hum of the electronics grated on him. Despite the surrounding chaos, he faced the hazy image in the portal.

Talaunia came to his side, slipped an arm around his waist, and spoke in hushed tones. "It's good that she will not be alone. Theran and Pretaris will help her transition." Lifting a hand, she closed the portal.

His left arm slipped around Talaunia, and he held her tight to his side. His right hand rubbed over the bare wall behind the arch. Jaw rippling with tension, chin quivering, he couldn't hold back the torrent of emotion any longer, and the tears broke free, leaving glistening trails down his cheeks.

Today the throne passed to Varunia, and abdication has lifted a great weight. Acting as Queen was an honor, bound to a heavy burden. The Mother, as well as our identities, are ever-changing. May Varunia be graced with wisdom and strength to lead us through the next era.

—Councilor Kryntan

Fifteen

Vile business, indeed.

Sean sat staring over the gardens, unfocused and numb. The sun struggled to announce its arrival. Heavy clouds resisted the light, casting the world into gray tones, perfectly in tune with his mood. A cup of coffee sat untouched on the corner of his desk, lacking all heat and appeal.

The blood-covered medallion Djain had taken in the battle rested in his palm. He absently traced the edge of the flame-shrouded cross with his thumb, contemplating what would dive men to such fanaticism. How could anyone cling to such a closed view of the world, where encounters between those holding different beliefs were measured in blood and lives. He thought of other symbols of hate, icons spanning history, often the sacred images of religious zealots trying to convert the world through force.

A soft knock sounded, and Sean turned in his chair.

Talaunia lingered in the open doorway. "We're about to start, if you want to join us."

Tossing the medallion onto the desk, he bolted from the chair. "Och, you couldn't keep me away."

The medallion rolled, plinking as it came to rest against the crystal pyramid.

Rage etched deep gouges across his face, and his eyes blazed in pained fury. "I should have been there!"

He was transfixed on the medallion leaning against the smooth crystal. His lips twitched, curling into a snarl. Seizing the metal disc, he hurled it across the room. The wood inside the empty bookcase splintered, and the hated symbol bounced out, coming to rest in the middle of the floor.

"Better?"

"Not particularly." He lifted his eyes to hers. "Why did I waste all that time? I should have been training!"

She remained silent, watching him, knowing the question wasn't meant to be answered.

He adjusted the pyramid, fingers lingering on the memento, until his desire to find answers moved him around the desk. Crossing toward Talaunia, he trampled the medallion. "Where are we doing this?"

"Training rooms. We are going to put up a circle."

"Sounds prudent, all things considered." He paused, finally seeing Talaunia, taking in her state. Her eyes were red and puffy, and it was clear she had been crying.

"She was already lost before we were called," she said. "Nothing you, or I, could have done would have saved her." She moved closer to him, and he tensed, looking at her from the corner of his eye. "I know better than to push things right now. I'm here if you need a friend—I may need one too." The pain of her loss honed her words like a razor's edge. "You aren't the only one that lost her." Her eyes fell to the floor, and she tucked her hands behind her back, wrestling with her own emotions. "Anyway," she whispered, "I'm here."

Shame flooded through him, stinging his eyes. His voice was almost swallowed in the raspy exhale. "I know . . . thank you." He chewed on his thoughts until they tumbled free. "You know, it's not just about her."

Her eyes found his, "I know . . ."

He stepped to her side and offered her his elbow.

She stared at him, eyes brimming with pain, and he knew he had added fresh wounds to her loss. She released her breath and slipped her fingers around his arm. "We should go. We're already late."

They made the trip to the training room in silence. Inside, the friends of the fallen had assembled, a mass of anxious bodies, eager to witness the interrogation. The place was drowning in a foul, mournful mood, and Sean's attitude matched it perfectly.

The guard Talaunia had captured in the morning's encounter sat at the center of the chamber. He was bound with cord and silver chain to a steel-framed chair. Two more sleep amulets hung from his neck, one layered atop the other, keeping the man comatose. A pair of large, black duffles lay on the floor at his side, their contents sealed away beneath heavy flaps.

Djain had already cast the circle, and the Guardians Sean remembered so well stood somber witness. Djain stood within the protective dome, all business. His slacks were crisply pressed, sleeves rolled up, with his shirt hanging open at the collar, prepared for the labor ahead.

Gadyen stood at Djain's shoulder, clothed in a slate-colored angarkha.

Noting Sean and Talaunia's arrival, Djain tipped his head. "Your timing is perfect."

Ryan nudged through the crowd, shouldering up next to Sean. He was shirtless, and his chest was wrapped in bandages. His left arm was bound against him and cradled in a sling.

"What did they say?" Sean asked, eyeing Ryan's wounds.

"I'm fuckin' benched for the next week."

Gadyen seized the sleep amulets, ripped them from the captive's neck, and tossed them to the floor.

"A week isn't bad. Humans take six," Sean offered in half-hearted encouragement.

Ryan's eyes cut toward Sean. "I don't give a fuck! I want to be out there hunting these bastards, not stuck here wanking with the wrong god damned hand!"

The room was now focused on Ryan, and he noticed. "Any volunteers to help me out?"

Sean shook his head.

Talaunia leaned forward. "Ryan. Shut up. You can bitch and moan later, but we have things to learn if you want to avenge Axylia, Conner, and Jaime."

Sean's focus snapped to Talaunia. "Jaime, I thought we got him out in time."

She shook her head. "He tried to hang on, but it took us too long to get there. No one could have saved them all—" Talaunia swallowed. "I wish she wouldn't have tried."

Inside the circle, the man jerked awake, letting out a horrid cry when he discovered his bonds. He thrashed and struggled against the chains, desperate to find a way free.

Gadyen swung, and the back of his hand connected with the man's jaw.

The crack of the blow was sharp, and the man's head snapped to the side and wobbled. Lifting his chin, the man glared at Gadyen through a dazed expression.

"This is not a dream," Gadyen said. "You are not caught in a night terror."

The man's eyes cut around the room, his neck twisting this way and that.

"You are a prisoner. Taken this morning from the banks of Galikere."

The man settled, staring daggers at Gadyen.

"You are all that remains. Others tried to thwart us, but we returned their souls to the netherworld. Now, ask yourself, will you comply and make your final moments pleasant, or will you force me to be persuasive? You set the tone for our discussion. Let us begin with something easy. Tell me your name."

Ryan struck the protective bubble. "Fuck being nice. Bleed his ass already!"

Djain fixed Ryan with a warning glare.

Ryan's chin dropped, and he backpedaled, reclaiming his place beside Talaunia and Sean.

The prisoner's focus shifted from Ryan to Gadyen. Realization of his inquisitors' race rushed over him, changing his demeanor from feigned nonchalance into outright fear. "Oh shit, oh fuck no. No way." The man's bigoted views bubbled up, curling the fear on his face into revulsion. "Demon!" Driven by the terror in his chest, the man thrashed against the chains.

Gadyen raised his hand to strike another blow.

Flinching from the threat, the man stilled.

"You leave me little choice. I require your name."

The man bowed his head, closed his eyes, and said a quick prayer. Glowering at Gadyen, he hissed an incantation.

Gadyen drew back his hand again, but Djain touched his shoulder. "Let the man finish."

Puzzled, Gadyen lowered his hand and stepped back.

The man completed his spell, becoming distraught when nothing happened.

Understanding came to Gadyen, and he spoke to the man in a calm, even voice. "We've encased you in a protective circle. You cannot invoke external magics here."

The man cursed and tried his spell with more zeal, getting the same empty results.

"Truth. It is all you will hear in this space. Do not doubt me." Gadyen stepped closer. "Now, you try my patience. Give me your name."

The captive spat at Gadyen, then sighed in defeat. Resignation settled on him, leaving him looking haggard and worn. His nose twitched in anger, and in a last effort of defiance, he spat out two words.

Everyone looked at one another, trying to sort out the language.

The man's head rolled back, eyes turning up into this head, his whole body convulsing under the effects of a frothy seizure. Seconds later, he fell still.

Djain smiled.

The room filled with angry shouts. Those gathered expressing dismay at being cheated out of the answers they sought.

Djain called Gadyen to him and pointed at the man's body, giving him quiet instruction as the room's commotion continued.

The circle sparked near the top, energy pulsing along the arc, and the room stilled. Confused chatter swept through the crowd as they tried to figure out what was happening.

Djain lifted his hands to calm everyone. "The situation is well in hand. If you are squeamish about death or gore, consider turning away or leaving."

Again, the circle pulsed with power, this time near the earthen candle, and the visage of the Guardian solidified momentarily.

Gadyen crossed to the corpse and unbound the right arm. He tore the cloth away from the shoulder, grabbed the arm by the wrist, and yanked. A wet, sickening pop sounded as the upper arm tore free of its socket. He pulled a knife from his belt and sliced into the limp arm, encircling it below the shoulder. Wiping the blade on the man's hair, he tucked the knife away and ripped the arm from the body.

Gasps rose at the savage act, blood slinging from the end of the arm, painting an arc across the floor and splattering along the magical barrier.

Twice more, the ghostly form tried to escape the circle, and each time remained trapped in the mystical cage.

Djain spoke again, attempting to calm the onlookers. "The circle is not only for keeping things out but for keeping them in as well!"

Gadyen continued dismembering the arm, tearing it apart at the elbow, and laying the forearm and hand across the corpse's lap. Grabbing the humerus in one hand and using the other, he peeled the flesh from the bone. It sloughed onto the floor with a sickening, wet sound.

Several people raced for the door, hands clamped over their mouths, while others dry heaved.

Gadyen turned the bone, inspecting his prize with pleasure.

Djain moved the canvas duffles, creating space to kneel between the body and his tools. Loosening the strap, he peeled the closure back, pulling items from the bag and placing them within easy reach. A set of three black candles, a long silver spike reminding Sean of an awl, a sealed glass jar filled with blackened earth, a silver knife, and an iron chain were all placed on the floor.

Looking around the room, Djain gave another warning. "The magic I am about to invoke is dark. I do not use it lightly. If you do not wish to witness such grim work, leave now."

A couple of those still struggling with their queasy stomachs welcomed the opportunity to slip out. Others shifted, uncomfortable, but were unwilling to turn away.

Reaching up, Djain plunged his hand into the open flesh at the corpse's shoulder. Taking hold of the exposed deltoid muscle, he squeezed and pulled until he had torn part of it free.

A smattering of groans sounded from the observers. A handful hid their eyes, several choked on their stomach contents at the gruesome sight.

Blood ran down Djain's hand, dripping from the chunk of flesh. Using the hunk of meat as a pen, he scrawled symbols across the floor in the man's blood. Once satisfied, he tossed the misshapen chunk of flesh into the sodden pile of loose skin and muscle Gadyen had peeled from the upper arm.

Next, he placed the black candles one by one, creating a triangle around the markings on the floor, the tip of the triangle positioned across from him. He reached for the jar, opened it, and took a handful of the black soil, sprinkling it over the bloody symbols between the candles.

Taking the blood-smeared arm bone from Gadyen, Djain picked up the awl, scratching symbols along its length. As he worked, he explained. "This man thinks he has bested us, escaped our questions by freeing his spirit from his body." Djain motioned around overhead. "But he is trapped by the Guardians that protect us." He wiggled the bone. "And he left behind things that are already accustomed to housing his spirit."

He continued to etch shapes along the bone, and the spirit's attempts at breaking free of the circle became frantic, causing the whole of the shell to shimmer and spark as it bounced from one point to another. "So now we will use what he left behind to draw him right back into a waiting vessel, and for good measure, we will bind him to our service."

Setting the awl aside, Djain took another handful of the black earth and rubbed it over the bone. It mixed with the lingering blood and pressed down into the etched symbols, making them stand out against the bone's pallor. Placing the bone in the middle of the triangle, he turned, checking that all present were maintaining control. "Please be still and quiet; this is not something I wish to make a mess of."

Lowering his head, he closed his eyes and took a series of deep, slow breaths. Moving his left hand, he brought the candle on his left to life. His right hand moved, and the candle to his right took flame. Opening his eyes, he focused on the far candle until it too smoldered and gave birth to a fiery tongue.

His resonant voice filled the room, delivering the incantation with absolute surety. "By your blood and to your bone, thy spirit, now be bound. Evermore to mind my will, else your essence come unwound." He repeated the phrase a second time, reaching for the knife. With the third recitation, he drew the knife across the fatty part of his palm, driving the blade deep. Purple smoke billowed around the wound, spiriting away the blood that dripped toward the floor. Holding his hand over the bone, he forced a few drops of his blood to connect as he finished the chant.

Before his voice faded from the room, the assault on the circle ceased. Djain placed the clean knife back in the bag and pulled out a small cloth bandage, wrapping it about his hand. "You will show yourself now," he commanded while rising to his feet.

The image of the man in the chair hovered in the air between the candles, his translucent visage glaring daggers at Djain. "Answer this, spirit. Who is it you serve?"

"You," the single word spat from the man's mouth with utter distaste, the voice cold and distant.

"And what is your name?"

The spirit squirmed and tried to resist, but the rules it was now bound by forced it to comply, so it answered. "Spirit."

Djain's eyes narrowed, and he bent, plucking the iron chain from the floor. He draped it in loose coils around the bone, and the spirit stilled, snarling as he watched. "I am not playing, nor will you. What is your full name? The one given to you by your parents while you occupied that body." Djain pointed at the limp corpse with the bone.

The spirit's head snapped to face the body with the gesture, and the ghostly form struggled against the invisible chains by which it was bound.

Djain gave the iron chain a sharp tug, tightening it around the bone, and the figure's legs and arms snapped to its sides.

After a prolonged silence, the spirit's face pinched, and he spoke. "Victor Nikolaevich Ivanov."

Letting the chain fall slack, Djain allowed Victor to move inside the summoning circle unrestrained. "We are getting along well now, Victor."

Victor spat at him again. "Half-breed!"

"Careful, don't forget who holds your chain."

Victor snarled.

Gadyen addressed the spirit. "Why did you seek the mask in the shrine?"

"I don't have to answer you, demon!"

"Demon, am I? Perhaps I should sample the bouquet of bigot." Gadyen dipped a finger in the corpse and licked the blood from his finger. "Not an exceptional year. To rank for my palate, though, I may make an exception. Take your corpse to a crypt and lay with it, desecrate you thoroughly."

Victor darted at Gadyen, slamming against the walls of his prison. Hatred contorted his face as he watched the vampire caress the chest of his corpse. "Stay away from my body, you foul fuck!" Victor's fist bounced off the invisible walls, sending ethereal light rippling around his cage.

"You wish me to leave your tepid, malodorous flesh alone. All you need do is comply. I believe a question still lingers, unaddressed."

Djain rattled the iron chain, and Victor threw himself against the barrier again.

"We were told you mutts were after it and to stop you," Victor hissed. "Like we needed to be told to keep it out of your filthy hands."

Hours passed, and little by little, the room emptied, leaving only a handful of onlookers to keep vigil with Talaunia, Ryan, 'and Sean. It became apparent within the first minutes that Victor was little more than a foot soldier, having no information on the inner workings of The Order. Still, Djain and Gadyen continued to press him, bend his spirit, wringing every facet of information he held from beneath his racially bent rants.

They confirmed the Order operated in regional cells and uncovered that each unit was assigned a medium. Communications and orders all came through the spirit realm. Recovered artifacts were packaged and sent via armed transport to Athens, Greece, though Victor couldn't give an address, even when his binding bone had been placed into Angelic Fire.

Regarding Victor in silence, Djain and Gadyen shared a glance. "I think we have learned all we can for now. Victor Nikolaevich Ivanov, you will take yourself from my sight, and we will not see you unless I call."

The spirit vaporized, and Djain wrapped the iron chain around the bone before tucking it into the canvas bag. After thanking each of the guardians standing watch, he released the circle, and the hum of power in the room dissolved, leaving it with an empty feeling.

Djain grabbed the medallion from Victor's corpse and tossed it at Sean. "Another for you to use as a focus."

Sean grabbed for it and missed.

Talaunia's lightning-quick reflexes snagged the necklace from the air before it collided with his face.

"Thank you," he said, taking the object and slipping it into a pocket.

She slipped her hand around his arm, and though he tensed, he did not pull away. "Let's get you out of here."

Djain indicated his agreement. "It has been a trying day. Go home and rest."

Sean did not have it in him to argue the point, so he lifted a hand in a half-hearted, parting wave and let Talaunia lead him from the room. She turned him toward the empty portal arches lining the back wall, and he shook his head. "I've still not been shown how to set an anchor point at the cottage, so I'll have to hire a car again."

"I'll call a car for us." She said, her eyes fixed on his reactions. He faced her, his gaze distant, and she saw no resistance in him. "I will come and show you how to set up an anchor."

He squeezed her arm to his side in quiet thanks. "I want to get my computer and a few things from my office before we leave."

Talaunia motioned ahead. "Then let's get to it."

Reaching his office, he picked up the medallion from the middle of the floor and placed it and the one taken from Victor into his satchel. There was a small stack of books left on his desk by Jason, which he collected along with the crystal pyramid.

He lifted the bag to find Talaunia leaning against the desk, watching him with a hawkish interest. "You pick that up for sentimental reasons, or are you planning a trip?"

Sean shrugged. "Perhaps a bit of both. Time will tell."

She sighed, retaking his arm. "You realize this means I am staying with you tonight?"

The tension rolled back into his body, and he pulled away. "All I need is the anchor point."

Her lips pressed into a straight line. "The crystal stays here, or I stay with you. Those are the only options you have. You are not to project without someone with you, and I'll be damned if you are doing it alone in your current state. I've already lost too much today." She turned and blocked his path, hands going to her hips. "Choose."

His hand covered the top of the satchel protectively. "There is a second bedroom in the cottage; you can stay there if you must."

With a curt nod, she stepped back to his side and looped his arm again, this time not letting him pull away. "Let's get you home then."

Today I inherit a throne that I am not eager to occupy. Nevertheless, it falls to me, and I must discover ways to ease the growing rift among our people. The Bright Ones are glowing beacons of beauty, and many have walked beside them in the Heavenly Gardens, becoming bewitched. Kryntan and Syrdan encourage this behavior, and rumors of gluttonous gatherings bursting with unrestrained primal passions grow in number. Meanwhile, the tiniest organisms birthed by the Mother flourish in Her depths, changing the taste and feel of the air above the waters they inhabit. Our focus should be upon their needs, not the yearnings the Angelic Host stirs in our loins. If some measure of compromise evades us, I fear for what the future may hold.

—Queen Varunia

SIXTEEN

A BIT OF SOLACE FROM AN UNEXPECTED PLACE.

Before Talaunia and Sean reached the lift, a blur of wings and color shot out, making several frenzied laps around Sean's head. When the whirlwind of color stopped, Frost was hovering before Sean's nose with his chest puffed out and an arrogant glint in his eyes. Looking down his nose at Sean, his shoulders drew back, and he snapped his command. "You have been summoned. Follow me."

Sean remained where he was and shared a puzzled look with Talaunia as the pair watched the pixie flutter back toward the lift.

The doors slid open, and Frost drifted in.

Talaunia and Sean eyed him quizzically.

The doors hissed and started closing.

Frost darted back out of the lift, narrowly avoiding getting his foot caught in the metal panels. "Fairy farts!" Hovering before Sean, Frost poked him in the nose several times. "I. Told. You. To. Follow. Me."

Talaunia laughed, despite the dour mood hanging over the group.

Wrinkling up his nose and twitching it around, Sean shook his head. "Why?"

Frost scanned him as though he were touched, and motioned toward Sean's hair. "I think that fiery hair of yours is melting whatever brain you have. I already told you because you have been summoned!"

With a heavy sigh and in no mood to play games, Sean snapped. "By whom?"

"Oh," Frost said, wings buzzing faster. "Didn't I say?"

"No, Frost, you didn't," Talaunia said.

Frost ignored her. "The Traxidor's wish to speak with"—he jabbed Sean's nose, casting a sidelong glance at Talaunia—"you."

Talaunia radiated energy, and anxious tension shot through her, tendrils of it spiking into Sean's arm, causing him to turn and look at her. "Of course, we'll be right there," she said.

Visions of the regal elves that dismissed him after being ordered away from Axylia's side drew his lips into a tight line. "Aye. Lead the way."

Frost glared at Talaunia before snapping his focus back to Sean and stammering in frustration. "But—but The summons was for you alone!"

Talaunia stamped her foot. "Listen here, you little gnat. No matter how much you want to dress up and play the part of a fairy, you're still second class, just like me. Now shut those paper-thin lips of yours and lead the way."

The speed of Frost's wings rose to a high-pitched squeal, and red sparks sputtered and fell from him. He stared at Talaunia with unmasked anger.

Sean blew a puff of air at Frost to pull his attention back from Talaunia. "If they want me, they get her, too."

When he stopped tumbling in the air, Frost's furious gaze focused on Sean.

"You can lead us both, or you can go back and report your failure," Sean said. "You choose."

Frost screeched in frustration, beat his wings in the air with vigor, and punctuated his tirade with a shower of multi-colored dust. "Let's go!"

Talaunia and Sean shared a look, then a laugh, while waiting for the lift to return.

Frost cursed and pounded his tiny fist on the lift doors, creating a small pile of pixie dust on the floor below. When the soft baritone chime sounded, he barked, "Finally!" Zipping into the car as the doors opened, he hollered. "Keep up!"

After exiting the lift on the thirty-fifth floor, Talaunia and Sean were in no rush. Exhausted by recent events, they strolled through the gardens, letting the restorative properties rejuvenate their energy.

Frost returned for them several times, leaving trails of brightly colored dust in his wake each time they failed to match his blistering pace.

"Play the part of a fairy?" Sean asked as they passed beneath another of the garden arches.

"Yup. The fairies are the size of humans, have thicker, feathery wings, and the elite among them act as a protective guard for the Elven queen and her closest advisors." Talaunia's lips pursed in thought. "You know, the Traxidors should have a team of guards assigned to them. We should have been summoned by one of them." She glanced at Sean, and he could see the apprehension in her eyes.

Directing his gaze toward Frost, Sean shrugged. "Perhaps the little guy got a promotion after all."

Talaunia laughed. "Pixies are too scatterbrained to be trusted with such work. If the Traxidors sent him, it means they have their guard on another matter, and that makes me nervous."

"Why does it make you nervous?" Sean asked.

Frost zipped back to hover before them both. "Why is not your concern. We have arrived. You will wait right here. After I have announced you, you may enter. Be respectful." Frost moved to the archway, struggling to get his anger in check. The colors of the dust that rained from him shifted from red to orange, almost reaching a goldenrod shade before he moved through the arch.

Sean moved to follow, but Talaunia held him back. "You should wait. They can get pissy when their courtly rituals are ignored, and they are going to be angry enough that you brought me along."

Heading her advice, he stayed by her side. "Is there a history here I should know?"

A scowl formed on Talaunia's lips, and she sighed.

Before she got the chance to answer, Frost's excited voice called from inside the hedge. "Mr. Sean Byrne—and—" The voice hesitated before continuing in agitation. "And the exiled, Talaunia Daejor."

"Here we go!" She tugged on Sean's arm gently, and together, they entered.

This section of the Elven pocket dimension differed from any other Sean had seen. To the left and right, pillows formed quarter circles along the hedge wall. Several elves were lounging in the grass and leaning back upon the cushions, lost in conversation among their various groups. Over their heads, branches had sprouted from the hedge at varying intervals, where delicate fabrics in an assortment of bright colors lay draped across the boughs.

Across the way sat another covered area, but the pillows there rested on large mushroom tops that sprouted from the trunk of the most massive tree Sean had ever seen. The tree had to be eighty feet across, and its canopy rose far above and covered the entire area. Brilliant flowers with luminescent shades that spanned the spectrum adorned the hedges and grounds around the Traxidors, who were seated atop the mushroom stools. Pixies fluttered about tending the flowers while Frost hovered near the couple, his haughty stance and ill-colored dust declaring his mood.

Talaunia picked up speed, almost dragging Sean across the open center of the area.

At her approach, the Traxidors rose.

Pretaris stepped forward. "You have no place here! Go, seek a home among our dark brethren!"

Letting loose of Sean's arm, Talaunia tore across the remaining distance to stand nose to nose with the female.

Sean's brows rose as people around the room moved from their lounging positions, standing, their anxious murmurs filling the space.

The pixies stopped flitting about, and all eyes focused on the two ladies.

"I do not belong among the dark! Nor does my father or the rest of my family!" Sean had never seen Talaunia so riled. Her fists clenched into tight little balls, the tips of her ears turned bright red, and she was practically vibrating.

Pretaris was the perfect picture of icy composure.

"You cannot even contain yourself long enough to bring a proper petition, and you expect what? That we will rescind the banishment of your line based upon your remarkable display of decorum?" Pretaris lifted a single, thin, questioning brow.

Talaunia stamped her feet and screamed in the lady's face. "If you were in my shoes, you'd be infuriated too. My family was banished because my father saved your brother." She pointed at the regal male, standing by Pretaris's shoulder. "And your lover! I just watched a friend die because of your damned rules!" A disarming calm settled over her, and she continued in icy tones to rival her opponents. "It is heartening to know the future of our race lay in the hands of one so cold. One who would rather watch a family suffer loss than consider there may be times rules can be justifiably broken."

"Your exile shall remain another three millennia should you disrupt our court again." Pretaris moved her eyes from Talaunia to Sean, and her gaze softened. Shoulder checking Talaunia, she stepped past her to greet Sean. "We will not hold this outburst against you, as you are still learning of our ways. Helping you understand is why we have asked you to come. Please dismiss your dreadful companion and sit with us."

Sean gave Talaunia a pleading look, and she exhaled in a huff. "Fine, but I'm going to be right outside, waiting!" Crossing to the arched hedge, she took one step beyond and turned, planting her hands on her hips right before the door and taunted Pretaris with a smile.

Pretaris lifted her gaze to the plants, and the archway shook, knitting itself together across the opening, making it appear as though it never existed.

From beyond the wall, Talaunia screamed in frustration.

Even while wrestling with the strain of facing those who had dismissed him, he had to resist smiling.

Unlike the sharp glances they had exchanged in the sunken temple, the elves welcomed Sean with comforting smiles.

"I am Pretaris Traxidor, and this is my mate, Theran. Come, sit and let us share with you some of our ways, and perhaps give you some comfort."

Agreeing, Sean moved with her back under the cloth shades, where Pretaris and Theran took their places on the mushroom stools. They watched Sean, leaving him to decide whether to stand or take a seat on the ground before them; he opted for the former. Shifting from foot to foot, he worked to contain his agitation. Looking around, he noted that the everyday bustle had returned among the pixies, and the other elves were no longer paying them any mind, lost in their relaxation.

Theran spoke, often swallowing to soothe and clear his throat, his voice harsh and gravelly. "First, we hope to offer you comfort. Know we saw her home, and she rests among her ancestors."

Sean's jaw tightened. "Thank you. I'm glad she wasn't alone, even if—"

Pretaris saw Sean's pain as he struggled to find the best way to express himself, and stepped in, her voice brimming with compassion. "Though you still wish you had remained with her."

Sean inclined his head again.

"You must understand, there are times and places for things, and not all things exist in the realm of your understanding," she chided.

Though her words made Sean feel like a child being reprimanded, they were spoken tenderly.

Coughing, Theran placed a hand on Pretaris's forearm. "We have been told you asked her to draw life from you to sustain herself."

Speaking of Axylia caused a knot of emotion to form in Sean's throat, and he swallowed it before replying to Theran. "Aye, I did. And still wish she had."

Pretaris shook her head in slow arcs. "Understand. Rending life from one with a soul is forbidden. Those who dare cross that line are banished from our society and their entire line with them. Our dark brothers took such actions, and they were naught but a blight upon the Mother." She paused, taking a long moment to study Sean before continuing. "Had she done this, the act itself would have destroyed her still, much like the impetuous Talaunia."

Before Sean could respond, Theran cut him off. "There is more." Brow pinching, he swallowed, patting Pretaris on the arm, encouraging her to continue.

"When we draw on life, a bond is formed between us and the life force we tap. Being bound to the Mother as we are, drawing life energy from plants is a natural act. We can understand what we have taken and strive to leave the plant healthy. We know what the Mother demands of us, and we are willing to serve her needs in return. Many of those who spend their lives caring for plants and forests are Elves. Living under glamors to care for the Mother."

Theran leaned forward. "Had Axylia sustained herself by drawing from your life force, she would have been bound to you, subject to your will and needs." He grimaced and swallowed hard, Pretaris reaching to settle him.

When she turned back to Sean, she continued. "A sharing of life energies is something we do only with our mates. Binding ourselves to each other. Each drawing on the other to form a bond that is shared, entwined." Everything about her emphasized her compassion. "I hope this grants you understanding, allows you to see why she could not accept your noble offering."

Sean mulled over their words. "In my mind, I comprehend what you're saying, and I thank you for trying to explain. But in my heart, it may be some time before I can understand."

Pretaris smiled. "Wise words, young Mr. Byrne."

"If I may," Sean lifted his chin to meet her gaze. "Is it true that is why Talaunia's family was banished? That her father healed another using the life force of others?"

Theran regarded him with a clouded expression. "Long ago, a quartet of our darkened kin breached the boundary of their prison and set themselves upon the home of our Queen."

Pretaris squeezed Theran's hand. "The fairy guardsmen were the first to fall in the onslaught. Dark ones with the power to heal used their bonds as weapons, ripping life from those who rose against their revolt. The life energy they drew was not needed, and so they dispersed it into the winds, wasted." Pretaris drew a breath while she considered how to continue. "Savjel, my brother, was meeting with the queen, along with Theran, and Dresin, Talaunia's father, when the assault reached the council room door."

"I was the only warrior among us, and I placed myself between the unseen forces and the others," Theran interjected. "Dresin moved the queen to a private chamber at the back of the council room and took a position before her door. Savjel leaped atop the table in the center of the room, preparing to face the coming battle." Lifting a hand to draw down his tunic's high collar, Theran revealed a pair of jagged scars on either side of his neck. "Shadowy arrows flew like nettles in a strong wind as the door gave way, piercing me through the neck, shoulder, side, and leg. The mystical bolts vaporized, allowing blood to rush from my wounds. In moments I lay in a pool of blood, gasping for every breath."

Pretaris leaned into Theran, holding her gaze on Sean. "The Realm of Shadows and things touched by its power are toxic to us. Nothing grows there, and the creatures that walk that darkness do not thrive on the same energies as you and I." She looked to Theran, the memory of the event still bringing pain to her eyes. "Theran's wounds were tainted with ash from that dark place." She focused on Sean with intensity. "You have never known terror until you feel the one you are bound to hemorrhaging away their life, without knowledge of where or why."

"Without thinking of himself, Savjel rushed to my aid, laying his hand on my chest and pulling life from the abundance of plants that surrounded us. Then it all went wrong. The four dark ones turned and pulled the life from every plant in the room, turning them to withered husks and leaving Savjel nothing to use in healing me." Theran coughed and cleared his throat.

"It was then that the four drove their shade-touched blades through my brother," Pretaris said. "Like poison to us is the ashy death of the Shadowlands, and with nothing to heal him, he fell atop Theran, their blood mingling as they both neared death."

"Blackness fell over my eyes, though I could still hear the sounds of battle around me." Theran turned a loving gaze upon Pretaris. "I still maintain it was our bond that kept me from expiring that day."

"When it seemed certain the quartet was going to reach the queen, Dresin turned the tide. In a fury, he ripped the life from all four attackers, feeding the energy back into Savjel and Theran. He saved the queen and two people whom I hold most dear, but he broke one of our most sacred laws."

Theran gave a sad smile. "None of us wished to send him away, to banish them from the kingdom. The queen even met with her council and discussed a pardon because of the circumstance, but the wisdom of the elders declared no exceptions would ever be made, or the law would erode in time."

Pretaris sighed. "We are to treat him and his family as we would any who violate the law, even though he is a hero. Though they refused to weaken the law, the elders made an exception, allowing for his family's eventual return, but their exile is yet to pass three millennia."

"That seems quite some time," Sean offered.

"From your perspective, it seems an eternity," she admitted. "You must understand, we live eons. For us, three thousand years does not seem more than mere seconds to you."

"So, in your view, it's not such a long time, considering the infraction," Sean said.

"Precisely." Pretaris leaned in and spoke in hushed tones, a veiled appreciation shining in her eyes. "When the day arrives that we welcome Dresin and his line back home, it will be a cause of such celebration. Until then, Talaunia will have to be patient. She is still full of youthful vigor and carries that impatience with her.

Nevertheless, she must wait to see her betrothed again."

Sean blinked, his head tilting, an unexpected knot forming in his stomach. "Betrothed?"

"Quite so, but she need not fret over it. Once banished, all arrangements were terminated. The young man she was to marry has been pledged to another. A new mate will be found for her upon her return. Please see she understands. I would, but we are required to shun those in exile."

Sean rubbed his hands over his face. "I will see that she gets the message." He gave each of them a bow. "Thank you for your hospitality and for teaching me about your people and the situation. Is there any way I can aid you?"

Theran and Pretaris shared a long look that conveyed more than Sean could read on their faces, and he wondered if their bond was allowing them to communicate by some form of telepathy.

Theran rose and shook Sean's hand. "Nothing at this moment, but we expect to see you again soon. May the Mother be with you in your travels, Mr. Byrne."

Pretaris stood in a graceful, fluid movement. "Do find rest and solace. I fear you will be called upon again all too soon."

A whole new set of questions unfolded, and Sean's brow puckered with their urgency, but before he could open his mouth, Frost was looming before his eyes and poking at the tip of his nose. "Out you go. You've taken enough of their time."

Shoulders dropping, Sean turned and headed back across the open green space. Before him, the hedgerow shifted and moved, branches and vines turning back in on themselves until the perfect archway had reformed. Talaunia shot to her feet, seeing him coming, the fire of her questions blazing in the intensity of her gaze.

< ᛉᛟᚾ ᛁ�ᚱᛟᚨᛗ ᛏᚺᛗ ᚾᛁᚨᛗᛋ ᛉᛟᚾ ᛏᛟᚾᚲᚺ >

Talaunia peppered him with questions about his visit with the Traxidors for the entire trip back to Stony Brook Cottage. She spent the better part of an hour after their arrival, continuing her interrogation, prodding him for every conceivable detail.

"Why didn't they show more remorse for betraying my dad after he saved Theran?"

"Did they seem sincere about looking forward to welcoming him home?"

"How dare they think I only want to return for an arranged marriage! That boy was destined for the relationship scrap pile long before any of this happened!"

While she focused on what she had missed, Sean boiled some water and made spaghetti. It turned out a little overcooked. He found a jar of canned sauce, cracked the seal, and dumped it into a saucepan. The aroma of tomato, basil, and garlic filled the cottage as it warmed. Consulting a guidebook in the drawer, he pulled a Pinot Noir from the wine cabinet and provided glasses for each of them.

290

As soon as the food was set before her, all questions stopped.

Sean laughed, watching her consume the pasta with the same zeal that had driven the questions about the Traxidors.

She glared, pointing her fork at him.

"Hey now, I didn't realize how hungry I was either." Lifting his fork, he dug into the mound of slippery noodles on his plate.

Once they had finished gorging on the pasta, Sean insisted Talaunia teach him how to create the portal anchor.

"Since this isn't a property we own, we can't create the anchor inside, but we can place one on the grounds. We wouldn't want to use it someday and interrupt someone's intimate getaway."

Sean's lips showed the hint of a smile. "That would be interesting."

Taking him by the hand, she led him to a small stand of trees along the river. "Here, we are close, but out of the way, should things be happening in the area."

She pulled a metal disc from her pocket and handed it to Sean.

"What's this?" he asked.

"This is an anchor. Some places, you can put the symbols on a wall, or some other inanimate object that will not grow or change." She held out her arms, indicating the wooded lands around them. "But here, everything grows, moves, shifts. So we attune a small, fixed object to act as the anchor."

Pulling out her phone, she opened an app Sean had not seen before. Standing at his side, she explained, "This connects to our database of portal locations." She selected an option on the screen to mark a new place, which prompted for the required information. She had to take a picture, provide a name, the geo-coordinates of the site, and the app responded with a series of symbols for the new location.

"Now, activate those symbols on the disc," she instructed.

He studied the device, looking for any clues to guide him.

Talaunia encouraged him to think about his training.

He smiled, pricked his thumb with a pocketknife, and dabbed blood in the grooves along the disc's edge. Mystical patterns appeared, glowing crimson across the round metal surface. He pressed his bloody thumb to each glyph in the order they appeared on the screen.

The disc vibrated.

Her phone chimed and went black.

"Good. Now, wherever that disc is, this portal will take you. So, bury it," she said, tamping the ground with her foot.

"I don't have anything to dig with!"

"You have a knife!"

"I'm not going to dull my blade digging in the dirt!"

"Fine, I'll do it for you this time!" She gave him a wink, took the disc from his hand, and dropped it on the ground. Roots erupted, knotting themselves around the metal, encasing the device before pulling it down into the earth.

"Cheater," he teased, and she responded with a wicked grin.

Moving back into the cottage through the late afternoon sun, they returned to the sitting area, and Sean pulled out his bag. The distraction of the Traxidors and food had been welcome, but placing the contents of his satchel on the table only reminded him of everything that had been troubling him.

Talaunia eyed the crystal pyramid. "That was a gift from Axylia, wasn't it?" she whispered.

"She didn't even leave a card. It was a mystery for a while." He ran a finger along its side, memories of her bringing a touch of sadness to his face. "If I had doubts about the struggle I have found myself in before, they are long past. Having seen the Order's brutality firsthand has made this my fight, too."

She sank onto the sofa beside him, placing a hand on his shoulder. "Don't do anything rash," she said, moving the medallions away from him. "You can look into this tomorrow. You need to rest."

His jaw tightened, and his head twisted. "I need to train! I need to find the pieces of the Cube before they do! Reading these damn books isn't enough. They contain speculations, scraps of information. I've found a few texts that may pertain to the hiding spot within the Abbey, but we need to know more! We need to see what's going on with our own eyes."

"I agree, but you are in no state to try tonight. You are tired, emotionally turbulent, and unfocused. All sorts of things could go wrong."

Sean pointed at the second room. "If you won't help, you can go wait in there."

She narrowed her eyes in brazen defiance. "If that is what you wish." Bolting up, she snatched all the medallions from the table and darted into the room. The door slammed behind her, and she threw the lock into place. Calling back through the door, she taunted. "Knock yourself out. Without a focus item, you'll wind up watching a dog getting groomed somewhere in Kentucky!"

He heard her flop on the bed; her continued grumbling muffled by the closed door. Picking up a book, he opened it, only to slam it back onto the table, unable to concentrate on the text. He glared at the door in frustration. Forcing his attention back to the pyramid, he held it and drew his fingertip along the smooth, sloped side.

Straining to focus on what he knew of The Order, he sought them out. With effort, he let his anger go and pushed the day's loss from his mind. He wrestled with his desire to prevent future loss until he centered himself. The hours ticked away and eventually he felt the familiar tug that had pulled him along before. Letting go of his physical form, he followed, and the comforting surroundings of the Stony Brook Cottage faded away.

The Goddess has blessed my petitions! Lilith now bears the seed of Iblis, the first of a new breed. The anticipation of meeting this child causes me to burst with joy! I expect wondrous things await this new life!

—Councilor Syrdan

Seventeen

Sean stood in a dank, murky fog. Around him, figures struggled to take shape. Their half-formed features contorted in grotesque ways as the churning haze ripped them apart. Muddled voices born of pain and despair cried out, directionless, needy. The ever-shifting haze blotted out his feet and the ground below. He was standing on the rigid support of pavement one moment, and the padded give of a forest floor the next.

Afraid to move his feet, he remained stationary, becoming completely unsettled.

"Something's not right," he muttered to himself.

Eerie voices echoed in mocking tones. *"Not right, not right, not right."*

The mist thickened, creeping up his thigh.

A graveled, unfriendly voice drifted from the haze. Its single word drawn out in a lingering plea. *"Hungry."*

Sean twisted, hunting for the speaker. Several sharp pricks stung his inner thigh and Sean slapped his leg, rubbing away the sting. *"Och!"* When he pulled his hand away, the smoke swirled back in, encasing his leg, piercing him again.

"Hungry," the voice drawled from the shadows.

Needle-like jabs peppered his lower legs, each prick spawning a tiny jolt of pain.

Other voices joined the first, some deeper, others high and shrill. *"Me too,"* screeched one. *"More,"* growled another.

Panic swelled, urging him into motion, and he groped blindly through the mist. The ground shifted to loose gravel, and his right foot slid, almost toppling him face-first into the soupy haze.

Around him, the voices grew in number and volume, building into a frenzied chorus of otherworldly tones.

"Famished," a high-pitched wail called from behind

The hairs on his neck stood on end, and gooseflesh erupted along his arms.

Spinning around, all he could see were shifting shadows and empty mist. He took off in another direction and discovered a pair of slitted yellow eyes keeping pace on his right.

Sean planted his feet to stop, but the ground had morphed again, and there was no purchase to be found on the slick ice. He crashed to the ground, landing hard on his ass, his breath rushing from his chest. Gasping for air, he felt blood spread down his arm from the splits at his elbows.

"Feast," came a gleeful call, and dozens of feelers snaked from the mist, encasing him, digging under his skin.

Phantom vines wrapped around him, burrowing in.

He struggled to catch his breath. More leaching barbs attached themselves, and he could feel his energy being stolen.

The joy of the feeding frenzy escalated around him.

Far above, brilliant lightning crackled through the mist, lighting it from behind and giving the bubbling clouds an eerie glow.

Below him, the ground transformed into sharp flint rocks.

A peal of thunder rolled overhead, resonating in his chest, and making the world around him quake.

Light shot toward him like a falling star, burning away the fog as it approached.

The voices taunting him became a mix of elation and fear, feeding with renewed intensity.

Sean cried out in anger against the assault, but his struggle for breath had stolen his voice. His scream escaped his throat in a raspy rattle.

The shooting star slammed into the ground, and the world around Sean exploded. A wave of pressure washed over him, forcing everything through a unifying metamorphosis.

The mist was driven away, breaking the bonds connection between him and the creatures draining his energy.

Beneath him, the floor became a polished black surface. At regular intervals, spires with long channels of angelic script rose into the empty blackness overhead. Walls of ghostly green flame spread between the pillars, sealing Sean within their bounds.

Outside the fiery curtain, the mist reformed. Shadowy figures stalked the barrier, probing for a way through. Anguished calls rose and fell as they brushed the jade tongues of fire. The cries of their hunger grew into pitiful whines, and Sean's skin crawled. Recalling the sense of helplessness that overwhelmed him while in their grasp, a frightening chill gripped his heart.

The unified chorus of a thousand voices shook the world. *"Why do you not grovel in thanks before your savior?"*

Sean spun.

A looming figure stepped through the barrier of flame. Ghastly tongues wrapped the frightening form in a cloak of living fire. The face, hands, and body radiated such brilliant light, no features were visible beneath the glowing cowl. Wings unfurled, regal and blinding, causing Sean to lower his head and turn away.

Shielding his eyes, Sean tried to identify the new arrival, wondering if his situation had improved. *"You drove away whatever those things were. For that, I thank you."* Pausing, he squinted at the brilliant light spilling from the massive feet standing before him. *"I'm still not sure if I've been saved."*

The voices laughed.

Sean covered his ears, but the voices came from everywhere, resonating in his head.

"You are nothing but apes playing with powers you cannot comprehend, stumbling through places you were never meant to venture. Surely you and your kin know you cannot hide. The Host of Heaven sees all."

Sean's stomach twisted, and he took in the towering inferno standing before him. Squinting, he strained to find some shape within the brilliant white glow beneath the hood. The light's intensity burned his eyes, forcing him to look at the cooler hues of the woven tongues within the being's cloak. *"I've met one of your kind before. You look nothing like him."*

Beyond the scorching fence of flame, the cries of hunger intensified. Along the horizon, Sean noticed other blinding lights streaking at odd intervals from somewhere far above, racing toward unseen targets, brilliant comets falling from the sky. Others rocketed from below, piercing the dark veil of shadows and returning to the obscured light far overhead.

Amid the Bright Ones' streaking trails, faint glimmers traveled, their dim lights shining in an array of colors. Rising and falling through the murky plane, some with purpose, others struggling to make their ascent.

"Your simple mind still struggles to understand. The laws of the physical do not bind the astral." The chorus of voices struck Sean like a wall of sound, and despite his efforts, he couldn't escape its force. *"Flesh and bone do not shackle the spirit in this place. Here, truth is found."* The Bright One circled Sean with a predatory gate. *"I will open your mind, sear it with knowledge; then you will understand and make yourself prone and tremble in our presence."* A blazing hand stretched from beneath the flaming robe, the tip of a finger coming to rest upon Sean's forehead.

Sean was frozen by the sudden chill burning through him. Events flooded his memory, filled with tactile aspects, and his senses overloaded. The sweet smell of the forest after a rain, stifling humidity, a group of Elves moving through vibrant, colorful vegetation. Daylight vanished, and he was now in a clearing, more stars than he had ever seen peppering the sky. Beneath the heavens, a cry of passion from a slender Elven woman broke the stillness.

Heat swept through Sean, and he knew this woman; her scent, the texture of her skin, the taste of her upon his lips, and with that carnal knowledge, came her name, Lilith. Her bare breasts heaved, and she ground herself against an unseen man. Time blurred, and the couple shifted. The man, a Bright One, tossed her to her back, plunging himself into her, his unfurled wings powering each thrust. Lilith called his name in the vision, *'Iblis.'* Others joined them until the field became an orgy of bodies given over to primal urges.

The world smeared into an array of colors before settling into a welcoming room made of enormous leaves and adorned with flowers. A cry of pain sounded from Lilith. Legs spread, she bore down. The swell of her abdomen and agony on her face made her labor apparent. Excitement and concern charged the air, heightened by the crowd gathered outside awaiting news of the birth.

Again, Sean's senses exploded, bombarded with images of time racing through his mind. He swore in defiance, his words lost in the onslaught. The smear of history slowed again, settling on an elf with dusky skin and a dark light in his eyes. Xeron was the Elven man's name. Beside him stood his mother, Lilith, stern and defiant as an army of elves followed them through the thick forest.

Civil war erupted among the elves. Trees burned, blood ran thick on the ground, anguish and loss gripped the world. Time twisted, and the battle raged on, grief deepened, and hatred grew. The Mother became angered by Her children and the oceans churned with Her ire. The world quaked, and storms lashed out in fury upon both armies, and Sean's spirit struggled under the crushing weight of the Mother's pain.

Time jumped, and Sean found himself amid the ritual that banished the dark elves and their compatriots. The Bright Ones were joining with the Elves to bring the destruction and pain to an end. The moment the magic was invoked, Sean's soul felt barren as Lilith, Xeron, and their armies were ripped from the world and banished into the Void. A deathly chill overwhelmed him, and in blurring motions, he watched as the ice laid claim to the lush forests. Sean ached, understanding why the elves thought they had destroyed the Mother.

Another jarring battery of images crashed through his mind. He saw himself hurling the bloody mark of The Order while Talaunia watched without judgment. He flashed to Athens and soared over the bluest waters, racing toward the Greek isles, where a natural cave turned into a mountain fortress filled with a collection of artifacts to rival the vaults below the Quari Group. The Order's mark was emblazoned on stands and wall hangings. Atop the center table, four pieces of the onyx cube lay bound, prevented from reattaching themselves. Behind the individual parts stood Lilith with her son Xeron.

The Bright One lifted his finger from Sean's forehead, and the visions vanished.

Sean's head was swimming with questions that disappeared beneath the iron grip of the Bright One.

Lifting Sean by the throat, the chorus of voices exploded, grating Sean's overstimulated senses. *"When next we command, you shall not defy."*

Sean flailed, struggling to grasp his assailant's arms.

The Bright One threw Sean against the walls of the cage, and the green flames flared brighter, searing him everywhere the tongues touched.

Sean fell to his knees and collapsed to all fours, not wanting to move or allow the back of his body to touch anything. An acrid stench wafted from him, and a blinding foot caught him in the ribs, sending him soaring back into the wall of flame. He wretched, gushing a stream of stomach contents that arched and splattered over the obsidian ground, before falling face first onto the black stone.

The powerful voice bellowed, *"Now prostrate yourself before me, and swear obedience."*

Sean shook his head, pushing himself up onto his knees. *"No—I'm not yours, Vitan."* Pain cracked through his voice, and he curled in upon himself.

Vitan took Sean by the neck and waist, hurling him across the space. The flames parted, and Sean slammed into the stone beyond the barrier's protection. Cries of glee pierced the air, and the vapory tendrils lashed about him, devouring his energy.

Moving to hover over him, the light from Vitan dimmed until Sean could make out the cold smirk etched on his face. *"Swear your loyalty. Pledge yourself to my will. Only then will I show you my mercy."*

A roar of pain ripped from Sean's core. He thrashed against the leaching spirits, but their stinging bite held fast.

"Why suffer such tribulation and torment?" Vitan waved a hand, and the vapors were driven away from Sean's head. *"One simple word can end it all."*

Jaw set, Sean's eyes were slits of pain and anger. He spat out an emphatic, *"No!"* and curled up, another pained scream escaping. His energy dropped, and the world about him dimmed. Somewhere far above, another explosion of light caught his eye.

Vitan sensed it too, and he scowled toward the Heavens. The blinding light within him flared back to life. *"He is mine!"* the chorus of voices bellowed, and the stone trembled.

The light from above blazed toward them, bearing down and growing as it neared. *"No more!"* sounded the thunderous reply.

The sound impacted them with such force, Vitan's wings were pushed downward, Sean was driven against the rock, and the mist scattered.

Vitan growled at the approaching light, and the flaming blue cloak covering him faded away until he was nothing more than a bright form. He lifted his wings, and when he drove them downward, the air cracked. In a blur of light, he rocketed skyward. The two forms collided in a blinding flash. All darkness was banished from the area, illuminating the twisted and ghoulish forms hiding in the mist. The light was followed by a concussive wave that cracked the stone beneath Sean.

When the flash cleared, Sean focused on the two figures locked in combat far above. Light spilled from each of them, exploding in arcs as they landed blows, sending showers of sparks in every direction as they tumbled toward him. The sounds of their battle grated on his senses. A twisted and disorienting cacophony of falling stones, shattering glass, and crumpling metal rang with every blow, sounding to him like crashing vehicles and demolition.

The pair hurtled toward Sean, and he scrambled to the side, narrowly escaping their impact. Shards of obsidian stone showered the area, and light burst from the crater with the intensity of the sun. The mist drew closer, tendrils reaching for Sean, driving him toward the edge of the pulsating pillar of light. The clash's chaotic sounds slowed, and the light flickered and vanished, leaving Sean unable to see in the sudden darkness.

Flinching, Sean twisted away from the first contact, scrambling over the sharp bits of rock beneath his palms. He cast his gaze about in the darkness, straining to focus on anything. Before him, the vague outline of a pale face framed in flowing red hair took shape.

"Shhhh," the soft, calming shush of a parent stilled his soul. A pale, freckled hand caressed his cheek. *"Calm now, Pet."* The voice was a smooth alto, filled with reassurance and comfort, and he found it familiar and soothing. *"I have summoned aid. It approaches."*

In the distance, the cry of a hawk sounded. Sean blinked, finding it much easier to focus on the round face before him. This woman was exuding a subdued aura of light, and Sean struggled to remember why her green eyes felt so familiar and calming. Around him, the darkness receded, and below him, the obsidian stone became a lush mat of clover.

Smiling with the understanding of a parent, she spoke again. *"We'll meet again soon."* A small fire appeared beside him, the warmth causing every part of him to ache as it soothed the deep chill left in him by the mist. *"I have missed you so, child."*

A memory stirred, faint and unclear. Grasping at it, Sean asked in near disbelief, *"Nanna?"*

The hawk's call sounded again, and Sean looked upward to see a dark form circling overhead. Raven black, it shimmered in the dim light, and streaks of silver gleamed in its feathers. The lady glanced upward, then fixed a loving gaze on Sean. *"For now, our time closes. Trust those to whom I've guided you."*

The hawk sailed down and landed in the clover. Its head turned to the side, and it fixed its gray eyes upon the lady. Sean blinked, and in the next instance, Ms. Iliescu stood glaring down at the pair of them in stern disapproval. *"Alorn, thank you for summoning our aid."*

Alorn rose and gave Ms. Iliescu a grin. *"He and I were destined to reunite, though it is sooner than expected."* She turned a playful and chiding grin toward Sean. *"More gumption than sense, it seems."*

Ms. Iliescu agreed while Sean scrambled to stand.

"I leave him with you," Alorn said. *"I must tend to another matter."* She stepped over to Sean and placed a kiss on his cheek. *"Soon, child. You and I will break bread, and you may ask all your questions. Until then, try to listen; this world is not one to stumble through."*

Sean watched her rocket toward the heavens, her light blooming about her as she ascended.

Ms. Iliescu stamped her foot, and a doorway appeared. Fixing Sean with a hawkish gaze, her hand shot out, taking him by the ear. Twisting it like a handle, she pulled. *"This way home, Mr. Byrne."*

"Och!"

When she opened the door, Sean could see the Stony Brook Cottage on the other side. It was odd to see himself sprawled on the floor, convulsing. They had pushed the table and divan to the side of the room. Djain stood in the kitchen entry, leaned against one wall, and Talaunia knelt at his side, holding his hand. Kneeling at his head with a knit shawl draped over her shoulders was Ms. Iliescu, her hands placed on either side of Sean's head.

Twisting on his ear again, Ms. Iliescu gave a firm tug. *"Time for you to go home."* She pulled him through the door, and together they plummeted back into themselves.

The number of our kind carrying the first generation of this new species grows by the day. Initially, there were few, but now the estimate reaches into the thousands. How many cycles did our people frolic with the Bright Ones, with no hint of life sparking from the lusty unions? Now, as though some fundamental barrier has been removed, more couplings result in pregnancy. Councilor Arianelis and I intend to investigate.

—Councilor Daejor

EIGHTEEN

Sean found the steely gray gaze of Ms. Iliescu boring into him when he regained consciousness. Her long bony fingers pressed against the side of his head; thin lips set in disapproval. "I shall order you a fine hanging rope, Mr. Byrne. Perhaps next time, you might opt to save the rest of us the worry and bother."

Releasing Sean, Ms. Iliescu sat up, pulling the shawl over her shoulders. Her gaze softened, and she lifted her head, reading an unspoken question in Djain's expression. She let out a resigned sigh that made her slight frame seem to shrink even further. "Very well, I will train him, though I require tea. Perhaps within its calming influence may be found the fortitude to endure such an undertaking."

Djain's concerned gaze twisted into a crooked grin. "I will see to it." He pushed off the wall with his shoulder and evaluated Sean. "I hope you are rested." Lowering his voice, he cautioned. "Do not ignore her assignments. She can be quite creative in disciplining underperforming students. Take it from one who knows." He shifted his eyes, looking at Ms. Iliescu with respect and adoration. "She will push you to feats you never imagined possible and leave you exhausted. But you would not find a better instructor anywhere." His soft laughter remained as he disappeared into the kitchen.

With a gentle squeeze of his hand, Talaunia pulled Sean's attention. Energy flowed through her touch, tingling as it spread through his chest, and he could see the relief pushing the worry from her violet eyes.

"Welcome back," she said. She dropped his hand and delivered a series of swift strikes to his chest, punctuating her now irritated tone. "Don't you ever do anything so stupid again!"

Sean lifted his arms to protect himself against her fury. "Hey—wait!"

Talaunia's blows subsided, but the pummeling of words continued. "Wait? Do you realize you could have been lost in the astral plane forever? That you had no tether in the physical realm? Without Ms. Iliescu, we never would have seen you again!"

He stared up at her, seeing the fear she tried to mask behind the ire in her expression, and he knew the loss of Axylia amplified it. "Well, I—"

Another single blow landed. "Of course you don't realize because you never wait for training! You bluster headlong into everything. Well enough!" She took his hand between both of hers and squeezed. "I've half a mind to have Sarah make me a poppet of you, so I can bind you up and keep you out of trouble."

"Ouch!" Sean yelped, his free hand snapping to the side of his head.

"Let me help with that project, Dearie." Ms. Iliescu held several strands of Sean's hair between her fingertips, which she offered to Talaunia with all seriousness.

Sean snatched at the hairs. "Hey now!"

Talaunia was quicker, gathering them up and spiriting them away before Sean could see where they went.

They could hear the kettle filling in the kitchen. The gurgle was masked when Djain chimed in. "I can provide you a sample of his blood if needed."

"That will make one potent poppet," said Talaunia. A wicked light filled her eyes, and her voice eased into a provocative tone. "Would prefer him under a different spell—but I'm not opposed to taming him first."

A pale bloom of rose touched Ms. Iliescu's cheek, and she gave Talaunia the faintest of smiles. "Now, now, dear. Let's keep your youthful fires to more appropriate moments."

Curious amusement spread across Sean's face as he watched the color spread over Ms. Iliescu.

Ms. Iliescu lifted her chin. "I understand pleasure, Mr. Byrne, in all its forms."

Sean shook his head to hide the smile spreading over his lips. "Of course . . ." His gaze turned to Talaunia. "No poppets!" He looked at their interwoven fingers and felt the energy fluttering in his chest. "Thank you. I feel so drained. Not physically tired, but more—"

"Spiritual." Ms. Iliescu interjected. "The creatures in the lower realms of the Astral are lost there. Cut off from any sources of renewal, much as you would have become if you had remained there much longer. They stalk unwitting travelers and drain them of spiritual energy, sapping their souls and turning them into twisted husks."

Sean shook his head, letting out a dispirited sigh.

"Depression." Ms. Iliescu pursed her lips. "The most common manifestation of those who have had their spiritual energy drained."

"This will take me a couple of days to repair. You must not go roaming the astral again until you are restored and trained," Talaunia said. "You and I will remain here for the next several days, and I will use the surrounding woodlands to restore you."

Sean gave a noncommittal grunt and squeezed Talaunia's hand in thanks. "But what about the Order? What about continuing my research on the Abbey and what we might find there? We can't allow days to pass."

Djain returned, carrying a silver tray. On it sat a large silver kettle with steam pouring from its spout, several small porcelain cups, an assortment of tea bags, a pyramid of sugar cubes, a much smaller container of milk, and crackers. Hooking a small table with his foot, he slid it toward the group, causing Sean to hurry out of the way and into a sitting position between the ladies. Djain placed the tray on the table. "You will spend the next few days here. You should accept it. No matter how dire the situation, I am not inclined to disagree with these two. You still have access to the library via your computer, and any books you require will be brought to you."

Ms. Iliescu poured tea for each of them as Djain settled himself on the opposite side of the table. Even sitting, he dwarfed the rest of them, balancing the seating with his presence alone. As she poured, Ms. Iliescu continued. "Tomorrow, we will take the first steps in teaching you how to traverse the Astral safely. We will begin here, using the outermost edges of the Astral to venture into the minds of others. Master how to walk the memories of another, and the Astral will become a safer place for you to explore."

Talaunia edged closer to Sean, lifting his arm; she draped it over her shoulder and leaned against him. Her hand slid around his back, the other up his shirt, sending the healing energy directly into his chest over his heart.

He stiffened at the unexpected intimacy of her touch, but decided he enjoyed the comfort of having her near, and relaxed.

Unable to shake the thought that he was betraying Axylia's memory, he felt fickle.

Talaunia laid her head back on his shoulder. "While we all take a moment to relax, tell us what you experienced." Talaunia glanced at Ms. Iliescu. "Was she there?"

"She was. And she was tending him when I arrived." Their gazes lingered on Sean, showing an intense interest in what Ms. Iliescu was saying. "The paths are not yet chosen, but this one will hold great sway in the days to come. Let us hope his impetuousness will not bring calamity upon us all."

"Are you speaking of my Nan?" Sean asked.

"Yes," Talaunia said, her finger drawing patterns on his chest beneath the shirt. "What did Alorn say to you?"

"Nothing relevant to what we are doing. She said we would talk soon and that I could ask all my questions then." He sighed, reaching for the tea with his free arm.

Ms. Iliescu cleared her throat. "And he should stop being reckless and listen."

Sean rolled his eyes.

Talaunia smiled.

Djain tilted his head, a curious glint in his eyes. "Now. You can tell us about your misadventure."

Sean groaned, and Talaunia nudged him with her side. "You aren't getting out of it, so you may as well tell your story."

Sean recounted his evening, starting with the argument with Talaunia.

"You'll learn to listen to me," she chimed in, tapping on his chest with a finger.

Ms. Iliescu took notes when he spoke of releasing and moving into the Astral. Djain watched him with curiosity as Sean recounted the fog and creatures. He told of Vitan's arrival and how he had not known it was Vitan, detailing how different the Bright One had looked and sounded. He continued through the demands Vitan had made; the visions forced upon him, and how tangible his experience with them had been, finishing with the confrontation between Vitan and Alorn, and the arrival of Ms. Iliescu.

Djain leaned back, his brow lowered in thought. "If Lilith and Xeron are here and aligned with the Order, we must prepare for far worse than what we encountered at Galikere."

"Why is Lilith so important?" Sean asked.

"She was a leader among the Elven people and the first to give birth to our halfling cousins," Talaunia said. She winced and balled a fist, the discussion prickling at her.

"Lilith is known as the Mother of the Dark Ones, the Elevari," Djain said. "She broke away from their traditions, forming a faction around her beliefs of power and control. Lilith commanded the opposing forces during the Elven Civil War, and I am told, was banished to the Void alongside her son and all the others like him."

"That explains a few things," Talaunia said. She shifted, so she sat upright, no longer entwined with Sean, and he stared at the space between them. "Sean and I spoke with the Traxidors. They sent a pixie to summon us, and there were no fairy guards with them when we met."

"I believe that is nearly enough to corroborate Lilith's presence," Ms. Iliescu intoned. She pursed her lips and turned her stern, gray gaze upon Djain. "If the Traxidors are aware of this, why did they not inform us?"

Djain shook his head. "We must change how we are operating." He rose, pulled his phone from his pocket, and dialed, pointing toward the bedroom door. "Talaunia, a portal to Ops, if you would."

Talaunia hopped up, moving to open the portal, and Djain spoke into his phone. "Send a messenger to the Traxidors. I want a meeting within the hour." He dropped the phone, shifting focus to Sean. "Apologies for the invasion, but if you are to be homebound, your team will be here often and will require access to operational data."

Sean was perplexed and looked to Talaunia, who shrugged at him and worked to open the portal.

Djain moved into the kitchen, issuing orders about remote operations into his phone.

Hearing Djain's conversation, Talaunia created the portal and moved into the dining area, taking hold of a pair of chairs and shifting them to the side.

Realizing she was working to clear the space, Sean pushed himself up.

The long, thin fingers of Ms. Iliescu gripped him by the shoulder and pulled him back down with unexpected strength. "You stay and rest, Mr. Byrne."

Talaunia echoed Ms. Iliescu's command with a look before shuffling the remaining chairs to the side of the room.

Hearing snippets of what Djain was saying, he asked. "Extended protections?"

With a grunt, Talaunia heaved against the massive, solid wood table; it shifted about three inches, and she groaned. "Protections for families, to make sure the Order doesn't go after them," she said.

Djain saw Talaunia's effort and stepped over, leaning into the tabletop with his thigh. Together, they shoved the table against the back wall of the room. "Thank you," Talaunia said, upset at having needed help.

Djain lifted the phone away from his mouth. "A pleasure." Taking in the space she had created, he lowered his head in appreciation. "And thank you."

Her lips twisted upward, and she echoed his words. "A pleasure." With the table out of the way, she stacked the chairs on top of its broad surface.

Sean jumped when a hand truck came rumbling through the portal, carting a rather large road case.

Ms. Iliescu smiled. "Mr. Byrne, we must work on your awareness."

Talaunia stepped to the side. "In here with that." She pointed the delivery team to the empty area where the table had been. A moment later, another pair of two-wheelers arrived, loaded down with equipment, along with a half-dozen technicians.

Sean shifted himself toward the patio. The spacious atmosphere of the cottage now felt cramped. From his space near the open door, he watched the team transform the dining area into an array of monitors and consoles.

Once everything was operational and data was streaming in, Djain thanked the delivery crew and sent them back through the portal with the spare case parts and hand trucks. The cramped feel of the space evaporated. "I must go meet the Traxidors. I will return with new information as soon as I can. Until then, the three of you take care of one another." Swinging his head around, he brought his imposing focus to bear on Sean and half teased. "And by the Ancestors, stay put!" With that, Djain stepped into the portal, closing it behind himself.

Talaunia pulled a chair over to the console and made a few adjustments. Soon the screens were filled with maps, blips, dots, and a status window that gave the latest report from every location, color-coded and all green.

Sean was shocked to realize how many operations were active worldwide, a dozen by his count, though his eyes were growing blurry as the wear of the past few days settled on him.

Ms. Iliescu placed her tea on the service tray and rose. Outside, twilight had descended, and she stared off into the stars, her gaze going distant. With a sigh, she frowned. "I must rest." She moved toward the room Talaunia had used the night before. "You should rest as well. Good evening."

The door closed with a quiet click as the lock snapped into place.

Sean's brown pinched. "What was that?"

"I expect she saw something she didn't like. She is a seer, like Pretaris."

Sean struggled to stand. "I wonder what she saw."

Talaunia hurried to his side, helping him stabilize. "Enough about that. Let's get you into bed," she said. Her words were compassionate and lacked her typical sultry innuendo.

He turned his head, considering the changes he had seen in her. "Thank you for not—well, you know."

"I told you I'm not completely insensitive," she said, leading him toward the bedroom. "Besides, I don't want to make this next discussion any more difficult by adding unnecessary layers of meaning."

"What discussion? What are you talking about?" He came to a halt in the doorway, eyes narrowing in suspicion.

Talaunia sighed. "I will be staying in your bed with you tonight. I need to keep in contact with you to continue fixing your poor choices."

Sean's eyes narrowed further. "I already assumed you would be with me. Why might it have—unnecessary layers of meaning?"

She pursed her lips in resolve, returned his stare, and spoke in clinical tones. "Because we are both going to be naked."

He rolled his eyes and moved into the room. "Whatever. Between you, the ritual, Ryan's tendency to walk about with his tadger flapping in the wind. I'm over the self-conscious bullshit." He turned to face her again. "If you say it's needed for recovery, fine. So be it." He paused, shuffled his feet, and studied the floor. The emotional undercurrents of Axylia's loss; learning the truth about his mother and father; having his worldview upended into something he still struggled to comprehend; all of it churned within, tinging his voice, giving it a pleading tone. "Don't cross those boundaries. You have been a good friend today, and I need that right now."

She rested a hand on his arm, and the other she used to lift his chin, locking their gazes. "No tricks."

He allowed her to help him disrobe, and she placed him on the bed where he lay on his side, facing the river. The soft moonlight gave a pale glow to the sheers covering the windows, turning them into the perfect canvas to display the leaves' shadowy figures. Behind him, he heard her clothing fall to the floor, listened to the brush of it over her skin as she peeled the layers away, and he resisted the sudden urge that swelled in him to turn and see her. Sean pulled a pillow from under his head and clasped it to his chest, curling up around it. Guilt raced in to taunt him as the memories of Axylia were now mingled with images of Talaunia.

The bed didn't move as Talaunia slipped under the light sheet. She eased up behind him, slotting her lithe form around his, nesting herself against him. Her arm wrapped around his chest, and she could feel the tension in him, the quickened pulse from his inner struggle. She pressed herself against him, and tapped into the life all around them. Everywhere their bodies touched, living energy flowed. She moved her lips beside his ear and spoke in hushed, breathy tones. "Let go. Rest. I've got you."

Sean trembled in her arms, the weight of everything he struggled with bringing far more discomfort than the wounds she sought to heal. He closed his eyes, silently begging for sleep to take him.

Eventually, it did.

Excerpt from the Elven Volumes of Living Knowledge
Celestial Cycle 20.969255
in the First Reign of House Varunia

Councilor Daejor and I have uncovered the cause, the catalyst, that began this rash of pregnancies. Two of our own, Councilors Kryntan and Syrdan, working with like-minded Bright Ones, created a ritual, significantly influencing the creation of life.

I am horrified at this discovery. The systematic destruction of life in the Heavenly Gardens, stealing the living energy of those glorious plants, and using it to fuel the ritual. A third party joins the couple, a voyeuristic toy, watching the sexual congress while being mercilessly teased, but never pleased. At the moment the man erupts, the watcher steals the life of the nearby plants, merging it with the burning lust roiling inside themselves, and pouring that mangled energy into the woman's womb. Thankful for the help, the mating pair then tend to the watcher's desires.

Never have I felt the need to keep the truth from our people, but the Council finds itself in that precarious position. To deceive by omission is a great injustice, but this knowledge would fuel the mistrust aimed at the unborn. Until proof exists, marking them in some dark way, this secret must be maintained.

—Councilor Arianelis

NINETEEN

Sean pressed his eyelids closed, attempting to block the glow of daylight. He hadn't rested well physically, and on more intangible levels, he felt hollow. His dreams had been disconcerting. Faceless nightmares ripped Axylia, Becca, and Jaime apart while he watched, helpless to intervene. Their souls were shredded and consumed by the shapeless apparitions, while his unskilled blows landed without effect.

Talaunia remained pressed against his back, arm draped over his side, and fingers splayed across his chest.

Instinctively, his hand covered hers, and he choked on his guilt.

Talaunia's breath washed over his ear, warm and feathery. "The warrior rises." She shifted, holding him tighter. The healing energies sparked at every junction of their bodies, continuing to flow in a steady trickle. "Slaying demons in your dreams? You seemed unsettled last night. Do you feel any better?"

He was thankful she was there, and clutched at her hand, despite his shame. The dichotomy of his emotions washed over him, and he nodded into the pillow, not trusting his voice to remain steady. "Aye. Some."

"We can talk about it."

The soft heat of her breath sent thrilling chills from his ear, making him ache. He shook his head, squeezed her hand, and slipped from beneath the cover. Despite his cocksure attitude the night before, he reached for a pillow to cover his erect form. "Washroom," he said.

He lingered in the shower after washing, allowing the warm water to run over his body while he wrestled with his thoughts. Though he resolved nothing, when he finally left the shower, he felt more centered.

Returning to the bedroom, he discovered Talaunia had already departed, leaving behind a neatly arranged pile of fresh clothing.

He sat on the edge of the bed and stared at where she had lain the night before. Confusion blurred his thoughts, so he pushed the images away.

Talaunia popped her head in the door. "Almost ready? Your food's getting cold, and we have a lot of training to do today."

He lifted the clothing. "Aye, thank you. I'll be out in a moment."

She closed the door, leaving him alone with his thoughts and the feeling of betrayal that haunted him every time Talaunia crept back into his mind. Not wishing to get lost in that trap, he hastened to dress.

He made his way to the common area, seeking a distraction. The divan and small table they had used the night before had been pushed up against a wall. In their place was a small round rug, dotted with pillows around its edge. In the center of the carpet sat the silver serving tray, and steam rose from the kettle.

Ms. Iliescu poured a fresh cup of tea. "Were you not recovering, Mr. Byrne, I would scold you for wasting away the hours. We have so precious few."

Her words still raked across his conscience, stirring his guilt over his inability to help those who had fallen. He sought the clock and discovered it was already well past ten. The scent of food struck him, making his stomach growl.

Ms. Iliescu arched a brow. "By all means, tame that monster before we begin." She waved her hand toward the kitchen as if she were shooing him away. "Go on now."

Familiar voices echoed down the hall, and he followed them to the kitchen.

Talaunia was sitting on a counter, a sprig of mint twisting between her lips.

Ryan leaned against the opposing counter, holding a plate piled high with sausage and bacon. He lifted his chin, greeted Sean, and crammed a strip of bacon into his mouth.

Talaunia pointed at the buffet spread across the bar. "Compliments of Papa. Eat up. You'll need your energy."

Sean gawked at the array of foods: bacon, sausage, mushrooms, oatcakes, grilled tomato, fried eggs, haggis, toast, baked beans, and potato scones. His eyes lit up at the traditional Scottish items mixed in among the rest, and he grabbed a plate, sculpting a mountain of food to rival Ryan. "I can't believe they made haggis and tattie scones."

"You're welcome," Talaunia beamed. "I told them to include those. I thought you might find them comforting."

Sean looked at her from the corner of his eyes, unable to hide his smile. "Thank you."

Talaunia eyed the overloaded plates and herded them from the kitchen. "You can eat in there. We need to get started."

"Dammit, I'm going to want more," Ryan objected, moving toward the serving platters.

Talaunia grabbed the hairs at the nape of Ryan's neck before his hand found the tongs. "Then you damn well know where the kitchen is, don't you? Move!"

Unwilling to face a similar fate, Sean scooted out ahead, leading the way back to the common area.

Ms. Iliescu directed each of them to a seat as they arrived, placing Sean's back to the status screens glowing in the dining area. As they ate, Ms. Iliescu outlined the day's goals, and what was expected of Sean.

Before Sean finished eating, she made him attempt his first circle casting. His invites to the elements were choppy and unsure. The mystical barrier formed around them, but it was unstable and lacked strength, so she made him dismiss it and begin again.

He lost count of how many times they worked through the ritual. Each time, Ms. Iliescu provided subtle guidance, and with each iteration, he improved, eventually learning to give urgency and authority to each element. They devoted nearly two hours to the exercise, but he was producing a quality circle with little guidance.

"Well done, Mr. Byrne. Now, prove to me you are capable of repeating it without aid," Ms. Iliescu demanded.

Sean bristled at having to do it again, but complied. The others turned away so he couldn't look at them for reassurance. Without the distraction of their scrutiny, his rhythm and flow improved, adding another layer of surety to the ritual. When the new circle popped into place, it hummed and rippled with energy.

The others studied the circle, tested the boundary, and shared rapid glances.

Sean watched the quiet evaluation with growing apprehension. "What have I done wrong now?"

Ms. Iliescu shook her head. "Nothing. This is an auspicious beginning, and we will be quite secure working within this circle. You may finish your meal if you wish before we continue."

Talaunia positioned herself next to Sean. Her face glowed in approval, and her hand rested on his back.

Relieved to have gained Ms. Iliescu's approval, Sean looked at the food. "I'm good."

Ryan leaned over and snatched Sean's plate. "Then you won't care if I finish this off for you."

Ms. Iliescu snapped. "This is not a barn, Mr. Washington."

Sean laughed. "You go right ahead."

Ryan lifted his chin in thanks. "Fuck yeah," he said, biting into a chunk of haggis.

"If you two are quite through, we shall push on."

Sean settled, a faint smile forming as the tension of the past hours eased away.

"Don't wait on my account," Ryan grumbled. "I know all this shit! I'm only here because they didn't have anywhere else to put my lame ass." A low growl punctuated his disdain at being injured, and he went back to eating, taking out his frustrations or a plump sausage.

Talaunia laughed.

Ms. Iliescu stared daggers at Ryan before delving into Sean's next lesson. She went over the basics of chakras, discussed how to align them, and instructed him on how to cleanse his aura.

All the while, Ryan murdered one piece of food after another until the plate was empty. With a smirk, he placed the empty dish on the rug and leaned forward, sticking out his tongue to lap at its surface until it was spotless.

Ms. Iliescu smacked him with her notebook. "If you insist on eating like an animal, I will insist Papa feeds you from a trough!" Ryan laughed, and Ms. Iliescu's shoulders shivered, the thought of it all sending a chill down her spine. "Enough of this foolishness. It is time to concentrate."

Talaunia glared at Ryan and he tossed up his hand in mock surrender, and settled down.

The guided meditation was next on the agenda, and Ms. Iliescu spent half an hour leading the session. When Sean relaxed and prepared, she taught him how to rise into the first layer of the Astral and hover in the room above the group. She transitioned with him, taking the hawk form he had seen her use before. *"How did you do that?"* he asked, his voice only resonating in the Astral.

"Vitan told you the truth. The Astral is not bound and constrained by the laws of physics. As you see yourself, so shall others. Try."

At her encouragement, he tried visualizing himself as other creatures. He sprouted monkey ears and a tail, but they faded as quickly as they appeared. He attempted to mimic Ryan's bear form but only managed the forward paws.

Ms. Iliescu encouraged him onward. *"It takes practice, Mr. Byrne; keep trying. Do not imitate others, but find the form which calls to you. The first manifestation will happen when you find the truth inside yourself."*

He visualized many forms, some with more definition than others. Eventually, the image that had spoken to him all his life popped into his mind. He smiled, his astral body quivered, and he transformed into a sleek silver wolf.

"Excellent, Mr. Byrne. Now, move about the room, test your legs." Ms. Iliescu's voice dropped to a hushed

excitement, and she spoke to Ryan and Talaunia on the physical plane. "A wolf! He has manifested a wolf!"

Ryan and Talaunia congratulated him.

Sean bounded around the room, moving through objects without effort or resistance in his Astral form.

"Come now, Mr. Byrne. Let us move on to our next lesson. Safely exploring the mental landscapes of others." She explained how willing participants were ideal, and how Ryan and Talaunia had volunteered.

Reforming her Astral visage to mimic her physical form, she encouraged Sean to do the same. She led him to the edge of Ryan's mind, shrinking with each step.

After some trial and error, Sean reduced his size to match hers, until they were the tiniest reflections of themselves as they approached Ryan. A field of energy formed a barrier around his mind, preventing their passing.

In the physical realm, Sean heard Ms. Iliescu speak.

"It is time, Mr. Washington."

The energy field rippled, and a doorway formed in the protective shield. Side by side, the two Astral forms stepped through.

A forest spread before them, creatures of all shapes and sizes darting through the wood. Ms. Iliescu led Sean to a clearing where acorns lay strewn about the matted ground. *"Pick one up,"* she directed, and Sean complied. Before them, in a mix of hologram and silent film, a scene played out. A child, Ryan, when he was a toddler, was playing in a steel-framed, iron-linked cage, surrounded by deformed and broken toys. Sean's sense of morality bristled, and his heart ached for Ryan, unable to imagine keeping a child in such a cold cell. Then clarity came. Baby Ryan laughed, and when he did, he shifted into a bear cub, pawing, gnawing, and batting all the frayed toys about the pin. Sean laughed.

Ms. Iliescu told Sean to replace the acorn, and they made their way back through the forest, out the doorway, and it vanished behind them. She led Sean to the edge of Talaunia's mind space. Talaunia sensed their approach, and an archway formed, open and welcoming, and they passed through with ease.

They walked alongside a slow-moving stream, the water a shimmery reflection of the beautiful foliage overhead. *"Pick a stone from the water."* Ms. Iliescu prompted.

Sean waded into the cool water, bending to retrieve a smooth, speckled stone.

A pair of boots materialized, blocking his way.

Talaunia crouched before him, pointing at another rock in the stream. *"Might I suggest this one?"*

Ms. Iliescu used her appearance as a teaching moment. She informed him that anyone might appear within their mindscape at will, wielding absolute control of the environment. *"Even when invited, Mr. Byrne, one must always be on guard."*

Sean studied Talaunia, caution nagging at him, as thoughts of her training methods rushed through his mind.

"It won't harm you," Talaunia promised. *"It's a memory I want you to see."*

Sensing the truth in her promise, Sean bent and picked up the stone. The water sparkled and brightened, shimmering images projected across the surface in muted watercolor. The memory sprang to life on the slow-moving current. Axylia and Talaunia sitting together, the best of friends. Laughing, sharing stories, and discussing one another's hopes and dreams.

"I wanted you to know things were not always as they seemed with us," Talaunia said in hushed tones. *"I miss her too."*

Emotion rippled over his Astral form, and Sean crashed back into his physical body. Rubbing the back of his head, he groaned. "Ouch."

Ms. Iliescu blinked several times. "Emotions, Mr. Byrne. They can be a help or a hindrance."

Talaunia tried to wipe away a tear without being seen, but Sean caught her, giving her a tender smile. "Thank you for sharing that."

"I can show you more later. Call it training exercises, if Ms. Iliescu wishes," Talaunia offered.

"An acceptable plan. For now, I think it best we all took a break." Ms. Iliescu turned to Sean. "Mr. Byrne, if you would release the circle."

Sean performed the ritual closing, and the room's energy dissipated, returning to nothing more than the mundane hum of electronics. Outside, twilight had descended, cloaking the grounds in thickening darkness. "I didn't realize we were at that so long."

Talaunia helped Ms. Iliescu to her feet, then kicked at Ryan. "Be useful. Take the dishes to the kitchen."

Ryan gathered the morning dishes. "Fine, but someone better get food here soon." He continued to grumble as he headed off down the hall. "Keep me waiting, and I'm going to bear-out and go fishing in that fucking river."

Talaunia took Sean by the hand, energy flowing into him as soon as their fingers entwined. "How are you holding up?"

Sean studied their hands. "Better than I expected to be last night." His eyes met hers, he eased toward the door, tugged at her hand gently, and she followed. Stepping out into the darkness, they wandered down to the bank of the river and lingered by the shore.

"What's on your mind?" she asked. "Something's troubling you."

"Why haven't you or one of the other healers helped Ryan, like you are helping me?"

"We can't. Well, we could, but bad things happen. Trying to speed up an already magically enhanced healing tends to get you into third nostril territory. Things get out of sync, and the body reacts poorly. It's best to let him heal at his natural pace."

He kicked a pebble, sending it into the river. "I see."

"Somehow, I think that isn't what you wanted to ask." She gave him a reassuring nudge. "You can ask me anything."

Sean turned. "Why did you share that memory with me?"

A sense of vulnerability was present in her tone. "Because it was the easiest way to bridge the trust gap. Even walking through my memories, you were wary that I was setting you up." She lifted their hands, wrapping both of hers over his. "I wanted to make sure you understood, she and I were not always at odds. There was a millennia-old friendship buried underneath our barbs. Who knows, perhaps in time, Axylia and I would have found it again."

"What caused the rift?" he asked, gazing at her from the deep shadow of his brow.

Her lips pressed into a tight line. "Aside from my family's expulsion from the Sanctuary because my father saved hers?" She shook her head and gave him a slight smile. "A boy. We both wanted him, and it tore us apart. In the end, it didn't matter; he had no interest in either of us."

"I think he was a fool." Sean swallowed thickly, forced himself to look away, and focused on the ripples moving across the water.

Talaunia fixed her gaze on him, trying to read what the darkness masked. "That is kind of you to say." She stepped up to his side, and his arm curled around her waist.

A sharp whistle sounded from the open doorway, and Ryan called out. "Papa's coming. He wants us all in here, now!"

From the swirling eddies on the face of the deep to the highest precipice in the Heavens, let my thanks to the Mother and the Goddess be known, Xeron is born. Lilith brought him into our presence amid the living energies of the Heavenly Gardens, with friends swarming about offering care and support. Iblis was absent, but his mark upon the child was clear as Xeron bears his father's eyes. Rejoice, we have overseen the creation of a new being, with energies unlike any we have seen before—I eagerly await the maturing of his gifts!

—Councilor Syrdan

TWENTY

All eyes in the Operations Center turned when Djain entered the room. Greetings sounded, smiles lit faces at his arrival, and he took the time to acknowledge everyone. Scanning the room, he found Jason at an array of consoles. Moving through the stations with purpose, Djain spoke before reaching the desk. "You found something?"

Jason's head bounced with excitement, and he pointed at the screen. "This guy. Silverman-66!" His finger tapped the screen several times and little rainbows appeared and vanished beneath the pressure. "Man, he has been replying to Reddit posts in the New York area for a while now. Only ever seems to show up when witches are asking for help or advice on how to deal with other witches who have betrayed them."

"What makes you think he is tied to the Order?" Djain asked.

"It's his phrasings, man!" Jason picked up a cup and tipped it back, making a face when it turned out to be empty. "Check this out. Any of these alone won't catch your eye. Take them as a whole, and it turns into a digital beacon!"

Jason read through snippets of several responses until Djain interrupted him. "I understand. Then we are ready to activate our plan?"

With a cocky grin, Jason pointed at an open portal across the room, a pair of figures wavering unfocused on the other side. "Dude, we are so ready! Sarah went to get Lamiri, and I expect that's them now."

As if on cue, Sarah stepped through the portal. She was dressed in a form-fitting black dress that ended above her knees, black net hosiery, and a pair of short, militant-looking black boots. She gave a wave across the room to Djain and Jason. "Found her!"

Stepping into the room behind Sarah was Lamiri Reid. A stunning nineteen-year-old with umber skin, golden brown eyes, and long, black hair fixed in thin braids, pulled up into a ponytail and bound by a multi-colored scarf. Several necklaces spilled over the front of her loose-fitting white top. Her wrists were covered with bracelets, each adorned with dangling bangles and bobbles. Multiple rings glinted from each of her hands. She wore a pair of snug burgundy pants and short, stylish boots that zipped up the side.

Djain waved and motioned the pair over before picking up the phone on the desk. Punching in an extension, he listened, dropping the phone from his mouth as the ladies reached the desk. "Welcome. We will speak in a moment." Before they could respond, he lifted the mouthpiece. "Rhoin, please bring the Whisper Stones to me in Operations. Thank you."

Turning a welcoming smile to the ladies, Djain hung up the phone. "Apologies, but I wanted to ensure we were not delayed." He focused on Lamiri. "It is good to see you again. How is your sister taking to her new position among the Trio?"

"Like I'd know," Lamiri sighed. "You know how sisters can be—a damned pain in the ass." She shook her head, a hint of frustration in the act. "I don't get to see her much now. She's off traveling, fulfilling her duties as part of the Witches Council, and dealing with one issue or another. It seems she's always on Trio business anymore." Her eyes found Djain's. "I miss her."

Djain placed a hand on her shoulder. "I empathize with your situation. Let us hope you two are reunited soon."

"Don't seem to be much chance of that with where I'm about to go," Lamiri said.

"Have you told your sister what you've volunteered to do?" Sarah asked.

"Oh, hell no," Lamiri laughed. "She still treats me like a toddler that needs to be under constant supervision." She fixed each of them with a feisty glare. "And she can stay in the dark until this is done. Understood?"

Jason laughed, glancing at Djain. "Dude, you are about to get in so much shit!"

Djain glowered at Jason. "I hope that is not the case."

"If Nekeisha wants to go a few rounds about this, I'll make sure she does it with me," Lamiri said. "I know full well the risks of trying to infiltrate the Order as a spy, and it was my decision to go."

"Now that we are all on the same page about that topic," Djain said, glancing from Jason to Sarah. "You two, tell Lamiri what you've found and how you plan to get the Order to approach her."

Jason went over the pattern he uncovered in the Reddit threads, and Sarah jumped in. "When you return home, you'll post into the chat we know he frequents, asking for help."

"Is there something specific that seems to catch his interest that I need to mention?" Lamiri asked.

Rhoin stepped through the portal to Djain's private office and shuffled his way toward the group.

"Well, that's where it gets tricky," Jason said.

"He seems to have a soft spot for people who are betrayed by their coven," Sarah offered. "Since secrecy is the top priority here, we can't quite ask your coven to help."

Rhoin reached the group and offered Djain a pair of rings. "Here's tha rings. Need ya ta give Victor a lesson in obedience. Ass keeps tryin' ta haunt the office, an' it's gettin' on my last nerve."

Djain took the rings, turning them over in his hand. The bands were each surrounded with a set of inset stones, and Djain appeared pleased. "Thank you for bringing these."

"Who's Victor?" asked Lamiri.

"Dude, you missed that," Jason said. "We captured Victor. He's a footsoldier for the Order. The idiot killed himself trying to escape, but Papa was like, 'I don't think so!' and bound Victor's spirit, turned him into a ghostly helper."

Lamiri's eyes widened. "Damn."

"Anythin' ta get away from that snivelin' specter," Rhoin grumped. "Anythin' else I can do before I return?"

Shaking his head, Djain bent and patted Rhoin on the shoulder in a supportive gesture. "I can make something up if you like."

Rhoin gave a dismissive wave to the thought. "No need ta go ta such troubles." He turned and shuffled off. "I've endured far worse!"

Djain chuckled. "That you have, my friend. I will address our troublesome guest as quickly as I can."

Rhoin lifted a hand, acknowledging and thanking Djain in the simple gesture, and crossed back through the portal.

Djain turned back to find the other three staring at him and the rings. "We will get to these in a moment. You were telling Lamiri the plan."

"Uhm . . . yeah. So. Since we can't ask your coven for help, Jason and I will go back to New York with you," Sarah said.

"We'll be playing the part of your coven turned vile oppressors. We'll even do a bit of casting against you to give your tale a ring of truth," Jason said.

Lamiri was apprehensive. "I know I'm a badass bitch, but I also know that I can't take on the two of you."

"No worries," Jason said. "You're gonna tell them that the coven was young witches that are fuckin around with stuff they don't understand. That you tried to warn them, but they turned on you, and now they are trying to attack you so you can't rat them out."

"Then we can mess up the stuff we throw at you. Make it reek of power, but be nothing but noise," Sarah said.

"No," Djain interjected.

"He's right," Lamiri said. "It's fine if you want to throw a few 'make the walls quake' type spells that fall short, but you need to throw some things that will be actual curses."

Jason and Sarah both seemed a little less keen on this idea.

"Listen to her," Djain said. "If you are playing the part of young witches, then the things that are real do not have to be heavy hitters, but she needs to be facing actual threats. If everything she faces is smoke and mirrors, she may be sniffed out before she even makes it past the recruiter."

"Exactly," Lamiri confirmed. "Even if some get through, I grew up around this stuff. I'm no stranger to fighting off the effects of hexes. You two best bring the pain. Once that starts, I can make the post and try to get their help."

Fixing both Jason and Sarah with evaluating stares, Djain asked. "Can you two handle this with the new rules of engagement?"

Sarah and Jason debated the matter through looks and expressions, but in the end, both were committed to the new plan.

"Alright," Lamiri said. Pointing to the rings in Djain's hand with a growing smile. "Now, tell me about my new bling."

Holding the rings in his palm, Djain let the group examine the bands. Each ring was inset with alternating translucent and blue stones. "These rings contain gems called Whisper Stones. This set is made of sapphires and clear quartz. They are a matching pair, and they enable the people wearing them to communicate over a great distance, even across different realms, by concentrating on the ring and speaking."

"Dude, that's awesome," Jason intoned. "Why haven't I heard of these before?"

"Because they are rare items. They take a great deal of time and energy to create and can only be imbued by someone favored by the spirits of the Air." Djain handed a ring to Lamiri. "You can whisper, speak, yell; it does not matter. So long as you are focused, your message will be delivered to the wearer of the other ring, just as you speak it. Sounding as though you are right beside them."

"Will other people hear what I say?" Lamiri asked. She slipped the ring over her finger, her lower lip protruding because it was many sizes too large; until it shrank to a perfect fit. Impressed and pleased, she held her hand up to admire the ring.

"Those in earshot will hear you. But only the recipient will hear your words on the other end, and when they respond, only you will hear theirs."

"Who will wear the other ring?" Lamiri asked. "You?"

Djain shook his head. "No, not I. Rather, the leader of our Special Projects team, Sean Byrne. Time will not currently allow for introductions, but I will ensure you meet before you undertake this journey." He slipped the second ring into his pocket. "You three have a lot of work ahead. Go. Get settled. Tomorrow, you may begin setting our plan in motion."

Taking a step back, Djain watched the group discuss their strategy as they moved to the archways across the room. When they had vanished, he checked the clock on the wall, considering his next move. Crossing toward the passage to his private office, his eyes narrowed. "Oh, Victor . . ."

EXCERPT FROM THE ELVEN VOLUMES OF LIVING KNOWLEDGE
CELESTIAL CYCLE 21.14068
IN THE FIRST REIGN OF HOUSE VARUNIA

Creating this new life, our mixed-blood kin, raises the need to label ourselves, if for no other reason than clarity. After a lengthy discussion among the populace, the Council has found consensus. We shall be known as the Elven people and those born with Bright One lineage shall be called the Elevari.

—Councilor Arianelis

Twenty-One

The group was sitting on pillows around the rug in the living area when Djain's presence announced his arrival. He appeared a moment later, moving through the patio door at a brisk pace, his brow lowered, with Gadyen close behind.

Djain moved straight to the console and made several adjustments. Many of the status markers shifted into a ruddy orange color.

Gadyen checked on Ryan, settling in at his side.

A low rumble of concern sounded from the others gathered.

Djain moved to sit with the group. "Do not fret. Those stations have already received additional help, and their actual status has not changed." Djain continued with the informal update, shifting into a comfortable position on the pillows. "We have redefined the indicators to more readily identify where unexpected encounters might occur. All field teams know what has transpired and are on alert."

Ms. Iliescu turned her gaze from the status screens and signaled her approval.

Ryan pressed the back of his fingers into the rug, cracking his knuckles, eager for another skirmish.

"As you know, Jason and Sarah have been searching online covens, chatrooms, magazines, any place that the Order may hunt for potential members. Yesterday, they found a Reddit user that appears to be recruiting, promising help to witches in trouble." Djain's eyes swept around the group. "The posts all came as replies for pleas from persons in the New York area."

Gadyen leaned forward with interest. "Go on."

"I have sent Jason and Sarah to our New York office, where they will assist another witch, Lamiri Reid. She has been given a Whisper Stone and told to contact Sean for help or with any information."

"What's a Whisper Stone?" Sean asked.

Djain held out a ring to Sean, and he accepted. "Place it on your finger," Djain instructed.

"Whisper Stones are rare objects infused with power," Gadyen offered, watching Sean slide the ring onto the middle finger of his right hand. "While wearing one, all you must do is think about the ring, and anything you speak, be it whisper or shout, will be carried on the winds to the one holding the matching object, regardless of how far away they may be."

Djain held up a hand. "I do not wish to get sidetracked on this topic for now. I only wish to inform you. Jason and Sarah left this afternoon with Lamiri and will be in touch as things develop." Pointing to the ring on Sean's hand, "Tomorrow, I will work with you on how to use the stone and help you make introductions to Lamiri."

Talaunia was agitated with the distraction of the rings, and injected herself into the discussion. "And the Traxidors? Did you meet with them? What did they have to say about what Vitan revealed to Sean?"

Djain focused on Sean. "Normally, I would not hold this conversation in a public forum, but time demands an exception. Please accept my apologies ahead of time." Giving focus to Ms. Iliescu, he asked. "How has his training progressed?"

"Trying at times, but he has made acceptable progress. You should see his circle casting; I think you will find it of interest. We have covered the basics of manifestation in the Astral, and with much prompting and trial, he succeeded in full transformation."

Djain head tilted. "What form?"

"A silver wolf," said Ms. Iliescu. She paused, choosing her words. "We have made a short and successful incursion into both Mr. Washington's and Ms. Daejor's minds, though our Mr. Byrne lost focus, falling back into his mundane form."

"That is unfortunate. We will need to work on his focus." Djain's brow lowered. "Anything else?"

Talaunia was biting her lip in frustration as Djain continued to ignore her questions.

"No. We had taken a break when we received notice of your arrival," said Ms. Iliescu.

Djain was apologetic but pressed on. "I trust your break was enough. I know it has been a long day, but I fear we have quite some distance yet to go."

"What about the Traxidors?" asked Talaunia, unable to hold her tongue any longer. Sean reached for her hand, but she pulled it away, still focused on Djain. "Don't try to appease me."

Djain turned his focus on Talaunia, a fiery rage burning in his eyes. He leaned across the circle. "Do not push me, Elf. Your kind has been harboring secrets, and their silence cost us unnecessarily!"

Every eye locked on the pair.

Talaunia blinked, sitting back, confused and hurt by the anger directed at her. "What secrets? I—" She stopped, anger flaring to life in her chest. Her tiny form leaned into the circle, brushing noses with the hulking frame of Djain. "I don't know a damned thing about their secrets! I'm anathema to them! And I've been nothing but loyal to you. Do you think I have kept you in the dark about something? Held something back that you needed to know?"

Djain's jaw locked. He drew in a breath as the others held theirs. Sean could almost hear him counting to ten as he released the air. Leaning back, Djan's jaw relaxed, but the tension remained in his frame. "Apologies, child. I left a confrontation with the Traxidors prior to my arrival, and you should not suffer my anger."

Talaunia's chin lowered once, curt, sharp, and she sat back. "Glad we got that settled. Perhaps you should tell us about what you've learned from those treacherous do-gooders, Papa."

Everyone breathed, and Djain gave Talaunia a short-lived smile.

"The Elves will neither confirm nor deny any knowledge of Lilith's presence on Terra," Djain said, a finger tapping in agitation. "After much deliberation, what I have gleaned is that their oracles have prophesied Lilith's return since the birth of humanity. They foretell a coming war between the Elven races that will hinge on human influence. And I have verified that the Fairy Guard is nowhere to be found."

"So, we don't know shit," piped up Ryan in frustration.

"Perhaps now you understand my agitation. Circular arguments were leading nowhere." Djain pursed his lips and exhaled. "While the Elves and I have long held an alliance, they have never quite trusted me, even when so much of what we do at the Quari Group furthers their goals."

Sean leaned forward, the history fascinating to him. "Are they distrustful of everyone, or is it caused by something specific?" He lifted a brow, focusing on Talaunia.

"There must be a reason," she said. "We are a trusting people until actions make us otherwise."

Ms. Iliescu cleared her throat and set her gaze on Djain. "You knew this day would arrive. It is time for others to know your truth."

Curiosity flashed across the faces gathered in the room.

Djain considered each of them. "Agreed." He cleared his throat. "I believe Sean already harbors suspicions about what I will be sharing. It is hard to hide such things from an archeologist when you hand them personal items of antiquity."

Sean stared at Djain, contemplating the contrasting things he knew of the man. "I find it hard to reconcile your age and that of your belongings unless you have discovered time travel."

"In a manner, I did," Djain said. "Though unintentionally, I must add."

Murmurs rose from the others, but Djain held up his hand. "I was born in 1153. My mother was a powerful witch, and my father remains chief among those who command the air. When I was born, the villagers made threats rooted in fear and ignorance. Those threats led to my mother being burned alive for sleeping with devils. I would have burned alongside her had Morjan not intervened."

Lifting a hand, Sean tilted his head, puzzled. "It wasn't your father I saw in that vision?"

"What vision?" asked Talaunia, with Gadyen and Ryan echoing the same question, their voices out of sync.

"I saw Papa in his home one winter's night and witnessed a brief exchange with him, and the man I thought was his father," Sean offered. His eyes settled on Djain, and the pair shared a knowing smile. "His sister was in the vision as well."

The group's attention had swung to Sean, with Ryan, Gadyen, and Talaunia pressing for more details.

Ms. Iliescu's quiet authority halted their inquiries. "We have strayed from the true topic of this discussion.

I suggest we focus on Papa's tale and not on random visions of children."

Apologies sounded around the group.

Talaunia locked eyes with Sean. "I'll hear of it later." She gave an apologetic glance to Djain. "Sorry, Papa. Continue."

Djain shook his head. "Morjan acted like my father. He was a feared shaman, worked the darkest of magic, and none of the nearby villagers dared cross him, though they stole to his house in the dead of night to beg his aide. I was raised alongside his child, Oai'Quari, who arrived within a year of my rescue. He once told me that a blazing spirit had settled him where we lived. The area is now a glacier, approximately two miles southwest of Oppstryn, Norway. Years later, the spirit revisited him and bade him rescue me. As a reward, the spirit took his seed, returning it to him as a daughter, giving him both his children."

"Where was your father, Morjan, from if the Bright Ones relocated him?" asked Talaunia.

"He was raised in the Caribbean," Djain said, smiling at Sean as they watched the others piece together things Sean had already uncovered.

Gadyen arched a brow. "Was Oai'Quari a direct descendant of a Bright One?"

"Yes," Djain answered without hesitation. "She was a shifter who took the form of a black panther. She was mesmerizing. Understand that she and I were alone in this world. Reviled by the villagers and father put us in positions that required us to depend on one another. We became inseparable. One. I had begun my twentieth year when our father died, and the villagers' fear waned with his passing. They knew we practiced the same magic as Father, and they came to us in the darkness, crying for us to ease their woes. They saw our power, but they saw our youth and inexperience as well. It bolstered them, and eventually, they came for us."

Djain leaned in, "I knew the moment Oai'Quari fell, I felt it as though a part of me had been cleaved off. At that moment, I ripped open a portal. I intended to step into the Realm of Shadows, a dangerous place, but one with which I was accustomed. I intended to move through the shadows and emerge back into Terra, well away from the attackers. It was not the Shadows I entered but the Elven Sanctuary. The Elves set upon me in a fury, demanding to know how I came to be in their sacred place. Years they detained me, questioned me, until they grudgingly accepted my tale, and we formed our alliance. They would aid me, and I would help them restore the Mother."

"How long were you there?" Talaunia asked in hushed tones, knowing, as each of them did, how time flows differently between the realms.

"A little over 83 years," Djain said. Seeing the puzzled expressions around him, he clarified, "Elven years. When I returned to Terra, almost a millennium had passed. The world I knew was no more. Where once a blacksmith forged you a tool, and fletchers made your arrows fly straight. Now horseless carriages roared past, and food was something you picked up from any number of shops, no weapon required."

Ms. Iliescu looked at Djain fondly. "I met Papa the day after he returned. I had been working with the Elves already, and they asked me to assist him. We were a scattered and unorganized group before Djain built the Quari Group, but that is a story for another time."

Djain focused on Ms. Iliescu, his gaze filled with admiration and respect. "The world would not be what it is today without the wisdom imparted to me by Ms. Iliescu," he studied the small group. "We need to look at the past." His gaze settled on Sean. "We need to examine the night Oai'Quari died. The Traxidors mentioned her passing and my entry to their realm several times, but refused to discuss why. There is something about that night we must discover."

Sean's brow lowered in concentration. "What do you need me to do?"

Looking at Ms. Iliescu, Djain asked a question that made the room explode in chaos. "Can he lead us all to the event through his gift of sight?"

Ms. Iliescu's countenance darkened, and she shook her head as Ryan, Gadyen, and Talaunia erupted in excited questions.

"Can that be done?"

"I didn't know that was possible!"

"Fuck yeah, let's go check this shit out!"

They talked over one another, bickering about who would get to try it with him first until Djain's deep voice bellowed, "Quiet!"

The room stilled, waiting for Ms. Iliescu's response. "Walking your memory is this not an option?"

Djain shook his head. "My memory is limited to what I witnessed, and I have lived that night many times. I do not think the answer lies within me."

Her shoulders fell, and Ms. Iliescu appeared tired. She fixed her gaze on Djain. "It can be done, but he cannot do it alone. He can barely lead himself about, much less maintain a group." Her eyes drifted to Sean. "If you lead, I can bind myself to you and tether the group to me, allowing us to follow."

The nervous energy in the room shot up.

Sean shifted, thinking of the task placed before him and the excitement bubbling over within the others.

"What do we need?" Djain asked.

"If you have something tied to that night, it would be helpful," said Ms. Iliescu. "Otherwise, it needs to be something from that time. He will need a strong focal item if he is to succeed."

"The pyramid Axylia gave you," Talaunia offered, rising. "I'll get it."

Djain rose as well. "Everyone, take a few moments. I must make a call. When I return, we will find the truth." He lifted his phone. "Rhoin, might you have a few moments?" His voice faded as he stepped out onto the porch.

Ms. Iliescu set about making fresh tea.

Gadyen pulled Ryan to the side, checking him over and making a more thorough inspection of his healing.

Sean sat in silence, trying to prepare for what he was about to attempt.

When Talaunia returned, she placed the pyramid on the rug in front of Sean. Sitting at his side, she put her hand in his. "I'm here."

Sean's lips betrayed the comfort he found at having Talaunia near, and he closed his eyes, drawing in a deep breath.

Talaunia joined him, followed by Ryan and Gadyen.

Upon returning with her tea, Ms. Iliescu's eyes warmed with approval. After settling herself in, she took them all with her in a guided meditation.

Rhoin entered the patio door and moved to Djain, placing an object in his hand. "Anything else ya need?"

"This is all. Thank you for bringing it to us," Djain said.

Rhoin gave a bow. "I'll leave ya all to yer work." And without another word, he waddled right back out into the darkness.

When Ms. Iliescu was satisfied, they were all prepared; she opened her eyes. "Now, the actual work begins." Turning her attention to Djain. "What has Rhoin brought you? A strong focus item I trust."

Djain extended his hand, dropping a small stone which dangled from an aged leather cord. The polished stone had a glyph chiseled into its face. "I made this for her. I completed it in the moments before the attack; she never saw it. When the chaos started, I draped it over my neck. It was with me until the end."

A somber silence weighed on the room as Sean reached out and took the necklace from Djain. He cupped the weight of the stone in his palm and wrapped the coarse leather around his hand, closing his fist over the treasure.

"Think of the moment it was finished," Ms. Iliescu instructed Sean. "Imagine the satisfaction of completion, the anticipation of presenting it as a gift."

Sean's eyes drifted closed, and he concentrated on the stone. He imagined how he expected Djain to feel in those moments before his world went sideways, and the stone responded. It vibrated, and the energy pulsing in his palm was familiar. "I have it."

"Hold it, let it fill you," Ms. Iliescu instructed, her eyes going white. An unusual tickle teased at his mind. "Connect with my energy, Mr. Byrne."

Brow drawing down in concentration, he focused on the unfamiliar sensation, reaching for it with his energy. Like an electrical jolt running through him, their auras linked. "Oh, wow. That is different," he said.

"Concentrate, Mr. Byrne. We cannot have a repeat of earlier," Ms. Iliescu admonished him. "Now, everyone, join me. Rise into your Astral forms."

Sean slipped out of his body with ease this time, dawning the guise of the silver wolf. Ms. Iliescu was in her hawk form, and there was a brilliant strand of energy flowing between them.

Ryan and Gadyen appeared in unison. Ryan manifested in ursine form, while Gadyen reminded Sean of a ball of lightning, a blinding core with deadly arcs dancing over the surface.

Talaunia caused Sean's concentration to falter. She appeared as herself, with a strapless gown hugging the curves of her lithe form. It curled outward at mid-thigh, sparking images of a multi-layered bud opening. An Astral breeze lifted her hair, and she floated, weightless and breathtaking.

Ms. Iliescu turned a hawkish gaze on Talaunia and let out a shrill cry in the Astral.

Talaunia shifted into the form of a squirrel sitting on her haunches, a picture of innocence.

Ms. Iliescu glowered at her and huffed.

Djain followed them all, his powerful upper body appearing from out of a cloud, dissolving into the roiling storm that carried him. It reminded Sean of the spirits that had observed the ritual at Djain's invitation. The image was clearer here than it had been in the circle, and thoughts of djinn popped into his mind.

With Djain's appearance, Sean watched tendrils of energy reach out to each of the others, as it had him.

"Feel my energy searching for yours. Connect. Link with me, so we may be bound on this journey." Ms. Iliescu was meticulous in the details as she forged the bonds.

Sean could sense each of them as they tethered themselves to Ms. Iliescu, their energy rippling along the delicate thread he shared with her.

When the process was complete, she turned to Sean. *"Now, Mr. Byrne. Focus on the vibration of that time, of that event. Lean on the energy of the crystals, let them strengthen you, guide you."*

Sean sat before the pyramid, his wolfish muzzle pressed to the carpet. He stared into the crystal facets, allowing the familiar vibrations to course through him. Letting go, he followed, and time melted away around him. Centuries of progress vanished until his paws found stability in the snow. He was outside an old, stacked stone hut. One he had seen before.

Excerpt from the Elven Volumes of Living Knowledge
Celestial Cycle 97.18341
in the First Reign of House Varunia

Regardless of the reprehensible manner in which the Elevari children must be bread, and despite the impact of their creation on the Heavenly Gardens, they trudge ahead boldly. After many cycles lost to debate among the Council, we have agreed. Councilors Kryntan and Syrdan may continue to spur the growth of this new species unopposed. In exchange, they must require all of their recruits to tend the Gardens and restore two new plants for each sacrificed for their debauchery. As this replenishes the Gardens and ensures their continuing germination experiments, all parties appear mollified, if not entirely pleased.

—Queen Varunia

Twenty-Two

Time heals nothing.

The sun hung low on the horizon, golden light reflected off the snow swirling by the heavy wooden door of the home, and the hush of approaching night settled over the area. Across the clearing, Sean could see a bearded man watching the dwelling from the long shadows cast by the trees. He was dressed in heavy furs, carried a two-handed ax, and across the distance, Sean could sense his fear.

A second figure exited the woods, joining the sentry in the shadows, and soon a third followed.

The astral forms of Sean's fellow travelers arrived at his side, and Sean pointed at the growing mob pouring in hushed haste from the forest. *"It's beginning."*

The rumble of thunder sounded from the core of clouds surrounding Djain, watching the men closing the distance on the structure. *"I am inside, happy, waiting for her to return so I can surprise her."*

"She isn't here?" Ryan asked.

Djain pointed behind them. *"Oai'Quari is in the village to trade. A portion of them came for me while she was away, and others attacked her while she was in the village."*

The group approaching the house had swelled to eleven men, each brandishing bladed weapons. Nearing the structure, they split up. Two groups of five flanked the entrance, using snowbanks as cover, leaving one man to approach. The lone figure drove the hilt of his axe against the wooden barrier three times and backed away several steps.

The Astral group pressed closer, watching the door swing open. Warm, orange light flooded the opening. A tall, dark form ducked and stepped into the snow. His bare feet sank into the icy crystals, necklaces of bone and teeth hung around his neck, along with the stone disk Sean held in his hand. The Djain in the doorway was physically identical to the one they all knew, and the voice was unmistakable; yet his eyes lacked the maturity and wisdom of the man they called Papa.

Djain's eyes swept over the tracks in the snow, and he folded his arms across his chest. "What brings you out before darkness has fallen, Skarde?"

"Devil child, hold your tongue, or we will pierce it with iron before sending you to meet your mother," Skarde said.

"I only see you, Skarde. Your brothers lack the nerve to crawl from their hiding places." Djain flashed a taunting smirk and took a single step backward into the doorframe.

The others cursed and moved out, forming a half-circle around the entryway, each giving bigoted jabs. Djain backed into the house and closed the door. The slotting of a crossbar sounded, and several men rushed forward. They brought their weapons to bear against the stout barrier, splintering its surface and sending fragments into the air.

The men in the back produced flint and steel. Soon torches were ignited and tossed onto the thatched roof. The flames spread, and black smoke billowed from the home.

Djain slipped out a window at the rear of the structure, holding the staff Sean had seen him carry once before. He rushed along the path leading into town, ignoring the throng of men seeking to turn his home to embers.

One attacker spotted him and sounded the alarm, charging after him. One by one, the others came to understand. Abandoning their assault on the home, they joined the chase.

The Astral party followed Djain, watching him check over his shoulder before vanishing into the cover of the forest path. As he ran, he pulled out a dagger and drew the blade across his forearm. Crimson blood rained from his fingertips, speckling the snow. The cries behind him were lost in the spine-chilling screams that ripped from the village ahead. Djain drew symbols across his chest in blood, and around him, four spirits took form.

The party shared glances as they watched the events unfold, but their Djain remained focused on watching things play out from a fresh vantage point. Nearing the gates, he pointed to a well-concealed, hooded bowman, blocked from view anywhere but from above. *"That one I have never seen before."*

His comment made the others realize they were not here to watch what had happened to Djain, but what had happened in places Djain couldn't see, but it was difficult to pull their attention away.

When past Djain reached the gates, he issued a command to the four spirits.

Each spirit entered a guard, possessing them, turning them on their fellow gatekeepers, and Djain walked over the bloody ground, entering the town unopposed with an armed guard at his side. He ripped a bit of cloth from his pants and bound his forearm as they watched the chaos of people running from the local tavern. "Oai'Quari is in there. Make me a path."

The possessed guardsmen ran into the throng, hacking and slashing anyone in their way. The betrayal added to the chaos, and Djain ran up to the doors and into the Inn. Sean tried to watch the events in the square, but the rest of the Astral party passed into the building, and the tether tugged him along.

Atop the bar, Oai'Quari stood transformed. Strength and power rippled beneath her sleek coat. Rivulets of crimson ran from her shoulder, mingling with the blood bathing her maw and paws. She leaped through the air and landed next to Djain, nuzzling him before turning to judge the threat.

Bodies lay everywhere, some still alive, others nothing but dismembered bits.

Djain lifted a hand and patted her behind the ears. "We need to get ourselves free of this village. They mean to put us to the fire."

The massive cat sneezed and bolted for the door, barreling through the next wave of attackers, knocking them back, and charging out into the snowy street.

Djain followed a step behind, dashing out into the chaos.

Women scattered before Oai'Quari, but those she hunted fell beneath a savage mauling.

One spirit returned to Djain, and he directed it into another villager.

Planting his staff into the dirt, Djain wrapped his hands around the shaft. He muttered under his breath, and around him, the winds churned and swirled.

In moments, the villagers had to lean into the wind to keep their feet, struggling to escape the nightmare they had loosed upon their village. It made them easy targets for Oai'Quari.

The buildings creaked and moaned under the relentless assault of wind, and Oai'Quari sprang to the stillness at Djain's side.

Debris filled the air, piercing the flesh of those caught in the gale. The guard shack collapsed, followed by the livery. Wailing cries for mercy mingled with the wind, but Djain bore down on the staff, whipping the winds into even greater fury. All the years of abuse at the hands of these people had found its path to vengeance, and it was untamed.

The next moments unfolded in a blur of motion, and they would have missed it if not for the Astral form of Djain. *"There!"* He pointed into the gale.

Amid the carnage, a solitary bowman stood amid the tornadic winds. Unaffected and unharmed. He stood behind Djain and drew his bow, taking aim at the center of Djain's back.

Oai'Quari saw the man and lunged, placing herself between Djain and the shot that defied the howling storm.

The arrow drove itself deep into Oai'Quari's side, and she hit the dirt, motionless.

Djain crumpled to a knee, screaming her name and clutching his side.

A sound best likened to a banshee's wail ripped through the world, and in a heartbeat, it was gone, and so was Djain.

The wind died, and the heavy clouds overhead shed fresh snowflakes as the powder whipped up by Djain fell to the ground, dusting the field of corpses.

Around them, the town was gone, save one small building that stood unscathed. The storm no longer obscured the archer that had taken the fatal shot. When he pushed the cowl back from his head, a narrow face emerged, rugged features and bushy black hair with pointy ears and a pair of white feathery wings. The man turned and whistled, signaling it was clear.

The snow was falling in heavy, wet flakes.

"That is one of the Fairy Guardsmen," Gadyen stated.

"I can't believe it," said Talaunia, horrified.

The door to the building opened, and a slender figure stepped out, flanked by two men wearing the Order's medallions. Heat flushed through Sean. He knew this woman intimately, though they had never met.

"Concentrate, Mr. Byrne," came Ms. Iliescu's command.

Sean fought to keep control, the ripples of the emotional wave threatening to topple him and send him plummeting back into reality. Restoring his focus, he pointed at the strange woman. *"That is Lilith!"*

The group with Lilith regarded the sky and the building intensity of the falling snow.

"Are you sure?" asked Ryan.

"He is sure," replied Djain, his voice distant. *"This is an example of unbalanced magic. This storm is going to bury this entire area. It is the first place I excavated when I returned to Terra. I found this scene unchanged, frozen in the aftermath of my rage."* Around them, the storm was already approaching whiteout conditions. *"It is time we return."*

Ms. Iliescu led them all back to the cottage, helped remove the Astral bonds, and was the last to descend into her mortal form. She blinked, and her eyes rolled, her gray irises returning to peer out at the group. "That was altogether draining."

"For all of us, thank you," Djain said. "I know you may have seen more than you expected, learned things you might never have guessed. Our unity now is more needed than ever."

The revelations shook Talaunia, and her voice quavered. "There are traitors in the Fairy Guard . . . ."

"Lilith is back on Terra," said Gadyen. "And based on Sean's vision, it seems clear to take this as confirmation that Xeron has also returned."

"They will try to bring over more of those fucking freaks from the Void," growled Ryan.

"And they are planning to use the Quari Cube to do it," said Sean.

"We will not let them succeed," said Ms. Iliescu. "I have seen what they will unleash if we do not intervene. The Void, into which they were cast, had no life, held no magic, yet was populated with creatures requiring both to survive. Many of those banished are no more. Devoured by their brethren long ago. Those that survive are the strongest, some twisted into nightmarish forms, molded by the chaos they were left to steep in."

Djain rose. "Rest. Tomorrow we no longer fight to avenge those we have lost, but to save those we yet have."

Whispers circulate among the Elves once more, and mistrust of the Elevari grows. Some among the Elevari children are gorging themselves on living energy from the Heavenly Gardens, creating a euphoric, dreamlike state. This discovery was made by finding Elven children suffering from the effects and investigating the cause. Councilors Kryntan and Syrdan see no reason for concern, and Councilor Jerandyl agrees. The laws of restoration are being maintained, and there is no lasting damage to the Gardens, though how may the soul be marred with such callous consumption of life? We all await Queen Varunia's decision.

—Councilor Daejor

Twenty-Three

I WILL NOT BOW; I WILL NOT BREAK.

Sarah watched the people crossing the intersection of Broadway and Houston from the shadowed depths of the office window. The room was being absorbed by the darkness settling between the buildings. The streets below traded the light of the sun for the uneven pools spilling from lamps, vehicles, and windows.

Beyond the glass, Manhattan hummed. Its sounds underpinning everything with a steady thrum of energy. A sense of life charged the atmosphere, an electricity never experienced within the gardens surrounding the Quari Group headquarters in Cordath.

"I love this town," Sarah said.

The signal light outside changed color, casting a red glow over her powder-white face.

Jason sat on the tile floor, double-checking the sigil he had spent the afternoon drawing on its surface. Since their arrival in New York, he had watched her gaze with longing on the concrete world surrounding them. "It suits you," he said after some consideration.

"It would blow to see you go, but have you thought about asking for a transfer?"

She pulled her focus from the bustle beyond the window and stared at Jason. The intrigue of the idea burned inside her until she extinguished it with a shake of her head. "I can't. Too much to do there," she said without conviction.

"You know it's never going to happen, right?" Jason asked, with all the compassion of a friend intent on making you see your blind spots. "Especially now, with Axylia gone."

"I'm sure I don't know what you mean."

Jason shook his head and laughed. "We've all seen it. The lingering stares, the yearning glances, the way you light up and fidget when she looks your way. And we've watched you try to hide your jealousy when she is fawning all over Sean."

Sarah was horrified. "What do you mean? You've all seen?"

"I mean, you don't hide it nearly as well as you think."

"Do you all talk about it?" Sarah asked, embarrassment darkening her cheeks, even under the powdery make-up. "Does she know?"

"I don't see how she couldn't know. But relax. None of us talk about it," Jason said, trying to reassure her. "Kind of an unspoken understanding that if you want us talking about it, you'll bring it up."

Relief flooded through her, followed by anger. "Then why the fuck are you bringing it up now?"

"Because it's clear that you and this city vibe," Jason said, pushing himself up off the floor. He crossed to the desk beside Sarah and picked up several candles. "And because I'd like to think you might find some happiness if you'd let yourself stop fixating on her." Moving back to the middle of the room, he placed the candles around the sigil. "It's a great big world, Sarah. I'm only saying it may be time for you to leave the nest and see what you find in it."

Her shoulders sank, and she stared at Jason with his floppy hair and concert t-shirt. She had never thought of him as anything but content. Sure, he was grumpy if anyone prodded him from bed before 9 AM, but he was still happy. She turned her gaze back out the window. "Maybe—"

Jason made another circuit around the sigil, this time lighting the candles. He crossed to another desk and gathered the remaining items needed to work the hex. When everything was ready, he moved to her side and spoke again. "Not like you have to decide tonight, just thought it was something you should think about." Giving her a friendly nudged with his elbow, he prodded. "Come on. We've got work to do."

With a heavy sigh, she agreed and turned her back on the call of the city that was resonating in her bones.

〈 ᛟᛣᛣᛟᚱᛏᚢ ᚺᛁᛏᛁᛗᛋ ᚠᛒᛟᚾᛏᛉ ᛁᚾ ᛃᛟᚱᚢᚱ ᚾᚠᛗ 〉

Lamiri crammed a handful of candles into her bag before moving to the bookshelf. She cast a glance over her shoulder at the laptop, cursing under her breath.

Nothing had changed on the screen.

She plucked a couple of her journals from the shelf and her favorite tarot deck, cramming them into the bag with the candles. Dashing around the room, she searched for the assorted bits of life she had to take with her if she was going to run.

The past three days had been akin to living in a witchcraft war zone. Sarah and Jason had been faithful to their promise and had come at her with both barrels. She had not slept in thirty-six hours, and the constant barrage of spell work was wearing down her latest round of wards.

Leaning on the bed, she stared at the screen, willing it to change, but the liquid crystal display taunted her with its steady glow.

As planned, once Jason and Sarah started their assault, Lamiri had asked for help in a local Reddit forum. All kinds of replies streamed in, some more helpful than others. The more she described her situation, the faster the would-be helpers crawled back into their holes.

It took almost two full days before Silverman_66 had responded. He sent her private messages outlining steps she should take to ward and protect herself until they could discuss her situation in more detail.

For the past day, she had followed his instructions, giving him her cover story, while Jason and Sarah went above and beyond what was required to sell it. Lamiri was afraid, and if she didn't get help soon, she would be in serious trouble.

She smacked the screen again, and the last messages wobbled before resuming their stoic stare in the face of her panic.

```
Sexy-Hexy > It keeps coming, non-stop!
I'm afraid my wards are going to fail
soon.
Silverman-66 > I have spoken with my
coven, and they would like to help you.
Sexy-Hexy > Thank you! Thank you! Thank
you!
Silverman-66 > We have a meeting place
nearby.
Sexy-Hexy > When can I meet them?
Silverman-66 > I will set up a time and
provide details when everything is
ready. Prepare a small pack of
necessities. My coven leader has
offered to host you until we end this
attack. Be prepared to meet her
tonight.
```

"Fucking help me, dammit," she raged, spinning back into her mad flight through the room, packing a few more necessary things to take with her when she fled. She was stuffing a bra into the bag when she heard the laptop chime, and she dove over the bed to read the message.

```
Silverman-66 > Washington Square Arch,
8:00 pm, have your bag.
```

Lamiri saw the time glowing in the lower corner of the screen: 7:44 PM. She cursed, slammed the screen on the laptop closed, shoved it and the charger into her bag, and scrambled toward the door.

Weinstein Hall was less than a five-minute walk from the arch, but she didn't want to be late. She closed her door, checked that it was secure, and hit the stairwell, running as though her life depended on it.

< ᚾᛗᚦ ᚠᛈᛁᛁᛗᚾᛏᛁᚱᛗᛋ ᚠᚦᚠᛁᛏ ᛁᛟᚾ >

Sarah stared at the sigil. "You don't think this is going too far?"

Jason shook his head. "We were told to sell it, so come on. Let's sell it."

Kneeling opposite of Jason, she sighed. "So help me, Jason. If I find out we've hurt her, I'm going to kick your ass."

Jason waved her off. "If she's got her wards up, this will do nothing but cause some near misses. Come on. We know she's made contact. Hopefully, we'll find out she's made it into the group soon, then we can start backing off."

Forcing herself to focus on the spell, Sarah began the incantation, and Jason joined in.

< ᛁᛟᚾ ᚠᚱᛗ ᚦᛟᚱᛏᚾᛁ ᛟᚠ ᛁᛟᛁᛗ >

The energy around Lamiri shifted, and she paused on the stairs long enough to double-check her wards, cataloging her bracelets, rings, and necklaces.

She stared at the Whisper Stone and almost reached out to Sean. They had talked several times over the past days, and she had come to trust he would reply when she called, even when she woke him. However, they had agreed that she wouldn't reach out again until she was inside the Order.

Pushing herself away from the wall, she moved down the stairs. The tread on the next step was loose, and she tripped, stumbled, and careened face-first into the wall on the next landing.

"Son-of-a-bitch!" She wiped the blood from her nose, descended the remaining flight of stairs with added caution, and exited through the lobby.

Stepping across the threshold of the building's main door, a terracotta pot filled with dirt hit the pavement and exploded, scattering bits of soil all over her boots.

"Sorry," someone screamed from the window overhead.

Lamiri spun and flipped off the building's facade, stepping back into the path of a cyclist.

The rider yelled and swerved around her. Their handlebars caught the strap of her pack, jerking her off balance, and sending the biker into the metal guard around a nearby tree. The momentum caused Lamiri to wobble and stumble into the street, arms windmilling to regain her balance.

Tires squealed, and she tensed, the taxi sliding to a stop, its bumper pressing against her knee. The driver laid into the horn, and the blaring sound caused Lamiri to jump as it drowned out the expletive-filled rant coming from within the car. When the horn stopped, the guy leaned out the window. "Get the fuck out of the road!"

Lamiri dashed out of the street, disaster looming with every step she took. By the time she reached the Washington Square Arch, her hands were trembling. She leaned back against the cool stone, clutching her bag to her chest. "I'm here," she panted. "I'm here."

She watched people wander past until an older gentleman approached her. Lamiri placed him in his mid-60's, with short white hair and a well-trimmed white beard that practically glowed against his ruddy cheeks. "Miss? Are you feeling well?"

Lamiri waved him off. "I had to catch my breath," she lied.

The man stopped right before her, sizing her up, his glasses and jacket making Lamiri think he looked like a professor.

"If you are certain you are okay," he said, drawing it out to add emphasis. "I'm always happy to help someone in need."

She would have sworn she saw his brow lift in question, and she blinked. "I'm here to meet someone. Thank you for the offer."

"Perhaps I should keep you company until they arrive," the man said. He extended his hand. "I'm Doctor Silverman, Alan."

Lamiri blinked. "Are you Silverman_66?"

He laughed, a warm, welcoming sound that put her at ease. "My students tell me all the time that username is a little too on the nose." He left his hand extended, hovering in the air between them.

"Oh," she said, taking hold and pumping his hand. "So, you're a professor at NYU?"

Alan regarded their hands with amusement as she held tight, continuing to work the handshake. "Correct. Religious studies, if you can imagine."

She glanced around, watching for the next calamity aimed at her. "I can't tell you how happy I am to meet you. Things have gone downhill since this afternoon."

Concern touched his eyes, and he enfolded her hand between both of his. "You are trembling. What has happened?" he asked with sincerity.

She told him of all her near misses, and he dropped her hand, pulling a small necklace from his pocket. It had a tiny jar attached to it, filled with bits of this and that, and he plucked the little cork plug out. "Spit in this, recap it, and put it on. It is a damned powerful protection charm. It will mask you and reflect anything targeting you back to its caster."

She followed his instructions and felt the charms warding effects wrap around her. She wished she could see the look on Jason's face when his latest spell bit back, but she suppressed that spike of glee, for now. "Thank you."

"It is a pleasure," he insisted. "Now that we have you out of immediate danger, how would you like to meet a few more members of my coven? Perhaps they can persuade you to join us. We have a long history, spanning back to the creation of the pyramids. You won't find any young, green witches souring the well with us."

"From what you've told me already, I can't imagine not finding a place among you," she said, glancing toward the fountain at the center of the park. "Where do we need to go?"

With amusement in his eyes, he inclined his head toward the arch behind her. "Right here!"

Turning, she found a portal had opened in plain sight, but no one seemed to take notice.

"Won't they see?" she asked in a panic.

He laughed, and peace settled over her again. "The charm masks you, remember? It is a perception filter of sorts. They could walk right past us and not even know."

She blinked, dumbfounded. "I've never heard of such a thing."

"One of many fantastical things we can show you," he said, motioning toward the portal. "Shall we?"

"Oh, hell yes," she said. Glancing at the stone ring on her finger, she added, "I'm in!" Without a backward glance, Lamiri stepped into the world of the Order.

< ᚪᛟᛚᚱ ᚲᛟᛏᛗᚨᛏᛁᚪᚾ ᛁᛋ ᚾᛈᚨᛁᛏᛁᛗᛋᛋ >

Talaunia closed the book that Sean was studying. "It's almost one o'clock in the morning. Time for good students to rest."

Sean sighed. He opened his mouth to grumble, but Lamiri's voice caught his attention. Though her message only contained two words, they were charged with excitement. His lips curled upward. "She's in!" A momentary relief that some part of their plan had worked eased the weight he shouldered. Knowing this to be only one step in the battle to come, he twisted his head to look at Talaunia. "Perhaps we should rest while we can."

< ᛣᛟᛐ ᚳᚠᛏ ᛉᛟᛩ ᚠᛐᚣᛏᚾᛁᛏᛉ >

Sarah and Jason both stopped casting at the same time. An odd, unsettled feeling was building about them. The radiator against the wall made a strange sound, bucked, and bounced on the tile, vibrating and chattering.

"Oh, fuck me!" Jason dove toward Sarah and tackled her, both landing behind the desk on the far side of the room.

In the next instant, the radiator exploded. Glass shattered out of every window, raining on the pedestrians and vehicles below.

At a distance, sirens sounded.

Jason laughed and checked on Sarah. "You alright?"

Scrambling to her feet, Sarah took a quick inventory of herself before giving confirmation. "Yeah. I'm good." She turned, checking out the damage. The floor had cracked in every direction around the remains of the radiator, and the plaster on the walls was marred and missing in places. Ceiling tiles hung at odd angles. Bits of wiring and insulation dangled from the broken ceiling, swaying in the dusty air. Sarah laughed. "I think she found help."

"Let's hope that means she's made it in," Jason said. Then, taking in the room's state, he added, "You get to tell Papa about this."

Over the last two cycles, only Elves have been caught and punished for abusing the living energies in the Heavenly Gardens. The Elevari make no effort to hide their continued addiction to excess life, though we can find no evidence linking them to the acts. In my heart, I know something is amiss, but my visions are muddled and offer nothing useful in uncovering the truth. Goddess, help us see past the veil of secrecy that keeps our eyes focused in the wrong direction.

—Councilor Traxidor

TWENTY-FOUR

SWEET . . .

Sean hit the mat hard, the thud of his sudden stop echoing from the walls of the training room. He groaned, rolled onto his back, and flung his arms out to his sides; they were drenched in sweat and sporting several new scrapes. "I yield," he panted. "No more. That's all I've got for the day."

"It better not be all you've got. You still have that dinner with your mother tonight." Talaunia reminded him for what seemed the hundredth time. She stood over him, her forehead covered in a light sheen, and her copper hair damp from the exertion of their sparring session.

He knew she wanted to go with him, hear the stories, and lend her support, but he kept her dangling. To his surprise, she had not pressured him for an invitation. She had been perfect in keeping her advances in check since Axylia's death, though he could see her biting back quips, and it sharpened his fondness for her.

"Fine," he said at last. "Let's go get ready. We don't want to be late." He had only delayed the invite to watch her squirm. He wanted her there for this conversation, afraid other secrets might come spilling out, and if they did, he would welcome her presence.

She was practically living with him at the moment. He had thrown himself into training. Spending his mornings with Ms. Iliescu, lunch in the library, making lists of books for the librarians to gather for him, and afternoons in the training room with Talaunia, Gadyen, and Ryan. Of an evening, he poured over the research materials and read well into the night. He was exhausting himself, only sleeping an hour or two each night. Talaunia stayed with him through all of it, making sure he ate regularly, and when he slept, she would lie beside him, restoring the damage he was doing to himself, enabling him to keep going.

He lifted a hand, and she took it, beaming and pulling herself against him. "About time you asked."

Once on his feet, he waved her off. "Please, you knew I'd cave and let you come."

She laughed, and the sound was bright, making a bit of joy bubble up in him. "Already have my dress picked out," she said with confidence.

"Then let's get out of here. We could both use a shower."

"I'll get the portal. You grab our stuff."

Sean gathered his satchel, the pile of books he was lugging to the cottage to read, and the bag she had her regular clothing tucked into before meeting her at the portal. The tell-tell ripple of the air let him know the connection was active.

Talaunia gave him a mischievous grin, and he paused. "What? I don't trust that look."

She laced her arm around his. "Come on, time's wasting!"

Still wondering what she was up to, he followed her through the portal. Rather than stepping into the forested twilight around the Stony Brook Cottage, they were standing in the entryway of a darkened apartment. Hardwood flooring stretched down a short hallway that had a pair of closed doors midway along its length. The walls were bare, and the large room at the end of the hallway appeared empty as well, though something gave a subtle blue cast to the dark mahogany flooring.

"Talaunia, where are we?"

She flipped on a light and tugged on his hand, guiding him down the hall. "Don't you recognize your flat when you see it?"

They entered the main room, and its lack of furniture gave it a cavernous appearance. The outer wall was made of glass panels and covered with floor-to-ceiling blackout curtains. A built-in shelving unit with space for a large flat panel covered one wall, and before it, a remote operations console with its buffet of screens hummed. The opposite wall contained a broad pass-through, opening the space between the sitting room and the kitchen. A bar sat on one side of the opening and a stone countertop on the other. The kitchen was comfortable, well-sized, and already fitted with a glass cooktop and oven. The dining area was at the opposite end of the kitchen, and it held a folding table and matching chairs. A collection of papers lay on the table, along with keys, and Talaunia pushed him in that direction.

"How could it be my flat?"

"Papa has had someone working on your housing issue since Vitan rendered you homeless. When they found this one, he said it was perfect and made the arrangements. It has two bedrooms, two full baths, a utility closet, hardwoods in all the living areas, and a gorgeous view overlooking Hyde Park."

"I can't afford a place like this!"

"You don't have to." She beamed at him and pointed toward the papers on the table. "This is the latest property purchased by the Quari Group. And it's yours as long as you are an employee." Shuffling the pages around, she continued, "Papa wants you to pick out the furniture. Circle what you want, and he'll have it delivered and installed for you."

"I—don't know what to say." Sean placed the things he was carrying on the bar and wandered through the remaining rooms, checking out the additional living space. The spare bedroom had a small bed already in place. A black dress with matching clutch was lying on the bed, a pair of pumps on the floor below. He glanced at Talaunia, and she smiled, saying, "I told you so" with her eyes.

In the master bedroom, he found a bed matching the one at the Stony Brook Cottage. The closet held his clothing, and what remained of his belongings, few as they were, had been wrapped and stacked in labeled boxes along one wall.

Talaunia leaned against the doorframe, basking in the unexpected wonder and happiness on his face. "You'll find a way to thank him. For now, clean up and change. We don't want to be late."

She slipped from the room, and Sean ran a hand through his wavy red mop of hair.

"My place," he said in wonder, sweeping the room again with his eyes as a smile spread over his face.

Excerpt from the Elven Volumes of Living Knowledge
Celestial Cycle 218.963712
In the First Reign of House Varunia

May the Mother and Goddess have mercy upon us and guide our futures. Evil walks among us, championed by Councilors Kryntan and Syrdan, and the throne will pass into Syrdan's control all too soon! The Elevari completely vanished from those found and brought for punishment. We have discovered the cause. If any two Elves, or Elevari, share their energies, it creates a bond, bringing one into subjugation of the other. The Elevari have taken to mating with Elves, coxing them to draw on their life force to heighten the experience, then force the now bound Elves to siphon the living energies and feed them back into the Elevari, keeping themselves floating in their intoxicated state, and leaving the Elves to suffer the punishment.

—Councilor Daejor

TWENTY-FIVE

. . . AND SOUR

Sean knocked on the door of his mother's flat, his lips pressed so firmly together they almost vanished. He was still wrestling with how to confront her with all he had learned, not wanting to diminish any of the revelations, but knowing that whatever came out last would become the focus of the discussion.

Talaunia squeezed his arm, watching his thoughts collide and grind against one another. "Just ask her what you want to know. Stop chewing on your questions like some kind of cud."

His head turned enough to glare at her from the corner of his eye.

The door opened, the aroma of cumin and spice washing out into the hallway. Narah beamed at her guests, pulling Sean in and giving him a warm hug. "It seems I've not seen you in ages, a sheòid."

Sean returned the hug, stiff and awkward. "Aye."

"How long has it been?" Talaunia asked, giving a dainty curtsey in greeting.

Narah laughed. "Almost three weeks now." She stepped back, motioning them inside. "Come in, come in! We have a standing Sunday dinner, but between his new job and the shop, we've missed a few."

Sean and Talaunia stepped into the spacious one-bedroom apartment. It was decorated with things that appeared to be straight out of the Victorian era. The curtains stood open, giving a view of the opposing building, and the street if you stepped near the panes. Pictures of Sean dotted the walls, each displayed in vintage frames.

There was no television. A record changer sat where you would find the flat panel screen in most homes. The speakers sat nestled within the floor-to-ceiling bookcases that framed the spinning player. The organizational system seemed a tad eclectic, mixing printed volumes and vinyl albums. A lilting melody played in hushed tones, giving atmosphere, but not infringing on their conversation.

A bar separated the kitchen area from the main living space. There was an empty fruit bowl on the bar, and a glass case containing a beat-up wooden sword. A framed Polaroid sat beside it, of Sean standing inside an open wardrobe, wielding the blade like a superhero. Talaunia's eyes lingered on the image, and her face lit up. "I love that picture. You were dashing into battle even then."

Color flooded Sean's cheek, and he shook his head. He motioned between the women. "Talaunia, this is my mum."

Narah smiled at Talaunia. "We've met."

Sean's brow lifted, and Talaunia nudged him with an elbow. "I told you I spoke with your mother when we were conducting our background investigation on you."

His preoccupation with the topics he had to discuss with his mother had kept the obvious connection from registering. Chastising himself, Sean moved toward the kitchen. "Are those tacos I'm smelling?"

"What else would I make for our reunion, and for whatever is troubling you?" Narah's eyes settled on Talaunia, a brow lifting, asking with her eyes if she had shared the truth about Sean's father.

Talaunia cut her eyes to Sean and inclined her head.

"Let's eat. You can tell us about your trip," Sean said, ignoring his mother's comment.

Narah studied the way Talaunia's gaze lingered on her son, a knowing smile touching the corner of her lips. "I see," she said to no one in particular. She guided Talaunia toward the dining area. "It seems he wishes to eat first."

Talaunia paused next to Narah. "He's been mulling this conversation for nearly a week now. I'm thinking it's going to take a pry bar to get the words out of his mouth."

Sean turned and glared at them. "It's going to get cold. Get in here."

Narah leaned toward Talaunia, speaking in a conspiratorial whisper. "He's always been this way. Usually ends with me having to coax it out of him." She gave Sean a motherly stare. "When it comes to defending others, he has the heart of a lion, but his own needs steal his courage."

Sean pulled out a seat and stood behind it, staring at the women.

"Don't you worry, tonight, I'll prod it out of him," Talaunia said.

"That would be quite a pleasant change," Narah confirmed.

Narah guided Talaunia toward the dining table before stepping into the kitchen.

The plates had already been set. A pair of buffets were sitting at the center of the table; one held the cold items, while the other had steam pouring from beneath its silver covers.

Talaunia stepped in front of the chair Sean was holding.

He sighed, moving her chair forward as she sat. "I thought you were supposed to be here as friendly support."

The blender came to life in the kitchen, the harsh crackle of ice hitting the metal blades hinting that something more was coming.

"I am. To help you do what you need to do," she lifted her chin, her eyes seeking his over her shoulder. "And to be there to help you process everything when it's done."

Sean moved to stand behind his mother's chair, eyeing Talaunia.

Narah swept into the room with a small serving tray carrying three tall, frozen margaritas. "I couldn't think of a better drink to match with tacos," she said, placing a glass before each plate. She gave her son an appreciative smile and stood before her chair, letting him help her settle.

Slipping into his seat, Sean plucked the covers from the service. His eyes moved between the women, who trained their expectant focus on him. "I'm not trying to delay things. I'm famished."

They both rolled their eyes, and the dinner settled into a strange imbalance. Sean gorged on taco after taco, uncomfortable and avoiding the discussion of his father while the two ladies enjoyed themselves, most often at his expense.

Narah spoke of her trip, giving details on the exquisite pieces she had seen and the few items she had purchased for her shop. "My fall cruise is coming up soon," she said, trying to draw some reaction out of Sean. "You know how much I love my cruises. I will depart on the 10th and will return on the 22nd. Things have been so busy of late. I'm looking forward to having the chance to recharge."

Sean's head tilted, and with a furrowed brow, he looked at his mother. "Well, doesn't that have all new layers of meaning . . ."

An awkward silence hung between them until Talaunia turned the discussion to Sean's past, drawing tales and stories from Narah that added layers of embarrassment to Sean's discomfort.

After finishing his meal, Sean dismissed himself from the table to make another round of drinks, prickling at the giddy laughter that followed him. He was pouring the fresh margaritas when his mother hit a nerve.

"I'm glad he's found someone who understands his work. He struggled to maintain relationships during his schooling. Spending extended stretches in the middle of nowhere, with limited connection to the outside world, does not lend itself to budding relationships."

The pitcher hit the counter with a little more force than it should have. Sean snatched up the glasses and moved back toward the ladies with fire in his eyes.

Talaunia was shaking her head. "Oh, no. While I've made my interest known, he's not ready."

Narah arched a brow. "Not ready?"

Sean placed a drink before both ladies and plopped back into his seat.

"You have a charming, passionate, gorgeous young lady seeking your affections, and you are not ready? What have I missed?"

"So very much," Sean said, wincing at the terse tone he had used.

He took a drink and started with the night of his promotion. He left out the details about the Quari Cube, but all the highlights were there. Learning of the Realm of Shadows and the reality of its creatures, the things she had convinced him were imaginary. Projecting into visions. The encounter with Vitan and subsequent branding of his bones. He ended with the loss of Axylia and the others.

By the time his story ended, his mother held his hand, and Talaunia had shifted closer, resting her hand on his upper back.

"You cannot delay this any longer. Talk to her," Talaunia urged in a whisper.

Sean's eyes moved over his mother's features, studying her in earnest. His eyes settled on hers, challenging and hard. "Through all of this, parts of my past have been uncovered, things I find it difficult to process. I've found that my grandmother is a Bright One, and you are a succubus. I have heard that you left my father and told me fanciful tales of a man—a man who never existed. All the while, my father was alive, living in Manchester!" Sean pulled his hand away from his mother and leaned back in the chair. His head shook in subtle arcs. "How could you hide so much from me? Lie to me all these years?"

Narah's eyes saddened, and she reached for his hand again. "Sean, understand—"

Sean lifted his hand, swinging it to the side, cutting her off. "I understand why you did these things when I was a child. I wasn't old enough to understand. You were protecting all of us." His breath hissed and his eyes narrowed. "Why did you leave me to discover it all on my own, under such trying conditions? Were you ever planning to tell me the truth?"

Narah lowered her head. "I could make excuses if that will help you come to grips with everything, but that is all they would be." Her eyes sought Talaunia, who gave her a warm smile. "The first time we talked, I knew I had already waited too long, and that I had to tell him." Her eyes slid back to Sean's. "But I wrestled and struggled with how to bring it up. Every Sunday, you were here, and we spoke, and I couldn't find the words. How do you tell someone such truths when they believe your species is nothing but a myth? How do you tell them the horrors you saw haunt them in their youth were not imagined? Would that bring those old fears roaring back to life? Would that leave you frozen in fear of every dark corner and shadow again?"

She reached for Sean's hand again. "I know. I should have told you years ago. Even weeks ago would have been better. And I can't express how much I regret you had to discover these things in such a way." Her eyes returned to Talaunia. "But I am thankful you discovered them with someone who cares for you."

Sean allowed his mother to gather up his hand, and he met her eyes, finding them brimming with a glossy mist.

Talaunia rubbed his back, reassuring him he wasn't alone.

Sean's lips pressed together, an uneasy silence replacing the conversation as he held his mother's gaze. His emotional struggle was clear in the subtle twitches of expression that broke through his mask of composure. He squeezed his mother's hand, cleared his throat, and rose. "Thank you for your honesty tonight." He bent and kissed her cheek. "I love you, but I cannot be around you right now. I need time. I'll call you when I can." Locking a pained gaze on Talaunia, he set his jaw, turned, and walked out the door.

Narah watched him go, her entire frame shrinking, showing just how much his departure had taken out of her. She turned to Talaunia, eyes shimmering as she fought back the tears. "Go after him, dear. He needs you."

"Thank you for having us over. I hope we can do it again when things are less tense," Talaunia said, pushing back from the table. She rested a hand on Narah's shoulder in understanding before rushing to catch up with Sean.

Lifting her glass, Narah took a sip.

A siren's voice floated from the record player in the main room, '*For he comes, the human child, to the waters and the wild, with a faery hand in hand . . .*'

And Narah's tears flowed unhindered.

EXCERPT FROM THE ELVEN VOLUMES OF LIVING KNOWLEDGE
CELESTIAL CYCLE 228.965227
IN THE FIRST REIGN OF HOUSE VARUNIA

The mistrust of the Elevari has ripped through our people like wildfire. We strove to keep the manipulations of the Elevari out of everyday discourse. Still, as with all hidden things, eventually light shines upon them, and you must face the ramifications. The Houses divide, families split and the Elevari push against us, defiling our very connection to the Mother out of spite. I fear the seers have not been led astray, but have seen where this great division must lead.

—Councilor Jerandyl

Twenty-Six

Aftermath.

Sean stared out the window of his new apartment. Talaunia was correct about the view, though he found it did little to provide comfort or distraction from his thoughts. Talaunia's offer to take him to see his father echoed in his mind, and he wrestled with the challenges that were tethered to the idea, snares threatening harm to everyone in his life if the situation was not handled with care. Every outcome led him to places he knew he couldn't go. Even so, the need burned inside.

Talaunia remained at his side. Silent. She held his hand in hers, their fingers twined together, providing an undemanding, unwavering presence of support.

They lingered there, taking in the beauty of Hyde Park, until Sean broke the silence. "Take me to see him?"

She knew his focus was still somewhere out there, above the park, and she could sense he wasn't yet ready to face anyone, so she kept her gaze trained across the treetops. "When would you like to go?"

"Tomorrow."

"As you wish." She kept her eyes forward, but smiled to herself. "I'll have a car pick us up from the office tomorrow evening."

He squeezed her hand, turning to look at her. "Thank you." Pulling away, he turned and moved into his room.

"You're welcome." She watched him close the door and sighed. She knew he would lack energy and focus the next day, but she wasn't going to invade his space tonight without invitation.

< ᚼᛟᚾ ᚠᚱᛗ ᚠ ᚷᛁᚠᛏ >

The following day was a disaster. Sean was tired, distracted, and irritable, and every misstep only added to his frustrations. Seeing himself failing tasks he thought already mastered chafed against his desire, his need to improve.

He tried studying the growing stack of books, but couldn't retain anything, reading the same passages repeatedly. Giving up, he headed to the training room, but by noon, Djain ordered him home to rest and sent Talaunia along with him.

Rather than going home, they summoned the shuttle service early. Talaunia produced a ring from her bag and slipped it on. Sean watched her copper hair lengthen and become fuller, shifting to a lustrous brunette, and her sandalwood skin lightened to a golden amber tone. Her violet eyes darkened into an earthy brown, and her pointed ears vanished into smooth curves that hid behind the waves of her hair. In seconds, she had transformed from Talaunia into Kate, the guise she had used to capture his attention before the promotion.

"Looks like you finally get that date," she said with a wink.

Their car arrived, and they set out on the long trip to Manchester. Talaunia made him lean against her, singing slow-moving songs until he fell asleep. The drive took them almost four hours, and he slept for three of them, leaving his mood much improved, though still dour.

Entering the tavern, Sean pulled her into the first available seats. "I want to meet him, but I cannot tell him who I am. Too many things can go wrong trying to explain."

"I understand. You just leave it to me—and play along. Tell him you're doing research if he asks. That's close enough to the truth." She stood, pointing at him. "Now stay put."

He nodded, and she moved with grace up to the bar.

She started a conversation with a man in the shadows at the far end while she waited for their drinks. In no time, she was returning, drinks in hand, and the stranger in tow.

"Hey, Sweetie," she said as they approached. "This is the man with that wild story. He said he'd be happy to tell you himself because, you know, he's going to do it so much better than I can."

Sean stood and offered his hand. "I'm Sean. I hear it's quite a tale."

"The names Ian. Ian Byrne," the man said in a slurred Scottish brogue. He appeared pleased with his poor Bond impersonation. "An it'll put the fear of God in ya too, laddie.

Sean's eyes scrutinized every aspect of the man, appreciating the firm handshake they shared before sitting. He stood about five foot ten, almost two inches shorter than Sean, but they both had the same build about the chest. Though Ian was wearing a cap, Sean could see the bright ginger curls peeking out from beneath, a few shades lighter than Sean's. Ian's face was lined, deep wrinkles giving the impression he wore a perpetual frown. His cheeks and nose were reddened from his long-term drinking, and there were dark lines under his eyes, which matched Sean's in color. He wore a three-day growth on his chin, his ginger scruff speckled with white.

Leaning on the table across from them, Ian finished his drink. Setting it on the pressed cardboard coaster, he stared at Talaunia, tapping a finger on the table.

"Oh! Yeah! You start the story. I've already heard it. While you do, I'll get you another." She winked at Sean and slipped back up to the bar.

Ian smiled, thought it never reached his eyes. He watched Talaunia take every step toward the bar before he turned back to Sean.

"Knew a las tha' looked like tha' once. Be watchin' yer back with that one." His eyes moved back to her standing at the bar. "What's yer interest in me story, lad?"

"I'm researching Scotland's unexplained phenomena. She mentioned hearing your tale some time ago. I was hoping to get a first-hand accounting, if you don't mind."

Ian shrugged. "Keep tha' whiskey flowin', an I'll tell ya all I know."

Sean settled in to listen.

Talaunia returned to the table with the fresh drink. "I've asked him to keep your glass filled." Slipping into the seat next to Sean, she wrapped her hand in his.

Pointing to their interlocked fingers, Ian inclined his head. "Narah an' I started tha' way. 'twas all bright an' 'appy. Young, an' lovin' tha' feelin' of bein' in love." He closed his eyes, and his demeanor softened. "I can still see her, every sultry curve, every charmin' freckle. Tha way she moved, tha way she spoke, was like she was workin' her magic on me."

Ian's eyes fluttered open, and Sean could see the spark that thinking of her still stirred in him.

After taking a long pull from the glass, he ran his hand over his mouth, working to extinguish her memory. The hard lines of time deepened on his face, and his shoulders sagged under the weight of his past. "Tha lass an I were 'appy for tha longest. We shared a home, an' she made it me castle. My queen, keepin' tha home fires warm while I slayed wha' needed slayin' and provided fer us." He drained his glass, setting it down hard enough for the bartender to hear the ice rattling in the cup.

Fishing in his pocket, Ian produced a well-worn black box covered in crushed velvet. He opened it. The white gold ring and respectable diamond sparkled in the low light. "We were so 'appy. She was startin' ta show, an' eatin' tha strangest things. I wen' an' got this here ring fer her. We wen' ta go an celebrate the wee one, an' it 'twas a nigh' of joy. I ask'd her ta be me misses, an' she said. 'Aye!'

The bartender placed a fresh glass on the table, and Ian eyed it, reaching out with unexpected quickness to catch the barkeep by the arm. Tipping back the highball, he downed it all in a single go. "Now ya' can fetch me another."

Turning his attention back to Sean, Ian shook the box. "Put this ring on her finger meself, an' it was tha end of me 'appiness. Before we made it back ta tha home, she wen' ta shakin'. I thought somethin' was wrong with tha bairn, but she'd hear none of tha'. Then we reach home, an' when I try ta kiss her, tha lass changed inta tha devil before me eyes."

Ian's next drink arrived, and this time he was more controlled, sipping on the spirits as he worked to corral the ghosts haunting his mind. "Tha lass's eyes turned into ghastly white specs. Horns, wings, and a tail all sprung out of her from nowhere. Her perfect skin turned inta black hide, an' she sucked tha life from me, like a bloody demonic leech."

Snapping the ring box closed, Ian tucked it away in the safety of his pants, draining the glass. "She put tha ring back in me pocket an' vanished, leavin' me fer dead. Somewhere out there is a half-breed demon child tha' I sired. An' every day I have ta think about wha' tha little bastard might be doin', who it might be hurtin'."

Locking eyes with Sean, he leaned in, "An that's me tale, lad." Ian's gaze cut to Talaunia. "Be makin' sure ya damn well know what it be yer beddin' afore ya go an' turn yerself inta her meal. Saint Mary's is jus' down tha road. Perhaps ya ought ta swing by afore takin' tha' one back ta yer home."

The bartender showed up with another drink for Ian, and Sean tried to engage him in other conversation, but he had told his story and now had no interest in doing anything but finding the bottom of a bottle.

Ian went back to his place in the shadows at the far end of the bar, taking his fresh drink with him.

Sean watched him go, a new sadness weighing on his heart.

After paying the tab, Sean offered Talaunia his arm. They walked along the street for a time, and she left him to his thoughts. Their progress was slow, Sean appearing to study the ground. When he lifted his head, Saint Mary's spire loomed in the next block. "Maybe I should take you in for confession. If you burst into flame, it might save me a great deal of torment."

She looked up at him, finding the hints of a smile on his lips. "It is nice to see this part of you break the surface again."

He folded his other arm across his body and covered her fingers with his hand. "I cannot thank you enough. That wasn't pleasant, but a necessary step for me to move past this. Now I have a better grasp of what my mum faced."

"You should call her tomorrow."

He shifted his head from side to side, uncommitted to that path. "I'm exhausted. We need to find a place to make a portal." Facing her, they locked gazes. "And I have much to think about before calling her."

"Understood." She held his gaze until he relaxed. Tugging, she led him between two buildings where the shadows were impenetrable from the road. "This will work."

He watched her open the portal. "You know, at some point, you need to teach me how to access my place."

She laughed. "Tomorrow."

"Tomorrow," he said.

Together they stepped into the entryway, and she closed the portal, leaving Manchester behind.

Sean took her hand. "Would you stay with me tonight? I could use . . ." His words trailed off, lost in his inability to decide what it was he sought from her.

Leading him down the hall, he could sense her unspoken understanding. "Anytime."

< ᛦᛟᚢ ᚹᛁᛚᛚ ᛒᚨᚾᛁᛋᚺ ᚾᛖᚷᚨᛏᛁᚡᛁᛏᛦ >

Over the next several days, Sean's focus improved, and with the group's help, his training accelerated. They fell back into the overloaded schedule, all of them relying on Talaunia to keep Sean restored and healthy after they broke him down each day.

September rolled into October, and autumn settled in around the gardens, turning the world into a wash of oranges and golds. Djain requested daily updates on Sean's progress, pushing each of his trainers to demand a bit more of him with each passing day.

Ms. Iliescu was pleased with Sean's progress. His circle casting had become second only to Djain in power and consistency, though he still did not entice the Elemental Guardians to manifest their presence.

Talaunia was still not ready to move him beyond the basics of using prepared spells, potions, charms, and other similar devices. While he had improved, and she was no longer forced to direct his every move, he was still fumbling on his decisions and too often burned through far more items than necessary to accomplish the desired outcome. She knew this was a process one had to experience and work through before understanding could be found. Until he stopped approaching it as a problem separate from himself that he could solve with logic; had the realization that magic was an extension of himself; understood that everything around him was interconnected; he would continue to struggle. She kept working with him, encouraging him, waiting to see the fundamental comprehension of magic resonate with him.

Ryan and Gadyen were both pleased with his progress. Ryan focused on teaching him how to defend and protect himself in a scrap, and Sean emerged with new bruises every day from their physical encounters. Gadyen taught him weapons, sticking to short swords and daggers, teaching him form and defensive strategy. While Sean often left their sessions covered in nicks and cuts, he had shown remarkable improvement, and Gadyen was confident that he could defend against all but the best of blade wielders.

Lamiri made regular contact, but had no new information. She had been accepted into the Order's New York coven, but had discovered nothing of use.

Narah departed from Southampton aboard the Zen Dreams on the 10th of October. Talaunia insisted Sean see her off, and together, they accompanied her to the docks. Tension lingered between them, Sean continuing to struggle with forgiving her lifelong deception, leaving them both with a sense of unease at her departure.

Jason and Sarah returned from New York on the 14th of October and presented a model of the Abbey created in their downtime. The labyrinth of underground passages lacked the colorful walls of the above-ground structures. Still, using radar sensing satellite images, Jason had constructed the most probable layout of the catacombs beneath the Abbey and identified the best place to attempt ingress.

The following days were consumed by analyzing the structure.

Sean pointed out the places most likely to house the tomb they sought, outlined the clues unearthed in the books and journals he had studied, and showed them a stack of prophecies that held tidbits of information needed to access the shard. The writings contained clues he could only put into context on-site after seeing the architecture and stonework. Until then, he couldn't isolate the correct one.

Jason cautioned that the map he had made of the catacombs was only an estimation. Many levels existed, one atop the other, making it difficult to tell how many there were and how deep it ran.

By the 16th, Djain decided they would undertake the recovery mission the following Sunday. According to Sarah's analysis, going in late on a Sunday gave them the best statistical odds of moving in and out unseen.

On the 19th, Djain thanked them for their efforts and sent them home early to rest and recharge. "Go. Enjoy your evening. Tomorrow night, we claim another piece of the Cube."

I cannot shed this burden with enough haste, yet I fear what Syrdan will do when he takes the throne. For good or ill, I have performed to my best, and I must yield the seat. Mother and Goddess watch over us.

—Queen Varunia

TWENTY-SEVEN

The rough stone of the catacomb walls was pitted and covered in crags, dressing the corridor in angles and shadows, which the torches' flickering light failed to breach. The stale air had lost its foul flavor in the hours spent searching the passages beneath the abbey. Despite their persistence, the crypts refused to reveal the cube's location.

Gadyen searched the darkness, a weariness in his eyes. "Another dead end. We must turn around. Be sharp. More wraiths are lurking in the shadows. I can sense them."

Djain turned to Talaunia, motioning with one hand. "Watch our back. We dare not allow another surprise."

Less than pleased, Talaunia relented without a fight. She turned away from Sean, who stood doubled over with his hands on his knees.

Sean groaned when she drew her hand away, breaking the energy flow. He motioned for her to keep going, slipping a vial from his belt, and dislodging the cork. After drinking the contents, he searched the surrounding shadows, trying to mask the old fears creeping through his mind. "I'm good. Let's find that bloody marker and get out of here."

Djain lifted a brow, pointing back down the passage with his chin. "You heard the man. Retrace our steps."

The quartet moved back along the forgotten corridor with tortoise-like speed. The disturbed dust on the ground mapping their intrusion.

Gadyen moved out ahead of the others, his hair reflecting the golden colors of the quivering light.

Talaunia scanned the darkness behind them, holding two silver daggers low and at the ready.

Sean chastised himself for the disaster this outing had been. He had lost track of the number of dead-end passages they had scoured. They had been set upon by things coming out of the darkness twice already, and though he worked to overcome the distraction of his past, those memories still haunted him. So much was riding on him, and he was failing.

Gadyen paused, pointing at a symbol engraved on the lid of a sarcophagus. It was small, tucked in among the carvings of leaves on the stone, meant to be overlooked. "Here. It is no wonder we failed to spot it on our first pass. The etchings are nearly worn away."

Sean grunted and moved to Gadyen's side. Leaning on the stone crate, he ran a finger over the symbol and concurred. "This is it."

Djain eyed Sean's stance. "How badly was he hurt?"

Talaunia evaluated Sean, concern reflected in her eyes. She returned her focus to the darkness behind them, scanning the shadows. "Wraith's hit hard." She cast another worried glance at Sean. "If he takes another hit, we're leaving." Head swiveling, she fixed Djain with an obstinate stare. "With or without you."

Gadyen snapped the thick stone slab atop the casket with a single blow, the sharp crack echoing along the passage. Pleased with himself, he shifted pieces of the broken top off to the side.

Sean glowered at Gadyen. "We don't have to destroy the history. Let's try to leave it intact."

Djain dipped his head, showing no sign of resistance to Talaunia's assessment. "If you say we must, then we must." His eyes moved from her to the black emptiness of the passage beyond.

Talaunia and Djain each pointed to the shadows behind the other, calling out in warning. Multiple wraiths detached themselves from the darkness, coming at the group from both ends of the corridor.

Another wraith rose from the shadows of the open grave, and Gadyen took a step back, drawing his sword, the blade's metal singing as it was freed.

Sean leaned against the alcove wall, pressing his back against the stone for support. He drew a knife from his belt, the flickering light reflecting in dull glints off the blade's carbon steel.

Djain was set upon before he could turn, the fetid vapor of his attackers wrapping about his body. Drawing a bone-handled knife, he sliced along the length of his forearm. Blood swelled out of the wound, and purple smoke formed all about his arm and the blade, devouring his blood before it could fall to the ground. His sonorous voice boomed, the words of his chant rebounding from the stone surrounding them, muddling into a constant rumbling cacophony. His face contorted, the wraith's claws digging into his back, the shroud of their darkness tightening around him.

Talaunia spun, silver blades slicing at the dark shapes behind her, causing them to cry out in fury and pain. Turning in a deadly dance with her assailants, she struck out at their shadowy forms while dodging their blows.

Gadyen's movements were only a blur, the blade slicing through the misty form of the wraith with ease, but it did nothing to slow the creature.

Sean pushed himself forward, driving the tip of his blade toward the back of the wraith attacking Gadyen. The edge passed through unhindered, and his momentum pitched him forward. He took a stumbling step, having to grab the sarcophagus to steady himself.

The wraith ignored Sean, focusing its assault on Gadyen.

Talaunia connected with her target, planting both daggers into its fetid chest. Its wail lingered in echoing refrains after it crumbled into nothing before her. Her other mark hissed, skirting around her to join its companions attacking Djain. Spinning, she saw Gadyen's futile struggle. "You need magic or silver!"

The wraith that ran from Talaunia attacked Djain low, digging its claws into the meat of his thigh. Blood was dripping from every wound and more purple smoke formed with each drop. Djain continued to chant, several spirits taking form around him and throwing themselves into the battle.

Sean dropped his steel blade and fumbled about with the vials on his belt, pulling two free. One contained a viscous, transparent liquid, and the other a shimmering powder. "Gadyen! Strike these!"

Sean tossed them in the air behind the wraith, and Gadyen struck. He stepped into the wraith's murky form, sword moving in lightning-quick strokes through the shadowy creature and shattering the first vial. A thick liquid ran over the blade, specs of it showering the area.

The wraith screamed as the spray of droplets landed on its back, burning through its form. Gadyen struck the second vial, and a cloud of silver dust filled the air. The wraith threw itself back, sliding over the coated blade, a horrifying wail coming from it as it burst into putrid smoke.

Talaunia dug both of her blades into the back of the wraith that had run from her, twisting them, digging them deeper into its murky form until it gave a howling scream and disintegrated.

The spirits around Djain wrestled with the other wraiths, peeling them off him. Djain held out a hand, fingers asking for the sword. "Gadyen!"

Gadyen's face contorted, specs of red appearing over his ashen skin, angry and oozing. Hearing Djain's request, understanding registered, and he tossed the blade through the air.

Djain's hand closed around the leather-wrapped hilt, continuing the motion of the blade and swinging it into a deadly arc that bisected each of the remaining wraiths.

Ethereal vapor filled the air, and everything stilled.

Djain spoke in a foreign tongue that Sean could not understand, and the spirits that had come to his aid bowed in deference before fading away. Taking in the state of them all, he shook his head. "We must become better if we are to win this war."

Talaunia turned to Sean, but he waved her off, pointing at Gadyen.

Gadyen sank to his knees, his face contorted in pain. Faint tendrils of white smoke rose from each of the wounds speckling his skin. Turning a pained gaze to Sean, he asked, "What was in those vials"?

Sean winced. "Holy oil and silver powder."

Talaunia knelt beside Gadyen, examining the large number of wounds covering his upper body. "This is going to keep burning him until we can clean it off," she turned her gaze to Djain.

Djain's brow furrowed, but he signaled his understanding. "Set a marker so we can return to this spot, and I will open a portal back to Operations."

Talaunia pulled a small metal device from her belt and moved toward the sarcophagus.

Gadyen lifted a hand to stop her, catching her by the wrist. "No."

She knelt beside him again. "We can't leave you like this."

"Agreed." Gadyen glanced at each of them, rehashing his decision before speaking. "Urine," he prompted. "I can rinse in urine, and we can press onward."

Sean made a face.

Djain tilted his head. "That is well beyond, Gadyen."

Gadyen was resolved. "It is what is required. We must recover this piece of the Cube before the Order, and I refuse to cause our failure." He turned his pained gaze upon each of them before pressing his insistence through clenched teeth. "Now, honor my request. I have smelled of worse things in my time, and stinking of urine is preferable to enduring this pain."

Talaunia stepped back. "Alright boys, you heard the man. Put him out of his misery."

Djain shrugged. He shifted the loincloth aside, took hold of his cock, stepped before Gadyen, and released his bladder, directing the flow toward the other man.

Gadyen lowered his head, letting the warm liquid spill over him. He worked the liquid through his hair, across his face and upper shoulders before Djain stepped aside and let the cloth fall back in place.

The three of them watched Sean in expectation, and after a brief hesitation, he stepped forward and unfastened his jeans. Gadyen rinsed the rest of his chest and arms with Sean's aid before stepping back from the steaming puddle on the stone floor.

After tucking his member away, Sean fastened his pants and tipped his head toward the sword. "Don't forget that."

Gadyen eyed the blade with unease. "Consider it a gift. I dare not have that near me now." He slipped the leather strap holding the sheath from his back and offered it to Sean. Droplets of golden moisture dripped from it as it hung suspended between them.

Talaunia grabbed the sheath and slung it over Sean's shoulder before he could protest. Djain picked up the sword and slipped it back into the sheath. "Guess that's settled," Sean offered.

Djain shoved the last bit of stone from atop the crypt and peered inside. Skeletal remains lay within the sarcophagus, draped in what remained of a monk's robes. The cloth was riddled with holes and a thick layer of dust. Spiderwebs were interlaced amid the bones, creating a mess of sticky tendons. Atop the breastbone lay a dust-covered medallion bearing the mark of the Order. Sweeping the alcove that housed the monk's remains, Djain asked Sean. "What is our next step?"

Sean leaned against the stone wall of the coffin again, peering over the edge.

Talaunia crossed and covered his hand with hers.

A warm, appreciative smile spread over his lips, the energy tickling as it flowed from her touch. "Thank you." After a moment, he lifted his head, studying the architecture of the crypt itself. "There was an old poem with a refrain that I believed referenced this spot," he pulled his hand from Talaunia's and fished a set of papers from his pocket. Unfolding them, he shuffled the pages until he found the one he was seeking.

Sean placed it atop the skeleton.

Gadyen shined a light on it, and they all leaned in to read.

Mighty warrior ever guards,
O'er the home of onyx shard.

Prove your worth, pass 'neath his gate.
For it be there, you learn your fate.
Hark! I hear, still yet he calls,
His challenge ringing 'long stone walls.
'Come to me if thou be brave.
Cross my sword! Best me knave!'

"This is not a warrior," Gadyen pointed out, motioning to what remained of the man in the box. "Have we identified the incorrect crypt?"

They all shuffled back several steps, examining the alcove again.

Djain watched in silence, studying the room about them, letting those with the experience in such things take charge.

Talaunia stayed back, giving Sean space to work. She had learned over the past several weeks that he operated well under pressure unless she was involved. Her presence caused his focus to wander, so she kept her tongue in check, trusting he would call her if she were needed.

Gadyen moved across the corridor to the stone coffin on the other side. It was simple, with minimal carving work. In the middle was a raised shield with a name chiseled across its breadth. Brushing his hand over the engraved lettering, he removed the dirt. "Ambiorix."

Sean's head snapped up, and he stared at Gadyen. "Ambiorix?"

"Is that name important?" Djain asked, glancing between the men.

"Historically, yes. Ambiorix led an uprising against the Romans when they wintered among the Belgic Tribes," Sean said. "He is considered a hero to this day." Sean eyed the stonework and the sarcophagus. "I'd say he qualifies as a great warrior, but this is almost certainly not the grave of Ambiorix."

They moved to Gadyen's side as a group, Djain giving orders, placing himself and Sean at one end of the stone lid and Gadyen and Talaunia at the other. They shifted the cover with combined effort, twisting it sideways and toppling it off into the hallway floor.

Inside were the desiccated remains of a soldier. The man was dressed in ancient chain mail that drooped around his withered frame. A simple metal helm had fallen off his head and now leaned against the top of the coffin. His hands were clasped around the hilt of his sword, which pointed toward his feet.

Talaunia's brows rose, setting her gaze on Sean. "Well, Darling, how are you going to cross swords with a dead man?"

Sean leaned against the stonework and rubbed his head.

Talaunia slipped her arm around him, drawing herself against his side, and he draped his arm around her shoulder.

Eyes filled with appreciation, he faced her. "Great question. I'm open to any thoughts, but the answer is likely woven into the lines of the poem itself."

Djain studied the remains. "Is this Ambiorix?"

Sean shook his head without hesitation. "No. This fellow is from the time of the crusades. Ambiorix pre-dates this guy by a thousand years."

Reaching over, Djain drew the sword from the scabbard on Sean's back.

Gadyen took several steps back into the hallway, staying well clear of the blade.

Djain placed the blade across the tomb. "We must start somewhere. No reason we should not begin by testing the obvious while Sean thinks." He repositioned the sword along the length of the crate, and nothing happened. "Who has another idea?"

"Place our sword in the coffin, so it touches his blade when it crosses," Talaunia offered.

Gadyen shrugged, a hint of amusement touching his lips.

Djain changed his approach, following her suggestion. The faint ring of metal scraping against metal sounded each time he repositioned the blade. He moved the sword into every position and angle he could imagine, all to no avail.

Sean studied the hallway's structure, the inset of the opposing alcoves, repeating the phrasing of the old poem over and over, contemplating the physical forms in relation to the words.

Talaunia saw Sean sink to his knees in the middle of the narrow hall, and she moved towards him. "Sean?"

The others turned as Talaunia knelt beside him, taking his hand.

"I'm alright," Sean said, attempting to reassure them, but the weariness was obvious in his voice. He felt the tingle of living energy in his fingers and gazed at Talaunia, his appreciation showing in his eyes. "I think I have the answer. I'm preparing to test my theory."

Djain crouched before him. "What have you unraveled?"

"The first two lines are obvious." Sean sighed. "A warrior is guarding the shard. And the final two are a challenge; some test or trial has to be overcome to gain access."

"And you believe the key to accessing the challenge is in the other lines," Gadyen stated, eyes moving over the arched top of the passage.

Sean locked eyes with Djain. "What gate can one pass through where they could still hear the challenge being issued?"

Djain's brow lifted. "I see. Are you sure you are prepared for this? We can return at a later time if we must."

Talaunia and Gadyen exchanged glances.

"I'm sure," Sean stated. He squeezed Talaunia's hand. "Just don't let go, and keep watch for me."

"Of course," she responded without hesitation, still unsure of his plan.

Gadyen drew in a slow breath and tilted his head as understanding came to him. "The Astral," he said to Talaunia. "The warrior and his challenge are in the Astral plane."

"We will watch over you," Djain said. "Proceed with caution."

Sean gave himself over to their protection, closed his eyes, and drew in a deep breath. Over the previous weeks, Ms. Iliescu had escalated his training in this area, and he found it paid off. It only took him a moment to calm himself and find his center. Resolved to find a resolution to this puzzle, he rose, easing out of his conscious form until the Astral realm appeared in a haze.

The blur of a spectral blade flashed before him, and Sean fell back from the boundary, watching it light up as the knight struck the membrane between the two men. Ms. Iliescu's lessons ran through his mind, the knowledge she had been forging within. The rules of physics did not bind the Astral. He wasn't limited to the fragility of his mortal form when on this plane.

With confidence, he flashed through the barrier, rising as a giant before the warrior. Tower shield held in one arm, a heavy spiked mace in the other. Sean's eyes blazed from beneath the horned helm that rode atop his head. *"Yield now, and I will spare you,"* he demanded of the spectral warrior.

Around them, a ghostly version of the tomb took shape. The alcove housing the warrior's body set into one side of a grand arch and the monk's into the other, and Sean recognized it as the knight's gate.

Beneath the monk's grave was an iron grate, held fast by many spiritual locks, and operated by a lever that ran to the middle of the passage. *"I do not wish to fight you,"* Sean implored. *"I only wish to secure that which you guard. Protect it from those seeking to harness its power for ill."*

The warrior did not respond with words. Instead, he charged, thrusting his sword.

Sean deflected the blow with his shield, knocking the man backward. *"Please do not force me to bring you harm. I know you have held your post with diligence."*

Again, the warrior charged, and Sean deflected the blow. *"Concede your post. Go, find rest."*

The man charged again. *"Never shall I yield!"*

With a heavy sigh, Sean deflected the latest attack. *"So be it."*

Tightening his grip on the handle of his mace, he waited for the warrior to lunge again. As expected, the spectral guardian came at him, and Sean turned it aside with ease. He twisted, bringing the mace around in a sweeping arc, burying it in the back of the warrior's head.

Had the warrior been mortal, the wicked metal spikes would have driven through the helm's thin metal and buried themselves deep within the man's skull. Being in his astral form saved Sean from witnessing that gruesome scene. Staggering forward, the guardian collapsed to his knees.

The warrior's sword fell to the ground and burst into vapor. His arms fell limp at his sides, bits of astral energy lifting away from his head.

Behind him, Sean heard a lock snap. One by one, he watched each of the shackles securing the grate vanish, falling away as the warrior separated into slivers of spiritual haze. When the fullness of the warrior's spirit had disintegrated, the entrance was free, and Sean was alone in the spectral gateway.

Sean fell back into his body, eyes blinking open.

"Did you succeed?" asked Djain.

"Aye," Sean said, upset with what had transpired in the Astral. He held tighter to Talaunia's hand. "Gadyen, can you get the warrior's sword, please?"

The bones snapped and splintered under the force of Gadyen's grip, and he wrenched the sword free of the dead hands.

Sean let go of Talaunia and crawled along the middle of the hallway, sweeping his hands over the floor. "There is a slot between the two crypts. His sword is the key, the lever, to open the path."

Djain and Talaunia joined Sean, searching the floor.

Talaunia spotted the thin slot nestled between two stones.

Gadyen put the tip of the blade between the stones and drove it downward. The sound of mechanical latches groaned beneath the floor. Stone ground against stone, and a faint cloud of dust rose from the monk's tomb.

Gadyen jumped to the edge of the grave and peered over the side as the noise subsided. The skeleton was gone, and the base of the coffin was now sloped, leading into darkness. "I think we have found the way."

Without Gadyen holding the blade in place, it was pushed back up, and the grinding started again.

"The ramp is closing," Gadyen informed them.

Talaunia tried maintaining pressure on the sword, but couldn't drive it into the slot on her own. Sean came to assist her, and together they managed to seat it again.

Everyone turned to Gadyen. "It is open again."

The grinding slowed and came to a stop.

Djain rested a hand on Sean's shoulder. "You and Talaunia keep the sword in place while Gadyen and I explore the passage."

"We should come back with more support. You two will be alone down there, and there are certain to be more traps," Talaunia objected.

Displeased with Djain's plan, Sean backed Talaunia, "She is right." Leaning against the cross-guard of the sword, he added. "I need to be down there with you. Isn't that why you brought me along?"

Gadyen remained silent, focused on searching the darkness below. He lit up another torch and dropped it down the ramp, illuminating the mouth to another passage.

Djain shook his head, more in dismissal of their arguments rather than disagreement. "I understand your objections." He turned to Sean. "You have already been injured. You keep leaning on things to stay upright. If there are dangers to be faced, Gadyen and I will face them." He gave him a reassuring pat on the shoulder. "If we find anything requiring your expertise, I will send Gadyen back to take your place."

The displeasure on Sean's brow did not ease.

Djain focused on Talaunia. "Stay vigilant. Care for him as best you can in the circumstance."

A fire lit in Talaunia's eyes, a wicked grin spreading over her face. "I'll not let anything take what's mine."

Sean shook his head, the corner of his mouth creeping upward into a crooked smile. "So we're back to that again, are we?"

"I've been patient enough, and we are in a setting where one finds their treasure," Talaunia said with a wink.

Djain chuckled. "Do not forget where you are." Crossing the corridor, he gazed into the passage below. "Come, Gadyen, let us find our treasure."

Gadyen hopped over the side of the box and slid down the ramp, picking up the torch he had dropped when he reached the bottom.

Djain followed, vanishing into the open maw of the grave.

"However, shall we pass the time, Sweetie," Talaunia teased as their waiting game began.

EXCERPT FROM THE ELVEN VOLUMES OF LIVING KNOWLEDGE
CELESTIAL CYCLE 1.138491
IN THE FIRST REIGN OF HOUSE SYRDAN

Syrdan is furious. While she sits on the throne, enough of the Council opposes her views and agenda to render her powerless. Discussions and votes on her policies follow predictable splits, with only Councilor Kryntan supporting the Queen's proposals. Unrest fills the souls of our people, and violence erupts between the Elves and Elevari with the slightest provocations.

—Councilor Daejor

Twenty-Eight

Djain and Gadyen explored the tunnel beneath the crypts. The air grew damp, the stone walls gave way to bare earth, and the paved floor vanished beneath thick mud. Heeding the whispers of apprehension, caution guided their descent, making their progress tedious and slow.

Gadyen studied the earthen walls along the path. "There is an opening ahead."

Djain squinted, staring into the inky darkness. "I can see nothing. What I would give to have your vision."

When they reached the door, Gadyen brought them to a halt. "Guard yourself as we enter here."

Djain inclined his head. The torch's golden light reflected off the ash-gray skull painted on his face, giving it a sinister, fiery sheen. "Go!"

The pair took the door together. A rusted iron gate slammed closed, sealing them in. Behind them, the sound of grinding gears echoed along the tunnel, originating from somewhere far above. Ahead, somewhere in the darkness, a chugging cough was silenced by the sound of gurgling water.

Gadyen tested the strength of the iron grate. "This is no obstacle. Let us see what secrets this passage yet holds."

Djain regarded the gate, deferring to Gadyen's opinion. "Lead on."

⟨ ᛒᛖ ᚲᚱᚨᚾᛞ ᚠᚠ ᚨᚱᚾᚱ ᚠᚲᚲᚱᛗᚲᛀᛋᚺᛗᛗ�∤ᛏᛋ ⟩

Talaunia had teased Sean as they waited, trying to draw him out of his agitation at having been left behind. Her plan failed. She fell back to discussing the next steps of their training, under the guise of ensuring he wasn't left behind again. "Are you ready to increase the intensity of your exercises? There are many other skills you still need to learn, more advanced things than potions and charms. Like creating spells and harnessing your power."

Sean changed which hand held the sword. "I am. We need to find more pieces of the Cube as well. I could try to summon Vitan, but I have little faith that would bring us anything useful." He reached for her hand again, thankful for the energy boost she was providing as they waited. "I believe you still owe me another walk among your memories. I need the practice."

Several weeks had passed since Sean had first been taught to walk another's memories. The continuation of that training had gotten lost in Ms. Iliescu's insistence that he master the finer nuances of projecting before delving deeper or venturing out on wide-scale hunts. Between training, research, and dealing with the revelation about his father, his progress on walking another's memories had stalled.

"You have my word." Her lips curled upward in a playful smile. "However, I'm going to impose one rule."

Sean eyed her with suspicion. "What would that be?"

"I get to choose every other memory that you view," she purred at him, adjusting her grip on the sword.

Rubbing his shoulder, he grumbled. "I think this qualifies as my physical training for tomorrow." He focused on the open crypt across the hallway. "How long have they been gone?"

"Not as long as you think," she laughed. "And don't check the time, or it will make it worse."

A mechanical ratcheting sounded beneath the warrior's bones, followed by the grinding, screeching sound of rusted joints forced into motion. The ring of a hollow metal bar striking stone joined the unfamiliar sounds. Talaunia and Sean both craned their necks to see the corpse.

The jawbone fell open, and the entire skeleton shuddered, sending spiders scurrying over their webs. A disembodied voice whispered, its breathy sounds rebounding from the stone in hollow tones.

Talaunia and Sean stared at one another, a sense of dread filling them, brought on by the shared realization that something unsettling was about to happen.

The world fell into utter darkness.

< ᚨᛟᛚᚱ ᚲᛚᚱᛋᛗᛋ ᛒᛖᚲᛟᛘᛗ ᚨᛟᛚᚱ ᛒᛚᛗᛋᛋᛁᛏᚷᛋ >

Gadyen took a step to his right and vanished, and Djain paused, waiting. Seconds later, Gadyen reappeared, excited. "A blind corner, hiding the entrance to the room beyond. Come see!"

Djain followed him through the tight passage that dumped them out into a small room. A dim blue glow lit the space, coming from row upon row of obsidian stones, carved with magical symbols that radiated power.

At the center of the cave sat a large fountain. Water sprayed up into the air, fell back into its bowl, and poured onto the floor.

"It seems we must find the correct one before you drown." Gadyen motioned to the hundreds of shards placed around the room. "How shall we begin?"

Djain eased around the room, water splashing and sloshing beneath his heavy footfalls. His hand hovered over the stones. "I must hold them."

Eyes sweeping over the myriad fragments, Gadyen braced himself, resolved amusement lacing his words. "Let us see what they throw at us next."

Djain grabbed the first stone, starting the long process of sifting through the shards.

< ᚠᛟᚱᚷᛁᚨᛗᛖᛏᛖᛋᛋ ᚦᛁᛚᛚ ᚺᛖᚨᛚ ᚨᛟᚢ >

"Talaunia?" Sean called, a touch of panic in his voice at being swallowed up by the darkness.

"Still here," she said, relieved that he was as well.

Sean's voice trembled with nerves. "What bloody well happened to the lights? Why'd this wank pheasant turn them off?" He kicked out at the stone crypt in the dark, slamming his toe into it much harder than he intended. "Fuck!"

"Calm down, Sweetie. We're in this together . . . whatever this is." She chuckled, a hint of nervousness in the bright tones.

To keep his mind from falling into fears from the past, he tried to lighten the situation. "Just so you know, I may have broken my toe."

"Then I'll fix it for you," she reassured. Her lips curled into an unseen, teasing smile that colored her voice. "Then I'll punish you for breaking my things."

"Thanks," he said and meant it. "Now, what do you think happened to the lights?"

"It's a magical darkness," she said. "I can hear the crackle of the torches, and they're still lit."

Sean slid his hand over the sword's cross member, trying to find Talaunia in the dark. Something brushed against his leg, and he jumped, losing his hold on the blade. Startled, he yelped, and it echoed in the darkness. "Bloody hell, Panji, now is not the time!"

"Panji isn't here; she's patrolling the Shadows," Talaunia said. She voiced his name, questioning and full of concern as the weight of the stone pushed against the lever and the blade shook, rising. "Sean?"

The sound of grating stone filled the passage. The ramp Djain and Gadyen had descended growled its desire to seal its secrets away.

"Fuck me," Sean said, groping in the dark, trying to locate Talaunia again. He couldn't even make out the shape of his hand before his face. "Talaunia?"

"I'm here," she called back, an edge of panic creeping into her voice.

A dull, scraping sound was coming from the surrounding darkness.

Sean called out, "Marco!"

"What?" Talaunia asked. "Who is Marco?"

The darkness echoed his nervous laugh, and Sean moved toward her voice, searching for her and the sword. Once located, they shoved the blade back into the slot, and the grating sound reversed. Holding to the hope that things would now calm, he attempted to keep the stress of the situation out of his tone. "It's from a game I played with my mum when I was a wee one. One person calls out Marco, the other Polo, and you try to find them by following the sound of their voice."

"I will have to remember that." Talaunia chuckled, more relaxed now that Sean had somewhat settled himself. Things appeared to be back under control, even if the dry scraping sound coming from all around them was getting louder.

Djain discarded one stone and picked up another. The process was slow, and the water was rising much faster than he was clearing shards. With every stone he disturbed, the rate of flow increased, and it was lapping at his calves already.

"At this rate, you may well drown before finding the correct one," Gadyen said. He had relaxed, dozens of stones had been discarded, and nothing new had happened.

Djain's brow rose, his head rocked back and forth, and he exchanged stones yet again. "Perhaps, but I trust our fortune will turn soon." Djain glanced at the water before eyeing the multitude of shards still waiting for his inspection. "It must."

< ᛏᚺᛖ ᚾᚨᛖ ᚨᚱ ᛒᚨᛏ ᛁᛋ ᚨᚱᛚᚱᛋ ᛏᚱ ᚲᛗᛗᛁᛗ >

The dry scratching sounds continued to intensify, increasing in numbers as time passed. "What the bloody hell is that noise?"

Talaunia squealed and let go of the sword so she could swat at her pants. "Ok, there is something in here. It touched my leg."

Sean sounded concerned, but smug. His voice strained as he struggled, failing to keep the sword depressed. "Not as crazy as you thought, am I?"

She laughed. "I rather wish you were."

"Me too," he confessed. The grinding of the stone signaled the closing of the door on Gadyen and Djain. "I hate to say it, but I think we need to worry about ourselves. They can make a portal out if need be."

"Agreed," she said. "Give me your hand so I don't lose you."

They both groped in the darkness until their fingers met, holding tight to one another. She squeezed his hand, and a set of bony fingers wrapped around them both.

In unison, they screamed.

< ᛕᛩᚾ ᛖᛁᚲᛗ ᛕᛩᚾᚱ ᛩᛈᛏ ᚲᚱᛏᚼ >

The water was sloshing about Gadyen's chest as Djain tossed another shard into the pool. Gadyen arched a brow and dove under the surface, scrubbing at his hair, face, and chest. He took his time, watching shard after shard splash into the water. Djain was cursing when Gadyen surfaced, his basso voice sounding hollow under the watery influence.

Djain turned to Gadyen. "Did you get the stench of us washed off?"

Gadyen's lips twisted in amusement. "We will not know until we return home." His eyes moved over all the remaining stones, but he refrained from commenting on their situation. "Ryan was already angered at being ordered to remain behind. We may see his darker nature if certain scents remain."

A smirk flashed over Djain's face. "That concern crossed my mind. We will deal with it should it happen. Ryan will understand." Djain paused his search, turning to Gadyen, head tilting to the side. "Eventually."

Gadyen laughed, though it was cut short by the muffled sound of stone slamming home. Turning in the direction they had come, his eyes narrowed. "I believe our way of egress has been compromised. I hope Talaunia and Sean are faring better than we are."

When Djain lifted the next onyx shard, the room shook. Several large splashes caused water to rain around the room. Portals opened in what seemed random places overhead, dropping giant eels into the floodwaters.

Gadyen moved with them, watching their motions as they swam around. "This will not be pleasant."

< ᚠᛟᛚᛗ ᚪᛟᚢᚱᛋᛗᚾᚠ ᚠᚾᛏᛏᚪ >

Sean tugged, Talaunia jumped, and they held tight to each other. The skeletal hand clung to them, its weight dangling from their grip, the bones closing with supernatural strength.

Talaunia brought the pommel of her knife down hard on the bony knuckles, and they cracked open. She pulled herself closer to Sean as the bones fell away, clattering off the stone floor in the darkness.

"Put your back to mine and swing that blade at anything that isn't me," she said.

Sean followed her order, trying to see any movement in the darkness. "Any chance of making us a portal out of here?"

Talaunia swung, the blade slicing through the air and finding no resistance. "Sorry. No. I can't see to make the symbols."

"I was afraid of that," he said. Feeling things crawling over his toes, he swung the blade downward, connecting with something substantial. "I'm afraid I know what that scraping sound is—"

"I wager you are correct. How many bodies do you think we passed coming down here?" she asked.

"You had to ask that question, didn't you?"

< ᛉᛟᛁ ᚠᚱᛗ ᛗᛏᛟᛁᚾᚷᚺ >

One eel went for Djain's leg, and Gadyen dove beneath the waves, catching it by the tail. It did little too slow the slippery creature, which pulled Gadyen along as it coiled around its prey. Blue sparks surged up Djain's leg, over Gadyen's arm, and the eel sank its razor-sharp teeth into Djain's thigh. Djain grimaced, and Gadyen jerked his hand away.

Holding the shard in his hand, Djain lifted it to his lips and kissed it before tucking it away. Reaching below the waves, he wrapped his massive hand around the slimy head. Bloodstained water swirled about them, the crimson stains darkening as he forced the jaws open, pulling the needle-like teeth from his leg.

Gadyen stood up as Djain uncoiled the slippery body and hurled the eel against the stone. More dark bodies dropped, splashing into the water. "Did you find it?" Gadyen asked.

"Yes," Djain said. "I think it's time we left."

Not waiting for further instruction, Gadyen crossed to the nearest wall, opening a portal to the training room in the Quari Group Headquarters. Gadyen and Djain waded their way through, water gushing around them, spreading out across the floor.

Djain closed the portal when his foot hit the building's modern floor. Half a dozen eels flopped about in the thin pool of water covering the center mat. "I will deal with this," Djain said. "You go to Ops and check the status of Sean and Talaunia."

The waters parted as Gadyen moved, taking the stairs to avoid the wait for the lift.

< ᚼᛟᚾᚱ ᚠᚾᛏᚾᚱᛗ ᛁᛋ ᛒᚱᛁᚷᚼᛏ >

The darkness was filled with the dull sound of metal striking bone and the rattle of bone chips crashing to the stone floor and bouncing from the walls. Talaunia and Sean leaned into one another; their backs pressed together as they fought the unseen foes.

The skeletons shambled along the hallway in the darkness. The bodies tangled and locked together, forming a reanimated wall that grew in thickness faster than the swords could dismantle them.

Sweat drenched them both, and Sean was finding it harder to fight. His earlier wound from the wraith was taking a toll on his stamina, limiting how far the adrenaline-pumping terror could push him.

Bony fingers scratched along the front of Talaunia's leather vest, and she swung the sword with all her might. The blade connected and wobbled, making a twanging sound that ended with a distinct snap. "Sean, Sweetie," she called over her shoulder, an unfamiliar edge of terror in her voice.

The blade in her hand had become so light, and she could only imagine that it snapped at the quillon.

"Yes?" he called back between ragged breaths and grunting swings.

"Don't mean to worry you any," she said, continuing to swing the handle. Her arms were connecting with the attackers bones more frequently than the broken weapon. "My blade broke!"

She felt his shoulder sag and the tension in his back release. His muscles hardened beneath her touch, and he swung the weapon with renewed vigor, calling out. "I'll try to keep them off us both!"

She turned, slipping her arms around his waist, beneath his tunic and leather vest. Her hands splayed over his chest, and she held on for dear life. Together, they turned in a slow circle, Sean beating his sword against the darkness and Talaunia feeding energy into him from the forest far overhead.

< ᚼᚱᚾᚱ ᛁᚻᚾᛗᚱ ᛚᚱᛁᚲᛗ ᚦᛁᛁᛏ ᚷᚾᛁᛪᛗ ᚼᚱᚾ >

Gadyen appeared in the middle of the Operations Center, but no one saw him. They were all focused on the stairwell door. He had blown through it at such speed; the handle was now embedded in the wall.

Ryan turned from the door, searching for Gadyen. "What the fuck happened?" His arm was no longer bound in a sling, but his chest was still wrapped in bandages.

Everyone turned to face the two men as they approached each other, understanding dawning on each face in its own time

Gadyen held out a hand. "What, we will discuss later. Who, we will discuss now."

Ryan came to an abrupt halt a dozen paces from Gadyen. His nose wrinkled up, and he growled, hands balling into fists. "Why the fuck do you smell like another man? No—men!"

Gadyen rolled his eyes and stepped forward, pulling Ryan to him roughly, pressing their lips together in a heated kiss.

Whistles and calls erupted around them.

When they separated, Ryan blinked, all the anger driven from him.

Staring at him with intensity and ignoring the jeers, Gadyen ended their discussion. "Later." He stepped away from Ryan, smirking, and watching him try to regain his composure. Capitalizing on the attention the two of them had gathered, he addressed the room. "Sean and Talaunia were separated from us. Have they returned or checked in?"

The entire center was back in action, people double-checking statistics, logs, portal activity, and many screens until a consensus was found. "We've no reports of them or their return."

Gadyen pointed at an empty portal. "I want a support team ready to return with me in ten minutes." People scattered about the room. "Portal team, get our Abbey location open and ready," he commanded, and another set of bodies headed toward the archway.

< ᚨᛩᚾᚱ ᚾᛁᚷᚾᛏ ᛁᛇ ᛏᛖᛗᛞᛖᛗᛞ ᛁᚺ ᛏᚺᛖ ᚦᛩᚱᚦᛞ >

Djain stood in the middle of the training room, facing an open portal with both arms extended, one calling and one pushing the air. The image wavering in the archway was filled with dense trees along a broad river. The air coming through the portal was humid and thick. It whistled as it was sucked through the narrow point at the top of the archway. It churned, whipping around the room, lifting the water from the floor and forcing it out the bottom of the breach. The eels flopped about, swept up in the frothing waters, and deposited into the far-away river.

When the floor had dried, Djain lowered his hands, and the winds subsided. Whispering a prayer of thanks, he closed the portal.

His hands dipped into a pouch at his hip, pulling the onyx stone with its strange markings from its place of concealment. He studied it lovingly, a sense of hope and longing in his gaze. "Nire Bihotza, I am closer."

< ᛏᛟᚢᚱ ᚾᛖᛗᛞᛖᛋ ᚠᚱᛗ ᛁᚾᚲᛟᚱᛏᚨᚾᛏ >

Talaunia poured energy into Sean, and he shattered bone after bone. They had stumbled through the darkness and found an alcove with a crypt. Placing themselves into the corner, they fought against the continuing press of the skeletons. Sean could feel the bone fragments piling up at his feet, and he continued to swing blindly, desperate to fend off the attack.

"Keep going," she urged him, her voice weakening.

A new pang of fear splintered in Sean's core, and he knocked her hands off his chest.

"Stop it. You need this," she argued, trying to put her hands back against his skin.

Another skeletal hand pawed at his shoulder, and he knocked it away, the tingle of her energy stirring in his chest. "Bloody hell, Talaunia! Stop!"

They wrestled amongst themselves until Sean had to disentangle his hair from an attacker's grip.

"No," she said, continuing to feed energy into him.

Sean leaned back into her, pressing her against the wall. "Dammit, quit!" He lashed out at the throng, channeling the fear her actions touched into the blows. "You will not do the same bloody thing to me she did!"

"You don't understand how important you are," she argued, taking a handful of his hair.

Sean yelled in frustration, feeling her pour energy into him through his scalp.

"I'm not that bad off. Stop fretting." She leaned closer, seeking to mask her fear in teasing words, but when she whispered in his ear, it sounded more of relief. "If this is to be our end, it's nice to know you care."

< ᚼᛟᚾᚱ ᛒᛗᛋᛏ ᛁᛋ ᛗᛏᛟᚾᚢᚼ >

"I'm fucking going this time," Ryan bellowed, standing before the portal.

The baritone chime of the elevator sounded, and Gadyen motioned toward the door. "Take it up with Papa," he said.

Djain stepped into the room. "What is the status?"

"There has been no contact. We await a healer, then we are prepared to return for them," Gadyen said, motioning to a pair standing by the portal, armed with various blades, bobbles, and potions.

Djain greeted the support team while crossing the room. "Myn, Rhoin."

Myn was Mindy Southampton, a powerful witch in her mid-twenties. Her dark chestnut hair fell past her shoulders, framing her round face, and her almond-shaped eyes were a rich amber, complementing the warm glow of her golden-brown skin.

Djain gave a brief rundown of what they had already encountered. Focusing on the heavy mace held by Rhoin. "Make sure you each have silvered weapons as well."

Rhoin grumbled and pulled a short, thin dagger from his belt, flashing it around before driving it back into its sheath. "This ain' my first trip down tha rabbit hole!"

Ryan paced back and forth in front of the archway. "We ready to go yet?"

Djain's eyes narrowed, watching Ryan prowl the area before the portal. "If you mean the support team. You will maintain your place here."

Ryan grabbed a chair, hurling it along the wall. "I'm sick of being left behind. I'm ready to fight!"

"And you will, once your injuries are healed." Djain pulled his shoulders back, pointing at the chair. "Now go pick that up and plant your furry ass in it before you anger me."

Ryan bowed up, a low growl sounding deep in his throat. His eye twitched, and with a huff, he spun and went after the chair.

"Good boy," Gadyen chided.

Ryan turned, giving him the finger, along with a scornful glare.

The lift chimed, and an older elf stepped onto the floor. He had white hair and sharp features, giving him a dour appearance. Joining the group, he asked in a gravelly voice. "Am I the last to arrive?"

Djain tipped his head. "Welcome, Aduin, and yes. Let's be on our way." Djain stepped forward and entered the portal, and the others followed.

< ᚪᛟᛚ ᛞᛗᛋᛗᚱᚪᛗ ᚪᛟᛚ ᛏᛁᛗᛗ >

Inside the portal, the party came to a stop. Blackness hung everywhere. "Light," Djain commanded, straining to identify the scraping sound he heard in the distance.

"Papa, we need to break this darkness. I have used two illumination charms, and they are failing," said Aduin.

"I cannot see my fire," said Myn. "I can feel the spell working on these walls. It's old magic."

"Can you counter it?" asked Gadyen. "I have heard that sound before. Corpses are walking these halls!"

"Necromancy, that's the strange current I wasn't placing," Myn said. "I think I can break this, but I will need some help and a jolt of life energy. I believe they have used the necromancy to prop up the spell, casting everything into the eternal darkness of the grave. Aduin, are you willing to assist me?"

Aduin's voice floated out of the darkness. "Tell me what you need, Miss, and I will do what I can."

"Myn. Please, call me Myn," she said. "First, we need to find one another."

"Blind bunch of beggars, the lot of ya," Rhoin grumbled. He shouldered his way through the group and pulled Aduin and Myn together. "If ya be needin' eyes, ask. I can bloody well see!"

Myn gasped, finding her breast cupped in someone's hand. "Oh," Myn exclaimed.

"There you are," Aduin said, pulling his arm back. "Pardon the hand."

"Don't worry about it. The unexpected happens when you grope about in the dark." She reached out and found his arm, dropping her fingers to lift his hand. "Besides, it's the most action I've had in months."

She knelt, pulling him with her and placing his hand on her shoulder. "Stay with me. I need to prepare; then we'll continue."

Holding out her pack, she spoke facing the wrong way, but Rhoin responded anyway. "Rhoin, can you find a black candle, a white candle, the mirror from the bottom of the bag, and if you can locate them, my ruby and clear quartz wands?"

Rhoin grumbled, fishing the items out of the bag, handing them to her, and naming each as it was found.

She placed them around herself, explaining her goal to her blind audience. "I'm setting up a sun-charged mirror, along with some crystals, to help amplify this. With luck, we'll get some light in here. Beyond that, I'm not hopeful. This magic is not something that is going to be shattered easily, and it's giving me the willies."

The whoosh of a butane lighter filled the darkness. "Ouch, damn, yeah, ok, the candle is lit," Myn said.

She reached up and patted Aduin on the hand. "I'm going to slice my thigh. I will let the blood pool around the mirror and soak into the crypt floor before starting. When I squeeze, you need to heal me. The more energy we can transfer through me, the better. The more that it overflows and charges the blood, the greater our chance of success."

She stared in his direction, seeing nothing but darkness. "Ready?"

Aduin shifted, resting his weight on one knee. "I will not fail you, Myn. Proceed."

Myn slipped a dagger into her thigh, wincing against the pain. She sliced through her denim pants and into her flesh. The blood came, a warm spot spreading down her leg to her knee.

She pressed the life-giving fluid into the voids between the rough stones, pooling it in the cracks and crevices, so it saturated the floor. In the darkness, she took Aduin's hand in hers, painting it crimson under her pained grasp.

Aduin reached into the forest overhead and tried to draw bits of energy from every living thing he found. Encountering resistance, he pulled harder until the wall that blocked the flow snapped, allowing him to flood Myn with a torrent of healing energy.

The wound on her leg swelled and knitted together. Myn hissed, her jaw clenched against the turmoil inside. "Keep going." The energy was bottled, building inside her with nothing left to heal. She strained, opening the paths of power within herself and channeling the flow into the sticky mess covering the floor. Her body became the conduit for energies it was never meant to hold, and a scorching scream ripped from her, echoing into the darkness.

< ᛋᚾᚲᚲᛖᛗᛋᛋ ᚦᛁᛚᛚ ᛒᛖ ᚨᛦᚾᚱᛋ ᛏᛦᛞᛖᚨ >

Talaunia gasped, the energy flowing into Sean cut off, and her grip on his hair released. "Oh, blessed Mother, no!" Panic coursed through her, and her arms flailed against the walls. She squirmed behind Sean, pleading. "Please, no—not now."

The battle had pressed against them so that Sean could no longer swing the sword, and he was forced to shove his dagger blades between bones and twist, rending bits and pieces from the attackers; at least, that was what he pictured in his mind. The pervasive darkness remained, hiding the truth of their situation from him. Feeling her sudden shift in tone and attitude, he called to her over his shoulder, a new knot of panic forming in his stomach. "Talaunia?"

"I can't, Sean! I can't!" She screeched, her fingers digging at the rock walls. "The Mother! I can't feel her!"

The knot in his stomach turned to a lead weight, sucking the air from him. "What?" His efforts against the undead mob slowed, and his swings weakened. "How?"

Talaunia wept, her words a wail in the darkness. "Fucking narrow-sighted elves! What the fuck did they do to her now?"

Feeling he was losing the battle, Sean turned, arching himself protectively over Talaunia, and she collapsed into a ball. Not knowing what to do or say, he held her tight, letting her emotions carry her away as the skeletal fingers picked at him.

The leather strap that held the bobbles and vials around his waist tightened until he thought it would cut him in half before it snapped. The sharp edges of the attacker's fingers sliced through his leather vest and pants. Bones wrapped into his hair, making his scalp ache, and the fingers dug into the skin on his back. Regardless, he remained curled into a protective shell over Talaunia, who appeared utterly broken.

A scream from somewhere far away echoed the length of the passage, and the skeletal hands stopped, drawing back from him. He sensed their retreat, heard their bony feet scraping over the stone, and he prayed that meant help was coming.

< ᚨᛟᚾ ᚠᚱᛗ ᛒᚱᛁᛋᛋᛁᚨᚾᛏ >

Myn's scream lasted what seemed an eternity. Her eyes turned a ghostly white, and the atmosphere shook. Light flooded the chamber, and Myn's eyes rolled back into her head. The candle went out, and she collapsed into a limp pile on the bloody stone.

Everyone blinked, now blinded by the sudden brightness. Gadyen was the first to recover, and he stuck his head back through the portal, calling people off the monitoring stations to help.

Djain and Rhoin were already moving through the passage toward Sean and Talaunia's last known position.

Aduin was checking on Myn.

Once the technicians arrived, Gadyen instructed them to transport Myn to the Elven Gardens for rest and aid. Urging Aduin on, they rushed after Djain and Rhoin.

Turning the first bend, they found them. Rhoin was swinging the mace in a sweeping arc. Everything he connected with shattered beneath the heft and force of his blows.

Djain was swinging his staff well above Rhoin's head and taking the skulls from the wall of skeletons before them. The entire population of the catacomb had been pulled from their slumber to protect the hallway, but they were no match for the power of these two men, now that they could see.

The hoard was diminished with every step, Gadyen and Aduin lingering behind and letting them work their well-choreographed assault.

< ᛉᛟᚾ ᚠᚱᛗ ᚠᚲᚲᛗᚲᛏᛗᛉ >

When the light returned, Sean was as blind as he had been in the darkness, only now he saw only blinding white. Once his vision recovered enough to make out forms, he saw the pile of dismantled skeletons around him. A twinge of guilt pricked at him for having destroyed so many graves, but it was washed away in the relief of survival.

He leaned out enough to peek around the edge of the cove they had taken shelter in and was horrified at the wall of death he saw making its way toward the other end of the passage.

Turning his attention back to Talaunia, he ran his fingers through her hair, brushing back the loose strands that were matted in blood and stuck to her face. "We're going to make it."

She was no longer crying. Her eyes had become hollow and distant, and she sat amid the shattered bones, rocking.

Sean pulled back to give her space, but her fingers clutched the front of his shirt, and he leaned back in, wrapping his arms around her.

She pressed into him and stilled.

Djain loomed over the alcove, taking in the sight of Sean curled around Talaunia, his bloody back and sides showing the aftermath of their ordeal.

Rhoin kicked the pile of bones out of the way. "Are ya alright?"

Sean shook his head. "I'll live, but something is wrong with Talaunia. She screamed about not being able to feel the Mother anymore and then stopped responding."

Aduin's face went ashen.

Gadyen arched a brow. "Do you know what has happened?"

Aduin shook his head and puckered his lips. "There is nothing I can do about it."

Djain leaned in, threatening, his gaze boring into Aduin. "What, exactly, can you not do anything about?"

Aduin shuffled his feet and pulled on his tunic. "I cannot restore her connection to the Mother. I can do nothing for her. She is an outcast."

Gadyen stepped behind the man as Djain turned to face him more fully. "Let us be clear. When you say there is nothing you can do, is this because there is nothing to be done, or is your inability only related to her status?"

Aduin shifted, his entire manner evasive as he repeated. "There is nothing I can do."

Gadyen leaned in, locking his iron grip around Aduin's arms. "Perhaps you should tell us precisely what has happened to her."

"I—I'd rather not."

Now nose to nose with the man, Djain wiggled a finger and toyed with the air. "This is no longer about your wishes."

Aduin gasped, his eyes expanding in fear. He managed a few words between breaths. "The treaty, you can't!"

Djain's voice exploded, making dust fall from the roof. "Do not presume to quote treaties and agreements to me! Not after the silence of your council cost us lives! They are already in breach and had best not cross me again."

Aduin opened his mouth to object, but Djain cut him off. "If they do, I will open a portal unlike any they have ever seen and march droves of the Mother's children through their precious Sanctuary. Now, speak!"

There was a moment of resistance in Aduin's eyes, and he tried to judge Djain's resolve. Whatever he saw banished all fight from him, and he caved to the demand. "I caused her condition."

Rhoin shook his head. "Idiots! I'm always surrounded by idiots!"

Gadyen spoke low, right into the man's ear. "How? Be precise."

Aduin sighed. "When I aided Myn, I did not consider that another might draw power. I tried to pull life from every source in the forest around the Abbey. There was resistance, and I didn't want to fail Myn—I didn't think another might be doing the same thing, so I forced my pull. It must have shattered her connection to the Mother."

Sean gaped at the man, horrified, his hold on Talaunia tightening. "So, you ripped her soul out, left it tattered, and now you refuse to help?"

"She is an outcast. I cannot," Aduin said without pause. He turned his focus to Djain. "You can take the matter up with the Traxidor's if you wish, or the Council, but I will have nothing to do with helping her."

Gadyen shoved Aduin up the hallway and turned to Rhoin. "Escort this—man—back to the portal, please."

"Forever babysitting," Rhoin grumbled. "Git yer arse movin', Elf!"

Aduin hurried up the hall, relieved to be away from Djain's anger, and Rhoin chased after him, chastising him with every step.

Djain observed Talaunia and Sean, drawing in deep breaths to quell his anger. After calming, he spoke with soft reassurance. "Sean, let me take her. We need to get you both out of here and to those who can help."

Sean's gaze lingered on Talaunia. Eventually, he agreed and tried to stand, but Talaunia's grip refused to loosen. Sean gave her a tender smile. "Alright. I'll carry you."

She shifted with him, allowing him to scoop her up, one arm wrapped around her lower back and the other tucked under her knees. When he stood, he took a few uneasy steps, the brittle bits of bone that covered the floor, making his footing unstable.

Gadyen and Djain each came to his aid, their strength doing more to keep him upright than his own, and together, they made their way back home.

Excerpt from the Elven Volumes of Living Knowledge
Celestial Cycle 1.319848
in the First Reign of House Syrdan

The actions of the Elves bring me shame, yet I understand the driving force behind their behavior. Fear. Willful abuse of living energies has become practically non-existent, with Elves only taking part when forced to by the Elevari to which they have unwittingly bound themselves. Now family members of the Elves actively hunt down the offending Elevari, administering the lashings with venom and fright. This is a recurring scene in the visions granted by the Mother, the precipice at the edge of darkness into which we are about to descend.

—Councilor Traxidor

Twenty-Nine

In a fit of indignation, Frost positioned himself in Djain's path. "I told you to stop!" His voice was shrill, and a cloud of orange and red dust trailed everywhere he flew.

Djain didn't slow, cutting a glance at the pixie and sending him tumbling on a gust of air. "Stay out of my way, little one. You do not wish to be in the midst of this conflict."

In a huff, Frost vanished into the hedgerow as Djain approached the arched entrance to the court. Ignoring the court's ceremony and traditions, Djain rounded the corner, stepping through the archway of living vines.

The atmosphere in the courtyard was tense. No elves were lounging in the peaceful setting. Many were on their feet, leaning into the conversations around them, filling the place with a constant murmur.

Frost was streaking across the open space, screeching and filling the air with brilliant color. "He's coming!"

A hush fell across all those assembled, and all eyes turned to Djain. He crossed the center of the courtyard toward the large mushroom caps that acted as the Traxidor's thrones with fiery purpose.

Pretaris was already on her feet, with Aduin kneeling before her, while Theran brooded under heavy brows from his seat.

To Aduin's side lay Myn, tended by a swarm of pixies. She had been cleaned and dressed in fresh clothing, but she was still unresponsive.

Stepping from beneath the canopy that covered their place of power, Pretaris met Djain in the courtyard's open grass. She greeted him in her usual courtly tone, cold and deliberate. "Have we abandoned all manner of decorum with one another? Has our friendship suffered so greatly that you will no longer honor the simplest of our traditions?"

Djain contemplated her question and gave a subtle bow of his head. "It is not our friendship that has faltered, but that of the alliance between myself and your people. As you stand in representation of that bond, it gives my actions unclear meaning." His steel-blue eyes locked on hers. "Make no mistake, I am enraged by the circumstances that bring me here tonight, but in no way do I mean to direct it towards Theran or yourself."

Pretaris reached out and took his hand, cradling it in her soft touch. "I understand your predicament, old friend. At times, position complicates my discourse as well." She turned and drew him along, maintaining her hold on his hand. "Come, let us discuss what has transpired and what may yet chafe, as friends, and dismiss formality; for now."

Djain followed. "Thank you, Pretaris. Your understanding is appreciated."

When they reached the others, Aduin shied away from Djain. Theran rose to greet him, and the two men clasped forearms. "Too often we meet as opponents of late," rasped out Theran. "I would that never the case, brother."

"As would I," Djain agreed, motioning towards Theran's seat. "Please, rest yourself."

Theran signed his thanks and eased himself back onto the bulbous top of the mushroom.

Pretaris turned a stern gaze on Aduin. "There is nothing more required of you." Lifting her eyes to the still hovering Frost. "Leave us."

Aduin rose, bowing several times before shuffling backward. He skirted around Djain and hurried from the courtyard, with Frost flitting about over his shoulder.

Taking in the activity surrounding Myn, concern etched itself across Djain's brow. "What did he tell you transpired?"

Easing herself to sit beside her husband, Pretaris spoke in hushed tones. "He spoke of misreading the situation, of causing traumatic injury to a member of your team, and in his effort not to fail, overtaxing another." She followed his gaze. "Myn will recover, but may well find certain energies are far more sensitive to her call now, and she will be more susceptible to others."

"How long?" Djain asked, watching the delicate dance of the pixies as they tended to Myn.

"Days, we expect," Pretaris said.

In unison, their heads turned, and they studied one another. Pretaris was the first to break the silence. "I know what you would ask of me, but you know I cannot. My heart breaks for her, but unless you wish Theran and myself to become outcasts as well, our actions are bound."

Tension rolled through his form, and he shifted his stance, wrestling with his words. "I know you risk much by even talking about her in these vague, indirect ways. Is there any help I might find for her, outside of your rules and boundaries? I care not how remote or difficult to find."

"She has been vital to us all, even as an outcast," Theran rasped out, swallowing to clear some of the thickness from his voice.

Pretaris stepped in, taking Theran's hand and squeezing it. "We know of no way to restore her bond to the Mother without the intervention of a gifted healer."

"Is there no way to force Aduin to correct the damage he has inflicted?" Djain pressed.

"If she were not in exile. As things stand, there is no chance of helping her." Pretaris studied the stars before speaking again in somber tones. "If she survives until her family is welcomed back, we will help."

Djain's head tilted, and his eyes narrowed. "She will survive."

An awkward silence fell among the three until Theran summoned the will to break it. "Is there anything further we can do for you tonight?"

Djain scanned the courtyard, taking in the makeup of those present and leveling a stern gaze on Pretaris. "This is the third visit I've not seen a single Guardsman present. Soon, we must discuss their absence."

The Traxidors shared a wary glance. "Not tonight," Pretaris declared.

"Not tonight," Djain confirmed. "I have answers I must find." He gave them a deep bow. "I miss our discussions on ritual and energies." For the sake of their friendship, he forced his lips to curl upward. "Be well friends, and may the Mother keep you."

"And you," they echoed in unison as Djain turned and strolled out of the courtyard.

When he was gone, Pretaris leaned against Theran. "You must go to the council, Love. If they stay their current course, we will lose him and all his people."

Theran drew in a deep breath and rose. Leaning in, he placed a lingering, tender kiss on her lips, his raspy voice sounding in whispers as their lips parted. "You are ever with me."

"In my blood and my breath," she replied.

As Theran turned away, she called after him, "Convince them, or I fear we are all doomed."

Excerpt from the Elven Volumes of Living Knowledge
Celestial Cycle 1.961374
in the First Reign of House Syrdan

We have yet to complete the first cycle of Syrdan's reign, and already things descend into chaos! Syrdan's half-blood grandchild, Xeron, led a band of like-minded Elves and Elevari into the Heavenly Gardens, seized Councilor Varunia, stripped her of her robes, and lashed her entire body savagely, laying open her skin from head to toe. Something must be done to bring these wild beasts under control!

—Councilor Arianelis

THIRTY

Lilith stood amid a field of lifeless husks in the Shadowlands. Her flowing green robe was spattered and smeared with viscera. The skeletal fingers of long-dead trees dotted the gray landscape. Piled around their blackened trunks lay a menagerie of bodies, the lifeless remains of shadow creatures, humans, and a few elves. They had been torn open, their organs spilling out and mingling with ash and dust. Their lifeblood oozed from the wounds, pooling around the gnarled roots and soaking into the ground.

Heavy black clouds hung low against the crimson sky, refusing to release their burden. The stale air moved, lifting Lilith's chestnut hair. Dried specks of blood dotted her bronze skin, and her honey-colored eyes were bright with satisfaction. Turning to face the fiery glow of the horizon, she lifted a slender hand, spoke an invocation, and touched the air.

Ripples spread through the air, the darkness of this realm fading, replaced by the shimmering image of feathery blue skies and a sweeping, weathered limestone balustrade overlooking the Aegean Sea. A lone elf with dusky skin and short-cropped hair stood facing the open waters from the railing. With the thrill of expectation in her voice, Lilith spoke with quiet confidence. "Xeron, it is time."

She watched Xeron turn toward the portal and give a bow. Determination etched on his face, he rose and moved beyond the fixed view of the portal. Lilith made space between herself and the breach by moving to the center of the killing field around her. Her gaze settled on the deep blue of the sea. Her nose twitched and crinkled, announcing the other changes that crept into her expression, a slow shift from the joy of victory to seething rage. She hissed, her words haunted with promise as they blanketed the battlefield surrounding her. "Soon, my children, it will be yours once more."

A shadow moved across the dimensional doorway, followed by a string of devotees to the Order. They flowed in, dressed in hooded robes and wearing the medallion dangling around their necks. Nothing could be seen of the persons beneath the cowls as they entered and formed a broad circle around Lilith. Moments later, Xeron came through the portal carrying a tray that held four pieces of the Quari Cube.

Stepping into the circle, Xeron paused before a hooded figure. Their gloved hand reached out from beneath the robes and took a piece of the Cube, cupping it before themselves on upturned, open palms. Continuing around the ring, Xeron paused at regular intervals. Other hooded figures claimed parts of the Cube, holding them with the same reverence as the first.

Tossing the empty tray outside of the circle, Xeron crossed to his mother's side. "We are ready."

Lilith studied him. "Not quite. Your brothers and sisters may not remember this face."

Xeron sneered, but obeyed. "Yes, mother." He pulled a ring from his finger, and his image shifted, the smooth and toned face of the young man melting into a pale shadow of itself. Half of his face melted to the bone, raw and seeping. The dusky skin of the other was so marked with overlapping scars that no smooth skin remained.

With adoration, Lilith admired him. "There's my boy."

Xeron's eyes moved from her to the swirling mass of clouds overhead, his displeasure at being without his glamor written across his features. "Let's finish this."

Lilith sighed as only a mother can, showing the depths of her disapproval and heaping on guilt in a single, unarticulated breath. "Very well."

Lifting a ceremonial dagger, the devout chanted in unison, and Lilith took Xeron by the hand. Closing her eyes, she pointed the silver blade up into the dark, swirling wall overhead.

The winds pick up, whipping to a frenzy behind the circle of believers. The cloaks snapped like flags in a brisk wind, pulling the fabric taut against their fronts. One hood after another fell away, revealing a mix of men and women, their hair lashing about their heads.

Lilith let out a primal scream.

In response, the voices of her followers grew in volume, and the wind gathered speed. The moisture trapped in the clouds overhead was ripped from its prison, falling in blackened drops like watery ink.

Xeron dropped to a knee. Keeping a tight hold of his mother's hand, he drove his sword into the blood-soaked earth.

Orange lightning streaked across the sky, and Lilith called to it, grabbing hold of the stored potential, ripping it from the sky, channeling it through Xeron and into the ground.

The acrid smell of burning blood filled the area, and Lilith released the lightning. She tugged at Xeron's hand, pulling him forward with her as the ground destabilized within the circle.

Tortured wails rose, the wind died, and the ground buckled and belched, the cries gaining volume the more unstable the ground became. The black rain continued to pour in torrents, painting them all in its oily sheen.

An arm broke through, grasping and struggling from the middle of the ground, and a second arm wriggled free. The fingers clawed and dug until an elf broke through the muck, coated in blood-drenched mud. Lilith and Xeron called, and the elf fought to reach the edge of the quagmire, where they helped pull her free, and she collapsed quaking and naked on the ground. Lilith knelt by her and patted her shoulder. "Welcome back, Gwenthil."

Two more elves popped through, and not even the slimy coating that covered them could hide similar injuries to those born by Xeron. The pair reached the edge when they screamed and were pulled back beneath the ground, another figure breaking through in their place.

The creature was only vaguely humanoid. Its maw gaped open, filled with bloody, needle-like fangs sprouting in every direction. Its long, forked tongue lapped at the foul air and two long arms, each ending in a set of four hooked claws, flailed for solid ground. It let out a shriek, and Xeron cursed. "A Malformed was near the portal."

Lilith struck Xeron's cheek. "The Malformed are still my children. His name is Malkar. Now help!"

Xeron glared at his mother before leaning out and grabbing hold of Malkar's arm. The creature's claws dug into Xeron's forearm, his blood welling up from the wounds, but Xeron held Malkar until he pulled the misshapen man free of the muck. Once free, Xeron beat the man alongside the head until he was free of the beast.

Malkar rose on his hind legs, standing hunched over, arms extended, knuckles dragging the ground, and from his backside, a long, whip-like tail flicked about.

Another elf popped up, and Xeron extended his bloody arm, offering them an anchor, with Lilith at his side, helping to pull the latest arrival to solid land. "Hold on, Zatel," she called.

Malkar rolled around in the bloody mud.

Gwenthil jumped up and squared off with him. Watching with a wary eye, she moved to maintain the distance between herself and the misshapen man. The two of them moved in a circle several times before Malkar grew tired of waiting and rounded on the nearest devotee.

Massive arms yanked the young man from the circle, Malkar's fangs slicing through his flesh and bone with ease.

Lightning flashed, and the man screamed, blood pumping from his shoulder. His arm was now missing, and his hand lay in the muck, severed mid-forearm.

The circle collapsed in an instant, and the ground solidified. Xeron fell backward, pulling the top half of Zatel with him, leaving a trail of organs, the rest of the fellow now lost somewhere in the Void.

Zatel choked and pawed at the ground, trying to find breath, but there was no hope.

Xeron pulled out a dagger from his belt and drove it through Zatel's skull, ending the man's suffering.

Malkar hunched over the dead man's body, ripping away bits of bone and flesh.

"No!" Lilith cried, slamming her fist into the ground. In a rage, she spun, sending a searing bolt of lightning into Malkar's back, disrupting his meal.

Malkar dropped what remained of the body and yelped, glancing over his shoulder before scrambling off into the darkness.

The devout gathered the tray and returned it to Xeron with all four cube pieces back in their respective places. Then they set about helping Gwenthil make her way to the portal. The group vanished into the realm of Terra, leaving Xeron and Lilith alone.

"One," Lilith said in anger. "We only freed one!"

"Two," Xeron corrected, dipping his head in the direction Malkar had vanished.

Lilith turned an icy glare on him. "I am not amused." She studied the circle before moving to close Zatel's eyes. "In truth, Zatel would have been the last. The portal was already failing before Malkar disrupted it."

Xeron grumbled his disappointment. "We have to find more pieces."

"We will." Lilith led Xeron by the shoulder back toward the breach. "And I believe we may have a way to strengthen our next attempt even without the complete cube."

Xeron arched a brow. "What have you discovered?"

"Word has reached me that there is a first-generation succubus living in London. Her name is Narah."

Xeron paused. "A child of my generation? That would be powerful blood to spill indeed." Staring off into the deepening darkness, he tipped his chin. "What of Malkar?"

Lilith followed his gaze into the distance. "Let him enjoy himself in the shadows. Terra is not a place suited for his kind. Yet."

Together, they stepped through the portal, and it faded from view.

< ᚪᛟᚢᚱ ᛋᚲᚠᚱᛋ ᛗᚪᚲᛗ ᚪᛟᚢ ᛒᛗᚪᚢᛏᛁᚠᚢᛚ >

In the depth of night, the skeletal fingers of a lone tree shuddered. Corpses rolled away from the trunk as roots creaked and stretched in the blood-nourished ground. At the tip of the tallest branch, a tiny bud pushed into view.

ACKNOWLEDGEMENTS

Foremost, I must thank my daughter, Coey, and my son-in-law, Isaac, for their unwavering encouragement and support. More than any others, they have trudged this path with me, listening to every change, and shining a light on innumerable issues. I love you both. Thank you for believing in the possibility and nudging it out of my head.

I would be remiss if I failed to thank the remainder of my family, in all its forms: blood, BAM, found, and theatrical. Many of you have suffered my rambling about creating family trees and histories for races that trace their roots to the earliest days of the planet's formation—and yet you remain in my life. Bear, Rain, Stacey, Diana, Nicole, James, Chase, Kiera, Fletcher— you're masochists, the lot of you!

One more group to mention. Those who trudged through the early drafts, and helped me turn this into something more palatable. Brittani, Ida, Emma, Anneliese, Eddy, Anne, and Adriana: Thank you! This would have carried many more holes, had less heart, rambled off into never ending, run-on sentences containing far too much description without your willingness to read and give feedback. I'll have book two in your hands soon!